She would try to remember landmarks along the rivers. She would try to make a map in her head, a map of a river twisting and rushing down through the dark mountains; and at the far end of that river map, she would see the inside log walls of her cabin, with the coats and pans and gun hanging from pegs where they had always been.

She would see, as she had seen so often from underneath, the pole rafters above the bed, the shingles becoming distinct in the morning light, or flickering with hearthglow at night, and the house existed complete and intact in her mind, every log and beam and peg and stone of it, more real and more significant now even than when she had lived in it and touched it with her hands and swept it with a rush-broom.

It was as if she had brought the real house with her in her head, so that Will could walk in through the door with his tools on his shoulder, his big frame for a moment a silhouette in the sunny rectangle of doorway . . .

By the same author:

LONG KNIFE

JAMES ALEXANDER THOM

FOLLOW THE RIVER

BALLANTINE BOOKS • NEW YORK

Library of Congress Catalog Card Number: 80-66552

ISBN 0-345-31210-4

Manufactured in the United States of America

First Edition: September 1981

First Mass Market Edition: November 1983

Map by Ron DiScenza

For Mari Silveus—
Under a Clear, Blue Sky

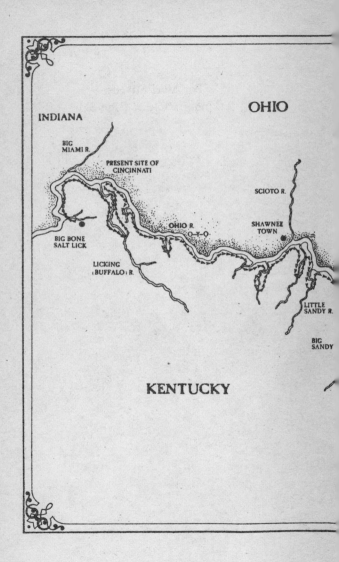

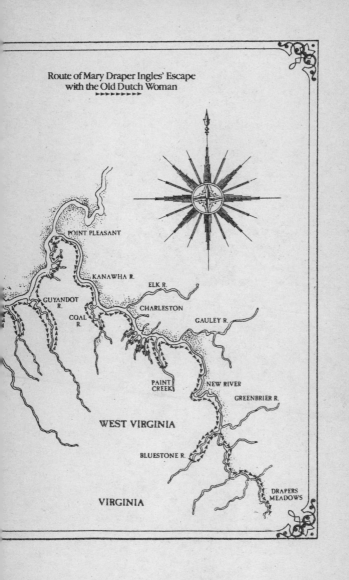

Route of Mary Draper Ingles' Escape
with the Old Dutch Woman
▶▶▶▶▶▶▶▶▶

POINT PLEASANT

KANAWHA R.

ELK R.

GUYANDOT R.

COAL R.

CHARLESTON

GAULEY R.

PAINT CREEK

NEW RIVER

GREENBRIER R.

WEST VIRGINIA

BLUESTONE R.

DRAPERS MEADOWS

VIRGINIA

CHAPTER
1

Sunday, July 8, 1755

SHE SHIVERED, DESPITE THE HEAT OF THE HEARTH, AND glanced again toward the sunny rectangle of the cabin door. No one was there, not a shadow. But she felt that same uneasiness that had returned to her several times this morning: a sense that if she had looked a second sooner there would have been a figure in the doorway.

It was not the nature of Mary Draper Ingles to be afraid in the daytime. Sometimes in the deep wilderness nights, when the wolves wailed and the owls conspired high on the Blue Ridge east of the valley, when the dying fire made shapes move on the ceiling and the restless sleeping children rustled their corn-shuck mattresses, Mary Ingles would feel frightened. But seldom was she fearful in bright daylight like this, when the valley was familiar and peaceful and the locusts unreeled their eternal dry shrills under the summer sun.

Mary turned back to the cookfire. Its heat baked her sweaty face. The little black iron stewpot with the rabbit in it was almost bubbling over now. She pulled it across the iron arm a little, moving it away from the hottest coals, so that the stew might simmer the afternoon away and be at its tenderest when William came back up from the fields. The old clock at the far end of the room ticked slowly.

She brushed a strand of sweat-damp auburn hair back away from her cheek. She braced her palms on her knees to help lift her weight from the low puncheon stool and stood up, wheezing with the effort. Her swollen belly, firm and turgid with life, tugged down at all the strong young muscles of her torso. She smoothed the faded homespun cloth of her dress down over the mound and cupped her palms underneath, a caress

1

and an appraisal. It would be happening any day now; she could feel that.

She paused there, looking through the sunny doorway, out at the lush meadows, over the dark green treetops, toward the ranks of somber Allegheny mountains marching away to the west where no one except Indians lived.

This little group of cabins at Draper's Meadows was deeper into the mountains than any other white community in Virginia. It was the first settlement west of what her husband Will called the Allegheny "divide." She and Will had been, indeed, the first white people wed on this wild side of the Blue Ridge. Five years ago, it had been: a pastoral wedding between the blue mountains with God seeming to breathe through the whole vast stillness of it. And they had lived prosperously and happily and in peace those five years. Their health was robust and both of their first two children had lived. The valley, fertile with limestone-rich soil where dense bluegrass grew and rippled, was irrigated by never-failing limestone springs, whose waters flowed down crystalline creeks into the lovely, twisting New River and thence out of their valley into the uncharted west. It was a place for health and high spirits, where one's first look out the cabin door every morning made the heart swell up. So, surely her uneasiness of this morning would pass.

Of course, Mary Ingles knew, a woman's feelings are at their most unsettled, their most skittish, when she is full of the humors of childbearing. She tried to smile away her anxiety. Even William had made light of it this morning, as he often made light of women's fears. This morning he had passed it off just that way, as the spookishness of a mother-to-be.

"Must'ee go?" she had asked him after their Sunday morning prayers, when the valley had still been full of the shadow of the ridge. "I . . . I be afraid, a wee bit."

And William Ingles had hesitated here in this cabin door with his cradle scythe over one shoulder, a bag of hoecake and a watergourd over the other. He had never before heard Mary profess fear in the daytime. "Why afraid?" he had said then, with that joshing smile of his, looking down at her swollen middle. "When Tommy an' Georgie come, y' squzz 'em oot slick as a grape-pip. And your ma's here to help. Bettie's here, too, who wasna before. And if 'ee start birthin', why, only send down for me, and y' know I'll come a-runnin', Mary darlin'."

So she had smiled him away down toward the grainfield, that great, dear, strong, hairy man whom she loved till her heart ached with the sweetness of loving, that man who kept her from being as fearful as she might have been here in the wilds with a lesser man. She had not tried to explain to him this morning that it was not the birthing she feared. Nor, really, was it anything else she could name. She had stood in the doorway and watched him join her brother Johnny Draper at the edge of the meadow, strong Johnny with his own scythe over his shoulder, and they both had turned to wave back at her as they disappeared—seemed to sink—below the rippling grass at the brow of the meadow.

They would have been working four hours in the barley by now, she reckoned—scarcely ever pausing, shirtless, pouring sweat, probably singing to give a cadence to the sweep of their scythes. She knew how they looked working because she had always worked beside them. This was the first year she had not helped with the harvest; her term was too close. But she could envision them as clearly as if she were down there. Those two were durable men and could work all day long, even in this July sun.

Her eye somehow went to William's long rifle, which lay across its two pegs on the far wall, beside the grandfather clock, a powder horn and bullet bag hanging under it, and again she felt the foreboding. Should not he have carried the gun down to the fields with him, as he had done in the first few years? Lately he had simply dismissed it as extra weight.

The Indians who had passed up and down through Draper's Meadows since their arrival here in 1748 had never annoyed them nor given them cause for alarm. Usually they were parties from north of the distant O-y-o River, going down to raid their enemies, the Catawbas, who lived farther south. For centuries they had used the New River as their war road through the mountains. They had caves in its cliffs and canoes secreted in its tributaries. But even in their war paint, they had always been friendly with this little vanguard of white families here in the valley. They would always drink spring water offered them in gourd dippers, smacking their lips and smiling, apparently trying to dispel any uneasiness their war-painted faces and their bristling weaponry might be causing. Sometimes they would take bread that was offered to them, eat it while nodding in appreciation, and then stand and raise their hands in a peaceful salute and continue down the ridges. And then the white people who had remained hidden inside the cabins with their flintlocks cocked, ready for the first unfriendly move, would ease forward the hammers of their guns and exhale in relief, hang up the guns and come out to resume their work or to watch the savages fade into the woods. Only twice had Indians caused any mischief in this valley: in 1749 when a band had raided the cabin of Adam Harmon to steal furs, and in 1753 when another party had stolen skins from George Hoopaugh and Jacob Harmon and killed their barking dogs. Those were old and negligible incidents. So William Ingles had got out of the habit of taking his gun with him to the fields. "More sensible, I'd say, to leave it here for *your* peace o' mind," he had joked to her once this summer.

True, there was war in the land now, in distant places along the frontier, war against the French and their Indian allies. And once, a few months ago, a young Virginia lieutenant-colonel named Washington, a serious-looking giant of a fellow but a gentleman withal, had passed through this valley with a small escort of horsemen, talking to Colonel James Patton, the valley's militia leader, about what was happening in the distant conflict. Colonel Washington had advised Patton to have his people on their guard for armed Indian bands with Frenchmen among them.

But the people of Draper's Meadows had seen no French-men, and only friendly Indians; and the weeks had rolled on, and the plantings had been done; the crops had grown, and edibles from the woods had been gathered and preserved, and Bettie Draper's infant son had learned to crawl, and Mary Ingles' baby had made movements inside her; those were the main concerns of the people in this isolated valley where war surely had no reason to come. Their King was two thousand miles away in London Town and surely gave no more thought to these distant subjects of his than they gave to him. If he was at war with France, how could it affect them here in this valley His Majesty had never even heard of?

Still, Mary would think now and then with dread about Indians. Her mother, Elenor Draper, was a widow because George Draper had failed to return from a hunting expedition ten years ago and was presumed to have fallen victim to Indians. And though Mary had never seen any Indian exhibit a hostile look or gesture in her life, their existence out there beyond the western mountains did nonetheless hang like a dark cloud on the horizon of her mind, the only thing that seemed likely ever to trouble this Eden folded between the mountain ranges.

But now Mary was here on a peaceful summer Sunday, cooking for her beloved William, as on any day; in a moment she would take the family's soiled clothes over to the spring under the big willow and wash them there in that delightful cool place where the water purled and gurgled and refreshed one's soul as well as one's heated body. Her sister-in-law was over there already—Mary could hear her slapping her family's wet clothes against the rocks—and they would talk while they worked.

Thanks be to heaven that Johnny found himself such a cheerful and pretty wife, Mary thought. Mary had come to love and admire Bettie Robertson Draper, in the year since Johnny had gone over the mountain and brought her back as his bride. Mary had been midwife for Johnny and Bettie's firstborn, and that did make a bond between women.

Aye, Mary thought, the dread now beginning to drift off of her soul as she tied the soiled clothes and a cake of tallow soap into a bundle, there's nought to fear in this good place. Through a window she could hear the voices of her sons laughing and murmuring as they gathered berries in a nearby thicket with their grandmother. Aye, Mary felt, surely all's well here.

And so, swinging the bundle of clothes over her shoulder as

easily as a man might, Mary went out the door of the cabin, preceded by her swollen belly into the sunny fresh air.

The moment her gaze fell over the settlement, she realized that what she had been dreading was about to happen:

Indians were running crouched and swift toward every cabin in the settlement.

Shwop! Shwop! Shwop!

Bettie Draper, kneeling on a flat rock beside the spring near her cabin, slapped her husband's soapy shirt several times against the rock, then dipped it into the pool of cool water, held it there a moment, pulled it up and twisted it to wring the water out. She was in the shade of a big willow whose gnarled roots bulged out right over the spring. The constant shade and the delicate green ferns growing around the spring kept the place pleasant on the hottest days. Nearby, spread to dry over sunbaked rocks beyond the shade, more of her family's laundry lay, creamy-white linen and faded gray homespun. She hummed as she worked, pausing now and then with an ear toward the house for sounds of her baby's awakening. Her husband, Johnny, had built both a front door and a back door in their cabin, and when both doors were open, as now, the breeze up from the valley could flow through the house and the baby could nap comfortably in his hollowed-log cradle, not waking fitful and flushed and sweat-damp as he often did in the night when the doors were kept shut. It was so cool in the Draper cabin, in fact, that sometimes on the hot days Mary would bring her two-year-old boy Georgie over to nap there instead of in his own bed. "By heaven, Bettie," Mary had said with a conspiratorial smile only yesterday, "one day after the harvest, you and I sh'll take my Will from both sides at once, and 'suade that old hardhead t' saw me oot a back-way just like't."

Shwop! Shwop! Shwop! John's spare pair of britches now. As usual with a button off one knee and a tear in the seat, she noticed. A hard-working and a hard-playing man he was, strong as a bull and just as heedless, and there was something to mend every week when he changed his clothes. But Bettie smiled. She rejoiced in any chance to do some little thing for him. Johnny was a prize of a man indeed.

Now wringing out the britches, Bettie looked up and saw Casper Barrier, a neighbor, coming up toward the spring with two empty oaken pails dangling by ropes from a yoke across his shoulders. Casper was a widower, bald and lonely, and Bettie had observed that he would always drop whatever he was doing to come fetch his water when there was someone doing laundry at the spring. And he would strike up a chat, all innocent enough, and stay there wistful-eyed for as long as the hapless laundress would listen, talking about how good his wife had been to everyone, and about how he would never find as good a one to marry, so why even leave the valley to seek? Well, I won't have much time t' hear out Mr. Barrier's woes today, Bettie thought, inspecting the tear in the britches. With mending to do and all . . . the Sabbath's no day of rest when ye've a man to care for . . .

When she looked up again, Casper Barrier was no longer walking toward the spring. He was lying face down on the footpath. A naked Indian, painted and shining in the sunlight, crouched over him, chopping into the back of his head. Casper's bald scalp was bright with new blood. There were other Indians running down the slope from the path.

A scream tore out of Bettie Draper's throat. She jumped to her feet. By instinct she sprinted toward the cabin, to get to her sleeping baby. She screamed again and again as she ran, screams that were not coherent words because there were no words for this.

In the corner of her eye she saw figures running as if to flank her, heard the slumping of their breath. She leaped with flying skirts upon the front-door threshold and into the cabin's shadowy interior. She snatched her baby boy out of the cradle and ran straight out the back door. *"PLEASE GOD!"* she was screaming now. *"HELP! MARY! ELLIE! INDIANS! THEY KILT CAS . . . OH GOD HELP! . . ."*

Colonel James Patton was sitting at a table inside the door of his cabin, writing a report to Colonel Washington—a report of nothing. The region, which he knew well because of his huge landholdings and his responsibility as militia chief, had lain in utter peace since Colonel Washington's visit; there had not been a tremor of disturbance anywhere on this western side of the Blue Ridge. Colonel Patton was in fact just now trying to organize the early harvest rather than any sort of military readiness. He had just sent his nephew Bill Preston down Sinking Creek to Philip Lybrook's house to ask him to come up and help with the barley cutting.

James Patton leaned back in his chair and looked at the page upon which he had been writing. He put the quill in the ink bottle and twirled it there, resting his other hand on his thigh. White chin-whiskers hid his broad chest. His chair creaked under the weight of his powerful frame as he extended a leg straight out under the table. Sitting cramped him, and he hated anything—ledgers and letters—that took him off his horse or out of the fields or woods and made him have to fold himself up to fit furniture.

On the table by his right hand lay a great antique weapon that he had kept with him ever since he had grown big enough to carry it. It was a claymore—a straight broadsword, as long as an ordinary man stood tall, and it weighed as much as an axe. It had been passed down through his family along with a legend that it had belonged to some ancestor who had been a Scottish Highland chieftain. Its hilt was made to be held by two hands, and an ordinary man needed two hands to wield it. But old James Patton, who was four inches over six feet tall, had always been able to swing it, with equal facility, by either hand, and could do so even now as a sixty-three-year-old widower. Though it was too precious to use as an everyday tool, James Patton had found occasion in camp or in the fields to lop down thick hardwood saplings or branches with this great weapon, usually in a single stroke.

The dazzling doorway suddenly was darkened. At the same moment, a woman's voice screamed outdoors. Colonel Patton looked up from his word gathering, and his heart leaped. Two painted Indians had entered, each with a raised tomahawk, and as James Patton grabbed the handle of his great sword, he saw others at the door.

The colonel wasted no time getting free of the furniture.

Rather, he exploded into a standing position, hurling the heavy table at the Indians with an upsweep of his left arm while the chair fell backward with a clatter behind him. The flying table slammed one of the braves back against the doorway. The second warrior had nimbly sidestepped, and with a gurgling yell he aimed a tomahawk blow at the old man's forehead. But the broadsword swished, glittering, and the warrior felt a strange tug in his shoulder and saw his forearm fall to the floor, spurting dark blood. It was the last thing the warrior saw; the great sword whiffed again and his head rolled on the cabin floor.

Another warrior was in the doorway. He saw the terrible old man advancing on him holding the long, bloody sword by both hands and roaring with fury. As the brave raised his tomahawk to strike, the old man grunted and swung and the sword came around and passed through the Indian's waist, parting everything but his spine. The Indian sagged, his bloody intestines spilling out.

Colonel Patton tried to ready his sword for the next Indian in the doorway, but at the end of his last great upward swipe, the point of the blade had jabbed two inches deep into one of the low ceiling beams. Blood ran down the blade to the hilt and reddened Colonel Patton's hands. And as he strained to free the weapon from the wood, the Shawnee on the threshold took aim and pulled the trigger of his musket. There was a roaring orange flash, and a musketball smashed through Colonel Patton's temple into his brain.

The Indians crouched in the doorway speechless for a moment in the blue powder-smoke and watched the white-haired giant begin to fall. One bloody hand slipped off the sword hilt, and then the other, and his huge body bumped to the floor.

The hilt of the embedded claymore thrummed up and down, spraying blood onto the corpse.

Bettie Draper was running hard now toward the Ingleses' cabin, her crying baby clutched in her right arm. She saw Mary Ingles standing dumbstruck on the doorstoop in the sunlight with a bundle over her shoulder. And the Indians, their presence now revealed by Bettie's alarm, broke their silence with yelps and howls. They sounded like a hundred devils wailing in the valley.

One of the warriors pursuing Bettie stopped in his tracks, aimed his musket and fired.

Her scream broke off in a gasp of pain as the musketball broke her right arm. The infant fell to the ground and Bettie spun away, falling to her knees. Her face was chalky with shock. She saw her baby lying sprawled in the grass a few feet away; she saw lithe, yipping savages running toward him with their tomahawks and clubs.

Bettie lurched back to her feet, ran to where the baby lay, scooped him up from the ground with her good arm and continued running.

Bettie's plight at last jolted Mary into action. She dropped her bundle of clothing and turned back inside the cabin. She grabbed Will's loaded rifle off its wall pegs and waddled back to the door with it. In the front of her mind was the urgent need to save Bettie and the baby; in the back of her mind was an awful question: whether the savages had yet found her own little sons and her mother.

The scene outside the cabin door made Mary, for the first time in her life, furious enough to kill.

Several warriors were having sport with Bettie's shrieking baby, tossing it back and forth between them, while another held Bettie by her dark hair and forced her to watch. She was on her knees, and her shrieks sounded as if they must be tearing out the membranes of her throat. One of the Indians was trying to hit the baby with his tomahawk as it hurtled through the air. The blade struck the baby and brought him to earth. Then the warriors scrambled for him as if they were playing some game of ball-scrimmage. They were laughing and howling; Bettie and the baby were screaming.

Mary's head was roaring with outrage. She tried to cock the flintlock hammer. Twice it slipped under her sweating hand.

Now one of the Indians had the bleeding screaming baby by its ankle. Lurching away from the other two, he swung the baby in a wide arc and dashed his brains out against the corner logs of the cabin. The baby's screams were punctuated by that awful squishing thud. Bettie's cries stopped also: she was beyond being able to scream.

In that awful silence the warrior, pirouetting triumphantly and holding the baby high overhead, its smashed skull dribbling blood on him, turned to find another white woman, this one big with child, standing on a doorstoop five feet from him with a cocked rifle aimed straight at his eyes. He froze. His mouth dropped open. Baby blood was spotting the ochre and blue paint on his face.

Mary pulled the trigger.

The hammer clicked. The gun did not fire.

She remembered then that Will always left the barrel loaded, but the firing pan uncharged, when he hung up the gun.

"No," she groaned. She simply stood there, resigned, the useless gun still at her shoulder, her eyes now darting wildly toward the berry patch for a last sight of her mother and sons. She felt strong hands grab her hair from behind and her head was yanked back and all she could see was the clear blue sky and the eave of the cabin roof.

She felt the the gun being torn from her hands and heard the Indians laughing at her.

* * *

Elenor Draper loved to take her grandsons berry picking in the summer, and herb gathering and mushroom and wild-grape hunting in their season, mostly because little Thomas had such an inquisitive mind and imagination. Tommy had been born here in Draper's Meadows and had never been anywhere else in his four years of life, but he was endlessly fascinated by the idea that his grandmother had once lived in a land far beyond a great ocean. They would reach carefully into the wild raspberry brambles and gently squeeze off the bright red berries, squeezing them ever so lightly so as not to crush them, reaching gingerly so as not to scratch their hands on the thorns, and as they did this with half their attention she would try to make him visualize what an ocean was. They had recited all this many times and surely would do it many times more, because his curiosity about the Atlantic Ocean seemed insatiable.

"Now, look'ee then to th' top o' that mountain yonder, Tommy-lad . . ." He stood up straight and looked where she pointed, his dark eyes squinting, freckled nose crinkling, a breeze moving wisps of his thick red-brown hair across his forehead. ". . . an' suppose now that was water all the way to there." He nodded in appreciation of that wonderful notion but waited to hear the rest. "And now suppose y' come all that way on th' water . . ."

"In a boat."

". . . in a boat, and then *ten times that far* . . ."

He held his hands up with his ten berry-stained fingers spread.

". . . Aye, an' then suppose ten times even farther than *that* . . ."

And little Georgie, two years old, trying to match his brother's concentration and understanding, held up his hands in imitation at the word *ten*.

". . . An' then still ten times *more* . . ."

Tommy nodded with satisfaction now, knowing those were the numbers of tens in her recitation.

"And beyond all that water, ten times ten times ten, with neither tree nor hill to be seen, y'd find a wee land called . . ."

"Ireland!" he cried.

"Ireland. And up in Ireland ye'd find a place called . . ."

"County Donegal!"

"County Donegal. And that is where y'r grandfather George Draper an' me come from on a boat, twenty-six years ago . . ."

"George! Me!" interjected Georgie, his namesake.

"Aye. When I were a young lass an' pretty just like y'r mama be now . . ."

"An' sh'll I ever go over the ocean to County Donegal?" That was the question Tommy liked to ask each time at this point in their reverie.

"Ye might; aye, ye might. But rather, I see ye goin' still farther th' *other* way. Ten times ten times ten," she said, pointing westward, "right over that mountain there, and on, Tommy, as we ha' been a-comin' bit by bit by bit since y'r grandfather an' m'self was young like y'r own mother an' father . . ."

She stopped talking suddenly.

Screams, wordless, terrified screams, were coming up from the cabins. Elenor Draper's face turned nearly as white as her hair. It was the voice of her daughter-in-law.

"What's wrong with Auntie Bettie?" asked Tommy. Little Georgie ran into his grandmother's skirt and hugged her leg. The awful tone of the screaming voice had scared him speechless.

"Come," Elenor Draper urged. She put down the pail of berries and grabbed the children's hands, hurrying them out of the brambles onto the path down to the cabins. Bettie must have hurt herself somehow, she thought.

Elenor and the boys emerged from the thicket onto the meadow by the cabins just as the Indian yells and gunfire broke out. She stopped suddenly, a shiver of terror pouring through her, and turned to drag the boys back into concealment.

But it was too late. Three Indians running with guns had seen them and now came bounding up the path with quavering mad howls.

Elenor Draper thrust the children ahead of her into the path among the berry bushes. "Go hide!" she hissed, then turned to face the pursuers.

She had nothing to fight with but her fingernails. Not even teeth.

The first Indian was upon her at once. His dark eyes glittered with the hunter's thrill. Old Elenor Draper struck into them with fingers hooked like claws. The Indian bellowed and, blinded, dropped his gun and tomahawk to capture her wrists. Then another Indian came close and she felt a blade go into her side, under her ribs. She heard her own gurgling animal growl as she sank.

She felt fingers pulling at her hair, pulling hard, felt herself hanging above the ground with all her weight depending from the roots of her hair. Naked, greasy brown limbs—legs and arms—moved around her, struggled with her. A knee smashed into her face and her nose caved in. Then she felt another blade slice into her scalp. Blood ran down over her eyes. She felt her scalp separate from the skull with a *pop* and then she was lying on the bloody green grass, a distance of ten times ten times ten from the green grass of County Donegal, all her life running hot and wet out of her.

Footsteps ran away through the brambles, faint and more faint until she could hear nothing but the rushing of an ocean.

Mary Ingles stood in the blood-spattered yard in front of her house. Her wrists were bound tight behind her with leather thongs and an Indian still held her erect by his grip in her hair. Her scalp anticipated the slash of the knife. She was praying silently, moving her lips.

Dear Heavenly God I do not want to die. But if Thou'll spare William and our sons and my mum I am ready to go in their place.

The shooting had stopped and the Indians had ceased their yipping. They were coming into the yard a few at a time from various places in the settlement. They were grinning, thrusting their weapons at the sky, laughing, some smeared with blood. Four warriors came down the slope from the little cabin of Henry Lenard, dragging him along on the ground by a noose. His hands were bound behind him. He struggled silently, in spasms of effort. Henry was an unmarried man, more hunter than farmer by nature, who had come to this valley with the Draper and Ingles families. He was a short and slight man, and the Indians dragged him with ease despite his kicking. He was not bloody, apparently having been caught unwounded.

Bettie Draper knelt nearby on the grass over her slaughtered baby, her shoulders quaking with a voiceless weeping. Her broken arm hung bloody and unheeded, as if she could not even feel it through the pain in her heart. Mary wanted to go to her but could not move. She stood and scanned the thicket, beginning to have a hope that her mother and sons had slipped away undetected during the attack.

Then she saw a movement in the edge of the berry thicket, and her heart surged. "Mum!" she cried. "Go back! Run!"

But it was an Indian who emerged from the foliage. He raised his arm and waved something gray and red. Mary looked at it as the warrior came near, and with a feeling that her soul was being crushed, recognized it as her mother's scalp. She lunged and wailed, only to be yanked back by her own hair so forcefully that she fell on her back to the ground, her bound wrists twisted under her back.

The Indian whom Mary had tried to shoot a few minutes before came and stood over her, grinning as if very amused. He bent and prodded the bulge of her belly with hard fingers. He said something, and the other Indian, who now had a foot on her neck to pin her down, answered with a short laugh.

The warrior quit prodding her belly and reached down for the hem of her skirt. He began drawing it up, until it was gathered under her breasts. The sun beat on her naked legs and loins and the turgid mound of her abdomen. She watched him with loathing and a rising panic as he reached for the waistband of his breechclout.

"Heavenly God!" she screamed. That they would rape a woman in full term of pregnancy, about to give the sacred gift of life, was to her an inhumanity even beyond murder. She shut her eyes and locked her legs together and prayed with all her soul for some miraculous strength, or death itself, to protect her from this final brutality.

She felt a pain at her navel: a sharp point of pain, pressing inward there. The Indians were laughing and talking. She was not being raped. Not yet. What . . .

She opened her eyes. The Indian was kneeling beside her and was watching her face is if he had been waiting for her to look at him. Her terror deepened when she saw what he was doing.

The savage was pressing the point of a knife hard against her abdomen, almost breaking the skin. He nodded at her, as if to say: *Now watch what I am going to do.* She had heard tales of pregnant women being slit open and their babies cooked and eaten by savages in blood lust.

She could not even pray now. She rolled her eyes back into

her head and tried to die. She felt the knife point moving from her navel downward toward her genitals. She felt the rough grass under her bare back. A warbler was singing nearby. And she heard Bettie Draper saying, barely above a whisper:

"Oh, no. Don't do that to her."

A rush of love swept through Mary. That Bettie in her grief could plead for me! she thought. The terrible moment suddenly took on a strange, desperate beauty. If Mary and her unborn baby were to die, it would not be in a truly loveless world, after all.

Several of the Indians were talking now, one in a great, deep voice. And through their voices Mary thought she heard Tommy's voice. The pain went away from her stomach. The foot was lifted off her neck. She opened her eyes and looked at the Indian, who was rising and sheathing his knife. Whether he had only been terrorizing her or had decided not to rip out her womb she did not know. A tall warrior with the air of a chieftain stood nearby and his was that powerful deep voice; perhaps he had ordered this to cease. Mary felt a swollen and almost delirious sense of deliverance. Henry Lenard was on his feet a few yards away, still tethered by the neck, his face mottled red and averted from Mary's sprawling nakedness.

And then there was Tommy's voice again. He was uttering a low, terrified moan. Mary looked around and saw her two sons. A warrior stood between them, holding each by the hair. Their faces were contorted and flushed and wet with tears, blood and slobber, and they appeared to be out of their senses with fear. Mary turned onto her side and tried to rise but could not with her hands bound. She lay now with the side of her face on the ground and looked at them. "Tommy," she said, surprised that she could produce a calm voice. "Georgie." She had learned to anticipate the worst and expected that they had been brought here to be slaughtered before her eyes.

"Tommy. Georgie," she repeated. They gave no sign of hearing.

The delicate, sweet voice of the warbler continued.

CHAPTER
2

"HOLD," SAID WILLIAM INGLES.

"What is't?" asked John Draper. They stopped and stood still, holding their scythes. Will squinted over the sun-bright field and listened. Nothing but the rush of the breeze and the rasping shrill of insects, and their own heavy breathing. John's torso was streaming sweat. His shirt was off, its sleeves tied around his neck so that it hung like a short mantle to protect his shoulders from the sun. He mopped his face with a corner of it and turned his head this way and that. "Y' heard somethin'?"

"A gun, I thought," said William. "Might be just my head a-poppin' in this heat, though. Y' heard nought, eh, Johnny?"

John Draper shook his head. "But I hear my guts a-grumblin' for victuals, an' I'm as dry as last year's gourd. Now't we be stopt, what say y' to a little grub and water?"

They grounded their scythes and went among their shocks of newly cut barley to the deep shade of a great elm in the middle of the field. They sat and leaned their backs against the trunk and drank water. Then they dug into their pouches for chunks of hoecake and began to eat. William's brindled chinwhiskers rose and fell over his sweat-soaked shirtfront as he chewed. The breeze made the wet shirt almost shivery cool.

"What crossed my mind, 'twere a signal Mary's started t' labor," he mused.

"More likely Hank a-shootin' 'imself some beastie f'r the cookpot," said John. "Mary's no sort to fetch y'outer th' field for a mere birthin'."

"True. Lest she was a-havin' trouble with it." He remembered her strange confession of fear that morning.

"Not Mary," said John around his bread. "Tougher'n either you nor me. Growed up 'longside me, just like a man. Y'know, how she c'd mount a horse in a leap. Jump over a chairback from a standstill. Naw. Like 's not she'll have th' baby on 'er teat and be splittin' cookwood with 'er free hand by th' time we're home." He chuckled. He was proud of his sister, and thought Will coddled her too much.

Will grinned. There was truth in Johnny's words. Mary at twenty-three was fit as green hickory, and a joy to behold. Wide enough in the hips to give birth easily, but slim and firm and smooth-skinned. William thought of her now with a longing and a tingling. It had been a long time since they had embraced that way, and Will Ingles was a vigorous and needful man by nature. When she was with child, Will would daydream a lot about their nakedness and her flat stomach that he remembered, and the surges of strength with which she would give herself to him.

And her eyes. In the firelight her eyes would blaze when they were doing that. Dauntless and willing and happy. Will and Mary had always rejoiced in each other and in the way they fit and in the way they loved. Folks often would remark that those two needed only each other and the rest of the world could go hang. But of course anybody who said that didn't know how important their land and children were to them. Now, give me my Mary *and* my wee'uns and my land, Will thought, and the rest *can* go hang.

His heart swelled with these feelings now, with longings that came from way back and went far ahead, as if spanning mountains. This was like the feeling of prayer to Will Ingles, to think of what he had and what might yet be. And in the heart of this feeling there was always Mary's face, those straightforward eyes, that golden down on her jaw, finer than peach fur, that stealthy smile that came at the oddest times and made three tiny dimples under each corner of her mouth. I wonder if most men pass as much time as I do with their heads full of their wives, he thought.

But again he remembered her anxious face this morning. She has a way of knowing things are going to happen, he admitted. When she had an instinct, he couldn't ignore it, even if he might try to laugh it off or say something to set her womanly qualms at ease. She just *knows,* somehow, like animals before storms.

"Johnny," he said suddenly, "y' might hop back to work or y' might nap, but I've got it in me t' walk up there an' look in on Mary. I jus' can't seem t' shrug it."

"So be it. As y' will, y'will, Will." Johnny chuckled. He liked to say that. Ol' Will. Always fussing over Mary as if she were frail and helpless. Still, better your sister's married to a man who cares too much than one who cares too little.

A copse of timber, marking the head of a wooded gully, jutted into the grainfield between the settlement and the elm where Will Ingles now left his brother-in-law resting, and the tops of its trees hid their view of the distant cabins. Will waded through the sunny fields toward the end of that timber, to go around it and then up. His leggings whisked in the high grain, and butterflies tumbled away before him. At the edge of the wood he saw a flash of brown: a deer plunging down into the gully.

I'm doubtless a fool, he thought, wasting an hour of good working light just to settle some head-spook Mary gave me.

But when he cleared the end of the woods, he saw smoke rising from among the house roofs, half a mile away. His heartbeat quickened, and he broke into a run up the long meadow, raced through a field of green corn and jumped over a rail fence.

By the time Will reached Casper Barrier's cabin and saw it burning, he was sure that Draper's Meadows had been attacked by Indians, though he had not seen any of them yet. He dropped to a crouch and moved with stealth, his pulse pounding in his ears. He crept to a corner of the cabin, hearing the busy crackle of flames inside, and peered around. Now he could see the knot of Indians, milling about in the yard up near his own cabin. There seemed at first glance to be perhaps twenty warriors, Shawnees, judging by their paint and ornamentation, some of them handling the settlement's horses, other carrying household items out of the cabins and sorting and examining them. They were in high spirits. Will craned and leaned forward, his nape bristling with anger and the chill of fear as he searched the clearing for a sign of Mary or the children. Then some Indians moved aside and he saw them, the abject little cluster of captives sitting, bound, among pots and kettles and blankets and other booty.

There was Mary; she seemed not to be hurt. She was kneeling on the ground, facing Georgie and Tommy, who sat on the ground near her. Even from this distance, Will could see that the boys' faces were pallid with fear. There too was Bettie Draper, her head hung far forward. Henry Lenard stood nearby, bound, an armed Indian holding him secure by a neck noose. Will looked for his mother-in-law and for Colonel Patton and Casper Barrier and Bill Preston and Jim Cull, all the other people who had been present at the settlement that morning, but could not see them. Either they had escaped or were lying dead somewhere, he guessed. He edged forward to the door of Casper's cabin to look in. The most pressing desire in his hammering heart was to get his hands on a gun. Then he could try to imagine what to do next, though there seemed nothing he could do against so large a body of savages. But with a gun he would be a little less helpless . . .

Two braves emerging just then from the smoky interior of Casper's house, their arms full of blankets and clothing and utensils, almost stepped on Will. Their eyes bugged and they dropped their loot and yelled. Will turned and bolted back the way he had come.

His feet thudded in the grass. He leaped the rail fence and plunged through the cornfield. He could hear both braves behind him, yipping, their bodies swishing through the cornleaves as they came after him. He was sprinting with all his power, but they were swift and he was not getting away from them. Bursting out of the corn and pounding down across the meadow, he glanced back and saw them coming, each with a drawn tomahawk.

He realized that he had started running directly toward the place where he had left Johnny Draper, as if Johnny might help him. But Johnny was unarmed, too. Mustn't lead them onto him, Will thought. He veered to his left, heading toward the wooded gully where he had seen the deer vanish minutes before. If I can get in there . . . maybe lose them, he thought. Or at least find a stick to . . . fight 'em with . . .

His legs were burning with exhaustion. His breath wheezed. But the Indians' yells were coming from a little farther back now; he had gained ground here in the open.

He plunged into the moist green shadow at the edge of the wood, down the gully. Leafy limbs lashed at his face and shoulders as he plunged headlong through them like a bullet. He could hear the rustling progress of the Indians in the woods behind him. They seemed to be gaining again.

A huge fallen ash lay on the gully slope across his path. Its great root system jutted up from the hole in the forest floor where it had been anchored. Will had too much momentum to veer around it; instead he leaped to clear the trunk. He did not leap high enough. His foot struck the top of the log and he somersaulted through space. He landed with a grunting thump on his shoulders in a shower of last year's dead leaves. Before he could regain his footing, the two warriors sped by, around the upturned tree roots and down the gully, disappearing into the underbrush below. They had not seen him!

Will scrambled to his feet and struck off at a right angle from the path of the chase. They would discover soon that he was no longer ahead of them, and they would double back. He would have all he could handle to shake them. Later then he could find Johnny Draper. Then the two of them would . . .

Would what? They were unarmed. They were helpless to follow and rescue Mary and Bettie and the children from so large a war party. And it would be at least a two-day trip back over the Blue Ridge to raise an armed company to go in pursuit—even if anyone would come . . .

God, O God Eternal, big Will Ingles thought as he trotted through the woods, feeling more hopeless and helpless with each step. *God tell me what to do!* In his mind he saw Mary's comely face and the faces of his boys and the old gray head of Elenor Draper. He knew it was likely that they all would be murdered before this day was out. His entire family! And not a drop of his blood would then pump through any other living heart!

Something kept telling him he should have plunged in among the Indians and fought and died with his family.

He plodded on through the woods, his soul crushed, and soon every step he took jarred a sob of guilt and misery out of him.

The warriors led their train of stolen horses out of the sunlight of the meadows down into the profound humid green shade of the forest and into a creek bed. They went westward in the ankle-deep water, which washed away their trail at once.

In bundles on the back of one horse were the bodies of the two braves Colonel Patton had killed with his broadsword. On the horse behind that one, Mary Ingles rode, holding her son Georgie before her. She rode unblinking, in a state of shock, her head wobbling on a limp neck with the horse's movements. She had hardly heeded the Shawnee chieftain when he had said, in English:

"Mo-ther will ride."

And they had put her on the horse, and had handed her little boy up to her.

Bettie Draper, in a trance of grief, rode astride the next horse, with Tommy behind her. He sat with his arms around her waist and the side of his face pressed against her back, his eyes glazed. Bettie's broken right arm hung bloody and untreated at her side.

The other horses were laden with everything the Indians had seen fit to carry away from the burning settlement: tools, clothing, pots and kettles, blankets, guns and ammunition. From the Ingleses' house they had brought virtually every movable thing except the grandfather clock; they had shied away from its mysterious ticking noise and left it standing by the wall.

Still secured by wrist-thongs and the noose around his neck, Henry Lenard splashed afoot down the stream. The other end of his noose was tied to the baggage on a horse's back. If he lagged, he would be jerked forward and fall, to be dragged almost under the horse's hooves. Thus he concentrated on his pace and footing and did not try to speak with Mary Ingles or Bettie Draper. Nor did he try to look back and

see whether their husbands were following. He simply behaved very well, knowing that his life depended on it.

The creek curved around the base of a mountain. After
progressing about half a mile, the party emerged into the
sunlight in a cleared patch of bottomland. Through the numbness of her soul, Mary Ingles was vaguely aware that this was
the little homestead of old Phillip Barger. This brook they had
followed, she knew, led to Sinking Creek, whereon Mr. and
Mrs. Lybrook lived farther down. And their house was the
last they would encounter. At the end of Sinking Creek they
would come to the New River, upon which, she knew, no
white man lived. Adam Harmon and his sons had a hunting
shack and a cornpatch there, but seldom stayed there. There
was too much Indian traffic on the New River.

The Shawnees stopped the horses a few yards from Mr.
Barger's cabin, which was little more than a hut. The tall
chieftain spoke to two warriors, who vanished into the corn
toward the cabin with their muskets at the ready.

Mary suddenly was aware that they were going to attack the
old man.

"Mister Barger!" she cried at the top of her voice. "Indians!" *In* . . ." her voice was choked off by a strong brown
hand at her throat. And as she tried to take in breath through
that powerful grip, she saw the snowy-haired old man emerge
into the sunlight at his cabin door, blinking, looking around.
He did not see the two Indians until they materialized on both
sides of him and pinioned his arms.

Then the chieftain called something to them. He drew
Colonel Patton's broadsword from its scabbard, which was
lashed to the side of one of the packhorses, and strode
through the corn. He stopped in front of the old man and said
something to the two braves, who then twisted the old man's
arms up behind him and forced him into a kneeling position,
bent so far forward that his silvery forelock almost swept the
ground. Holding the broadsword in both hands, the tall
Shawnee laid the blade on the back of Philip Barger's neck for
an instant, then raised it.

Mary Ingles shut her eyes and put her hand over Georgie's
face to shield his eyes.

Even at this distance, she heard it, the *swish* of the great blade, then the murmur of the Indians' voices.

When the chieftain came grinning back to the pack train, he held the bloody sword in one hand. From his other hand hung a cloth bag, stained red, something heavy and round in it. Mary tried not to look at it as the party proceeded down sinking Creek toward the Lybrook house. The warriors were in a cheerful mood now, laughing and chatting, as if the beheading of Philip Barger had fulfilled some last requirement of their bloody mission. Revenge, perhaps, for what another old white man had done to two of their brothers with that same big Scottish sword.

Colonel Patton's nephew, Captain Bill Preston, was at that moment leaving the Lybrook cabin with Philip Lybrook. They had shouldered the tools they would need to help with the harvest up at Draper's Meadows, said good-bye to Mrs. Lybrook and her small son John and started up Sinking Creek.

"Now I'd reckon," said Mr Lybrook, "we'd save us a half hour if we jus' cut across th' mountain here. They's a good path 'crost t' the Drapers'. If'n y' don't mind a wee climb."

"Lead on, Mr. Lybrook."

They left the creek bottom and turned into the forest and began a diagonal ascent up the steep mountainside along a well-worn deer path. Sunlight penetrated the oak and maple foliage and dappled the fern-covered slope, the mossy stone outcroppings. The climb quickened their breathing and they talked little.

"And how fares your uncle?" Philip Lybrook said after a while as they labored toward the crest of the ridge.

"As always," said Preston. "In the best of health and still working like a yoke of oxen."

"Good. And pray what says 'ee to th' Indian War?"

"That we hearabouts sh'll likely never get even a whiff of it... Whoa, now!" They had reached the stony spine of the ridge. Preston pointed toward Draper's Meadows. "Look 'ee yonder. They's somethin' big a-burnin' there."

"Aye!" Philip Lybrook began trotting heavily down the

mountain path. "Folly me lively. Might be we can help 'em put
it out yet!"

Mrs. Lybrook stepped to her cabin door at the sound of
hooves grating on the creekbed gravel. Her son Johnny came
running up through the garden looking back fearfully. He
grabbed her wrist and dodged behind her skirts to peer out at
the Indians and horses that had just halted in the creek.

"God help us," murmured Mrs. Lybrook. She had caught a
glimpse of blue and gray cloth and white faces among the
Indian party, and she squinted hard. "They've got Bettie and
Mary. Oh, God help us!"

Three of the Indians had detached themselves from the
group and were coming toward the house. They were smiling
and talking cheerfully and seemed not to be armed; but for
the sight of their captives, Mrs. Lybrook might have presumed they were friendly.

The tall, lithe warrior leading the trio raised his hand in
greeting as he came. His smile was handsome and pleasant
despite the parallel streaks of ochre paint across his nose and
cheekbones; his teeth were white in his russet face. Mrs.
Lybrook stood frozen with fear and doubt, afraid that she
would provoke them if she ducked inside for Philip's gun. And
Philip, she thought, dread building inside her: What have they
done to my Philip? He and Captain Preston surely would've
met these savages up along Sinking Creek, aye, but minutes
ago.

The chieftain emerged from the garden now and stopped a
pace in front of Mrs. Lybrook. He raised a cloth bag darkened
with blood and held it up to her. Johnny was quaking so hard
he was shaking her.

"Man here you know," said the Indian, glancing at the
laden bag and then back at her eyes. He thrust it closer to her.
He wanted her to take it.

Mrs. Lybrook was growing dizzy. All her blood seemed to
be draining to her feet; she felt certain at once that the bag
contained some grisly remnant of her husband.

Finally the Indian grabbed her arm and thrust the neck of
the bag into her hand.

She stood there holding it, holding its awful swinging weight, while the warrior said something to his braves. They shoved past Mrs. Lybrook and her son into the cabin and then came out carrying Mr. Lybrook's musket and a bag of barley, four big turnips and half a haunch of cooked venison—all the ready food that had been in the house. They spoke to their chieftain and went back toward the horses. Then he raised his hand again, still smiling that mocking smile, and turned away to go after them.

Mrs. Lybrook stood, she knew not how long, holding the bloody bag in her shaking hand, until its weight made her arm ache and she had to do something about it. She clenched her jaw, shut her eyes and prayed a moment for strength, and ordered Johnny to go into the house and wait. She took one last look after the party of Indians and captives, seeing a glimpse of Bettie Draper's white face turned back toward her just before they vanished into the leafy shadows. Then she opened the bag and peered down into it with God's name on her lips. She gasped and flung the bag away and sank to her knees in a turmoil of gratitude and horror as the bloody package thumped to the ground and rolled flopping to the garden's edge.

It was not her husband, thank the Lord.

But she knew that her soul was marked forever by the vision of old Philip Barger's bulging dead eyes staring up at her from among strands of bloodied white hair in the bottom of a stained linen bag.

CHAPTER
3

MARY GROANED AS THE HORSE'S PROGRESS DOWN THE BOULDER-strewn streambed jostled her. It was the first time she was aware that she had groaned; perhaps she had been doing so all afternoon. But now pain was working its way up through the numbness of her despair, the aches and stresses in her swollen belly forcing her to be aware of the real world they were passing through, forcing her to sit the horse consciously, forcing her to hold on to little Georgie, forcing the hideous images of the day out of her mind until they grew dim and dimmer like night-dreams retreating from daylight. She concentrated on bracing her stomach and back muscles to restrain the wobble and plunge of the mass within her, to protect it from violent motion. And gradually, as pain reminded her of her senses one by one, her view of the world expanded. Her skin began to tell her of the humid valley air, the trickling of her own sweat, the crawling of wood ticks, the bites and stings of mosquitoes and no-see-ums, the rubbing of the horse's hair against the inside of her knees, the whip and drag of leafy branches across her face and shoulders. Then the smells: the dank breath of wet limestone, the horse's sweating withers, the rotting of vegetation on the steep creek banks and the strong smell from her little boy in front of her, who sometimes during this ordeal had smirched his clothes.

And she began to hear: she heard Georgie's occasional little whimpers, the grating and splashing of hooves in the stream, the gurgle of its fast water over the rocks, the soughing of a breeze in the treetops high on the hillsides, the low, brief words of the Shawnees when they spoke to each other, the wet blowing of horses along the line and now and then Bettie

Draper's voice, groaning with pain, sighing God's name or
trying to soothe Tommy with some dubious reassurance.

The creek ravine was filling with deep shadow. Pinpoints of
late afternoon sunlight flashed occasionally through the foliage ahead. Under the horse she saw the pellucid creek water
curling and seething over brown and mossy stone; ahead
were the horses' rumps and swishing tails and their burdens
of loot, the flicking ears and bobbing mane of her own horse,
the dusky, muscular backs of the warriors and the rocky,
wooded slopes of the mountains that rose steep and gloomy
on both sides of the creek.

And then eventually under these proddings from her senses
Mary returned to the present enough to begin to think. She
thought of the unborn baby inside her, which surely would be
forced soon, by this eternal jouncing and by her legs' grip on
the horse's ribs, to give up its tenure in the refuge of her
womb and come forth into this hopeless world. She thought of
the attention Tommy and Georgie would need when this
march should stop for the night. She thought of Bettie's broken and bleeding arm, and wondered if she would be allowed
to try to treat it. She wondered whether Will and Johnny had
truly escaped the notice of the Indians, and wondered
whether they might be trying to follow. That wan hope rose in
her breast and would not go down.

She thought of her mother lying dead somewhere and scal-
ped near the burning settlement. And of Bettie's baby, slaughtered before their very eyes. She squinted and bit into the
flesh of her lip to keep that grievous memory from over-
powering her. She wondered about James Cull and Philip
Lybrook and Bill Preston, none of whom she had seen killed.
And then about Will and John again. If they all found each
other they might dare to follow us, she thought. But dear God
the heathens have brought every gun there was in the settlement, I'm sure; what could they do for us if they did follow?

And she began to wonder why she and her children, and
Bettie and Henry, had not been killed. Perhaps we're hostages against pursuit, she thought. Or we're to be ransomed.

Nay, she thought, more likely enslaved. Our children to
grow up slaves.

But she knew as well that they might have been spared only for the present, that they might be destined for those tortures of which all white wilderness settlers had heard. Maybe we're to be sacrificed, she thought. Or eaten. The legends of Indian brutality stopped at nothing.

She knew with certainty that their lives were in a precarious balance. If we make noise or slow 'em down, she thought, they'll kill us at once. Thank God my children are no crybabies, she thought. At a first wail they'd doubtless be brained.

I must tell Bettie these things if we get a minute together, she thought. In case she's not thought of them. So's she'll know how to conduct herself.

I would tell her now, she thought, but this chieftain seems to know our tongue. And I reckon they'd kill us if we tried to talk to each other now.

Mary did not know how far they had come. In her trance she had not been aware of time nor of landmarks. She could not remember anything about the journey since the murder of Mr. Barger. She had no recollection of riding out of one streambed or descending into another, and so she presumed that they were still moving downstream in Sinking Creek. But, she realized, we might have crossed a mountain and I'd not have noticed.

With a sudden surge of her heart, half of panic and half of hope, Mary Ingles realized a desperate need to know where she was.

If I know, she thought, if I remember the way, maybe I could find my way back! Something might happen and we'd get free. And if it does, we *must* know the way home. To be lost is to die. She had heard William state that warning. He was always warning her and the children not to stray out of sight of the cabins. Womenfolk just tend to get lost, he'd always say; it's just a weakness they've got.

If we're still on Sinking Creek, she thought, I could find my way back just by going upstream! It was a wonderful revelation. But if we've got off Sinking Creek, I'm lost.

Must watch everything, she thought. *Everything!* Must look back whenever we pass something, see how it looks from the other side. *Memorize* how it would look coming back! And never forget it! The new excitement of this was making her forget her discomfort.

She twisted and looked back. She saw the horses coming behind. She saw Bettie's pain-gray face and her hanging, bloody right arm. She saw Henry Lenard stumbling along grimly, the rope jerking at his neck. And she saw one of the braves in the rear guard staring intently at her, then looking back up the creek, then staring at her, looking angry. He said something to her in a sharp voice and reached threateningly toward the tomahawk in his waistband.

Mary scanned the landscape behind her quickly. It looked no different from what she had been seeing ahead. She faced forward. Must memorize, she thought. But I mustn't make them suspicious.

She peeked cautiously back over her shoulder again. The Indian was now looking back over *his* shoulder. I've made him uneasy now, she thought. Now perhaps he fears we're being followed.

Now Mary tried to remember everything she had ever heard the menfolk say about Sinking Creek and New River and the mountains to the west of Draper's Meadows, hoping to remember some clue that might indicate she was indeed still on Sinking Creek. The men had hunted down into the New River Gorge, and they had come back with awesome descriptions of cliffs and rapids and jumbled boulders and mountains rising so steep they blocked all but the midday sun. Mary never had been taught to read, and thus had an unspoiled eye and ear for pictures and sounds. She could remember almost everything she had ever heard, had learned ballads and hymns on first hearing and could remember the look of almost everything and everyone she had ever seen.

She remembered the menfolk saying that one could follow Sinking Creek about four leagues down from Draper's Meadows, and it would suddenly vanish from sight into the ground. But you could still follow its valley, about a league farther, until the creek came out of the ground between two steep hills and flowed into the New River in sight of a great sheer cliff curved like a horseshoe. Or you might, they had said, want to

find easier going by leaving the creek where it first goes
underground, and veer off to the left, straight west on an easy
deer path along the north slope of a straight-ridged mountain,
right down to the New River's edge. And there you'd be at an
elbow bend in the river with a palisade cliff on your right and
a natural stone arch straight across on the opposite shore.
There's a spring there with water that tastes like gunpowder,
and Adam Harmon's hunting shack is nearby, they had said.
Mary Ingles had envisioned all those landmarks as she had
heard them described. The Indians were going toward the
setting sun now, and so must be headed for the New River,
which was their roadway through the mountains to the unknown lands of the Northwest. Will always said he believed,
from things he had heard, that the waters of the New River
eventually reached a great river called, as he had heard it, the
Ho-he-o, or the O-y-o, hundreds of miles through the wilderness. But no one was sure of that, of course, except perhaps
the Indians, as no white man had ever explored down the wild
New River Gorge farther than ten or twelve leagues.

Mary turned over and over in her mind those remembered
descriptions of geography she had never seen, all the while
hugging Georgie in front of her and trying to hold her muscles
against the burning weariness. The great weight of her womb
felt as if it would simply tear loose and fall out of her onto the
ground, but for the broad horse's back she held between her
thighs.

Georgie seemed to be asleep, or simply dazed. His head
lolled back against her bosom and she stroked his hair. She
leaned forward and saw that his eyes were closed. The dried
blood on his face was flaking away. He had only been
scratched by briars and was not really hurt. Her heart
squeezed with tender concern. Pray t' God these heathens'
bloodlust has cooled, she thought, and they'll not hurt my
boys. Nor my baby when it comes.

Surely they will, though, she thought. A newborn babe can
only be botheration to 'em in flight. Be ready, she told herself; be strong enough to bear it if they choose to kill it.

But Lord, how can anybody be that strong?

But what matter if they choose to spare it or not, she

thought. It could hardly survive a birthing in this wilderness anyway. On this trail. With all this riding. It'll prob'ly die a-bornin'. She stopped a whimper of pain and despair in her throat.

Suddenly Mary realized that the horses were climbing. They had left the creekbed. She glanced back to memorize, if she could, their point of departure. They were on some kind of an animal path along the north side of a mountain. Behind her and below she could see a patch of water, but straight below there was only the brushy bed of a ravine.

We must have turned off where the creek goes underground, she thought.

Surely we cannot travel much farther this evening, she thought. Although there was more light up here on the mountainside than down in the streambed, the day was fading. She tightened her muscles once more against the enormous, sagging, aching weariness in her middle. The pain was wracking, pulling her attention away from everything else again. And her bladder, full now and pressed by the weight of the womb, aggravated her discomfort.

We must stop soon, she thought. I'm afraid they're going to try to reach the river before night. But we must stop. I must get off this horse soon or I'm going to just up and die.

They rode down into the river valley at twilight. Suddenly they were out of the dark woods and under an expanse of rose-tinged sky in a bottomland overgrown with grass and wild-pea vine, with a sharp bend of the glassy river before them. Bats were stitching silently back and forth across the sky, feeding on mosquitoes.

Even in her misery, Mary Ingles was awed by the strange beauty of the place. The river flowed from left to right across their way, then turned so sharply away that it appeared it must meet itself somewhere beyond the other dark shore inside the bend. At its sharpest crook downstream it cut under the very base of a perpendicular wall of fluted gray stone cliffs and columns and spires of stone three hundred feet high. On the inside of the bend stood a natural stone arch, gray amid the dusky woods, with a free-standing shaft of stone eighty feet tall beside it. It looked like an experimental landscape chopped out of solid stone and forest by some god trying to make a channel for a confused river. She had never seen such a place, even in the harrowing crossing of the Blue Ridge.

The Indians had grown cheerful, on reaching the river. They laughed and raised their arms and talked back and forth along the line. They brought the horses to a halt near a spring that gave off a strong mineral odor. This, Mary thought, must be what the men called the gunpowder spring. Adam Harmon's cabin must be hereabouts. The Indians drank from the spring, then led the animals down to the river's edge and let them drink there. Mary held Georgie tightly to keep him from pitching forward into the river as their horse stretched its neck down.

About fifteen of the warriors stood gazing over the river, talking in low and melodic voices. Mary prayed that they would make camp here, that they would let her dismount and relieve herself, perhaps bathe and soothe her children and talk to the other captives. She looked back at Bettie. Her sister-in-law now sat so slumped, her face pasty with pain, that it appeared little Tommy was holding her up from behind. It's a marvel she's not fainted, Mary thought.

"Mi . . . uhm, Mister," she said to a passing warrior. He looked up at her and she cupped one hand and made a drinking motion, then pointed around to the other captives. The Indian called something to the chieftain, who answered from the riverbank in a few words. The warrior detached a pan from one of the pack horses and filled it at the river. He brought it to Mary and handed it up to her. She held Georgie's head and put the edge of the vessel to his lips and was pleased that he was conscious enough to drink a little from it. Then Mary gave the pan back to the Indian instead of drinking from it, and again pointed to the others. He made a soft exclamation in his throat, then took the water to them one by one.

"Thankee, Mary," Henry Lenard called to her softly.

"Welcome, Mr. Lenard."

There. They had dared to talk, and the Indians seemed not to mind now. The warrior brought the pan of water back to

Mary and she drank the rest of it, and it was good; it was almost as refreshing as having been able to speak. The Indian nodded and smiled as he took the vessel from her. It was unbelievable that they who had wrought a massacre and burned a settlement in their savage passion a few hours ago could smile and behave like humans now. That seemed like years since; this seemed like a myth-story now.

"Bettie," she cried. "Bettie, ca' y' hear me, hon?"

"Aye," came her reply after a moment.

"How d'y do, sweet?"

"Oh, Mary. I want to die."

"Nah, nah nah nah, Bettie! Won't have that. We're goin' to be all right yet, dear, I do believe so."

"No. I'm going to die."

"Thomas!"

"Hey, Mama?"

"Y' don't let y'r auntie die now, or I'll give y' a sound hidin', d'y hear?"

After a moment of hestitation, the child replied, "Ay, Mama."

Mary smiled. Good Tommy, she thought. He's best off with a chore at hand.

It was odd how Mary felt now, with this unexplainable hope and good humor rising up in her, above all her pain and fatigue. I'm going giddy, she thought. But I'll vow, if these savages don't get murderous again, I'll get us out o' this somehow.

"Oh, I will die," Bettie moaned again.

"Y'do, Bettie, and it's *you* I'll whip," Mary said, feeling a bubble of outrageous hilarity in her breast. I mustn't go crazy, she thought.

Or maybe best I should.

The tall chieftain now was walking toward her, apparently attracted by the talk among the captives. He was not smiling, but he did not seem annoyed, either. He stopped and looked up at Mary with curiosity, then started to say something, but didn't. It was as if he were searching for English words he might not have. Mary was astonished that she felt no fear of him now. He was simply a person, a man standing here.

Though he held all their lives in his hands, for the moment at least, Mary was not afraid of him. But Georgie was. Mary felt the child stiffening his back against her in terror as the warrior stood by the horse. She stroked the little boy's hair and spoke to the Indian.

"Will we stay here, Mister? We *must* get down."

He pondered her words, then pointed to the north, up toward the high, jagged escarpment. "No. There. Mo-ther be still."

"Oh, please, not up th . . ."

"Mo-ther be still," he repeated, more loudly. Then he turned his head and studied the slope which led up onto the cliff. Mary watched his profile and studied his demeanor to determine how close she might be to the limits of his good-will. My Georgie's all beshit, she thought.

"I need to clean . . ."

"Be still!" the Indian spat at her. He looked straight at her and his eyelids narrowed. It was obvious that this was all his indulgence for now. He turned and called a command, and the group of warriors dispersed and took up their places along the pack train. Mary watched the chieftain as he strode forward to the head of the column. His back was straight as a wall, and she noticed that the back of his head was flat also; a leather band around his head held three dark feathers and they stuck straight up in back. His thick black hair, parted in the middle, was held neatly in place by the headband and flowed to his shoulders. He carried himself with that same erect confidence Mary had noticed in Colonel Washington and so Mary presumed that this warrior was perhaps the equivalent of a colonel.

We shan't have to mollycoddle them all, at any rate, she guessed. If we can keep this gent calm, I don't reckon he'd let the others do us harm.

And then she got an arm around Georgie, and cooed to him as the horses moved off again. She tightened her stomach muscles as well as she could and gritted her teeth and the column turned northward away from the river's elbow bend, climbing a steeply sloping ridge that led to the palisade's crest. The path was closer to vertical than anything Mary had ever ridden; the horse lunged and stumbled and scrabbled for footholds, and Mary had to squeeze her legs with all her remaining strength and grab handfuls of mane to keep herself and Georgie from sliding back over the beast's rump. Pray Bettie's still got strength to hang on, she thought. "Tommy," she called back, "hold tight, dear!" She couldn't hear his reply over the clatter of hooves and sliding rock debris. Below, almost straight below, the river gleamed like dull pewter through the black foliage. The Indians were almost invisible now in the gathering darkness, but nevertheless swarmed sure-footed as panthers up the steep ridge.

At last the slope became more gentle, then leveled, and they rode a few yards to the left into a deep wood that she reckoned must be on the very crest of the palisade.

And then, on this precipitous height, the column stopped, and the Indians began unloading horses. A warrior appeared beside Mary's horse and reached up and grabbed Georgie, who reacted with a moan of terror. Don't cry, Mary thought; don't cry out or he'll pitch ye over the cliff! The Indian set the little boy on the ground, and said something to Mary. With a wheeze of effort she leaned back and raised her aching right leg over the horse's withers, sat sideways for a moment praying her legs would support her, then slid off. She staggered and stumbled and held her ponderous abdomen when her feet hit the ground, but found her balance and stayed upright. Nearby, Bettie cried out sharply in the gloom, doubtless having hurt her arm in dismounting. Tommy's voice warned, "Don't die, Auntie Bettie!"

Indians led the horses off somewhere, and herded the captives into a group on a jutting, scrub-covered promontory of the ledge, then stationed a single warrior to watch them. On three sides of the huddled hostages, sheer cliffs dropped away. On the fourth side the sentinel seated himself on a rock with his musket across his knees. As the last silvery-gray of the gloaming faded out over the horizon and stars appeared overhead, the rush of water over rocks could be heard from far below. Beyond this narrow place, there was nothing but night and space. The captives kept close together, intimidated by the nearness of the precipice, and whispered consolations to each other. It was obvious that they were to be allowed no comfort but that of togetherness.

"A paradise down there by the spring, and they choose an eagle's nest for a camp," Mary explained.

"So 'tis," murmured Henry Lenard. "A safe place from pursuit, that's why."

"D'y' reckon anyone is followin' us?"

"Not likely, I guess. Who's to follow? Best as I could make out, they kilt Colonel Patton. I saw Jim Cull light out f'r the woods wounded, limpin' bad," said Henry. "That leaves but Will and Johnny and Casper to follow. An' maybe Bill Preston an' Phil Lybrook, who was down th' creek som'ers, an' maybe stayed safe."

"Not Casper," Bettie sniffled. "I saw 'em cut him up. I saw . . ."

"Let's us have a look at y'r poor blighted arm, Bettie . . ." Mary said, scooting carefully across the rock and closer to her. "I been frettin' about that all the livelong day . . ." She didn't want Bettie to start recalling the massacre.

"It's broke here. Ow! Oh! I can't stand touchin' . . ."

"Now, down at that spring, with water and a fire and a shred o' daylight left, I could ha' treated that up just sweet as c'd be," Mary commented. "But here . . . well, got t' splint it somehow, at least, darlin'. Mister Lenard, would y'be so kind as to feel around f'r a few sticks please, about a foot long, I guess. An' I'll get me some strips o' cloth here. Must tear the sleeve off y'r pretty dress, Bet, hon, t' get at you. Tommy, I must ask'ee to clean up Georgie a bit. He's messed himself, poor tad . . . and, Tommy," she added, "thankee for not letting your auntie die on us. That was a good lad . . ."

"I won't die on y' now," Bettie murmured. "Forgive me such talk. I just . . ."

"Ssshhh, now. Nought to forgive."

Mary ripped up the bloody sleeve of Bettie's dress and tore strips from her own skirt, and with a few lengths of branch Henry had broken off a shrub, they prepared a makeshift splint. "This'll hurt, now, Bettie. But just for a minute. Pull her hand there if y'd kindly do so, Mister Lenard, just a slow an' steady pull . . ."

Bettie's shriek split the night open and quavered out over the valley when Mary probed blindly into the swollen, bloody flesh of the broken upper arm as Henry stretched the arm. Mary steeled herself against the anguished wail and tried to guide the broken ends of the bone together, as she and Will had done once for Johnny after a log-toting accident had snapped his arm.

But there were no simple clean bone ends in Bettie's break. The musketball had shattered the bone and Mary could feel pieces of it adrift in the tortured flesh. A pity, she thought; it's going to heal up short. If it heals at all, she thought.

So, as Bettie went into a merciful faint, they braced the arm as well as they could in the splint, and Mary prayed that the festering might not get too well started before they could make a decent camp with a fire and hot water and maybe a poultice of some kind—what was that we used for Johnny's? she tried to remember; *comfrey,* that's what it was, comfrey— a poultice of comfrey leaves to draw the pus and poison out.

And at that moment a huge grab of pain in her own sore and strained pelvis reminded her of another urgent reason why they would need a decent camp any time now.

The captives awakened themselves and each other at times throughout the night with the mutterings of their nightmares and discomforts. But the marvel of it to Mary Ingles was that they had slept at all, on the bare, crumbling stone of the cliff-top, with the dew settling on them and chilling their skin. Mary had been tormented awake countless times by the pain of stone debris grinding into her shoulders or flanks or the side of her face, and especially under her weighted hipbones, and had turned over and lain there trying to drown thoughts of their desperate straits in the muzzy undercurrent of exhaustion. She had managed to doze now and then, and when she awoke in the indistinct predawn grayness, she realized that she had fallen at last into an utter oblivion of slumber, she knew not how long. She looked about and saw her children and Bettie and Henry lying like so many dew-damp corpses in the half-light, saw the vast, foggy abyss beyond the edges of the cliff and saw the form of the Indian sentry still sitting, as if in a trance, a few feet away.

The Indians, she saw, had not even indulged themselves with a campfire. As the light grew, she saw the warriors rise one by one from their beds of concealment, with their weapons, and she knew that they had slept—if they had slept at all—ready to do instant battle, if necessary, on this fortresslike cliff-top. They had both hobbled and rope-corralled the horses, in a grassy glade near the edge of the woods, no doubt to keep them from straying over the brink of the cliff during the night.

The Indian camp stirred to life in silence. The river muttered and rushed below. A cricket nearby creaked its monotonous repetitions. Mary painfully detached herself from the ground, hauled herself upright and stepped among the sleeping captives to a small corner of space where she could relieve her bladder. Not wanting to squat and bare her haunches under the eyes of the Indian sentry, she simply spread her feet apart, bent her knees until her skirt hem touched the ground, gazed out over the valley and emptied herself of a long stream, concealed from his eyes. When she turned back from it, the Indian had not moved nor altered his impassive expression, but she imagined a smirk of amusement. The thought irritated her. It seemed very important somehow, though she knew she was presuming things about the Indian character, that she and the others should exhibit all the dignity their destitute circumstances would allow. Somehow, she felt, dignity might be all that could keep them alive. It was a notion she had arrived at largely by watching the straight-backed carriage of the tall chieftain.

The sky paled. The mist began to grow pearly, then yellow, then began to separate into wisps and dissolve. Mary got the children awake and tended to them, persuading them through her own whispers and soft tones that they must not whine or talk too much. She aroused Bettie and Henry, managing to whisper to them also the conclusions she had reached about stoical and dignified behavior. "I don't care how ever much y' hurt, Bettie—nay, I mean, I do care—but however much, just be still and bear it. Once we get out of this, we two might just go out in the open somewhere and holler and caterwaul. But not so long as we're in the hands of a band of nervous savages. What say y' to that, Mister Lenard?"

"Right smart, Mrs. Ingles. Dignity it is."

She mused on his apparent willingness to let her, a woman, assume the natural leadership among the hostages. Perhaps, she thought, it's out of his respect for William.

William! she thought, with such a mighty compression of her heart that it nearly forced undignified tears from her own eyes.

A warrior brought a pan of food to the captives and took the place of the sentry. They ate while the Indians readied the pack train. Mary recognized some of her own hoecake, and also distributed a few sections of the rabbit she had been cooking yesterday—incredible that it was only yesterday! she thought—when the raid had so abruptly uprooted and scattered their lives.

The Indians bound Henry's hands again, and were about to tether him by the neck once more, when Mary took a chance on his behalf and indicated that the rope might be attached to his wrists instead of his neck. The Indians, to her surprise, simply shrugged and complied.

Now, she thought, I reckon he can stay more dignified thataway.

CHAPTER
4

THEY RODE OUT NORTHWESTWARD THAT MORNING, FOLLOWING ridge trails and creekbeds, sometimes not glimpsing the river for hours. Then they would come around the brow of a mountain and there far below would be a stretch of river with an island in it, or a stunning horseshoe riverbend glinting in the morning sun under the lowering mass of some great curving cliff-face. Then up another steep ridge and into the deep woods or across a high meadow with no river to be seen for still more hours.

When the river was out of sight for very long, Mary would suffer a dread suspicion that they were leaving it for good, and that they were being taken by some profound wilderness byway through which she could never find her way back for lack of landmarks. In those times she would glance back continuously, trying to find something to memorize. But those backward views were already becoming vague and muddled in her memory.

You can only count on the river, she thought. Dear God let it be true that they never stray far from this river, or we all are lost, lost, lost from the way home.

And then, just as she could hardly bear the dread another minute, a break in the forest would reveal the river, still coming along hundreds of feet below them; or sometimes, after they had descended a long ravine, they would suddenly come out from between two hills and find themselves right at the river's edge, with bluffs and mountains towering on both sides as they picked their way along.

Mary could no longer even estimate the distances they were traveling.

I must at least, she thought, start keeping a count of the days.

This day, she thought, which began on an eagle's roost above a stone arch in a sharp riverbend, shall be known as our second day out. Our second day out.

She committed it to her memory.

By the end of their second day out, the Indians seemed to have lost much of their anxiety about being pursued. They stopped in a glade and spent an hour burying their two dead warriors and chanting over them.

They did not ride late into the evening; instead they stopped at the base of a sheer cliff while there was still an hour of daylight. There were caves in the cliff, a few feet above the river level, and the warriors made the camp in one of these. It had a packed dirt floor, and old fire-beds made of circles of sooty stones. Pieces of Indian pottery and a few unbroken clay vessels lay here and there in the dim, cool interior, and there were old stacks of straight, slim, peeled poles and sticks which indicated that some industry—arrow making and canoe building, Mary guessed—had been conducted here in years past. In one corner lay pieces of arrowheads and a few broken stone axe heads.

Tommy and Georgie were quite taken with the cave, and were cheerful and quiet, despite their fatigue and their general wariness of the Indians.

The horses had been corralled in a grassy compound surrounded by dense brush at the river's edge outside the cave, and a rope was strung from bush to bush to keep them from straying. Mary saw the chieftain send two braves climbing, with their guns slung on their backs, up the face of the cliff, one upstream and one downstream a few yards. They vanished into the cliff above, apparently into small caves overlooking the approaches to the canyon.

Mary was scarcely able to move for the first few minutes after dismounting. Her back and pelvis were a mass of aches and stabbing pains, and her thighs cramped several times before she could knead out the muscles and straighten her limbs.

When she was at last able to rise, she waddled to the chieftain, who stood in the mouth of the cave surveying the river and watching his braves bring firewood into the cave. He looked at her without expression, without the slightest trace of friendliness in his eyes. His severity, and the great quantity of wood the braves were fetching, suddenly alarmed Mary. A notion jumped into her mind that some of the hostages might be burned for the Indians' entertainment. Or food! She felt a chill of the soul, and her legs began to tremble.

Of course, she thought. The less they fear pursuit, the less they need us. For a moment she was rendered speechless by the thought, and stood with her mouth gaping while the chieftain waited to hear what she wanted.

Be dignified, she reminded herself. *Whatever it is, be dignified.* She shut her mouth, stood as straight as she could and

stared straight into his black-slit eyes. Then she pointed at
Bettie, who sat with her back to a boulder, quiet and stoical,
but going an awful pale gray in the face with the pain of her
crudely splinted arm.

"Mister," Mary began, "I have to do something for her. I
have to find something—some medicine leaves, do you understand?—for her arm." Mary touched her own right upper arm
and then pointed again at Bettie. "And I need hot water."
Even while asking for hot water, Mary remembered tales she
had heard about savages ripping unborn infants from the
womb and throwing them into stewpots to boil before the
very eyes of their dying mothers. She remembered the warrior who had threatened to cut her open at the settlement.
Was this what they were planning, with all their wood gathering? At that moment a brave entered the cave carrying a large
iron sugaring kettle that had belonged to Casper Barrier at
the settlement, and again Mary had to bite inside her cheeks
to keep from whimpering. And as if to confirm her fears, the
chieftain let a suggestion of a grim smile move the corner of
his mouth.

But in the meantime, there was Bettie to be taken care of.

"Medicine leaves," Mary repeated.

"Mo-ther go there, be still," the chieftain ordered, pointing
to Bettie and the children.

"Please, Mist . . ."

"*There.*"

And so the prisoners huddled together near the mouth of
the cave and watched the Indians build two fires, a large one
and a smaller one. The warriors rigged a wooden frame over
each fire. They hung a small kettle over the smaller fire and
the big kettle over the larger fire. They brought vessels of
water and filled the kettles. The Indians had built and managed the fires so that they were virtually smokeless, and the
little smoke that did rise from them flowed up a natural draft
out of the cave mouth and up the face of the cliff.

Mary did not express her fears to Bettie or Henry. Perhaps
those or similar fears were haunting them already. But to talk
of them would only worsen the fright that was already as
much as they could bear in dignity. Mary settled the children

side by side in a niche floored with soft, dusty earth, and told them to take a nap before supper. It was like a down mattress compared with the flinty cliff-top of the first night's camp, and the boys' eyes grew heavy immediately and they fell into a sound sleep. God be merciful, Mary thought. If they're to be murdered, let it be in their sleep so's they won't see it coming. Then she turned to the care of Bettie's arm. Being careful not to unsettle the position of the bones, she untied the knots in the splint's bindings and laid back the sticks. "Some nice, for a riggin' done blind," observed Henry Lenard with satisfaction as he knelt and helped. "We can make a better, though, with some o' them sticks yonder."

"Aye," Mary said. "But I don't care f'r th' looks o' that flesh." The edges of the wound were swollen and were issuing a mass of greenish-white pus. There were bits of dirt and bark, even some dead gnats, in the pus, the result of their having dressed the wound by feel in the darkness. Mary knelt close, straining over her own massive, hurting belly, and sniffed the wound. The baby within her kicked, as if demanding more room. "Not stinkin' a whole lot yet. How's it feel, Bet?"

"Hurts somethin' unspeakable. An' itches."

"Well, by the Eternal, if these savages have got no humanity to a sick woman, I sh'll . . . Got to clean that. Raise up there, darlin'. I need your apron." She removed it, then rose with a wheeze and stood. She went dizzy, and had to grope for a handhold on a boulder. Her vision cleared. She carried the apron straight to the small kettle and, before any warrior could move to stop her, dipped it into the boiling water. She raised it out steaming and, tossing it from hand to hand to avoid scalding herself, carried it back to Bettie's side and stooped. "Hot, now," she said. "Don't jerk your arm." And, deftly folding it into a pad, she laid it on the suppurating wound and held it there snug with her palms. Bettie lurched at the contact of the heat, but she kept the arm still.

"Oh, merciful God," she groaned. "Thankee, Mary. Oh, I feel it's helpin'. Oh, leave it there. Oh, I feel it's just a-pullin' that corruption out . . ."

Mary gathered herself to rise. "Got to rinse it hot again." She swabbed the wound gently as she took the cloth away.

The chieftain stood between her and the kettle, frowning. "'Scuse me, Mister," she muttered, going around him. But he grabbed her arm and held her back.

"You not do," he said. "See this." He nodded to a warrior who stood over the kettle with an armful of various leaves and strips of green bark. As he spilled them into the boiling water, Mary recognized some of the plants as comfrey. "Go be still," the chieftain said, shoving her back toward the other captives.

Mary hardly dared to hope. She sat holding the sopping apron against Bettie's wound, feeling the baby kick within herself, and tried to watch the proceedings at the fires. Into the big kettle the Indians were putting barley and cutting pieces of the venison they had taken from Mrs. Lybrook's house. A short, slight, older warrior was bent over the smaller pot, stirring and mashing the plants in the water. The smell of a stew began to mingle with a sharp, bitter medicinal steam from the other kettle.

And then the Indian brought a piece of cloth and a gourd to the kettle. He dipped a mass of green slime out of the kettle and into the cloth, then folded the cloth over and over to contain it. Holding it gingerly by the corners then, he brought it to Mary and held it forth to her, nodding in the direction of Bettie's arm.

With a rush of gratitude, Mary realized that her remotest hope had come true: the Indians had prepared a poultice of the comfrey and other medicinal leaves and barks. "Thank'ee, Mister, thank'ee thank'ee!" she kept saying as she squatted down and plastered the slick, squishy compress over the bullet wound. "Oh, I can't believe this, merciful God, how thou work'st even through heathens and murtherers." Mary was almost ecstatic. Surely this poultice would be even better than the ones they had learned to use in the settlement. She hummed softly while applying it. The chieftain came over once and looked down at the two women. He did not ask anything or show any expression, but for the first time Bettie spoke directly to him:

"Y'll burn in etarnal hell, for what y' done t' my poor babe . . ." Mary grew alarmed for the possible consequences of such an outburst, not knowing how much of it the Indian understood; but Bettie added, ". . . may the Devil give y' a minute's respite, though, for this kindness. It feels better already, sir . . ." And then she lapsed back with a sigh and closed her eyes.

The chieftain looked at Bettie for a moment, then at Mary. "H'mm," he said, and went away.

The barley chowder the Indians had been cooking in the big kettle was savory, and there was plenty of it, and Mary felt her strength growing afterward. But the constant tending to the poultice, and to Tommy and Georgie, and the groaning weight of her own womb had her gasping with exhaustion by nightfall. The Indians removed Henry Lenard from the company of the women and children after dinner, and put him in a back corner of the cave with his hands bound behind him and his feet tethered to a log. Mary worried for some time that they might be planning to torture or kill him. But as the night deepened and the warriors settled themselves down to conversation and tobacco smoking in the glow of the cookfires, she presumed that he was being moved only for the sake of security, as he was, after all, the only one among them well enough and unencumbered enough to have a reasonable chance of running away.

Mary at last built and bound another splint, with the rest of the poultice dressing lining the inside, and when she saw that Bettie was deep in sleep, she lay back on the dirt between her and the children. She watched the fireglow shift shadow-shapes on the irregular vault of the cave above, smelled the tobacco and the dusty, musty earth-smell of the cave, and heard the Indian men's voices grow less distinct and the rush of the river rapids outside grow more monotonous, and tried to keep her slipping mind awake long enough to take stock of the day and what it had signified. Her eyes came open for a moment as a wolf howled somewhere outside, and a familiar, squeezing ripple of pain moved through her waist, then receded. It's not going to be long 'til we have another of us to care for, she thought. Then she went almost overpoweringly drowsy again.

But thank God, she thought. That they made a poultice for poor Bet means something.

It means . . . it means for now, anyway . . . they'd as soon have us alive as dead.

Then she slid away into dreams of Will and her mother and beyond.

Our third day out, she thought as the pack train toiled along the endless ridge of a mountain a thousand feet above the river, this third day out I'm afraid is going to give thee, William my love, a new baby y' may never see. I can feel it's like to be today, and only the Lord can say how soon.

By the middle of the day, when the sun was beating straight down on their heads and the forested mountain across the valley was shimmering in the baking sunlight, Mary knew her labors were starting. But being astride the lurching horse, the pains and fatigues of her body already being so general and intense, she was unable to measure the onslaughts as she had been able to with her first two childbirths.

Tommy, her first, had been an excruciating birth, with her whole pelvis feeling it was being rendered bone from bone, but it had been a quick and regular birth withal, the pressures coming according to a predictable inner clockwork of her mind. And Georgie too had entered the world in compliance with her sense of time, and much more easily, with hardly enough pain to remember.

But these two days on horseback, with the exhaustion, the hopelessness, the endless wobbling and plunging and thumping, had destroyed that sense of reliable interval; it was as if time itself had been left back at the settlement, standing there against the wall in that old ticking family clock the Indians had been afraid to touch. Now Mary was at the mercy of unannounced waves of weakness and dizziness. She would feel an awful fear of falling down the mountainside, then a wracking twist of pain inside the greater prevailing pain; then her vision would clear and she would find her face bathed in cold sweat, her knees needing to straighten, her heartbeat slowing from a gallop almost to a dreadful standstill.

The afternoon went on and on like that. She lost her ability to take note of the route, and even forgot to keep an eye on the river. Her hair hung now in sweat-dank strands. Once she opened her eyes from a near-swoon to find little Georgie twisting and craning to look back up at her. There were his alarmed dark eyes in his dirty face. "Mama hurt?" he said.

"Aye. But it's a-goin' away. Don't y' fret now."

They were down off the mountain and in a deep-shadowed, moist, still forest the next time she took any notice. It seemed to be evening and there were thousands of mosquitoes whining in her ears and nipping at her face and neck and arms. Georgie was crying and slapping violently at himself. "Hush, son," she commanded, alarmed that the Indians might kill him to shut him up. She fanned mosquitoes away from him and then raised her sweat-soaked skirt up around her waist and draped it over him to protect him from the swarm. Doing so exposed her own thighs to the insects, and they gorged themselves freely on her blood. Their bites were so dulled by her total agony that she did not even bother to slap them. And Georgie did stop crying. Once Mary heard Bettie wail behind her:

"Dear Lord, they're going to drive me *mad!*"

Mary felt a silent pop deep in her bowels, than a hot flood of wetness down between her thighs and onto the horse's hairy back. There goes the water, she thought. She knew she should have been off the horse hours ago. But to have hindered the Indians' progress she felt would have been a certain death warrant for the baby and herself. Must wait till they camp, she thought. Surely I can wait till they camp. The sun's down. Can't be long. Hold. Hold.

But then that inevitable moment came: that familiar, awful sense of unstoppability, that loss of control, when her will lost its sway over her muscles. She gave a low, gurgling wail and looked up and saw the black foliage overhead and wanted to reach up and pull the forest down upon herself.

Someone had lowered her onto the ground, or she had fallen without feeling it. She was on her back, on the forest floor. Bettie Draper was kneeling beside her, her good left hand using her skirt to wipe sweat and chase whining mosquitoes from Mary's face. The great dark trunks of trees converged into blackness straight above. There were no horses or Indians or children nearby now. Sometimes she could hear them in the distance. Another enormous surge went down; she felt her skeleton creaking open; she was turning inside out. Her heart fluttered. She held a cry behind her throat. She reached behind her head for a tree to uproot, but got only handfuls of dirt and leaves. She raised and spread her knees and strained and tried to expel that tormenting hot wet mass out of herself, to free herself from it, from the endless agony it was causing. It eased a bit, and she sucked night air and heard Bettie saying things to her and smelled excrement.

This alcove of the woods now had become like a dark room. Its walls were tree trunks. Its ceiling was black foliage with a hole at its peak where a star winked through. Off to her left, as if outside the room, there was a low, smoky fire burning, and men were moving around it. Indians. And now and then she would hear Tommy or Georgie say something, in little asking voices, and Henry Lenard would say something. Somewhere else outside the room a horse nickered and another snorted wetly. But here in this lightless imaginary room there were only Mary and her enormous act of expulsion, and Bettie on the edge of it saying things and praying aloud and doing half a job of midwifery with her one good hand.

Mary watched the star until another awful bone-stretching pressure went down and the star went out and her heart trembled.

I got through that one, she thought in triumph a moment later when the star reappeared. I got through that one; I can stand anything. Except this one that's coming now!

She stood that one, too, and exulted for a moment. Bettie was down there below her, touching and mopping, pulling and talking and sobbing. "Poor hapless tad; first thing 'twill feel in this life's a bloody mosquito bite. 'Sno fair, 'sno fair a-tall . . ."

The Indians were not helping in this matter. They furnished neither water nor cloth, and did not even come near. This was not a bullet wound, but a birth; it was a matter for the women. Mary was aware of that, in a moment of lucidity, and it made her angry. She looked at the star and hated men for all their meanness and hurtfulness and cruelty. Why is this happening to me?. she demanded as the hideous squeezing pain returned, what have I ever done? The star went away and then came back, and she was euphoric, and her heart grew soft and big at the thought of William.

"Fine head o' hair," Bettie was saying down there. "Y're nigh done now, Mary darlin'. Y're a fine worker, oh, truly y'are . . . Come on, now, little weanie, turn y'r lovely mama loose . . . That's good now, that's very nice now . . ." Bettie's voice broke with a sob, then, " . . . Oh, God love ye, Mary Ingles, 'tis a little jill, I do believe."

Beside the smoky fire they had built to baffle mosquitoes, the Indians stopped talking when they heard a baby's cry quaver in the nearby darkness among the calls of owls and crickets. They all looked to the chieftain, who stared in that direction and nodded.

He was very impressed. He had not heard the white mother cry out a single time.

Mary had to bite off and tie the cord herself because of Bettie's crippled hand. They dried the bloody slime and feces off the baby with their skirts. Bettie tossed the afterbirth away into the bushes. Mary unbuttoned her dress and put the baby inside against her skin and they covered it with Bettie's apron to keep the mosquitoes off.

The baby began suckling sometime during the night as Mary lay awake in the leaves listening to the breathing of the sleepers and the whine of mosquitoes and the stealthy rustlings of wild animals in the woods. It sucked hard on her sore nipple, making an exquisite pain, while the rest of her body ebbed into numbness and forgot its sufferings.

What shall we name 'er, Will, m' love? Mary thought as sleep began to overpower her and the stars she was watching through the treetop blurred. Elenor, after my mother? Or Bettie? Maybe Bettie Elenor Ingles. Now, that's a fine sound, aye? How say y' to that, my Will?

Before dawn the horses were spooked by the scent of a starving lame wolf, which crept to the edge of the camp and stole the afterbirth.

CHAPTER
5

WILLIAM INGLES AND JOHNNY DRAPER RODE WHIP-AND-SPUR
down Sinking Creek, at the head of a column of thirty armed
horsemen that Captain Buchanan had raised for them in the
upriver settlements. Among them were Will Ingles' younger
brothers, John and Matthew.

"Buzzards," Johnny Draper shouted over the thunder of
hooves.

"At Phil Barger's I'd say," yelled Will.

There was little left of the old man's headless body: shreds
of putrid flesh and the rags of clothing brown with old blood.
They turned the skeleton over and disturbed a thousand busy
maggots. They scraped out a shallow temporary grave and
put in the stinking bundle of bones and covered it up and rode
hell-bent on down the creek toward Lybrook's with the stench
still in their nostrils.

Philip Lybrook and his wife and son unbolted their cabin
door when they saw that the riders were white men. Lybrook
had hurried back over the mountain after he and Prescott had
discovered the burning settlement four days before. Mrs.
Lybrook told the militiamen what she had seen: the number
of Indians she guessed had been about twenty, though she had
been too stunned to count them or really even look. Yes, they
had had Mrs. Ingles and Mrs. Draper with them, and the little
boys. And a man on a rope, Henry Lenard, she seemed to
recall. Raccoons or something had carried away the bag with
Mr. Barger's head in it; one minute it had been lying there at
the edge of the garden where she had thrown it, and later it
was simply gone. Then she broke down and couldn't tell them
any more, but there really was nothing more to tell.

"Down Sinking Creek to the New River, then, I'll wager," said Will Ingles. His eyes were crackling, his mouth was bitten white. "Let's go. Lickety-cut."

Captain Buchanan's scarlet coat blazed in the sunlight. "Sir," he said to Philip Lybrook, "I reckon you know the place upriver called Dunkard's Bottom?"

"Aye."

"I recommend y' take your family and go there, with all your goods and whatever harvest y' have already. Folks are a-gatherin' there. They're a-buildin' a fort."

"We'll go, Cap'n. We've had enough for now."

The force rode on down Sinking Creek at as brisk a pace as the terrain would allow. William Ingles kept his eye on the sky for buzzards. At every turn in the river he expected to find the remains of Mary or Bettie, or one of the children.

There was no sign of the Indians' passage yet, as they apparently had stayed in the creek. One of Captain Buchanan's men was an accomplished tracker, a Tuscarora half-breed named Gander Jack, and he scanned the creek banks with hungry eyes for any sign that the Indians might have left the creekbed. Such signs, if there were any, would be faint because of the passage of four days since the massacre. But there had been no rain in the region, so there was hope that a spoor might remain.

Captain Buchanan rode up between Will and Johnny late in the afternoon. "We ought to ease off, gentlemen. We've rid hard two days. We'll burn the horses out."

"The trail's old enough, Cap'n. I don't want it to fade altogether."

"Then, too," the captain persisted, "I don't intend to run my boys into an ambuscade. I share y'r urgency, Mr. Ingles, but I advise caution."

Will reined his horse back. He knew Captain Buchanan was right. And he knew too that he should abide by the militia-man's wishes, not just for the sake of common sense, but because he was lucky even to have got his assistance for a pursuit so far into these parts. Buchanan had opined even before starting out that it likely would be a goose chase.

But whether it was a goose chase or not, Will had to try it.

It was his Mary out there in the hands of savages. And his sons. And Will knew that Johnny Draper was just as determined.

There was nothing to do but comply with Captain Buchanan, and keep him as long as he could. The captain certainly did want to rescue the hostages. And every man with him was eager to avenge the massacre. They were all together on that. It was hard not to go headlong. The Indians had four days' lead.

But they're heavy-burdened, with all they took, and with Mary pregnant, he assured himself; they can't travel fast.

Four days is a long lead, though, he argued back at himself.

Especially as they know where they're a-goin' and we don't.

"Sir, they left the ravine here," said Gander Jack. They had reached the place where the creek pooled and went underground. It was a well-trodden place, where deer and elk and bear apparently watered in great numbers. "Up that path, I'd guess, but let me range up yonder a-ways an' see if they come back down."

"My guess is they went straight west to the gunpowder spring," mused Will.

They followed the spoor along the mountainside. It had been largely obliterated by the subsequent passage of game, but an occasional print of a horse's hoof or moccasin led them on.

Emerging finally at the spectacular bend in the New River, the tracker reconstructed and described for them the war party's brief halt, then pointed out the route they had taken up onto the palisade. Captain Buchanan looked up at the towering natural fortress warily. "Reckon they might still be holed up in there?" he wondered aloud. "Hate t'go up there if they was. Looks t'me like a mean place f'r an ambuscade."

"No," Will Ingles sighed impatiently. "No reason they sh'd loiter hereabouts an' let us catch up."

"Except to ambush us," said Buchanan.

"Cap'n, they're a-totin' most o' Draper's Meadows. They got our families t'haul wherever they be a-goin'. I just doubt they got any inclination to wait about an' wage war on an

armed company. They don't even know we're a-comin'. I'll
stake my rep'tation on it, Cap'n, they left long since."

"I'll stake my *life* on it," exclaimed Johnny Draper, suddenly spurring his horse. He took the gunpowder spring in a
leap and galloped full tilt for the steep ridge leading to the
cliff-top.

"And so'll I," said Will, whipping his mount and thundering off in the same direction. His brothers John and Matthew
followed.

Captain Buchanan hesitated for a moment, a little ashamed
of his caution, but trying to seem indignant about their reckless behavior. Finally, when they had vanished up the ridge
without drawing any fire, he waved his column forward to
follow.

Atop the awesome bluff, the tracker described the particu-
lars of what had apparently been a combat-ready first-night
encampment. "Cold supper," he said. "No fires." He showed
them a trampled place liberally spotted with horse manure.
"Corral here," he said. "Hobbled 'em too, looks like." Then
he trotted like a hunting dog over to the cliff's edge, stooped
and came back. "Limbs all fresh broke off a bush yonder," he
said. "An lookahere." He held up a narrow torn strip of
cloth—part of a dress sleeve. Johnny Draper, with a rush of
emotion, recognized the weave. He snatched it out of Gander
Jack's fingers. "It's my Bettie's! They were here, Will! They
were this far!" He was grinning through his dark whisker-
stubble, his eyes almost desperately dancing with hope.
"Now, man," he said to the tracker, "lead on."

"Y' might want t' know," drawled Gander Jack, "that
somebody dribbled a lot o' blood on yon rock thar." He
twisted his mouth and squinted up at Will Ingles. He saw Will
go gray under his leather-brown skin, and saw Johnny Draper
do likewise.

"Well, but they be no bodies lyin' round, hey?" blustered
Johnny. "Heh! They're jes' fine, far as we know. How say y'
we move on an' find out f'r certain?"

Captain Buchanan looked very reluctant. He was in parts
unknown, in a region he and his volunteers didn't even know
their way out of, and their own families were holed up on the

Roanoke, east of the Blue Ridge, and all of them had crops ripening in their fields begging for harvest. If they went deeper into these mountains, and this Ingles and Draper got themselves killed in the heat of their quest, the whole troop might well be lost.

"Well," he said at last. "We've come this far. Let's give 'er another day, at least. But with all respect, Mr. Ingles, they's a lot of us stringin' ourselves way out for these kin o' your'n."

"By th' Eternal, Cap'n, well I know it. But you help me get 'em safe, an' I'll buy every man o' you a colonelcy. If it takes me th' rest o' my days."

Gander Jack lost the spoor the next morning in a maze of ridge trails and creeks. He simply and utterly lost it. And after leading the confused column up and down the same creek for an hour, finally beginning to locate its own hoof-prints, he announced, "I done the best follerin' any man could do. I'm sorry but not ashamed."

"Then, Mr. Ingles," said Captain Buchanan, "here we must turn back. My regrets, sir. My condolences on your families."

"No, wait," Will insisted. "I'm certain they'll stay in this valley . . . Down in there somewhere, I'll vow, they're a-ploddin' along. We could . . ." He paused, realizing how desperate he sounded.

"'Down in there *somewhere*'?" the officer repeated. He was trying to mimic the poor man, then was ashamed of his sarcastic tone. "Down in that valley somewhere, y' say," he added gently. "But, man, *look* at that valley. Y' could hide five armies behind any one of those mountains. And look 'ee. How many mountains? Looks t' me like about a thousand!" He stopped talking but kept sweeping his hand over the awesome gorge with its river twisting white and green so far below.

William Ingles really looked at the New River Valley then. He sighed and his head drooped forward. He remembered something his mother-in-law had oftimes chanted to the boys:

Ten times ten times ten.

"Very well, then, Cap'n. We've no right to ask more of you. Johnny lad, how say'ee? I fear 'e's right."

"Right f'r them, mebbe. But I'm f'r you an' me an' John and Matt goin' on alone, if that's th' way it has to be."

"Nay, Johnny. That's suicide f'r us and no help for our'n. Come ride along back with me, brother. 'Tween us we'll think of another way . . ."

Far down the valley, thunder muttered. Clouds the shape and color of anvils stood on the western horizon, under the descending sun.

"'Spect I could still recover their trail f'r you, gents," the tracker mused, watching the approaching storm. "But that would wash it away 'fore we could use it."

They nodded and let him pretend so. It apparently made him feel better.

Two days later the armed company was back at Draper's Meadows. They took a rest at the spring under the willow, and ate, and watched in wordless pity as Will Ingles and Johnny Draper poked among the burned buildings. They found the awful remains of old Elenor Draper in the berry thicket, and dragged her down in a blanket and dug a grave for her next to those where they had buried Colonel Patton and Casper Barrier and the Draper baby a few days before.

Captain Buchanan was getting impatient to get back toward the Blue Ridge. He walked about, switching his boot-tops with a peeled twig, and watched the two settlers confer solemnly over the graves. He had come to admire them immensely; they were apparently tireless and fearless. But their futile errand of rescue had cost him and his volunteers many man-days here on this wild side of the divide, and he was worried about how matters might be back at the eastern settlements. The countryside well could have been pillaged in their absence, and was but thinly defended while his force was out here on this vain pursuit. At last the captain walked down to the graves. He cleared his throat to interrupt them. "Gents, we'd best be off. We can do even less for these poor souls than we could for those out yonder."

Will Ingles looked thoughtfully at Buchanan's fatigue-drawn face. Then he said:

"Johnny and me and my brothers'll be a-stayin' here a

while, Cap'n. You fellers go on back. And with our deep thanks for your service."

"What?"

"We been a-talkin' us up a plan," said Will Ingles.

"Whatever it is, y' can't travel alone. Better let me advise y' to stay with us."

"We looked this place over," said Johnny. "Th' savages left a few tools; our scythes are down in th' barley field. We're a-gonna stay here an' harvest as much as we can pack out. We'll bring it to th' Dunkard's when we can. Reckon it'll be welcome there."

Buchanan flung down his homemade switch. "Damnation! I'd figgered you t'have a *little* bit o' sense! Come on, now. Riskin' lives for your families is one thing. Riskin' 'em f'r barley's another! Now, how can I let all th' fools hereabouts keep on after lost causes, when I'm supposed t'be *protectin'* 'em?"

"Well, Cap'n," Will Ingles said slowly, "might be what you see as a lost cause, we don't. Y'see, Johnny and me, we got us a notion we could ransom our people."

"Ransom?" Buchanan acted as if he'd never heard the word.

"Ransom."

"How can y' ransom somebody y' can't even *find*?"

"Well, first, of course, we'll find 'em."

"Oh, no, no, no, now. I won't let you stray off after hostile savages into parts unknown, with y'r heads full o' such vain idees. Not if I have t' hog-tie y' and carry y' back to the fort!"

"Just get along, Mr. Buchanan, an' leave this to us. We're no' fools enough to go a visitin' Shawnees. But the Cherokee Nation . . . " Will pointed to the southwest. " . . . They're peaceable. With us *and* with the Shawnee. We reckon there's a chance, just an off chance, we could go down to th' Cherokee, talk to 'em, maybe get their help. Might be *they'd* inquire o' th' Shawnee. Find the whereabouts of our people. An' make a ransom offer on our behalf."

Buchanan's face had gone long and sour on this. "Now, damn, Mr. Ingles. You surely don't believe you can . . ."

"Cap'n, I believe I can do anything that I have t' do."

Buchanan looked at Will for a minute, then bit the middle of his upper lip between his front teeth, hissed a sigh and gazed out over the grainfields of Draper's Meadows. The fields rippled in a gentle breeze. At length he asked, "How long d'ye reckon y'll need to harvest?"

"No more'n we can carry on two horses, a day."

The captain pondered. "It's fine lookin'. An' ripe if ever I saw ripe. Tell y'what I could do, gents. I could volunteer ye ten men under a sergeant—if they'll agree, I mean—t' help y' cut an' winnow. Then mebbe in two days y' could bring in enough to make it worthwhile. And have some protection while y're aboot it."

A slow grin opened in Will Ingles' whiskers. His eyes glimmered and danced. "Mister Buchanan," he said in a tight voice, "I mought yet come t' believe y're as smart a feller as me."

CHAPTER
6

MARY RODE WITH THE BABY GIRL AT HER BREAST, CRADLED IN her right arm, and fought off dizziness and nausea and a relentless piercing soreness. Seeping blood had soaked her skirt and the horse's flanks. Only by tangling the fingers of her left hand in the horse's mane and locking them there in an unconscious grip was she able to keep from slipping off the beast as they went up steep slopes and down precipitous ravines or splashed along in streambeds. Both Tommy and Georgie were now riding on the horse with their Aunt Bettie, Georgie in front of her and Tommy behind.

Mary believed she might well bleed to death. The morning after the baby was born in the mosquito-infested woods, the

Indians had loaded up the horses. Then the chieftain had come to where she and the infant lay on the bed of dead leaves, and had looked down at her and said:

"Mo-ther come?"

He had given her as simple and final a choice as that: If she had not been willing to try to travel, it would have been the end of her. They would have tomahawked her and the baby or simply left them to die in the forest. And so, hiding her agony behind a feeble smile, she had struggled up into a kneeling position, stayed long enough to catch her breath, then stood up, still clutching the baby to her bosom. She had stood there for a moment, swaying, feeling as if all her innards were going to fall out onto the ground. She had been too weak to walk, of course, and so they had put her on her horse and she had sat straddling it, feeling all bruised and oozy and smashed and rent apart there in her crotch, and for the first few minutes it had been so awful she had felt as if she were giving birth to the great horse itself.

And now it was their fifth day out and she had been riding that way for two days and she was still bleeding. She had been so faint that she had nearly forgotten to count the days. The river was there sometimes and sometimes it was not.

On the morning after the birth, they had come to a fording place where a creek flowed into the river, and there they had crossed from the east to the west side of the river, wading in swift water almost to the horses' withers; Mary could remember the cool water on her aching and swollen and insect-tortured legs. And she could also remember, vaguely, riding in a huge thunderstorm and downpour.

And now on this fifth day they had come by many an unexpected and confusing way. They had come down along the narrow bank of the river for miles, through bottomlands and over bluffs and ridges, at one place riding across the river in a canoe the Indians had hauled from a hiding-place, finally reaching the mouth of a tributary that flowed deep and fast from between bluestone cliffs into the New River. And as well as Mary could remember, they had turned westward off the New River to go up this tributary. She was confused by it, and knew she would have to remember this and try to sort it out if she ever again recovered the strength or the will to think about escaping.

Beginning to distrust her memory, sometimes unsure whether she had forgotten to count a day or had counted one twice, Mary decided to improvise a calendar of sorts. Among the items of booty the Indians had brought from the settlement was Mary's sewing basket, which had been given to her by her mother ten years before. From it Mary now took a long strand of wool yarn. Going back through her sometimes foggy, sometimes vivid memory, and comparing her recollections with Bettie's and Henry's, she recounted the days and marked each one with a knot in the yarn. She wore the yarn looped several times around her waist, where it served both as a calendar and as a belt to secure her deteriorating dress. Each morning, her first act upon awakening was to tie another knot in that woolen strand, thus keeping her memory clear to concentrate on backward glances at landmarks.

There were ten knots in the yarn when the party finally came down off a path that had carried them northward for three days along the arrow-straight ridge of a flat-topped mountain. Mary had not seen a glimpse of the river for four days. They descended through a dense forest and began following the narrow bottoms of a twisting, north-flowing creek. The bottom of the creek was all of many-colored, round pebbles. There were trees along the way marked with tomahawk cuts or circles of faded war paint. When they made camp that evening, at a delightful place where a spring poured down over a ten-foot ledge, the Indians went one at a time to the spring, stripped, and washed off all the traces of their war paint, as if it were a ritual here.

Mary's bleeding finally had subsided. Her legs and clothing were encrusted with dried blood. After the warriors had cleaned off their paint, she and Bettie went to the spring with the children. They bathed the dirt and sweat and blood off themselves in the musical rush of the falling water. Tommy and Georgie, naked, played on mossy rocks with the cool water spilling over their heads and shoulders. She heard them laugh for the first time since the Sunday of the raid. They were happy and carefree for the moment. Their dread of the Shawnees seemed to have been diminishing over the days, though both would stiffen and grow still when a warrior would approach directly or reach to lift them on or off the horse.

The pain in Bettie's arm was lessening, she said. The poultices had cured the infection and the swelling was down. At several camps along the way, the Indians had allowed Mary to go off in search of comfrey for the dressings, and had taught her to make a salve by mashing the steeped leaves in deer fat. She would wander out of sight of the camp, and sometimes would stand alone in the wilderness simply noting the strange experience of being alone and unguarded. The Indians seemed to feel sure now that neither she nor Bettie would try to flee, at this distance from the white settlements. Surely, she thought, we're more than a hundred miles from home by now.

But they would not let her go into the woods with her baby and two sons; they seemed to know that she would never flee and leave her children. Their vigilance over Henry Lenard did not diminish. They kept his hands tied except when he was at work camp building and wood gathering, and a warrior with a gun was always within a few feet of him.

Mary was aware that she was becoming the most favored among the hostages. When a fresh kill of game was made along the trail and a horse was needed to carry it, it was always Bettie and one or both of the boys who had to give up their mount and walk. Mary and her baby daughter were always permitted to ride, even though there were times when she would have welcomed an opportunity to dismount and walk for a change of posture. Mary suspected that her policy of cheerfulness and dignity was largely the cause of this deferential treatment, so she maintained it and encouraged the others to do likewise.

And now on this tenth day, sitting in camp beside the spring, with her week-old dark-haired daughter at her breast, Mary felt a presence, and looked up to see the tall chieftain standing before her in the twilight. Without war paint, his face was quite handsome and pleasant. In the first glance at his eyes, Mary imagined she saw a fleeting look of tenderness in his face, as if he had just hidden it upon realizing she could see it. Now he straightened his back just perceptibly and crossed his muscular arms over his bare chest and looked at her with the kind of satisfaction a proud man shows toward a good possession.

"Oui-sah. Mo-ther good," he said. "Mo-ther strong." He made a downward scooping motion in front of his loins, which she perceived to mean the coming of a baby. He paused as if working with words, then said: "Not make big voice." She presumed he meant that she had not screamed in her labor. She presumed that this probably was one of the reasons why she was being treated so well.

The chieftain smiled. "Look this," he said. "Shawnee mother." He assumed a comical expression, an imitation of dreamy blissfulness, and stepped away in what apparently was the waddling of a pregnant woman. Then he returned in the same walk, mimed an expression of surprise, squatted before her, both feet flat on the ground, and began grimacing and making straining sounds in his throat. For a moment Mary was incredulous; this grave warrior seemed to be trying to move his bowels right before her eyes. Three or four of the warriors had come near and paused to watch, amused. Then the chieftain convulsed suddenly with a loud sigh, and, still squatting, looked down and made the scooping motion again, between his thighs, held an imaginary something to his chest, stood up with a smile and tilted head, and pretended to run forward. He recrossed his arms then and stood beaming with amusement while his warriors chuckled nearby.

Mary found herself flushing, and she understood what he had demonstrated: an Indian squaw, pushing and squatting on the trail to give birth without even lying down, then scooping up her baby and running to catch up with the tribe. "Surely not," she exclaimed. But then she smiled with amusement at his antics, his strange, suddenly very human demeanor; it was as if something else had come off with the war paint. "Squatting!" she exclaimed, laughing. "Well, well! Mebbe I sh'll just have t' try it that way next time . . ."

Next time, she thought, suddenly almost crushed by a sense of sadness and longing. As if it had a memory of its own, the skin of her body felt the broad, wooly warmth of her husband's powerful torso. *William,* she cried silently inside. *Ever again?*

Bettie was sullen that night. She would not look at Mary while the new potion of salve was being applied to her arm. She would not talk.

"Bet, darlin'," Mary said at last, "y're distressin' me, girl. We can't afford to shut each other out; we've nowt but each other!"

Bettie turned accusing eyes on her. "Y' laughed with 'em." Her voice was flat with hostility. "With those murtherers."

Mary's mouth dropped open. First she was indignant. Then her soul flooded toward Bettie and she remembered the awful moment when they had brained Bettie's infant against the cabin logs. "Oh, Bet!" She put her arms around her sister-in-law and hugged her head against her bosom. "I'm only tryin' to keep us alive!"

Yet, true as that was, it suddenly sounded feeble even to her own ears.

It was so: she *had* laughed with the killers of her own family.

She had somehow forgotten—in the moment when that chieftain was being so very human—that these were the same people who had made a massacre on her own friends and family.

The north-flowing creek had returned them to the river, to Mary's great relief, and there were twelve knots in her yarn belt when they came in the afternoon to a shoal where the river was wide and ran shallow over a bed of rounded stones and gravel, and here they recrossed to the northeast bank.

After a tedious ride along this shore, involving the fording of two creeks, they came to a stretch of river bank where a strange odor pervaded the air. It was not the stink of dead flesh, exactly, but faintly like bad eggs. The Indians were obviously coming into a familiar place; they were talking much and in good humor.

At last they drew up near a small depression, where a murky spring bubbled out of the ground. The Indians held the horses' bridles tightly, and talked in excited tones while one of the braves knelt and struck flint and steel to make fire in a wad of punk. Blowing on it to bring up the flame, he then darted to the edge of the spring and threw it in, then darted back. What happened then was like a Biblical miracle: a huge tongue of flame leaped thirty feet into the air with a breathtaking *whoomp!* Horses lunged against their bridles and the women and children screamed and hung on to keep from being thrown to the ground, at the same time trying to shield their faces against the heat from the pillar of fire.

The Indians made big sport of it. The white people's terror gave them a moment of supreme amusement. They watched this phenomenon cheerfully. For a few minutes they made gestures hinting that they might throw the boys into the whipping yellow-orange tower of flame. Then, when the captives finally were in a good state of terror, the chieftain uttered a few solemn words and the party resumed its progress down the river bank. The Indians relished their joke for hours afterward.

The next day there was another noticeable agitation among the Indians. They talked rapidly among themselves, in low voices. They seldom stopped to rest, and seemed intent on getting to some particular place. All this had its effect on the imaginations of the hostages. The last few days, despite the rigors of getting through the wild landscape, there had been an almost reassuring monotony. The scare at the burning spring had shown the captives how comforting that monotony had been. There was a certain feeling of security in the predictability of the hours, in not having to dread new events. Now the prisoners were affected by the intensity of their captors' behavior, particularly their increased attention to firearms. Alarming possibilities grew in Mary's fancy. Were they coming into the territory of hostile tribes? She imagined her family once again caught up in a storm of war cries and gunfire and scalping. Or were the Shawnees simply getting near their own homeland and preparing for a triumphal return? That prospect was equally dreadful. While on the trail, the captives had enjoyed a sort of a state of grace, but at the journey's end, she knew, their fates would have to be decided. They might be burned at the stake, they might be publicly tortured, they might be butchered and cannibalized, they might be torn from each other and given into slavery.

While she, and no doubt Bettie and Henry, grew grim and terrified with such imaginings, the chieftain brought the column to a halt in a narrow ravine near the river's edge. He had the horses secured and made the captives dismount to sit and be quiet under guard. Then he supervised the checking of weapons and charging of flashpans, and led a dozen of his braves on stealthy feet out of the ravine and on up the river bank. They were obviously on their way to make an attack of some sort. Mary waited, almost breathless, in the sunflecked covert with her infant girl at her breast. Now and then she would glance around at Bettie and Henry, and their drawn faces and vulnerable eyes would only feed her apprehension. They were all waiting for screams and gunshots.

Half an hour passed in this loaded silence.

Then they heard the first gunshot, a solid *thud*, and its echoes came reverberating up the valley. There were four or five more shots, almost all at once, and their aftershocks came rolling between the wooded slopes. Mary's heart raced; her mouth was dry.

Then one lone voice called from up there, an eerie, exuberant wail. And at once the warriors who had been left behind to tend the pack train broke into cheerful chatter and began moving. They prodded the prisoners to stand up and walk, and led the horses out of the ravine to follow the route of the others.

The firing had been brief. But there had been no more shooting than that at the massacre of Draper's Meadows, Mary recalled, and it had been enough to devastate many lives. She was almost ill with the dread of what she might see.

About a half mile up the river they came in sight of the main body of warriors, who were milling around on a strangely white stretch of beach along the river's edge. Some of them were kneeling, others were standing or walking about. Forms

were lying on the beach. There was no sign of buildings. As they
rode closer, Mary saw that the kneeling warriors were bent not
over human bodies, but over the carcasses of several large
animals that lay dark against the dazzling white of the shore.

Mary had seen elk before, in the hills around Draper's
Meadows, and recognized one of the carcasses as that of a
great bull elk. He lay on his side, head twisted, his enormous
fork of antlers looking like some of the dead, bleached, bark-
less trees that stood around the edge of the white beach. The
elk's tawny flank was still heaving.

A few yards away lay a white-tail doe, slim and slight and
still, its blood staining the sand crimson. Beyond it was a
huge dark-brown bulk of a beast unlike anything Mary had
ever seen. It had a glistening mantle of darker hair over its
shoulders and its blunt, short-horned head.

The horses, growing nervous near these carcasses, were led
to the far edge of the beach and unloaded. The captives were
herded together, and Henry Lenard explained to them that this
had been a highly successful hunting foray instead of an attack.

"It's a salt spring," he said. "That sand's half salt, it is.
Look at all the tracks here'bouts. Game comes here to lick.
All kinds. That yonder, lookin' like a mangy bull: I do b'lieve
that's what they call a buffalo. Colonel Patton tol' me he saw
one once that had strayed a way up the New." He stood
staring at it. One of the braves came near, noticed their
curiosity and pointed to the beast. "*P-thu-thoi*," he said.
"*P-thu-thoi.*"

There was movement in the brush behind them. Two warriors emerged, each pulling at one hind leg of a small buck
deer. They dragged the dead animal to the center of the beach
clearing, leaving a narrow track of blood, which was dribbling
from its nostrils. Tommy and Georgie pressed close to Mary,
but watched with wordless fascination as the skinning and
butchering began. She saw Bettie watching, pale, as knives
ripped along through tough hide to lay bare white tendon and
red meat, and by the look of her eyes knew she was thinking
back to the massacre twelve days ago at Draper's Meadows.

As was Mary herself.

* * *

The baby girl sucked and pulled at the nipple as the sun came up. Little shocks of hurt and pleasure spread like ripples from Mary's breast through the rest of her body; the pleasures and pains became longings and regrets, became a total bittersweet emotion.

A large brown spider with black-banded legs had built a perfect net of web between two branches a few inches above Mary's head sometime during the night. Now the spider sat in the center of the web, its legs touching the radiating strands, waiting for vibrations that would signal the entrapment of some small insect in the far filaments.

The rising sun illuminated the web. Dew had covered everything during the night, and the spider's web looked like a piece of lace ornamented with a thousand tiny diamonds. Mary had seen a diamond once, in Philadelphia when she was a little girl, and had never forgotten that it had looked like a shattered rainbow. Now each dewdrop in the web was like a tiny trapped rainbow.

As Mary watched in her nursing trance, a small fly blundered into the margin of the web. The brown spider left its station in the eye of the web and raced out to the struggling insect, examined it, then with swift and industrious motions of its forefeet began rolling it in a shroud of filament until it was entirely immobilized. Then the spider went back to the center of the web and resumed its vigil. Mary shuddered.

She tied the fifteenth knot in her belt this morning. They had worked hard here at the salt spring. There was always the smell of woodsmoke in her hair and clothing. Fires burned day and night. The Indians had cut the lean flesh of the game animals into strips and hung them on frameworks of green saplings to smoke them into jerky. And they had put the captives to work, over another bank of fires, boiling down the waters of the salt spring in the stolen kettles to make salt. Thus far, working from dawn until dark, they had produced almost a peck of the white treasure.

Jerky and salt were being wrapped and packed with care, apparently for an imminent resumption of the trek toward the Indians' homeland, where it would be a part of the winter's food hoard. The pack train, which already had been heavily

burdened with loot on the trip down the river, obviously
would be loaded to its capacity from here on, and Mary could
foresee that she and her fellow prisoners might have to walk
the rest of the way.

However far that might be, she thought.

The long halt at the salt spring had been good for Mary and
Bettie and the children, despite the fatiguing work. Being off
the horse had given Mary's tortured abdomen and loins a
reprieve, and she was no longer bleeding or feeling torn inside. The flesh of Bettie's arm was healing well, because she
had been able to do her work at the salt kettles with her left
hand and protect the splinted one. Bettie had said nothing
more about Mary's accord with the savages. But Mary remembered her accusations and was careful not to displease
her in that way again. So now she had to conduct herself with
especial care, to keep from annoying not only the Indians but
Bettie as well.

Tommy and Georgie had been almost no trouble on the
trail, and were even less here. They seemed to find the hunting and butchering activities of the Indians supremely inter-
esting, and in the last two days had drifted from their
mother's side to spend more and more time helping the warriors with the game meat and hides. Tommy, whose chief
entertainment at the settlement had been listening to his
father's and grandmother's stories about distances and long-
ago adventures, seemed now to be caught up in the doings of
the moment. He's havin' adventure enough of his own now,
Mary thought. As for Georgie, his activities always had been
simply whatever Tommy was doing, and seemed to be so even
now. Often during the evenings at the salt spring, Mary
yearned to gather them close to her and tell them stories, and
otherwise to keep them from drifting from her influence into
that of the Indians, but it was not possible. She had no leisure.
Besides, the boys found the boiling of brine much less inter-
esting to watch than the preparation of game and the mainte-
nance of weapons.

In a way, that was just as well, as the infant girl needed
most of the energy Mary had left from the salt-making. Some-

times she would detain the boys and make them watch over the baby while she worked, but they chafed under this.

At the day's end, the warriors had been teaching Tommy and Georgie one of their own childhood games. From a strip of split green hickory and rawhide thongs they had made a perfectly round hoop, which could be rolled along the ground as a moving target for the throwing of small crude spears made of cane. The Indians encouraged them to play this by the hour, sometimes stopping work to watch and cheer their best throws. At home in the settlement, the boys had been assigned certain chores as early as they had been able to understand and do them. But Mary soon came to understand here at the salt camp that the Shawnees considered play a more appropriate pastime for boys than work.

They will make proper little savages out of them all too soon, I fear, Mary thought. And I doubt there's much I can do to prevent it.

Every day the Indians brought in more game, which they killed easily in the vicinity of the salt lick, and every meal was a feast of roasted meat, made more savory with salt. Mary ate it and loved it, and felt her strength returning. But eventually so much of even this succulent flesh grew monotonous, and she began to have yearnings for bread. One evening she obtained a bag of flour and some cornmeal from the booty the Indians had taken at Draper's Meadows, and made a dough with salt and water. She shaped thin wafers from the unleavened mass and baked them on stones. The Indians welcomed this food, whose preparation obviously was the province of their women and thus rare on the trail. Bettie nearly foundered herself on it, muttering around mouthfuls something about "the staff of life," and apparently did not mind this time that Mary had done something that pleased the savages.

They left the salt spring on the seventeenth day and continued northward on the right bank. The river ran broad and smooth now, curving less tortuously around the steep mountainsides. There were wooded islands in the river, and sometimes the party could travel an hour at a time along narrow bottomlands without having to climb into the hills.

Bettie's horse had been employed to carry some of the meat and salt produced at the salt lick, and so she and Tommy were afoot. Georgie was put on Mary's horse, to ride behind her as she carried the baby girl in her arms.

Mary wished she herself had been permitted to walk—not because she really wanted to, but because of the resentment this new arrangement was aggravating in Bettie. She plodded and stumbled through the brush and cane a few feet in front of Mary's horse, leading Tommy with her good hand, her dark hair and her slim figure in its torn dress and her splinted right arm right in Mary's view as a reminder of the inequality of their treatment. Bettie would look back over her shoulder now and then, her face unhappy and her stare full of accusation. Then she would face forward again, and for a while would seem to stumble more often and more heavily, lurch more violently, crash more clumsily into bushes, moan and mince more pathetically at the pain of gravel underfoot, as if to increase Mary's guilt at being the Indians' favorite. At least, so it seemed to Mary, and she was bothered by it.

"Bet," she began calling every so often, "Bet, I can walk. Would y' like to ride a spell?" Bettie would respond by not looking back. And Mary hurt inside, and was confused. But she suspected that the Indians would not have let them change places anyway. They had made a point of assigning the horse to her.

By evening Bettie would be sulking and silent, giving in only reluctantly to let Mary dress her arm. "Bet, darlin', don't y' see it?" Mary hissed to her one evening, believing she understood it now. "They *want* to divide us up. They *want* us to resent each other. Why . . . why . . . see how they've kept poor Henry off by himself. See how they've mollycoddled my boys, and lured 'em off from me with games . . ." It seemed so obvious now, now that she had seen it. It made sense to her. "Now, Bettie," she said in a confidential tone, "we must all stay one in heart, like the family we truly are. No suspicion, please, hon? We're us, and they're our enemy, I know that as sure as you. I'm sure Henry would agree with me, that's what they're a-doin'."

They were given no opportunity to discuss it with Henry Lenard, though. He was kept always at a far side of the camp or at the other end of the column. But from a distance, he watched Mary's special treatment and Bettie's discontent, and in his eyes, too, Mary thought she saw accusation.

It was distressing. Through no conscious fault of her own, she felt herself being isolated from her dear ones.

On the morning of the nineteenth day. Mary refused to mount her horse. She held the baby in her right arm and took Georgie's hand, turned away from the brave who was prepared to help her up with the children and started walking forward along the column. She walked up to Bettie and said, "That horse is free. I want you to ride it. I sh'd rather walk a hundred leagues than have y' look at me the way y' do. Come, Tommylad. Will y' walk wi' me?" Tommy glanced at his aunt, then fell in behind his mother.

The Shawnee chieftain watched Mary Ingles coming forward with her lips compressed and her head held high. He shrugged. Then he rode back and told the brave to help Bettie onto the horse.

All day they went that way. For Mary it was a great effort to walk and carry the baby and lead her two sons. She had to shift the infant from one arm to the other at increasingly frequent intervals. She panted and was drenched with sweat. Her shoes were falling apart. The soles flapped loose and threatened to trip her, and her toes and feet were bruised over and over by rocks and roots. But she walked, and would not look back at Bettie on the horse.

For the greater part of that day Mary was too preoccupied with what she was doing, and its possible effects on Bettie, to notice that the Indians once again were acting eager and excited.

In the late afternoon they were moving over the gentlest terrain they had yet encountered. The mountains were less steep and less high, and the bottomland was more than a mile wide. There were vast areas of cane and meadow.

The sun was almost on the western bluff, and Mary was automatically dragging one sore foot up before the other, her eyes on the spongy ground, when the Indians began calling:

"Spay-lay-wi-theepi!"

"O-he-oh! O-he-oh!"

Mary looked up and saw before her the widest stretch of water she had ever viewed. Far to her left, the river they had been following widened through the broad lowland and curved away between its bluffs to empty into a great blue-green, slow-flowing stream that appeared to be a mile wide.

She thrilled. This surely was the great Ho-he-o, or O-y-o, into which her husband believed the New River flowed. Dear Heaven, she thought, we're likely the first white folk ever to have come this way! Somehow, for a moment, that grand notion rose above everything else in her soul: the discomfort, the jeopardy, the remorse.

And it meant that, if ever there should be a chance of escape, she really could, as she had speculated over and over and over on the trail, find her way back to Draper's Meadows by staying on the river. Her happiness rose like a song in her breast.

Never had she seen such a beautiful or mighty river. It was so wide its far bluffs looked blue in the distance. They were flat-topped and covered with dense, dark forest and brilliant blue-green meadow grass.

They made camp that evening in a parklike stand of timber free of undergrowth, on the point where the two rivers converged. From the center of the camp they could see the surfaces of both streams glittering under the sinking sun. A gentle and soothing river breeze hushed over the point. The sense of spaciousness was heartening after the two weeks of struggle and confinement between the steep walls of the river gorge. Mary felt the same expansiveness of spirit she had always enjoyed on the rolling heights of Draper's Meadows.

The day on horseback, perhaps, and the pleasing site of their present camp, seemed also to have dispelled Bettie's resentments. She was her old self now. As they knelt by their cooking fire in the twilight, Mary told her what she had been thinking about the way back. Bettie listened, her eyes glittering now with excitement, now with fear. The prospect of such a trek to freedom through the wilderness they had already traversed seemed joyous but impossible. They whispered back and forth about it late into the night.

"But that river, Mary," Bettie exclaimed, nodding toward the O-y-o. "If they take us across it, how could we *ever* return?"

Mary looked toward the broad, black expanse of darkness where the river flowed.

"I only know this, Bet. If there be a way to go somewhere, there must likewise be a way to return."

CHAPTER
7

HER FATIGUE FROM HER FIRST FULL DAY AFOOT WAS SO GREAT that she managed to bring herself only half-awake during the night to feed and tend to the baby girl. And when she awoke at daylight, the rest of the camp was up and about; the horses were being loaded.

The short, slight warrior who had first helped make the comfrey medicine came to Mary as soon as he saw her awaken. He held an oblong basket about as long as his forearm, made of hickory and hide and thongs, with straps of rawhide attached. The Indian pointed to it and then to the baby, then made a motion of slinging it onto his back with his arms through the straps. Mary understood then that it was a device for carrying the baby on her back. The baby would be slipped down inside, its head outside, so that the mother could carry it while keeping both hands free. It was an ingenious device, its only drawback being that it would restrain the infant from any free movement. It even had a forehead strap to hold the baby's head and keep it from wobbling.

Mary nursed the baby and cleaned her, then slipped her, naked, into the basket, which was soft inside, being lined with the hair side of a doeskin. Its hickory-strip frame appeared to have been made in the same manner as the boys' target hoop, but then forced into an oblong shape, bound and covered. It was a clever piece of work, very strong and lightweight, and, with an eye for the utility she had come to appreciate as a woman of the frontier, she carefully noted its construction.

When she stood up, she almost fainted from the pain in her bruised and swollen feet and the tautness in her leg muscles. It was worse when the Indian loaded the baby onto her back. Oh, how I should love to ride today, she thought. But the Indians seemed to have redistributed the loads among the pack animals, leaving no place for anyone to ride now. Apparently she had forfeited her mount once and for all by choosing to walk the day before. One of the warriors lifted Georgie onto the top of a load of hides and he sat up there looking half-proud, half-scared, without an adult to hold on to.

"Don' 'ee fall off, Georgie," Tommy warned him gravely. "If 'ee do, *I* sh'll ride."

Georgie clutched his little fists desperately around a strap as the column started and the horse lumbered forward. Mary grimaced against the agony of each step. But within a hundred yards the exertion of walking had benumbed her pains to a throbbing ache that was much more bearable.

They traveled less than a mile, down into a place of thickets and swamp, busy with mosquitoes, where the Indians opened a stack of dry brush to reveal two hidden canoes. They hoisted the loads down from the horses' backs and loaded two packs at a time into each canoe, paddled the loads across and deposited them on the far shore of the New River, then came back for more. So, they were not going to cross the broad O-y-o here. The canoes apparently were kept here only for crossings of the tributary.

After the cargoes had been ferried over, the captives were put in one canoe with two paddlers and taken across. Then the canoe was sent back to bring over three braves at a time, while the other canoe was employed in the tricky business of leading the unladen horses to swim across the stream. Finally, both canoes were secreted in a creek mouth on the west side of the river, the loads were strapped onto the horses' backs as before and the column now moved up the left bank toward the mouth. The whole process had been executed with such efficiency and economy of motion that it had cost less than an hour.

The way was easier here in the valley of the O-y-o River. The bluffs were low and rolling, easy to cross when they had to be crossed, and most of the route was through the rich bottomlands, through soft-floored forests and sunny cane-brakes along the base of the bluffs.

They went straight south along the bank of the wide river for a day, covering what Mary estimated to be about twenty miles, and she plodded in a trance of exhaustion, starting, now and then, to catch her balance or waking to the whimpering of the baby on her back, or to the voices of the Indians when they would scare up bears or elk or deer along their route and send them scurrying for cover. Game birds would sometimes burst from cover like brown explosions, their wingbeats whirring and thundering, throwing the horses into panic. Georgie was nearly thrown at one such time, and cried for so long afterward that Mary grew alarmed lest the Indians grow annoyed and silence him.

The sun was low and reddening when they came to a vast, sweeping bend in the O-y-o. From here the river seemed to flow westward in almost a straight line, as far as the eye could see, between the opposing bluffs. The far reaches of the river faded into an iridescent mist below the sun, whose ruddy, blazing disk was mirrored on the shimmering river. Flocks of birds, clouds and arrows of them, wheeled and soared and dipped in the brilliant, pearly light, twittering and mewing their various calls far and near along the great valley. The grandeur of the scene stunned Mary, even through her fatigue. The column stopped here, and the Indians stood with their faces to the west, their skin and ornaments gilded by the evening light, their expressions serene and thoughtful.

Mary felt she was being watched. She turned her head quickly and saw the chieftain standing a few feet away gazing at her, his face and his lithe, long-muscled physique burnished by sunlight.

When her eyes fell on his, his gaze seemed to intensify momentarily, to flash darkly, and he continued to stare at her until she dropped her eyes and looked back over the river. She shivered. She adjusted the shoulder straps of the baby carrier, gently to avoid waking the baby, and wondered why this warrior watched her as he did. This time it had not been the same tenderness she had thought she had seen in his eyes at the earlier camp, but rather some kind of thoughtful study. She glanced back at him through the corner of her eye to find that he was still looking. Again she dropped her eyes.

She wondered about this man's special attention to her. He was, she knew, responsible for the lenient treatment she had been receiving for so long on the trail, but she felt she had earned that by her forbearance and cooperation. It did not explain why he studied her so.

It might well be, of course, she thought, that he's just never seen anyone with my coloration. Like as not, every woman he's ever seen has had the same raven hair and dark eyes as his. Even lovely Bettie has black hair, brown eyes . . . Surely I'm just a curiosity.

She had worked that explanation out reasonably enough. But in her breast she remained unsettled. She did not want to think too hard on the matter. Somehow, she feared, when this savage looked at her he was making decisions that might affect her future in a very personal way.

He might be, she thought, putting the thought directly into words, planning that I should be his.

This was an annoying thought. It made blood rush to her face and her skin prickle. By the Lord God, she thought, my Will would snap your spine if he caught ye bold-eye-looking at me thisaway, ye murtherin' snake.

She had a daydream then. Her eyes were seeing the glare of sunlight on the great river, but in her mind she saw Will Ingles, her Will with his great, thick knotted arm and shoulder muscles bulging with strain, squeezing the life out of this slender brown man, his arms around his middle, his skull pressed up under the Indian's chin, bending him backward, backward, straining the way he could strain for minutes at a time, levering out a stump or a boulder from a plowfield, until his skin grew pink and his veins stood out; she saw Will's arms like oak limbs tightening, saw the Shawnee's tongue protrude and his eyeballs bulge white until, with a muffled *crack*, the Indian's backbone broke; and then she saw Will fling the savage down like a broken twig and stand over him, flushed, sweat-drops glinting in his reddish chest hairs . . . Sometimes, she remembered, when Will would put himself upon her on summer days, taking pleasure with her in a sunny field or in the airless heat of their cabin while the boys napped, with that sudden great plunging desire of his, he would drench her with his sweat, and it would trickle tickling down her flanks and thighs, and when he would rise off her there would be sweat-drops glimmering in his body-hair like dewdrops on a spiderweb . . .

Her mind came back and she saw the river there before her, and her heart was pounding and she felt weak, weak in the way she felt weak after Will had lain upon her, or weak in the way she felt weak after she had watched him slaughter a pig.

It was strange that she felt this way now after those fantasies of love and killing: weak, spent, satisfied, avenged.

But she had come back to the present moment and was standing here, flooded with the sunglare off the river. And when she looked out of the corner of her eye again at the Shawnee chieftain, he was still standing there tall and hairless and slick as a snake, gleaming with bear grease, his black eyes still on her. His straight back was not broken after all, not even bent, and for some reason she was relieved to see him still standing there erect and perfect and, in his heathen way, beauteous . . .

Beauteous?

She could hardly believe that she had thought that: *beauteous*.

She was confused now by her thoughts, and she hated the Indian even more for having confused her so strangely, for having disturbed her so deeply.

She tried to put the daydream out of her mind. But her thoughts kept returning to it as camp was made overlooking that long river vista, as she nursed the baby, as she watched her sons throw spears at the rolling hoop, as she dressed Bettie's arm. Sometimes she would think of it in personal terms: about the chieftain and his drilling scrutiny of herself, about this matter of his beauty. Other times she would think of it in general.

They have the power to decide what is to be done with us.

She had never had such a thought before. It was not a way in which anybody should ever have to think.

"How far d'ye reckon they've brought us?" Bettie asked that evening as Mary worked with needle and thread in the remaining light to rejoin a sleeve to Tommy's shirt.

"Ten times ten times ten," said Tommy.

Mary laughed, and Tommy laughed. Georgie laughed after his brother. Then even Bettie laughed.

But then Mary thought of her mother, whose saying that had been. And then apparently all the others remembered, and they did not laugh any more. In her mind Mary saw the bloody scalp of her mother's gray hair.

"How far?" Bettie had to ask again after a while.

Mary pondered. She thought of the knots in her belt and tried to calculate how far they had come on a typical day. "We've been a-comin' three weeks now," Mary said. "Twists and turns, ups and downs an' all, surely we've done five or six leagues a day. Th' number that come t'my mind is two hundred miles or thereabouts."

"Two hundred," Bettie breathed. She was still for a minute, then sighed. "That's just about what I'd thought. My feet told me a thousand, but I known they'd be a-stretchin' the truth summat."

Mary smiled in the dimming light. Thank God, Bettie's humor was returning. Mary had had to worry a great deal about Bettie while it was lacking.

They followed the O-y-o westward the next day, perhaps fifteen miles. They were slowed by the fording of several creeks and small tributary rivers. They waded the shallower creeks, the Shawnees carrying the children over. At the rivers they brought forth hidden canoes. At each stop, Mary lifted the baby out of its carrier, rinsed out its swaddling cloth in the stream, wrapped it in a dry one and put it to her breast. The baby slept most of the time, perhaps lulled by the motion of Mary's walking.

Th' are such a good babe, Mary would think as she walked along the river bank behind warriors and horses, such a good, still and calm babe. She would think this as if talking silently to the little weight on her back, and a rich sadness would squeeze her heart. Keep looking back, little 'un; that's where y'r rightful home is . . . that I fear y'll never never see.

She could not let herself hope that the baby would ever see their homeplace or her father. It was better not to try to envision Will Ingles with this babe in his arms ever. Better to imagine it, in some vague way of imagining, as an Indian baby. An Indian baby, an Indian child. A white Indian woman.

Mary tried to foresee such a life, in her imagination, to prepare herself for that awful possibility. She envisioned a little girl huddled among animal skins on a dirt floor; than a naked woman shiny with animal grease, painted and tattooed, adorned only in bracelets and tufts of feathers, dancing obscenely with a savage leer on her stained face, being passed from hand to hand among warriors and chiefs, bearing half-white children, then growing haglike and white-haired, praying to pagan gods in some corner of the wilderness and someday dying unaware that she was to have been Bettie Elenor Ingles, daughter of William . . .

The baby girl's whole live thus passed in vague and wretched images through the dismal fancies of her mother, who plodded westward along the river bank toward an unknown destiny.

They traveled two more days along the shore of the great river, going generally in a northwesterly course. On the thirtieth day of their captivity, with a noonday sun beating down, Mary noticed that air of anticipation among the Indians again. When they stopped to rest, the braves got out their bags of pigments and mixed war paints, and decorated their faces and bodies. Mary looked at Bettie and saw in her eyes that old dark terror of the first days. Even Tommy and Georgie, who had grown familiar with several of the warriors, came to Mary's side and hung there watching. Their memories of old terrors were being stirred as they again saw the savages as they had seen them on that first day of blood and shock a month ago. Mary was chilled with dread, and hugged the boys close to her, feeling anew their awful vulnerability. "God save us," Bettie breathed beside her, "what d'ye reckon, Mary? It's no huntin' party now, for certain."

"Faith, Bet. Faith, now. But I don't know, I'll confess." They watched the braves work on Henry Lenard's bonds nearby, retying his hands behind his back and once again slipping a noose over his head. Mary tried to catch the eye of the chieftain, to see if she could somehow gauge their peril from the expression on his face. But when he paused to look at her, his face was as distant and unreadable behind its paint as if he were masked. Once again he was not a human.

The sight of a cornfield was so unexpected that they were halfway past it before Mary realized what she was seeing. It was the regularity, the orderly spacing, that caught her eye, which had grown conditioned to the random profusion of woods and thickets and cane. The sight of cultivation was such a shock perhaps, she realized, because she had never expected to see such a thing again. Bettie seemed to notice it at the same time, and turned to look back at Mary with wonderment in her eyes.

"If Will and Johnny could see this corn," Mary exclaimed. "It's every bit o' ten feet tall!"

And she realized now that she was looking too for buildings—that without having thought of it she was expecting buildings to be where there was cultivated grain. With an ache in her breast she realized that she had not seen a human dwelling in a month, other than caves.

And then alarm and confusion: They must be approaching a settlement! That would be the reason for the war paint. She had thought they would never again see a white settlement, after this long trek northwestward. But there must be one hereabouts. And the Shawnees were evidently planning to attack it now, and once again she suffered that awful sense of helplessness, knowing that she could not warn the settlers, whoever they must be, of the massacre and mayhem that were about to fall upon them.

She smelled woodsmoke before she saw it. Then above the shaggy tassels of the corn she saw it drifting up, faint against the dark backdrop of the forested bluff.

Strangely, the Indians had not deployed themselves for a surprise attack. Instead, they continued marching straight toward the source of the smoke, and, instead of subsiding into stealth, suddenly began hooting like owls and laughing.

The dwelling came into view beyond the edge of the cornfield. It was unlike any building she had ever seen, either in Philadelphia or on the frontier. It was the size of a small cabin, but was domeshaped and covered with slabs of tree bark. An animal skin, hanging on its doorway, was being held open by a black-haired woman who was naked except for a small deerskin apron and moccasins. A sturdy Indian man of middle years, without war paint or other decorations, was coming forward from the house to greet the party, smiling, his right hand held raised in greeting. An array of crude mattock-and hoelike tools and pointed sticks, evidently agricultural implements, leaned against a pole fence beside the hut. The place was pleasantly shaded by cottonwood trees, and its yard sloped down to the edge of the wide river, where two naked boys, about twelve or fourteen years old, had paused in knee-deep water, one holding a slim spear, the other a large, open-mesh basket of woven cane. On the shore near them a bark canoe lay upside down; in its shade a large yellow dog stretched and yawned and watched their approach. Mary understood now. There was not a white settlement here. They were apparently arriving at the outskirts of the Shawnee civilization. The warriors had painted themselves for their victorious return.

And despite the apparent tranquility of the place, Mary trembled with apprehension. The frank, silent curiosity in the eyes of these riverside dwellers, this silent, expressionless approach to inspect the captives, was ominous. She felt her vulnerability more keenly than she had since the day of the raid.

The Indian boys were sent across the big river in the canoe. The vessel angled downstream across the blue-green water, diminishing to a speck, then vanished between two low bluffs on the opposite shore, into what evidently was the mouth of a tributary. The warriors talked and smoked with the hut-dweller, glancing often across the river. The Indian woman regarded the knot of white hostages from a few feet away with a dark, veiled look that was not shy, nor friendly, nor really even hostile. Mary smiled at her as one young woman to another, but there was no response except a momentary, apparently unconscious, raising of the black eyebrows. After a while Bettie murmured something that conveyed the strange meaning of it:

"We're in their world, Mary."

By the middle of the afternoon five long canoes had come across the river and had been loaded with the booty from Draper's Meadows, the meat and salt from the salt spring and the warriors and their captives. There were five strong young paddlers in each canoe and the vessels surged swiftly in a single file across the sparkling river. For some time they were on the wide, smooth surface of water. Tommy asked: "Is this like an ocean?"

They entered the shade of the woods at the mouth of the tributary and went upstream. Along the bank there were more of the domeshaped huts, and many shaped like cones, covered with skins or bark. These stood close to the water, and their inhabitants, women and children and old men, came down to the river bank to look and then began moving in a crowd, apace with the canoes, talking excitedly and laughing and pointing.

The woods gave way then to cleared fields separated by pole fences. Some of the fields were in corn; others were full of pole frames leafed over with climbing pea and bean vines. Other fields were yellow-green with tobacco leaf, and some were covered with low, broad-leafed plants Mary did not

recognize. And as the canoes slid upstream, close to the
shore, a huge village of the cone-shaped dwellings and some
long, low lodges—bigger even than the houses Mary had seen
as a girl in Philadelphia—came into view above the cultivated
fields. She was dumbfounded by the sight of this unexpected
civilization, by the extent of its agriculture. Her old imaginary notions of Indian life, of small, ragged bands of murderous nomads scattered through the forests and living
unsheltered on the ground, were being forced out of her mind
by this impressive scene, by this now murmuring mob of
copper-skinned people moving en masse along the shore toward the town.

And they're all coming to see what's going to become of us,
she thought. We're the center of all this. She quailed at the
thought.

The canoe men deftly beached the vessels at a place that
seemed to be the end of a long, wide street or commons of the
town. The crowd of Indians, a moving, easygoing, laughing
mass of ruddy naked skin and pale deerhide garments,
pressed close to the canoes to gawk, then fell back a little way
on each side to make way as the painted chieftain sprang
ashore with a panther's agility. They cheered and clapped
their hands and parted to make way as he strode grinning
toward the center of the town, holding a musket aloft with one
sinewy arm and waving a scalp with his other hand. It was a
scalp with gray hair, but, Mary knew, not her mother's. No
doubt it was that of Colonel Patton. Mary trembled and felt
sick, sickened by the villagers' gleeful response to this grisly
trophy.

Each of the next three braves who leaped ashore was waving a scalp; each brought another outburst of cheers. Mary
did not want to look at the scalps, but found herself watching,
fascinated and horror-struck, as if identifying ghosts: that
small patch of graying brown hair would be what was left of
bald-headed Casper Barrier; those short white wisps, Phil
Barger. The little dark nest of curls, Bettie's baby boy. Mary
glanced back at Bettie, grateful to see that she was not watching this. Then she turned in time to see the long gray hair of
her mother's scalp being waved over the heads of the crowd.

And though she should have been expecting it, the shock of it went through her heart like a lance; for a moment her vision swam and she had to brace herself against a faint.

It was Tommy and Georgie who helped keep her from swooning. Intimidated by the mob—they had never seen more than ten people at a time—they pressed back against Mary with such voiceless, urgent need that they brought her out of her shock determined to protect them in any way she could.

Her mind was whirling with the confusion of the moment. Brown hands were clutching at the gunwale of the canoe; others seemed to be reaching for her and her children. The musky, earthy smell of the Indians was close and she had never heard such an uproar of so many voices, not even in Philadelphia town. The babble of the voices seemed to roll over her with waves of the Indian smell. It was not the sour, rankling smell of white people who have been too long in their clothes; it was not unpleasant in that way. It was simply the heat and the closeness of so many; it was their rude staring and their reaching, their incomprehensible tongue being uttered at once by so many voices, shrill and deep, masculine and feminine; it was their delight at the hostages' misery; it was that eerie *other-worldness* Bettie had spoken of on the other side of the river, but now amplified by hundreds. Mary and her three small children, like a knot of life, clung to each other in the belly of the canoe and cringed against the gunwale away from the people as hands reached. In the distance above the babble, she could hear the strong voice of the chieftain going away into the village, in a chant of boastful tone. He at least had favored her, on the trail; now he was deserting her to swagger away boasting, no doubt, about the scalping of old men and women and babies.

Mary grew angry then, and her anger gave her the strength and courage to face the mob and control her fears. *Dignity,* she remembered. *Be dignified.* It's worked thus far. "Up, laddies," she said as calmed as she could. "Up now. They want us to get out of the boat." With her hands gripping their upper arms, she urged them up and away from her and toward the reaching hands. And she, gathering her legs under her,

rose with the weight of the baby on her back and stepped
gingerly after them as they were lifted out, silent in fright,
onto the trampled grass and packed dirt of the shore. "Come,
Bet," she said, reaching back for her with one hand. Bettie
shook her head and cringed in the canoe, face in a grimace,
hugging herself with her left arm. "Up, Bettie, sweet. Be
dignified, now. Show them what a Draper is made of."

On the bank they soon were being pressed toward the
center of the town by the crowd, and it seemed that all the
hundreds of women and girls and boys had their hands on her,
abusing her or exploring her as a curiosity. Brown hands
snatched at her hair and pulled it, slapped her face, grabbed
and pinched her arms, ripped at her dress, raised her skirts,
tugged at the baby carrier on her back, felt her breasts, in-
truded on her person in every rude way. Faces kept looming
in front of her, laughing, hissing, baring their teeth, some
spitting at her face. There were old women with snow-white
hair and faces creased and cracked like boot leather; there
were pretty young women with saucy and derisive black eyes;
there were great broad women with moon-round faces and
hooded eyelids and gaps in their teeth, blowing their stinking
breath in her face or screaming shrill as whistles in her ears;
there were naked little children striking with their fists at her
hips and her groin. Ahead she could hear Tommy and Georgie
screaming, but they were invisible among the milling Indians.
On her back, her baby daughter was squalling. Somewhere
beyond the din of voices Mary could hear—or rather, feel—
the pulsation of drumbeats. Dust of the street roiled upward,
charged with afternoon sunlight, rankling in her nose, dry
and gritty in her mouth. Above the heads of the crowd she
could see the tops of village lodges and cone-shaped huts of
hide and bark, and leafy treetops shivering in the hot breeze,
and beyond that, a dazzling pearly blue sky. She yearned to
keep her eyes above the intimidating faces and pray to that
sky, but had instead to look down to fend off blows and try to
keep from being tripped.

In the center of the village the crowd suddenly opened, and
she was thrust forward, almost falling, into a cleared and
trampled space some thirty feet across. In it stood four up-

right posts, and at the foot of each post there were people sitting and lying. Their faces were turned toward her: they were white people.

They were in rags. Their hands were bound behind them and there were ropes and thongs around their necks, tethering them to two of the posts. There were six of them. Two women and a little girl were strung to one post, and three men to another. One man's face was covered with dried blood. He wore the tattered red coat of a soldier. Another's clothing was brown with old bloodstains but there were no injuries on his face.

Strong hands forced Mary's arms behind her and she felt thongs being wound and tied around her wrists, mercilessly tight. Tommy and Georgie were being bound by nooses to the third post, their hands free, still crying at the top of their lungs. Henry Lenard was already tied to that post, and at the moment Mary's eyes fell on him he was struck to the ground by one of the braves of the war party.

In a moment Mary and Bettie were secured by nooses to the fourth post. The mob drew back a few feet and stood in a circle surrounding them, and a change in the thumping of the drums suddenly depressed their shrilling cries to a murmur. Tommy and Georgie and the baby girl were still crying, and their voices rose above everything else now, wailing up and down in the stillness. Their wails were the center of everything now. Mary was both torn with pity and mortified. The Indians had begun laughing at them.

"*Thomas!*" she snapped suddenly, in that voice she seldom had to use. "THOMAS!" His cries stopped and she stared at him. Dust and tears streaked his face. "Thomas, hush Georgie up, or I sh'll cane thy hide!" Tommy swallowed and grimaced, his nose running, almost starting to cry again, but then rubbed his fists in his eyesockets and turned on Georgie. With threats and hugs and cajolery, broken with hiccups of strangled sobbing, he soon calmed the two-year-old. The circles of Indians had observed this interchange of authority, and began laughing softly, exclaiming in what seemed to be tones of approbation. Mary stood with her head erect and tried to look as dignified as she could with that last screaming voice still issuing from the baby carrier on her back. "Bettie," she murmured, "please, can y' try to quieten this babe, in the name o' God?" Bettie stood behind her and whispered and crooned. That, or the cessation of the hubbub, worked. The baby's squalling descended and trailed off and soon she was gurgling and cooing. Again the Indians in the encircling mob laughed appreciatively. Mary stood, flushing, aware of the hundreds of dark eyes on her. "Thank'ee, Bet. Oh, thank'ee, Thomas, and Georgie, dear. We must no' shame ourselves in any way, now. Good, good . . ."

She glanced at the post nearest by, where the strange women and the girl were tied. The older of the two women had risen to her feet and stood there looking at Mary and nodding. She was saying something. Mary sorted her voice out from the surrounding drone of voices. "Gut," the old woman seemed to be saying. "Gut. Gut."

She was a startling sight, this old woman. Taller and broader than most men, she stood with a proud stance and peered with pale hazel eyes out through a lank, tangled mob of white and iron-gray hair. Her cheeks were concave with toothlessness and her mouth was puckered and furrowed. She was grinning, displaying large, yellow, horsy upper and lower front teeth, which gave her the appearance, Mary thought, of a braying ass. A great wen sprouted black hairs on the right side of her nose. What had been a dress of linsey-woolsey hung here and there on her big-boned frame in strips and tatters, belted with a strip of deerhide, almost black with dirt and ashes. Her muscular legs, scratched, insect-riddled, wrinkled at the knobby knees, were visible through great rents which ran from the waist to the hem of the dress, and the left side of the bodice had been ripped open to expose a great, veined, brown-nippled dug that hung to her waist. Despite her remarkable ugliness and her devastated condition—she looked as if she might have been raked out from under a bonfire—there was something formidable and even noble about her. She was standing there, apparently unbeaten by the ordeals she must have survived, grinning happily straight at Mary and repeating, "Gut. Gut." Mary smiled at her. Here was dignity, and it was reassuring to see it among these helpless hostages.

The shout of a strong male voice drew the attention of the village Indians, and one side of the circle opened.

Five Indians walked slowly through the gap into the arena, led by a white-haired man wearing a red headband, which held at his right temple a silver disk with two eagle feathers hanging from it. A wide chest ornament made of rows of red beads and white quills hung from his neck, and his breechclout also was decorated with rows of red beads. He was of medium height, and stately, with eyes so deep-set and shadowed that he appeared to be blind. His mouth was wide and thin, drawn down at the corners in an expression of severity. Mary presumed that this man was the chief. Walking beside him—almost strutting—was the slender chieftain whose party had brought her here, and it was apparent that he had led the chief here to see what he had brought back from his expedition. Behind the two came two other finely dressed Indians of middle age whose air of gravity and self-importance suggested that they too might be chiefs of some rank.

The four stopped within the cleared circle, a few feet from where Mary and Bettie stood, and studied the captives while the young chieftain began a long discourse in rapid syllables and grunts, moving his hands in ways that, Mary imagined, were meant to illustrate brave fighting, risings and settings of the sun, high mountains and long distances. Now and then he would point toward one or another of the hostages, and he and the chiefs would look at that one as the narrative continued.

The chieftain talked a long time while looking at Mary. He made that baby-scooping motion, and she knew he was talking about the birth of Bettie Elenor. He looked proud, and Mary remembered what she had been thinking about this chieftain's special interest in her. He was not beauteous now and she wondered how she had ever thought he was beauteous, because he was in truth a murderous, painted braggart, ugly as Satan.

Mary saw the chiefs nod several times while they were looking at her. And they actually smiled and chuckled when the chieftain led them closer to Tommy and Georgie and talked about them. She saw him make motions that reminded her of the spear-throwing game his warriors had taught the boys. The people in the crowd, meanwhile, listened rapt to all this oratory, sometimes muttering, sometimes exclaiming, sometimes laughing, sometimes patting their palms lightly together as if applauding. Now and then Mary would turn to look at Bettie or the other captives. Bettie stood as if frozen, scarcely blinking, not looking at the chiefs, her lips white. Tommy and Georgie had calmed down and were mostly watching the chieftain. Mary wondered what they could be thinking of him. He had become familiar, even, perhaps, a friend, on the trail, and she wondered how much they still associated him with the violence and hurt of that bloody and flaming day a month ago at Draper's Meadows. Henry Lenard, now with a dark red abrasion on the left side of his face where he had been struck a few minutes before, sat on the ground and glared at the chiefs. It had been weeks since he had been allowed close enough to her to talk at any length, and she wondered what he was thinking of their plight by now.

The formidable old woman at the next post still stood, looking defiant and amused, sometimes staring at the chiefs, sometimes sweeping her gaze over the surrounding mob with hauteur or, for no apparent reason, flashing her yellow-toothed ass's grin at them. Several times, too, she brought her gaze to bear on Mary, and smiled each time she did so.

The chieftain seemed to run out of words suddenly after about ten minutes, and the old chief with the red headband then spoke in a deep, growling voice for less than a minute. When he finished, the crowd broke out in cheerful chatter, and parted again to make way for the departure of the chiefs. Part of the crowd began drifting away. Others stayed on, studying the captives with rude fascination, but now no longer venturing close to torment them. The sun was almost down into the treetops now, washing the scene with a glowing cross-light, heightening the purples and reds and blues and vermillions decorating the scanty clothing of the villagers. Scrawny dogs, yellowish and wolflike, wandered among the legs of the people, came and sniffed cautiously at the strange scents of the white people and went away, their tongues hanging pink in the hot evening air. Through the dust now came the distant shouting and laughing and crying of children, the drone of voices, whiffs of woodsmoke and the enticing fragrances of cooking meat and baking corn.

The old woman had come as close to Mary as her neck tether would allow—about five feet—and made a summoning motion with her head, grinning. Mary went toward her until the rope at her own neck stopped her, and then they both sat down in the dusty grass. The old woman apparently wanted to talk.

"Ya, nah," she said. Her voice was gurgly but loud. "You ben 'ahngry?"

"Angry?" Mary replied. "Well, more afeared than angry, but, yes, I . . ."

"Nah, I say 'ahngry!" The old woman opened her maw and pretended to chew and smack her lips. Then she raised her face and shut her eyes and sniffed the fragrant air with a blissful expression. "Gott, I 'ev altso! Dey vohn *feed!*" Mary had to listen carefully to sort out any comprehensible words from this thick accent, which was unlike anything she had ever heard. "Vair from, you?" the old woman said then.

"By the Blue Ridge," Mary said. "D'ye know of it?"

"Nah."

"And you?" Mary said.

"Fort Duquesne. You know dot?" Mary nodded. She had heard of it; Colonel Washington had spoken of it when he came through Draper's Meadows. It was a new fort, at the place where two rivers came together to make the O-y-o. It had been started by the British and captured by the French even before it was completed. "Indians, Francemens, kill whole English army by there. Las' mont'. One mont' ago. General Braddock. Not shmahrt enough. Whole army! *Blitzen!*" The old woman shook her head as if in wonderment at the recollection. Mary gathered that the old woman had been at or near a disastrous battle and had been captured then, perhaps brought here afterward by just such a band of warriors as had destroyed Draper's Meadows. So there really *was* a war with the French and Indians, as Colonel Wash-

ington had told Mr. Patton. She tried to imagine that. A war.
Whole armies and little settlements.

The old woman was talking again. "What?" Mary asked.
"You nem?"

"I . . . I am Mary Ingles." It was odd to speak her own
name in this strange world. "You?"

"Ghetel," the old woman seemed to say, "Ghetel. I ben
vidow from Herr Stumf." Mary could not follow this very
well, but made an effort to remember the strange name.
Ghetel, she thought.

"So, Ghetel," Mary said. "Here we meet, then. And what
d'ye s'pose will come of us next, eh?"

"I hope zupper," the old woman said.

They were fed, around sunset time, on a delicious hot
starchy porridge, tasting faintly of hickory smoke and corn,
and laced with nuts and strips of meat. Their hands were
untied and they were allowed to dip into bowls of the rich
food with their fingers and eat until they could hold no more.
The Indian women who had brought the food squatted on the
ground nearby and talked and watched them eat, then carried
away the empty bowls. The old woman named Ghetel wolfed
down great quantities of the stuff, evidently being as famished
as she had said she was. The younger woman and the little girl
tied to the post with her had eaten little. Those two did not
seem to be related in any way to the old woman. They did not
speak English at all, but wept softly and occasionally talked
in a croaking, throaty sort of language to the three men tied at
the next stake.

Through the twilight the captives were visited by Indians,
sometimes families of them, who came to squat on the ground
a few away and look at them. They watched Mary feed the
baby at her breast. At dark the last people went away and
the village grew still. There was the smell of tobacco smoke in
the air, and in the vicinity of a big lodgelike building several
hundred feet away, a fire kept burning and a drum bumped
monotonously. Mary went to sleep to that monotonous throbbing. She awoke once when a slice of moon was almost

straight overhead. The drum had stopped and the fire was out. Crickets and katydids unwound their screechy songs in the silver-edged darkness. Georgie was mumbling in his sleep. Mary turned over to take her weight off the aching shoulder and hip of her right side, moved the baby gently to place it near her head, then went back to sleep vaguely thinking about the tether around her neck.

The baby crying for food woke Mary. Morning sunlight was touching the treetops. Nearby, the old woman was looking at the infant and saying, "Shoosh! Shoosh!" Mary sat up to attend to her child and saw that the other prisoners were already awake, gazing fearfully around the village.

Mary took the baby out of its carrier and unwrapped it from its swaddling cloth. She shook the bowel waste out of the cloth onto the ground and used an unsoiled corner of the cloth to wipe the little girl clean. But the cloth was too wet with urine to reuse. And the other cloth, which she had had available on the trail, had been lost somewhere. So she held the baby naked to her breast. It suckled, making the strange sweet pain around her nipple. After a moment Mary no longer noticed the sour smell of the stale urine. She listened to the ngn, ngn, ngn sounds in the baby's throat and looked around the village.

A few Indians were up and moving among the huts. The old woman was standing up now, her feet wide apart, pissing a sibilant stream onto the ground. She smiled at Mary, quietly said something that sounded like Morgan, then went to dry ground a few feet away, sat down, stretched and yawned noisily.

Bettie was relieving herself, too, but trying to be more discreet about it. She was squatting with her skirts spread on the ground about her and looking around insouciantly as if to give the impression that she was doing anything but what she was doing. Mary smiled to herself. Of all the awful things we have, she thought, this lack of privacy is one of the worst.

She turned to speak to her sons, but suddenly her attention was diverted by a commotion of voices and drumbeats from the vicinity of the lodge. The prisoners all turned to look. Mary's heart seemed to jump into her mouth.

Scores—then it seemed hundreds—of Indians were pouring into the long open space between the lodge and the place where the prisoners were staked. Young and old, male and female, what seemed to be the whole population of the village came running, howling and laughing, from every direction. All of them were carrying sticks and switches. They milled around and then began forming into two parallel lines along both sides of the streetlike clearing, and began slapping the earth with their sticks.

Then, from the lodge at the far end of the street, between the long lines of people, came the chiefs she had seen the evening before, as well as several warriors and the chieftain she knew. With them were two white men, one lean, one stocky, wearing faded cloth hunting shirts, with bright red caps on their heads. As they came closer, these white men could be seen smiling brightly through their black beards. They did not seem to be prisoners. One had a pistol in his belt and one wore a sheath knife. Mary was confused by a rush of speculations. Were they envoys perhaps sent from civilization to barter for the release of the prisoners? Were they former captives now living as Shawnees? Or were they some of the Frenchmen Mary had heard of, the French who were said to be involved in the war?

They were speaking cheerfully with the chiefs as they approached. They seemed to be speaking in the Indian tongue.

The white men came into the clearing and moved among the captives, looking them over carefully. Their eyes were quick and merry. They were talking between themselves now in a different-sounding language, nasal and sonorous. Then they stepped back among the chiefs and talked and nodded briefly with them. Mary glanced at Tommy and Georgie, who were looking, transfixed, at the white men.

The main chief then said something in a quick, sharp voice, and a cheer ran along the two waiting lines of Indians.

Three warriors stepped up to Henry Lenard and hauled him to his feet. They untied the bonds at his hands and ankles and detached the tether from his neck. The chieftain then said loudly to Henry:

"Be naked."

Henry looked at him, confused. The chieftain struck him a resounding blow on the ear and repeated, "Be naked."

Henry hesitantly reached for his shirt collar and drew his shirt off over his head. Then he stood there holding it, and apparently he stood too long. The chieftain said something and two of the braves, brandishing knives, grabbed Henry, and in seconds had cut his breeches off and wrenched the moccasins off his feet. He stood there white as a fish, looking pitifully vulnerable, trembling. His panic-widened eyes flickered among his fellow prisoners as if appealing for forgiveness of his shame. Mary dropped her eyes.

"Lord in heaven," Bettie murmured, and she too looked at the ground.

The chieftain turned to one of the bearded white men and told him:

"Say English to him. What he do."

"M'sieu," said the man. "I regret thees. Mais . . . you 'ave to *run*—run, comprenez?—to that." He pointed toward the big building, which stood some two hundred yards away, at the end of the parallel lines of Indians. "When drum ah, ah, go, you run. Savvy thees?" Henry nodded. "You, ah, fall, you 'ave to run again. From here, comprenez?" Henry shifted his feet, tensed his legs and looked back. Mary was watching him again and saw that his usually weather-darkened face was almost as white as his scrawny backside.

A rumble of drumbeats rolled from the lodge. "Go! Vite!" the Frenchman yelled. At that moment the chieftain swung a swishing blow with a limber four-foot stick. It whacked so loudly on Henry's pale buttocks that Mary winced.

"*Yaaaa!*" Henry gasped, then yelled what he must have thought the Frenchman had said: "Go, feet!" And he dropped into a crouch and sprinted away. The Indians were howling now, and the air was full of the swishing and whistling of their sticks and switches as he raced past them. Mary could hear the lashing of the wood on his skin, and she cringed. She saw him raise his hands to shield his face and ears. This slowed him, and he was no more than thirty yards down the gauntlet when a well-aimed staff swung by a grown man smashed him to the ground. The Indians converged on him and slashed and whipped at him repeatedly for several awful seconds.

They let him up then and dragged him staggering back to the starting place and aimed him again toward the lodge. Blood was running from his right ear. His back and buttocks and legs were laced with bloody welts.

But now Henry Lenard's face was red with fury and he no longer looked scared. He crouched for the signal and stared with bugging eyes and bitten lips at the chieftain. "Let's go, great Injin," he hissed. "I'm set." Mary's heart was hammering in her neck and she could hear her sons whining.

The drum sounded. Henry, his eyes on the chieftain, shot out like a rabbit before the chieftain could raise his stick. And now he ran with his arms pumping, not bothing to protect his head any more. Mary prayed for him and watched him get halfway to the lodge before he was tripped and clubbed to the ground and again obscured from view by the milling Indians.

When he was brought back to the head of the line again there was scarcely an inch of his skin that was not criss-crossed with red marks, and his face was covered with blood. Again he stood defiant, looking with hatred at the chieftain, heaving now for breath.

"I'm set," he said again. The drum thudded and he lunged forward. Halfway down the line he was again knocked out of his course, but this time, after dropping to one knee, regained his footing and shot forward again. A man with a raised club stepped into his way, but was bowled to the ground by Henry's momentum before he could strike. Mary's heart leaped with joy when she saw the distant naked figure stagger to the lodge and heard the Indians give him a cheer.

"He made it!" she yelled to the boys. "He made it!"

The three men prisoners were next. Neither of the first two made it. The first fell to the ground within ten yards and drew himself up into a whimpering ball and took their blows until he passed out. He was dragged back to the stake and lay there face down, his skin entirely red with stripes and blotches and oozing blood. The second man made three tries, finally being

felled and beaten senseless a mere twenty yards from the
lodge. Then the man in the British army coat was stripped.
He was big and beefy. He stuck out his pugnacious jaw and
scowled at the Frenchmen until the drum sounded. Then,
instead of starting down the gauntlet, he roared, "God damn
y'r eyes!" and lunged at the thin Frenchman, catching his
throat in his big hands and nearly strangling him before he
could be pounded into insensibility with a war club and
hauled back to lie beside the other unconscious men.

The Frenchman sat on the ground, coughing and wheezing
and spitting, his face draining from red to white, then finally
stood up, leaning against his companion. Neither of them was
smiling now. The chiefs watched them patiently, exhibiting no
concern. Then the main chief spoke, and the Frenchmen
nodded. They turned now toward the remaining prisoners,
who were all women and children. The chief shouted something down the line, and all the men with their clubs and staffs
stepped back out of the lines.

Dear God, Mary thought. It's us next. Oh, not the young-
uns, please God. And not Bettie. She's hurt.

One of the young chieftains came into the clearing and
looked at the foreign woman, thoughtfully, and pointed finally at the big old widow. She stood up slowly, glaring at
them with hard-edge eyes. Braves untied her tether from the
stake, then cut the hide belt from her waist and ripped away
what was left of her tattered dress. She stood naked, a great,
gray-white ruin of womanhood, breasts and buttocks hanging
flat, her skin drooping in folds like a loose garment on her
sturdy frame. Her thighs were massive with muscle. As she
was led toward the head of the gauntlet, muttering an incomprehensible something that might have been a prayer, she
kept her back straight and was dignified despite the ugly, ill-
fitting suit of flesh that quivered with each step she took.
Mary felt a sudden, surprising welling-up of admiration for
her. Her own flesh felt the awful nakedness and anticipated
the shock and cutting of the switches. She doubted that she
herself would be able to bear it, and even though the Indian
men with their stout sticks and clubs had withdrawn from the
ranks to leave this sport to the women and children, she

foresaw herself falling and curling up to faint under the pain, just as the one male prisoner had done.

But you had a baby on the trail, she told herself. You knew then that any other sufferin' would be less.

But she was not so certain now.

If the old woman gets through it, I promise I will get through it, she told herself. I promise.

The old woman stood waiting, her back to the prisoners. Than, as if remembering something, she stiffened her spine and turned her head to look back. Her glance fell on Mary. She smiled her best jackass smile, gave a funny shrug, then turned her face again toward her tormentors. Most of them were grinning now, as if there were something less serious about the business of whipping women prisoners. It was as if this part of the rite would be more of an entertainment than a vengeance.

The drum sounded. The old woman started down the line in a strange, straight-backed, jiggling trot, elbows bent, fists up. The switches began whistling. The old woman seemed to be moving scarcely faster than a walk, raising one or another shoulder as if to shrug off the blows. The men were laughing and hooting, bent over with hilarity as the quivering mass of flesh jogged by.

But jolly or not, the whippers were not being gentle. The Indian women and children were, if anything, laying on their switches with even greater ferocity. If the object had been to pound the male victims senseless and keep them from reaching the lodge, now it seemed to be that the female victims should get there with the utmost suffering.

The old woman lumbered on, it seemed for an eternity. Then, halfway down the line, a stout Indian woman stepped out of the line with a thick staff cocked over her shoulder and brought it around in a sweeping horizontal blow aimed at the side of the old woman's head.

But the victim got an arm up, slightly deflecting the blow, which instead glanced off the top of her skull. And with a bellow of outrage, she stopped, turned on the astonished squaw, snatched the heavy stick out of her hands and rammed the end of it into her abdomen. Nearby squaws and children, who had tried to converge on her when she stopped, suddenly surged back. She was laying to, left and right, left and right, as if the staff were a scythe and her tormentors were blades of grass. Thus armed, she literally fought her way along the next twenty yards of the gauntlet, giving as many blows as she received. It was an uproarious amusement for the men. The little knot of howling combat moved slowly toward the distant lodge until the old woman's arms grew weary and her blows flagged. Soon she was disarmed, and Mary watched with pride and amazement as she resumed her slow trot to the end of the line under a renewed torrent of switches. The whole assemblage gave her a goodhearted cheer when she walked up and touched the wall of the lodge. "Quelle femme!" cried one of the Frenchmen. "Formidable!"

She was paraded back along the line in triumph, stumbling now and then, as the Indians laughed and whooped. Even the old chief was smiling when she returned to the head of the line, and she, despite her profusion of stinging welts and a stream of blood clotting her hair and running down her left temple, grinned back at him. One of the chiefs uttered some sort of command, and when the old woman had been brought back to her stake, panting and triumphant, a young squaw quickly appeared at her side with a clay pot and began working over her wounds with a greasy-looking gray-green unguent. "Gut. Gut," the old woman kept saying, wincing and sighing. "Gut. Gut." She looked up at Mary's admiring eyes and winked. "Vas not bad," she said. "You can do."

They came and took Bettie next. She stood with her eyes shut and groaned as they untied her. They had to rip open the right shoulder of her dress because of the bulky splint on her arm, then they peeled the garment down off of her body. Mary ached with mortification for her sister-in-law, and she thought of Johnny so far away, hot-tempered brother Johnny and how enraged he would be to know she was being exposed like this. Mary was shocked, too, by the gauntness of Bettie's once shapely body. Through the ordeal of their month on the trail, the perfect young curves and hollows of her flesh had melted away and now her ribs and shoulder blades, her hipbones and even vertebrae, jutted under her skin, accentuated by the hard midmorning sunlight. Mary was so crushed with pity for her that she could just manage to speak when Bettie's pain-haunted, fear-distended eyes looked back beseechingly over her shoulder.

"Faith, dear," was all Mary could call to her. "*Faith!*"

Bettie stood slim as a reed, beautiful as a spirit, at the head of the gauntlet, looking down the long brown lines of people and their now bloodstained switches. She looked too frail to run. And Mary suspected she had been too dazed to learn anything from watching the others run. Tommy and Georgie were watching intently, wordlessly, trembling from head to foot at their aunt's peril.

They can't kill her with switches, Mary kept reassuring herself. The worst to fear is falling and breaking that poor arm again.

Bettie was not as lethargic as Mary had feared. At the first thump of the drum she was away like a startled deer, and got by the first twenty or thirty Indians before they found their reflexes and began hitting her. The rest of the way down the line she continued so swiftly that only a fraction of them managed to lay their switches on her. There was a general murmur of admiration when she stopped at the lodge and was led back. She returned as if the eyes on her nakedness were as painful as the switches had been; she looked at the ground, and tried to cover her little pointed breasts with her splinted right arm and her groin with her left hand. When she was seated at the stake, the young squaw went to her at once with the bowl of ointment. Bettie's back and legs were striped with perhaps two dozen livid welts. There was one cruel red slash across her nose and cheekbone, and Mary realized with a shudder how close Bettie had come to being blinded by that blow.

"Bettie, I'm proud. And O so grateful."

Bettie was wincing as the squaw palpated her wounds and worked in the ointment. She nodded, and looked at Mary. Her mouth was drawn down in a grimace and her chin was trembling. Her eyes bulged with a hurt fury. She worked her mouth, but no words came out; instead, bloody spit drooled out of her underlip. She had been biting her tongue, Mary realized, in order not to scream.

I'm next, surely, Mary thought. Quickly she thought back

over what the others had taught her: Go your swiftest. Guard your eyes. Fight if you're blocked; the Indians admire that. Never mind the pain; it's getting stopped that'll ruin you.

But Mary was not next. The Indians now were untying and stripping the young foreign woman at the next stake. Her face and figure were comely; she was hardly more than a girl. Mary had presumed she was the mother of the little girl, but, seeing her naked now, guessed she was no more than fifteen or sixteen, perhaps a sister, or maybe not even related. They scatter and mix families as a whirlwind does the leaves of fall, she thought.

The nude girl was dragged sobbing and whining to the head of the gauntlet. She was abject, beyond any semblance of dignity or courage. At once she fell prostrate before the chief, trying to wrap her arms around his legs. But his face darkened with scorn and he kicked her in the face. A pair of bucks grabbed her arms and set her upon her feet. Blood burbled from her nose as she snorted between sobs. She was aimed down the line and the distant drum sounded. Instead of running, she screamed and cringed back against one of the bucks. He shoved her, and she pitched forward to the ground. The squaws at the head of the line converged on her with their whistling switches, and went at her as if to flay all the skin off her buttocks. She shrieked and rolled on the ground and flailed with arms and legs to deflect the lashes. *In the name of God, girl, get up and run!* Mary was thinking, and then she heard her own voice above the hubbub and knew she had been shouting it.

The girl did not get up. She had gone limp. After several minutes of the sickening swish and smack, the squaws were called off. The girl was dragged by her feet back to the stake. The squaw did not come to her with medicine. Apparently medicine was only for the courageous.

Now me, Mary thought. *I'm ready, dear Lord.* At that thought, she felt a deep calm. She held her baby at her breast and waited for them to come for her.

The chieftain came toward her. He stood over her and began orating. The chiefs came closer and listened. He talked for several minutes, once more making the scooping motion to signify her delivery of the baby.

My, how that seems to've impressed him, she thought.

The chieftain went on and on in his great, deep voice, accompanying himself with sweeping and pointing hands, posturing like a lord. He was some fine talker; she could tell that, even though she could not understand a word. The crowd was enjoying his performance immensely; they seemed to lean and sway like puppets beyond the ends of his moving fingers, looking rapt at him until he would direct them to look at her.

And *he* looked at her. When he talked with his eyes on her, he talked as a man does who is proud of something that he has.

He believes I'm his, she thought. He wants the people to know this.

Well, ye heathen, I'm not. I'm Will's, that's whose I am.

And yet in a way, she realized, this chieftain was an important person to her. She knew that she and hers might have been dead by now if he had not taken this proprietary interest in her.

And now as he stood here binding all his people with his eloquence, she had to admit to herself yet again that for all his savagery he was a splendid man, a man who, had he been born white, doubtless would have become with age a general or governor or some sort of leader in the civilized world. Cleaned of his warpaint, wearing soft, tan hide leggings and beaded breechclout, his coppery upper arms encircled by soft-gleaming metal bands, his long raven hair perfectly parted and combed, he was as trim and graceful a figure of a man as anyone she had ever seen. Being beardless and hairless as a woman, but hard and straight, he seemed keen-edged, like a new, sharp knife—a contrast, somehow to Will, burly Will whose outlines were softened by thick body hair, by unruly brindled hair and whiskers so close to the color of his skin that in certain lights his whole being looked fuzzy, out of focus. Will was wonderful to be against, all warm and tickly. It would be like lying with a sword, she thought, to lie with this Indian who now stood . . .

She flushed suddenly at what she had been thinking, realizing that the chieftain's eyes had been on hers while she was thinking it. God above, she thought, sweep such abominations out of my poor bumfuzzled head! I'm starting to think like a conkybine.

The chiefs were listening to him with grave attention, nodding and grunting. It dawned on Mary at last: He was arguing that she should not have to run the gauntlet.

He was interrupted by a loud yowl from the old woman. She was kneeling over the girl, an incomprehensible stream of language pouring out of her. She had turned the girl onto her back.

The old woman paused for breath. She looked at Mary. "Det!" she cried. "She iss det!"

Dead?

The chieftain stepped astraddle the inert girl and bent down. He lifted her eyelids with his finger. Then he stood up and looked at the chief.

"Nepwa," he said. He made a short, final horizontal sweep over her body with his hand.

The chief scowled at the naked corpse. Flies were walking on its wounds. Then he turned away and went to the head of the gauntlet. He made a short pronouncement. The two ranks of the gauntlet dispersed and came strolling up to crowd around and gape at the naked, bloody captives. Mary realized then that she was not going to have to run the gauntlet. Not now, anyway. Every fiber of her being suddenly seemed to melt. A tremendous shiver of relief passed from her scalp to her knees. Once again she had been delivered, and once again it was this proud and keen but murderous young chieftain who had caused her to be spared, for whatever his reasons.

She looked down at the dark hair of her baby girl, this child that was the only simple truth she could turn to: the daughter of Will Ingles. Mary placed her hand on the baby's tiny arm, and its miniature hand closed around her thumb.

Mary looked up at the chieftain then. He was looking at the baby's hand on Mary's thumb.

Then he raised his eyes to Mary's, and they stared at each other for several seconds, oblivious to the multitude of voices around them.

I wonder what his name is, she thought.

CHAPTER
8

THE THIN FRENCHMAN, WHOSE NAME WAS LAPLANTE, IN THE next two days explained certain things that Mary had already partially deduced.

LaPlante was the one who had been throttled by the big British soldier. His windpipe was bruised and he was low in vigor and spirits, and so he stayed in the vicinity of the prisoners, talking with them as much as his tender voicebox and limited mastery of their language would allow. He was a trader, he said, not a military man, and one who is a trader values information as much as he values goods. Thus he explained his penchant for talking and listening.

As he understood it, Mary Ingles had been spared the gauntlet for one or both of two reasons: the death of the girl had satisfied the chief; and Mary was highly esteemed by the warrior chieftain who had brought her here. His name, LaPlante told her, was Captain Wildcat. He was a very much favored chieftain of the Shawnee warrior sept, likely to be a great chief someday.

The captive woman and children had been moved temporarily into a roomy open-sided hut near the center of the village. The men had been taken somewhere else. By pointing at the torn rags of clothing and making sewing notions, Mary had suggested to Captain Wildcat that her sewing basket should be returned to her, and she had assumed the duty of repairing the women's clothes while their wounds were being nursed. While she sewed, LaPlante came by frequently to linger and attempt conversation. He watched her sew when he was not ogling Bettie's nudity.

The gauntlet, he told her, was a manner of trial, an initiation, for the prisoners, preliminary to their adoption by families of the tribe.

"You, Madame," he said, "you are, ah, you are *deja preuve* . . . how does one say . . . *worth-ee*. M'sieu Wildcat say thees."

Mary glanced into the hut. Bettie sat there, in profile. She had slept on her stomach or remained sitting ever since the running of the gauntlet. She could not bear to rest on her back, even though the squaw came in and refreshed the ointment on her back several times a day. The squaw had also taken over the care of Bettie's arm, which was healing very slowly.

Bettie had not met Mary's eyes since the day of the gauntlet, and had said nothing to her.

"I sh'ld rather been whipped by these people, than accused by my own," Mary murmured, talking more to herself than to the Frenchman.

"Eh bien," LaPlante said, then leaned close with an earnest look on his face. He was watching as she put the finishing touches on Bettie's dress. "Madame, I will say now, I propose to do commerce with you."

She looked at him suspiciously. "I don't get your drift a-tall, sir."

"We will do, how you say, partners. Ecoutez, Madame: Goulart and I, we 'ave, ah, ah . . . *bolts* . . . oui, bolts . . . of good cloth, with a . . . a . . ." He squinted with his effort to find the word. "Un moment," he said, raising a forefinger and getting to his feet. He disappeared. Mary shook her head and continued sewing. She stole a glance at Bettie, catching her glowering in her direction. What the devil d'ye suppose is in her mind now? she thought. Likely condemning me now for traffiking with enemies . . .

Far up the street, she heard Tommy yelp in delight. He and Georgie had been taken into the company of a group of little Indian boys of the village, six of them about their own age who belonged to three tribal families, and had been playing for hours with them. To the delight of the village bucks, Tommy and Georgie were holding their own in the running and throwing games they had learned on the trail. They could be distinguished at a distance by their whiteness. Like the

Indian boys, they were naked. Their rags of clothing lay beside Mary, along with the dress of old Ghetel, waiting to be repaired.

Mary was not sure now that the old woman's name was Ghetel. Each time she would address her as Ghetel, the old woman would raise her hand and say, "Nah, nah! Not Ghetel, *Ghetel!*" She would display her front teeth and press her tongue tip against her palate as she said it, and would point at her mouth with a gnarled forefinger.

"Ghetel," Mary would say.

"Ghetel!"

"Ghetel."

"Ach. Ghetel," the old woman would shrug, and then Mary would shrug and return to her sewing.

Now a shadow fell over Mary and when she looked up LaPlante and the other Frenchman, Goulart, stood before her. They each held one end of a bolt of checked cloth. "Thees," said LaPlante.

Behind the two traders stood a dozen or more Indians, men and women and girls who were admiring the material. The traders set the bolt on end and LaPlante turned down a corner of the fabric for Mary to rub between her fingers. It was a soft and strong flannel, very luxurious to the touch. The checks were bright blue and a clean, clear white.

"But what's this t'do with me?" Mary asked.

"Would sew shirt, eh? Make shirt. We would sell shirt to them." He inclined his head toward the gathering Indians, whose desire for the bright cloth was evident. "Very good, ah, price. For you, for us." Mary continued to look from LaPlante to Goulart and back, saying nothing. She had been too long and too recently involved in the survival of herself and her family to think yet about business.

"They say you are fine squaw," said Goulart, who was easier to understand than LaPlante. "A squaw is very useful. If useful, she is important. Alors, to have importance is to be treated well. It can be the, the *difference.*" It was as if he had read her mind about the matter of surviving and had connected it for her to the matter of business. The future of the captives was still an unknown.

"Very well, then," she said in a low voice, that Bettie might not hear. "We are in business."

When Mary worked with needle and thread and shears, her thoughts would flow through her like a song that changed but never ended. She thought much about Draper's Meadows, because most of the sewing she had ever done she had done there. And she thought much about Will, because most of her sewing had been for Will. She wondered often what William would say about this business she was in, and what he would say about her partnership with the Frenchmen.

They are only traders, she thought. They're not the kind of Frenchmen who bring Indians to kill us. Will's a most practical man, she thought. He does what's best for everybody and doesn't waste his mind on thoughts of enemies. He's not ever made an enemy as I know of. Even when he was constable at Roanoke.

Now Johnny, he's a different sort. A hotspur, and will let a grudge color his judgment.

I'm more like Will, she thought. That's a reason we're married good.

Married, she thought.

The sun-flecked white and blue of the flannel she was working on filled her vision.

I wonder how Will Ingles would look in a blue and white checked shirt, she thought. Pretty fancy! She smiled down at the cloth.

She remembered him as he looked when he would raise his arms to pull on a gray homespun shirt. She remembered his powerful thick trunk, thin white skin over hard muscle, and the reddish-brown hair all down the front of him. She remembered how his belly button would look, winking out through that belly-hair for a moment before the shirt would come down and hide it.

She remembered how his hairy belly felt against the skin of her belly: like a thousand little caresses just before his whole weight would settle on her and the bigger caress would start inside her.

Her loins remembered William and suddenly she was desolate and empty and bittersweet inside, and the blue and white pattern of the cloth shimmered and blurred.

She had to stop sewing for a minute.

After a few days the Frenchmen began taking Mary each morning to their trading post, near the center of the village. The post was another open-sided shelter, facing the street. In corners of the building there were several barrels and kegs, some metal cooking pots and kettles, boxes of knives and steel tomahawks and axes, a few muskets, a stack of gray woolen blankets and assortments of buttons, colorful glass beads and mirrors. There was also a great musky pile of pliant, well-cured deerskins and buffalo hides.

The Frenchmen had built a long puncheon table and placed it across the open front of the hut, to conduct their trade over, and Mary could lay the cloth down on this table to cut it without getting it dusty. That was why they had begun bringing her to the trading post. She would come over with the baby on her back, and while she was not sewing shirts she would nurse the baby. LaPlante had an Indian squaw, a girl of perhaps eighteen years, plump and pretty and easily incited to fits of strange, tearful giggling. Her name was An-Otter-Swimming-On-Its-Back, but she was called simply the Otter Girl. She had had LaPlante's baby a few weeks ago but the little half-breed had been feeble and had died. She was morose. She was a Chahlagawtha Shawnee whom LaPlante had married in a bigger Shawnee town many miles north where the Chahlagawtha sept lived. The Otter Girl at once fell in love with the baby white girl and wanted to know her name. Soon she was taking care of the little girl, fulfilling her own frustrated motherly instincts, cooing to her and fondling her while Mary worked, and calling her Bay-tee Ali-no.

Mary listened while she worked, and learned everything she could learn about where she was and what might happen in the future. The chieftain named Captain Wildcat, she learned, was from the Kispokothas, who were in charge of things pertaining to war in the Shawnee nation. This village in which they were now sojourning was called Lower Shawnee Town, and the river on whose bank it stood was called Scioto-cepe, the Scioto River.

Because of its location near the O-y-o River and its importance as a trading center, Lower Shawnee Town was inhabited by Shawnees of all the five septs, but it was predominantly a Maykujay Shawnee town; the old white-haired chief was a Maykujay. The Maykujays, Mary learned, were healers and seers and makers of magic.

Mary learned that the Shawnees as a nation were newcomers to the valley of the O-y-o. Years before, she learned, they had been driven from their ancestral lands in Virginia and Carolina by the Cherokee and Choctaw nations. They had gone northward then into lands on the upper O-y-o. They had lived there a few years until Englishmen came in and settled and drove out the game and called that land Pennsylvania. And now the Shawnees were here. They had become allied with the Frenchmen against the Englishmen, they said, because they were tired of being pushed back from one place to another and did not intend to give up these lands of the O-y-o valley.

Mary did her best to learn these strange names and facts, because she sensed that she and her family were not through being moved around and imperiled, and that anything she might learn about places and about the feelings of the Indians might be useful in keeping them alive. She sewed and listened to the Otter Girl chortling to the baby and repeated the names over and over in her mind.

She was surprised at the variety and complexity of the Indians' civilization. The people seemed generally happy, always busy. In reality, Mary had to admit, their life seemed easier and more diverse than the hard, spare life in the white settlements.

Otter Girl was beginning to absorb little Bettie Elenor into her own existence the same way the bucks had absorbed Tommy and Georgie into theirs. While Mary was sewing, swimming in the river of her dreams and fears, she would become aware now and then of Otter Girl's melodious voice softly murmuring endearments and lullabys to the baby, and she would look up from her needlework and see the baby's ivory-white skin against the flushed-umber skin of Otter

Girl's torso, held close and lovingly against the squaw's swollen, dark-nippled breasts. Mary was both comforted and disturbed by this bond she saw developing before her own eyes. That the infant was being showered with caresses and gentle voice-music that she herself could not give it during the work hours was a very good thing; she could tell that the baby would grow secure and quiet under such care. It was a far cry from the harsh and miserable circumstance of its birth in the woods. But sometimes Mary's own breast would ache for the baby Otter Girl was holding.

And then late one somnolent afternoon, when sunlight through the trees was dappling that tender scene, making trembling blue shadows on their velvet skin, Mary looked up and saw one slight, natural motion that made her heart plummet to the pit of her stomach:

Little Bettie Elenor was puckering and rounding her miniature red mouth; Otter Girl shifted the infant slightly on her arm and with her other hand cupped her breast and pressed its turgid nipple against the seeking mouth.

The baby attached itself instantly to this offering, drawing and smacking with relish, and Otter Girl's eyes glittered and her face melted into blissful repose.

The white face and the brown breast. And yet, Mary knew, they were now one. The Shawnee milk nourishing the English child.

Something between sadness and outrage told her to jump up and seize the baby from the squaw's embrace.

But stronger than that was the realization that she could not bear to separate them at such a moment.

For a while she tried to sew through a blue and white shimmer of tears. But gradually it became easier to bear.

Y've known this would come to happen, she told herself. It'll be best f'r us all, finally, I just know it.

But God help me if Bet ever saw it.

The first shirt Mary finished was for a buck who was the son of the village chief. He bartered for it with narrow bracelets that looked like pewter. Mary watched the transaction. The Indian wanted to give the Frenchmen one bracelet for the shirt. Goulart insisted on three bracelets. After a great deal of arm-waving by Goulart and solemn head-shaking by the Indian, Goulart took two bracelets and gave the Indian his shirt. The Indian broke into a broad smile then, slipped a long, slim pole in one sleeve of the shirt and out the other and then, yipping with delight, trotted down the street waving the shirt like a banner, showing off his rare new possession.

"Tres bien," Goulart said, grinning to LaPlante. He bent to show the bracelets to Mary, then gave one of them to LaPlante. "Argent," he said.

"What?" Mary asked.

"Argent," said LaPlante. "Ah, silvair."

"Silver?"

"Oui. Somewhere the Shawnee find silvair in the earth," Goulart said. "Only their chiefs know the place."

Mary thought about that. "Then you trade for silver, do ye?"

"Pas beaucoup. A little. Most they pay in furs. But not thees, ahm, season."

Mary thought some more. "Is a checked shirt really worth two silver bracelets?" she said.

The Frenchmen looked at each other and grinned. They began chuckling, low in their throats. "A shirt," said Goulart then, "is worth what one will pay for a shirt. That, Madame, ees commerce."

She thought some more. "Would the Shawnee pay two bracelets for just the cloth?"

Goulart shrugged. "Peut-etre . . . Non. No. Maybe one."

"Then," she said, "I reckon y'll be a-payin' me one of those bracelets for *making* the shirt?"

"Heu!" LaPlante exclaimed, then laughed. "Madame, that ees no' commerce!"

Mary looked at them through hard-edged eyelids. "And why's it not, pray?"

Goulart thought awhile. "Because, Madame, because you have no use for silvair here. And you will be here. Toujours."

"What is that, 'too-zhoo?'"

"That, Madame, is 'always.'"

Dogs barked somewhere. A whiff of roasting meat drifted

in. A fly came and walked on Mary's arm. She could hear the voices of Indian children at play. For a few moments she had been wondering if she might make enough as a shirtmaker to buy freedom for herself and her family. The possibility had gleamed like a thin beam of sunlight through a chink in a wall.

"Then tell me this," she said after a while. "What *am* I to be paid for the shirts I make?"

LaPlante and Goulart glanced at each other. Though they did not look alike—Goulart being stocky with a large and lumpy nose, LaPlante thin and ferret-faced—Mary thought they seemed to be twins in their avaricious souls.

"We have talk on thees," said Goulart. "We assure you, you will be pay well."

"But yes," exclaimed LaPlante.

"I sh'ld think so," said Mary. "Otherwise, I sh'ld have no reason to sew shirts, should I?" They nodded, a little abashed. "Then what," she said, "is my wage?"

"With each ten shirts you do," said Goulart, "we pay you one fine wool blanket."

Mary's mouth dropped open, then she set her jaw. "Nay," she said. "I'll not sew for that!"

"It is late in summer," Goulart said in a tone less friendly. "When the cold wind comes and the trees are naked, you and your children will count a blanket good pay."

"Silvair not keeps one warm," LaPlante said.

Mary saw the sense of it. "But not ten shirts," she said. "Four."

"Four! Sacre! Non! Eight, then."

"Six."

They looked at each other. They looked at the Indians who were gathering outside the hut to gaze at the cloth. Just then the chief's son trotted by with a big smile on his face, his new shirt fluttering like a flag from the pole over his shoulder. They shrugged.

"Eh bien. Six."

Goulart wanted to see the gold wedding band on Mary's finger. It was only a narrow little band.

"I am remarkable that the Indians did not take this from you," Goulart said.

"I'm glad they didn't try," she said. "It won't come over the knuckle any more."

"Sometime if that ees so, they will cut off the finger."

She shivered. "Well, then I'm glad Cap'n Wildcat got no such an idee."

"I would give you a blanket for that," Goulart said.

"Nay. 'Twon't come off."

"We could get it off with bear fat."

"Nay," she said, more stern-voiced now. "I mean 'twon't come off because I won't *let* it come off."

Goulart drew the corner of his mouth back and glanced at the ground. "Eh bien," he said.

She began to wonder then whether Goulart was a man who might cut off a woman's ring finger. She decided he could bear watching. He was a merchant, and therefore gold would mean more to him, she decided, than to an Indian.

Each new purchaser of a Mary Ingles checked shirt would parade proudly through the village exhibiting it. Mary became very industrious in the shirt-making business, working usually from dawn to dusk through the long August days, stopping only to commune several times a day with her children, talking to them about their father to keep them thinking of him. By the end of a week she had earned two blankets, one for herself and Bettie Elenor, and one to be shared by Tommy and Georgie. Then she started on a third half-dozen of the garments, with which she would secure a blanket for Bettie Draper. The Frenchmen were delighted with the arrangement. They were disposing of their cloth at a wonderful profit in silver and hides and war booty.

Bettie became less sullen when she saw the practical yield of Mary's activity. Already there had been two unseasonably cool nights, one of them dank and rainy, to impress on her the providence of Mary's business.

One afternoon when she was sewing in the shade, Captain Wildcat's voice came through the murmur of town sounds. He was nearby, and she looked up quickly for him.

He was standing in the street outside the trading post, talking to Goulart. He had come to buy a shirt, and with him was one of his warriors who also wanted one of the prestigious garments.

While Wildcat talked with Goulart about the price of shirts, he glanced frequently into the shadows toward her. It was strange how he looked at her now. She had never seen fear in his face and never had expected to, but now what was in his face looked a little like fear, or timidity at least.

No one else had ever looked at her quite that way—except Will. She had gone to the mountains very young, and she had never been courted by anyone but Will because there had been no one else at Draper's Meadows to court her. Will had looked at her with just such timidity during the days when he was getting ready to ask for her hand. She had realized then that he had looked fearful because he had been afraid she might refuse him. It had been the only time she had ever realized that a woman could have any kind of power over a man. Timidity, she remembered, had looked odd on Will Ingles because he was a fearless man.

Timidity now looked odd on Captain Wildcat, and for the same reason. He looked like a shy boy now, not like a strong, bold savage who dealt in lives and deaths and would be chief. Mary almost smiled at this, but it was too serious in its consequences. She was in no position to make light of his yearnings.

Wildcat was naked except for his breechclout and moccasins and jewelry. Even his sinewy, shapely muscled legs were hairless. They were oiled against insects and they gleamed with reflected sunlight, as hard and smooth as cast iron.

Even I got hairier legs than that man, she thought.

Wildcat and his warrior had brought familiar things to barter for the shirts, and the sight of these made her jaw clench.

The warrior had brought her own pewter tea kettle, one of her wedding gifts from her mother. A tea kettle was not enough for a fine and prestigious shirt, in Goulart's estimation, and so the Indian also produced a bullet-mold, which she recognized as Will's.

Damn you, she thought, looking at the warrior's face. This was the Indian who had held the point of his knife on her belly the day of the massacre. Mary had a notion that she might barter separately and directly with the Frenchman to get the tea kettle back in her own possession but decided she would not, because the need for blankets was more urgent.

Wildcat had brought Colonel Patton's huge broadsword to exchange for a blue and white shirt. Its blade was brown with rust now and tarnished with the blood it had spilled on that day. The beheading of Phil Barger flashed in Mary's mind, and she turned away and would not look at the weapon again.

A shadow came across her sewing.

"Coat must . . . hold Wildcat good," she heard the chieftain say. He had completed the purchase arrangements and now stood inside the hut, towering over her, feet wide apart in that stance men take to make themselves look brave, looking down at her, expressionless. He was standing under the highest part of the roof, at its front edge, but his head was almost touching it.

"I beg your pardon?" Mary said.

He did not understand this. "What you do?" he responded. Neither was understanding the other's words, and the resolution in Wildcat's face was beginning to crumble into confusion.

"What did you say about a coat?" she asked him.

"This," he said, pointing to the flannel, "you make . . ." He then drew the fingertips of both his hands from his shoulders down to his hips " . . . be like Wildcat."

"Fit," interjected Goulart from one side. "he mean it have to *fit* him *tres bien*."

"Oh, he's a dandy, is 'e now? Eh, well." She put off her lap the garment she had been sewing, gathered her legs under her and stood up. Under the low, slanting roof she had to stand very close to him, and, as if afraid of her nearness, he stepped backward, bumping the table. It was an unusually clumsy move for him, and she smiled, enjoying his embarrassment. She picked up a piece of ribbon she had been using

as a measuring tape. She advanced on him and he leaned
backward against the table.

Goulart had gone out into the street and was showing the
long sword to bystanders. Otter Girl sat back in the shadows,
nursing the white baby and covertly admiring Wildcat.

"Hold y'rself still," Mary told him, and raised the ribbon to
his left shoulder with one hand. He shied from it. "Be still,"
she said. She knew he understood that; he had said it to her
so often. Then she stretched the ribbon down along his arm to
his wrist, and at that point pinched the ribbon and then
marked it with a bit of chalk from her sewing basket. She saw
that gooseflesh had risen on his brawny brown arm where she
had touched him. He had a good, clean, musky smell. "Now
be still again," she said. She stretched the tape across his
chest from shoulder to shoulder. He was all gooseflesh now,
and his little dark brown nipples stood hard as if he were
cold. "Gettin' stirred, are ye, chief?" she muttered with a
nasty little half-smile, and he responded:

"What you said?"

"Never mind, chief." She wanted to laugh; the urge was for
a laughter of bitterness and mockery.

He could see that she was about to laugh at him, and the
look that flashed through his dark eyes at the moment she
glanced up was a desperate, angry, insulted look. He was not
a man to be mocked. She knew that, and she knew that she
had fared so well in captivity because she had never annoyed
him. The way he felt about her—whatever strange way that
might be—could still determine her fate; she knew that quite
well. And so, thankful that Bettie was not here to see this, she
suddenly stared into Wildcat's eyes with a serious intensity,
which she meant only to show him that she did not mean to
mock him.

It transformed him. The timidity, the hurt, vanished from
his countenance and now his face was hawkishly earnest; his
irises suddenly went deep and limpid, as if a reptile had
opened the protective veil over its eyes.

"Hear," he said in a voice low and intense. "White mo-ther
is good blood. Children good blood. Come with Wildcat to
Kispoko Town." He pointed northward, up the river.

To Mary, farther up the river meant farther from Draper's Meadows. That alone was enough to make her shake her head.

Wildcat's eyelids hardened; his nostrils flared. Then he softened his glare and grasped her upper right arm firmly. She looked down at his hand and kept looking at it. She did not like to be touched by this man. It unsettled her.

"Wildcat will be," he said, and then his next words shocked her like a blow: " . . . the father of your sons. They will be sons of a chief."

Aye, she thought after the flash of indignation had cooled down inside her, leaving her weary and almost ready to agree to anything that would mean security for her children and herself. Aye, one could go along with such an offer, I reckon, as there's no other choice to speak of but slavery or maybe death. There'd be no shame in it really, now would there?

Captives often became squaws; she'd heard of many. And this Captain Wildcat was no ordinary repulsive Indian to her; he was noble enough, for what he was, and he would be important in his tribe, and she and her children, she felt confident, would be well honored and cared for if she agreed to his desires.

Oh, not to worry about one's fate day by day, she thought with a heavy longing. Just to give up. One could be comfortable. One could . . .

He was still holding her upper arm, firmly but not hurtingly; she was still looking down at his hand on her arm. She sensed Otter Girl's attention behind her. But the girl could not understand their words.

Mary brought her left hand up slowly across her bosom now, the ribbon still pinched between thumb and forefinger, to put her hand on the hard, hairless brown wrist of the hand that held her. And as she brought her hand up, the sunlight reflecting from the bright outdoors glinted on the little gold band on her finger.

She took a deep breath. She put the heel of her hand on his wrist and shoved his hand away, still not looking at his face, just at her own hand now.

Bright yellow light flooded her eyes. His dark silhouette

had vanished from between her and the sunbeaten street. He was gone.

She stood looking at the ribbon for minutes. The sounds of the town, the voices, the barking dogs, which she had not been hearing for all those minutes, began filling her ears gradually as if she were approaching the village from a silent place out in the woods.

She took hold of the other end of the ribbon with her other hand and held the ribbon horizontally in front of her.

His shoulders are this wide, she thought.

During that week several war parties came in with white prisoners. Mary saw the wretches from a distance as they were led to the stakes. And each following day she would find herself alone in the trading post when the town's whole population would gather on the far side of the council lodge for the formation of the gauntlet. She would sew diligently, concentrating on her work, sometimes humming songs aloud to shut out the excited murmuring and wailing of the distant crowd and, especially, the chilling screams of its victims. The people of the Shawnee Town seemed never to tire of this cruel entertainment; only the feeble and sick excused themselves from it. Captives who had come earlier and had already endured the gauntlet were kept away from it. The Shawnees were skillful, Mary noted, at keeping their white captives separated in small groups. Even though she now enjoyed a degree of freedom to pass through some parts of the town, she never came within speaking distance of any whites other than Bettie and the old widow and the children. On two separate days she saw Henry Lenard at the far end of the street with the other white men who had been in the same circle of captives a week before. They were carrying rails, burdened as heavily as slaves.

As the village population swelled with the influx of war parties and prisoners, there was a detectable stir of anticipation. Long councils were held almost every day in the central lodge. LaPlante and Goulart would come from those councils full of vivid war stories they had heard. Men, some red, a few white, and some who could have been either, rode into the

town on lathered horses and went directly to the lodge. Mary
guessed they were couriers bringing war news. Parties of
warriors would ride or strut up the streets, some of them with
bound wounds, bringing no prisoners but displaying grisly
scalps at the top of long poles—in virtually the same spirit,
Mary thought, as the town bucks exhibiting her checked
shirts.

"Bettie," she exclaimed one evening. "That Otter Girl today went to stand in the line to whip prisoners. When she
come back there was blood on her hands, even specks of it on
her face an' 'er dress . . . and sweet as y' please she picked up
Bettie Elenor an' took 'er to 'er bosom as tender as ever I do.
How can . . . how can the same person . . ."

Bettie's eyes grew dark, veiled. "You saw 'em slaughter my
baby," she said. "Likewise I wonder how can you traffic with
'em. An' let y'r newborn suckle at a heathen's teat."

It was as hurtful as a slap, coming just now. Mary lifted her
chin and hardened her heart. "Bet, I advise ye, but f'r my
prudent conduct, y'd likely be dead now."

"Would I were."

"Blast 'ee, Bettie, for a snot-sniveler!"

When she was making Captain Wildcat's shirt, she was full
of curious, shape-shifting daydreams. Plying her needle in
tight stiches along a shoulder seam, she had a sense of the
hard, manly shoulder that would eventually be clothed by this
work. But the shoulder in the daydreams was not always
brown and hairless; sometimes it would be fair and freckled
and hairy: Will's shoulder, somewhere at the end of a long
river journey.

She would try to remember landmarks along the rivers. She
would try to make a map in her head, a map of a river twisting
and rushing down through the dark mountains; and at the far
end of that river map, she would see the inside log walls of her
cabin, with the coats and pans and gun hanging from pegs
where they had always been, and the old clock ticking; she
could remember all the marks of the broad-ax upon those
hewn walls, and the marks of the tooth-chisel on the fireplace
stones.

They burnt the house, she would remind herself sometimes; it's not there anymore. I looked back and saw it burning down. But she could not remember that burning very well; she would see vaguely, for an instant, the shake roof falling in with a roar of colorless flame in the sunlight, but that vision would go away and she would see, as she had seen so often from underneath, the pole rafters above the bed, the shingles becoming distinct in the morning light, or flickering with hearthglow at night, and the house existed complete and intact in her mind, every log and beam and peg and stone of it, more real and more significant now even than when she had lived in it and touched it with her hands and swept it with a rush-broom. It was as if she had brought the real house with her in her head, and if she could go there she could set it right back down where the charred chimney must now be standing, and it would be instantly complete again, so that Will could walk in through the door with his tools on his shoulder, his big frame for a moment a silhouette in the sunny rectangle of doorway . . .

And then the silhouette in her mind's eye would become Captain Wildcat standing before her under the low roof of the trading post a few days ago with his hand on her upper arm, making his proposal to her. She would look up from the blue and white cloth then, thinking that he would be standing there, but he would not be. It would instead be Goulart standing there in her light, scratching his armpit or groin, watching his partner sew the wonderful shirts, his eyes agleam with profits. Wildcat had not come back since she had pushed his hand away, and she felt vulnerable, as if a protective wall had been torn down between her and the mass of nameless, ruddy, cruel Shawnee faces.

Sometimes her daydreams would go up a river in the opposite direction: up this Scioto-cepe to Kispoko Town, and there she would imagine the interior of Wildcat's *wegiwa*, a sleeping-pallet of boughs and hides and blankets under one sloping wall, a fire-ring of blackened stones in the center of the dirt floor, herself and Tommy and Georgie and Bettie Elenor all living under his roof.

His squaw, she would think, putting it in words. *My children his children. Ingles blood Indian blood.*

Nay! she would think, her heart thumping and her face flushed with anger and embarrassment: *Nay. I'm Will's, that's whose I am, and that's whose I'll ever be!*

But even at that, when she would feel the first hint of autumnal coolness in the dawns of late summer, and think how far north they had been brought from Draper's Meadows, she might envision again that warm pallet, those fur robes, that fire-ring; unlike Draper's Meadows, it was a place possible to get to, and, despite herself, she would watch the street for Captain Wildcat and listen for his voice.

He's offered me protection and I've refused it, she thought. And she could be proud of herself for that. But she knew that it was still in his power to take her without her consent.

Sometimes it seemed that she was counting on him to do that.

"Tell Wildcat I've done his shirt," she said to Goulart one afternoon, folding up the biggest and best one she'd yet made. "Tell him he can come and get it now."

Goulart went away, and she sat waiting, her heartbeat racing. Goulart came back alone and took the shirt from her. "He tell me to bring it to heem."

She felt so alone and vulnerable now she could hardly bear it. She took Bettie Elenor abruptly from Otter Girl's breast and put her to her own. Otter Girl's eyes glittered with tears of hurt, but Mary ignored them. *Squaw,* she thought contemptuously at her. Then she sat the rest of the afternoon, not sewing, the baby at her breast as a soft armor against loneliness, trying to reassemble Will's face and form in her mind's eye.

Her body could remember the tickle of his hair and his weight upon her and the sour smell of his work-sweat and the breath-taking entry of his rigid flesh into her moist, wanting flesh; her body could still remember all this. But every day it was harder to see his face in her daydreams.

Then there was a long day of councils and drums. The Frenchmen came back from the council lodge late that day glowing with excitement and talking sonorously to each other with much waving of arms and gesturing of hands. They drank from cups of rum and discoursed for a long time while Mary sewed. After a while, she began to think she was hearing a familiar name, and she interrupted:

"Are you saying 'Washington'?"

They turned and looked at her curiously, then LaPlante replied: "Yes. That was the name."

"What of Washington?"

"Eh," Goulart said. "A chief of this town named Red Hawk. He was in the grand victory at Duquesne. He say that he aimed onze—ah, eleven—times at the Virginia colonel, Washington, most clearly, but his bullets do not kill him. Red Hawk says then he does not shoot at him again as the Great Spirit must protect thees Washington. Red Hawk says he believes this because his gun never misses its mark before."

The story made Mary shiver with awe. She envisioned the battle in her mind, and it was very clear, because she could remember the face of the young colonel.

"Eh, bien," Goulart was saying. "Few of your Anglais were so protected. For every Indian or French soldier who fell, twenty of your Anglais. A thousand of your officers and soldiers were shot, madame. *Sacre! Quelle victoire!*"

Mary felt a cold sweat. Surely, she thought, these are only Indian boasts and cannot be true. Surely.

The next day began with drums.

Mary was lying on her blanket in the open hut with the baby at her breast when the drums started thudding, regular and ominous. Something unexpected was happening, and her heart sped up as if to match the drumbeat. There had been some security in the routine pattern of the days at the trading post, and any disruption, like this drumming, could suddenly throw her fully back into the anxiety of peril.

The drums stopped within five minutes, but by then the whole population of the town was moving up the streets toward the center of the town.

"What d'ye suppose?" Bettie asked, up on one elbow

nearby. Tommy and Georgie were sitting up, too; Tommy was yawning and Georgie was rubbing his fists in his eyes.

"Nothing to do with us, pray," said Mary. But the public gatherings in the Shawnee Town always seemed to have something to do with the prisoners, and she had little hope that they would be ignored today. Then, when Captain Wildcat and another warrior chieftain—both in their new checked shirts—arrived at the lean-to, she was sure that another day of reckoning was at hand. Wildcat summoned them, drawing his palm toward his chest.

"All come," he said. "All."

Blinking and rumpled, they emerged from the hut, their hearts racing at that pace which an early-morning fright can induce. Mary looked for a hint of something personal in Wildcat's eye, but his eye was now again like the veiled eye of a reptile.

"Blankets," Wildcat said, again with that summoning motion. Mary stooped into the hut to gather and fold the two blankets she and the two boys had been sleeping on. Her sense of dread was heightened somehow by this. The blankets were their only possessions and they were being told to bring them.

"This too?" Mary said, holding up her sewing basket.

Wildcat nodded. Mary slipped the little basket between the folds of her blanket and put the baby girl in her carrier. She slipped her arms through the straps and picked up the blankets and came out into the open with the others. A light, warm rain was sifting down from a dull sky. Ghetel squinted up malevolently.

The chieftains led them toward the council lodge. Mary held Georgie's hand and Bettie led Tommy. They moved along with the crowd of townspeople. They aren't carrying clubs and switches, Mary thought. Thank the Lord for that. But notions of other tortures she had heard about through the years—rape, burning at the stake, death by slicing, dismemberment, disembowelment—kept crowding her mind and she had to fight them down with a wordless, constant prayer of faith.

They were taken into the council lodge. It was the most

spacious room Mary had ever been in, even bigger than the
livery barn in Philadelphia where her parents had taken her
once. It was at least ninety feet long and fifty feet wide. Its
roof was held up by an ingenious framework of upright tree
trunks overlaid with horizontal poles. Pale skylight filtered
down into the smoky gloom through a series of smokeholes in
the roof. The floor was smooth-packed, swept earth. The
smell of new wood, dirt, tobacco and Indian flesh was dense.

They were herded into the center of the floor, where some
two dozen white people, men and women and children, stood.
The skylight made their faces whiter, their eye sockets and
cheeks more hollow. The men's hands were tied behind their
backs. Henry Lenard raised his head in greeting when he saw
Mary and her party.

The captives were surrounded by a circle of sitting chiefs
and chieftains, behind whom a large part of the town's population stood. Smoking pipes lay on blankets before the sitting
chiefs, and a thin wraith of smoke curled up from a single clay
bowl of embers toward the hole in the ceiling. Mary felt as if
some ceremony had been going on before they were brought
in.

They stood amid the hum of voices for a few minutes, until
another group of prisoners—three men, one of them with a
head wound bound in a bloody rag—was brought in. Then the
white-haired chief rose in an easy motion from the blanket on
which he had been sitting, and raised his right hand. The
room grew still, and he began speaking. His voice was deep
and loud, very resonant in the cavernous lodge.

Then he stopped talking and stretched his hand toward one
of the young warrior chieftains, and sat down. As the chieftain rose and stepped forward, Mary saw LaPlante and
Goulart standing near one of the upright columns, looking on.

The chieftain walked among the prisoners. He stopped first
behind the sturdy man who had tried to strangle LaPlante at
the gauntlet. He grabbed the prisoner by his bound wrists and
the hair on the crown of his head, and forced him to walk to
one of the columns. Warriors turned the man's back to the
column, kicked his feet out from under him, and then quickly
wrapped a leather thong around his neck and around the post,

so that he now sat unable to move, unable even to slump forward. He grimaced against the tightness of his bonds, and Mary saw that his front teeth had been knocked out since the other time she had seen him. The chieftain talked briefly over him, turning to look down and spit on him twice. Then all the chiefs and chieftains grunted something in response. The chief snapped out a brief statement and some warriors came forth with a bowl and swabs. They cut the big white man's clothing off and quickly painted his chest and face black with a fluid from the bowl.

Then the chieftain selected from among the prisoners the foreign man who had curled up whimpering at the head of the gauntlet, and tied him to another of the uprights. After a few more minutes of discussion among the chiefs, he too was painted black. He sat looking skyward and sobbing, and it was that sight that made Mary suspect that the black paint signified death. It seemed that they were going to kill one because he was too brave, and the other because he was not brave enough.

Mary tousled the hair of Georgie, who was beginning to quake leaning against her leg. She stole a glance at Bettie, who stood braced and rigid and had probably not yet guessed the meaning of the black paint. Then she glanced at Captain Wildcat, but he was not looking in her direction. Finally she took a sidelong look in the direction of the Frenchmen. LaPlante was looking elsewhere, but Goulart caught her glance, and one of his eyes began twitching as if with a tic.

It might have been a tic, from stress. Or it might have been a wink of reassurance.

Mary could only pray that she had become too valuable a business asset to be painted black.

But by that token, what's to become o' poor Bet, she thought. She's o' no earthly use to 'em . . .

The chieftain then went to the third foreign man who had run the gauntlet that day, and pulled him out to stand before the chiefs. The chieftain talked briefly, got noises of assent from them and then had warriors take the man out of the council lodge. Next, the little foreign girl was brought out, discussed briefly, and then passed into the hands of a middle-aged Indian man who led her out of the lodge.

Ghetel was the next one to be pointed out. As she stepped out before the chiefs a murmur of good humor went up in the big room. The chieftain spoke, then the chief spoke again, and then another of the elder chiefs stood up and talked, looking at the old woman from time to time. Then he sat down, and a buzz of cheerful voices followed. The old woman was led, looking bewildered, out of the lodge.

Having thus disposed of all his captives, that chieftain resumed his seat in the square, and the chief turned to his left to address another of the warrior chieftains. This one rose and went among the captives, sorted out three, one at a time, and they too were taken out of the lodge. To Mary the process seemed like cutting horses out of a herd for sale.

This business continued for more than an hour, and the dwindling knot of captives stood mournfully in the middle of the lodge, awaiting fates they could not understand. No more were tied up and painted black, and the two who had been remained lashed to the posts. The soldier glared defiantly around, watching everything, his pale eyes stark and ferocious in contrast to the blackened face. The other kept his eyes closed and muttered constantly to himself.

At last Wildcat got up, and by this time the ony prisoners left standing in the arena were those from Draper's Meadows: Mary, with her baby on her back, Bettie, Tommy and Georgie, and Henry Lenard.

Mary looked down at Georgie. The boy was gazing at Wildcat with the kind of wide-eyed admiration and trust he had always beamed upon his own father. She glanced back and down at Tommy, who was gazing likewise. She heard Henry clear his throat nearby.

Wildcat went to Henry first. He pointed at him and began to speak. Today Captain Wildcat was the finest sort of Indian. There was nothing human about him today, nothing hesitant or shy or warm or humorous; he was a war chief of tomorrow, standing straight as a plank, glowing in a beautiful new blue and white shirt, slicked raven hair gleaming in the skylight from the smokehole above, filling the air with thundering words, with well-timed pauses, with graceful sweeps and powerful thrusts of his hands. Mary wondered what there could be about the culling of a slaveherd that would require such epic eloquence.

And the worst of it was that, for the first time, his oratory seemed never to refer to her. Not once had he glanced her way. Two warriors came to the center of the room and accompanied Henry away. He did not look back.

Then Wildcat stood by Bettie. He talked for a minute about her, then pointed to a round-faced Indian man of about fifty. The chief nodded and said, "Oui-sah." That, Mary remembered, meant "good." It was the only word she had understood through this whole transaction.

Wildcat grasped Bettie's left arm and disengaged Tommy's hand from hers. He pointed to the round-faced man.

"Go. Him."

Bettie's eyes widened, faltered, searched Mary's face. They glittered with sudden tears while her mouth seemed to try to form a question. Mary suddenly had the awful notion that she and Bettie would never see each other again. And Bettie's stricken expression seemed to say that she understood that too. At once they lurched toward each other and embraced. Neither was able to get a word out past the little strangling noises in the top of her throat. Then Bettie was pulled away. She went away into the gloom, an indistinct shape veiled by a sudden flow of hot tears. Tommy and Georgie were both piping questions Mary was too stunned to hear.

Mary raised her arm and put her face against the upper sleeve of her dress to dry the tears and mucus that had so suddenly poured from her eyes and nose. Above her own snuffling she could hear Wildcat talking.

When she had gotten herself under control, LaPlante was standing beside her. "Pas de rien," he was saying. "Pas de rien, Madame. You will be, ah, with *us*. In the store. Our, ah, partner. We 'ave, *arranged* so."

Anger and disgust brought her voice back to her. "*Bought* me," she snapped.

"Ehhhh . . ." LaPlante shrugged. But his eyes fell. Then he

looked at her again with a blazing smile. "So come, eh? We make shirts, eh?" He grasped her upper arm and, with a bow to Wildcat and the chiefs, started to lead her out of the square.

She understood, rationally, that once again she had been exceedingly lucky, that she had survived this latest perilous reckoning probably better than anybody. She was not to be put to death; she was not to be taken away to still another unknown place; she had not been given in concubinage to some savage stranger. But even this kind of fortune was not enough to outweigh her deep sense of insult: she had been *sold*, sold like a slave.

And a part of the insult, it shocked her to realize—she rushed to put it out of her mind—was that it was Wildcat, her protector and advocate in this alien world, this man who had spared her the running of the gauntlet, this man who had looked at her one sun-gilded evening on the O-y-o River with some deep personal thoughtfulness, this man who once had looked at her with admiration, even tenderness, and had said she was *oui-sah*, good; this man who once had held her arm and offered her a proposal; it was this man who had now simply *sold her off*, as if she were of no importance to him. He did not want her if she did not want him. And she was immediately ashamed of herself for having felt hurt by it.

She lifted her chin and looked coldly at Wildcat's eyes. He stood between Tommy and Georgie. He held each by one hand. His chiseled face gleamed in the white light from above and the look in his eyes was hidden in shadow. For just an instant they held each other's gaze, hers indignant, his inscrutable, and she reached slowly toward her sons. "Come," she said to them, still staring at Wildcat's face.

"No," Wildcat said quietly.

She squinted up at him. "What?"

"No," he repeated.

She looked down, confused, her hands still reaching for her sons'. Wildcat turned his head and spoke three syllables over his shoulder. A brave appeared behind him and took the boys by their arms and hauled them back out of the circle. Mary's eyes went rapidly from them to Wildcat's impassive face, then back to them, then returned to his face, confused and beseeching.

"Will be Kispokotha Shawnees," Wildcat said. "I take."

LaPlante and Goulart were standing behind Mary. They saw her begin to shake and crouch. She was either going to scream or get sick or attack Wildcat. They understood that she would do no good for herself, or them, with an outburst in the great council lodge. So LaPlante nodded to Goulart, and Goulart nodded to LaPlante, and each grabbed her under an arm. LaPlante clapped his hand over her mouth. They carried her swiftly, her toes just brushing the dirt floor, out of the lodge and into the misty rain.

They did not have to fight her.

She had fainted.

They rushed down the street toward their trading post with her limp body between them. From the rig on her back came the thin, purling wail of her baby, Bettie Elenor, whom Wildcat had not wanted. The baby had been jostled awake and was hungry. They gave her to Otter Girl when they got to the trading hut. Otter Girl stuck a ruddy nipple in her mouth and smiled down at her, and the two Frenchmen sat on the floor flanking their unconscious partner, the shirtmaker, ready to do whatever they might have to do to deal with her when she revived.

CHAPTER
9

THE SALT OF TEARS HAD FINALLY SCOURED HER VISION. SHE SAW everything in clear, hard outline now, no longer through a mist of hope, trust or sentiment. Her heart was as small and cold and heavy as a bullet. When Wildcat had taken her children away from her to Kispoko town, he at last had made her invulnerable.

Two days after the council in the great lodge, the Indians took the two black-painted prisoners to a clearing north of the town and tied them standing to posts. The men were naked and had been scrubbed by squaws with sand and gravel in a creek until their hides were pink. They had been purified for the ritual of dying.

Their wrists had been bound behind them, then attached by five-foot tethers which allowed them to walk around the posts. Around each post the town squaws had built perimeters of kindling wood, stacked waist high. They had also sharpened thirty or forty slender fifteen-foot poles, then laid them on the ground, radiating out like wheel spokes, their pointed ends in the kindling. This was the arrangement when Mary was brought into the clearing, along with townspeople, to witness the executions.

The sun had come out. It drew at the moisture left by two days of rain and the air was thick and humid. Mary's dress was sweat-soaked and stuck to her skin. Sweat ran in tiny courses down the dark and gleaming back of a brave who stood in front of Mary. She was determined not to watch what was to happen at the stakes. Although they would not let her leave, she intended to look at the back of the Indian, not at the condemned prisoners. They could not make her look. She had seen enough, in the massacre, at the gauntlet and at the prisoner market, to convince her that she had descended into hell. Somehow, without dying, she had come to hell. These Shawnee Indians were demons, and she had been fooled several times by their few little gestures of patience and good humor. But she could not understand what sins she was suffering for; she had never harmed anyone in her life, nor broken a commandment. She had never been proud nor gluttonous nor envious beyond those little degrees an ordinary person falls to day by day.

Squaws were carrying torches out to ignite the circles of firewood now. The crowd was silent, waiting.

No. Those two are truly in hell, she thought. I must be instead in purgatory. She had heard purgatory mentioned in preachments and had never understood it, but now she seemed to understand it. And she had never thought hell and purgatory could be in the same place, but it seemed they were here.

Watching the sweat stream down the Indian's back, she heard the kindling begin to crackle. Here and there in the crowd, voices whooped, male and female. The big soldier's voice burst forth with a powerful string of oaths, against bloody heathens, against greasy squaws; then the oaths stopped and were followed by a quavering bellow of agony. Mary smelled woodsmoke and felt the heat from the flames even here. The Indians around her fell back a pace or two. It was a hot day for such a hot spectacle. The Indian's back was not blocking Mary's view now, and for an instant she saw the soldier writhing against the pole, trying to press back against it to get as far as possible away from the perimeter of fire. His eyes were squeezed tightly shut; his teeth were bared in a grimace. The flames were scarcely visible in the bright sunlight; the firewood was turning black, and the naked man's figure was distorted by the updraft of heated air. Gray smoke piled into bright sky.

Mary shut her eyes and shrank backward into the crowd. Then she had to open them again because of waves of vertigo that made her fear she would fall.

The kindling had already fallen to gray and pink coals, still sending up a shimmering curtain of hot air. The soldier was on his hands and knees now, making a wet, grunting noise as he tried to cough out his scorched lungs. His hair was gone. Huge, glistening blisters had raised all over his body. The Indians were all yelling now, and squaws were stooping to pick up the long poles. Holding them by the outer ends, they began jabbing at the man's blisters with the smouldering points of the poles. Mary turned and wove among the spectators to get out of the circle, closing her throat to keep from gushing vomit. The Indians were now too absorbed to heed her.

She found her way back to the trading post. There was no one in the town. Off in the distance the blended voices of the crowd made a low hum, and now and then a high shriek would come to her. Probably they were at work on the second man by now.

Mary put Bettie Elenor to her breast now and sat rocking to and fro on her haunches, scarcely conscious of what she was doing. Flies buzzed. The baby sucked and swallowed, sucked and swallowed. Mary ran the thoughts of hell and purgatory through her mind again and again.

Finally she decided that those were vague and fuzzy thoughts, like hope and trust. The reality was that she was here on this earth and her husband was on this same earth, four or five hundred miles away across a mountain range, at the far end of a wilderness river, and that the only thing to be done if she were to continue her life as a real human being was to go there, where her husband was, to get there somehow or perish in the attempt.

Wildcat was gone out her life now, and she did not have to worry any more about pleasing him or displeasing him. She did not have to worry any more about whether she was going to be his squaw. She did not have to bother her head any more with the delicate and unspeakable doubt about whether she would have liked being his squaw. He had given her but one chance to accept him and had been too proud to claim her after she had refused. He had simply taken her sons from her, getting in that way the precious Ingles blood he had come to covet so, and had cast her away like a bean-pod.

She had been such a fool to care what he wanted or did, she thought now, such a fool, and in a way it seemed to her that she had been unfaithful to Will by even considering Wildcat's desires.

She had really never needed Wildcat anyway; she had only thought she had, she rationalized now. Through her own industry and her own character, she could have become important enough here in Shawnee Town to be her own protector.

I could do that yet, she thought. But I'm not going to. I'm no Shawnee, nor ever will be. I'm Mrs. William Ingles.

I turned aside from 'ee in my heart, William Ingles, just a wee mite aside—not so's y'd ever known it anyways, but a wee mite—but I'll make it up to ye, William, I swear I'll do that. I'll come home. I'll come home, and you and I somehow we'll get our sons back, or have new ones, and we'll make a new house like our old one, but with two doors 'stead o' one, and I'll work 'longside o' ye in the grain, as I always did, and someday we'll buy us some good checked flannel and I'll make 'ee a fine shirt to wear. I'll come home, Will. I'm no Shawnee squaw nor French merchant. I'm Mrs. William Ingles.

She began reviewing landmarks in her memory, trying to fix them again, as one tries to remember a waking dream before it fades.

I must think of them every day, she advised herself. If they jumble together in my head I'll have no chance at all.

Her heartbeat began to accelerate.

I could walk away from here now, she thought. She looked around the trading hut. There were tomahawks and blankets here. There was corn and dried meat. There were moccasins and hides.

And there were no two sons or sister-in-law here now to stay for, no attachments. The only things to detain her were the hazards of getting away from the Shawnee town undetected, and getting across the O-y-o, and then those hundreds of unmarked miles to go . . .

But how does one cross such a river? she wondered.

Sure there'd be a canoe unguarded somewhere.

But what about food?

What one can carry, long's it lasts. Then, why, it'll be fall soon: Nuts and berries, persimmons and paw paws, and game, if I could steal a gun, and then, well, we'd just have to see . . .

But . . .

She looked down on Bettie Elenor's head, at the whorl of dark silky hair on the soft skull, and felt the hungry pull at her nipple. She thought of the countless miles of stony river banks and creekbeds, and of the coming cold of autumn.

A babe would starve as I starved, and freeze as I froze, she thought.

She realized that of all the obstacles she could anticipate in the path of her escape, this delicate and helpless life was the greatest. Surely it would die on the trail.

Even more surely than I would die on the trail, she thought.

Her vision was clear, free of hope. Her heart was like a bullet. She erased the name *Bettie Elenor*. The baby at her breast had to become an object to her. Just an object. Her soul was still a huge gaping wound where her sons had been, as if a keen-edged knife had cut away a living part of her. She must see to it now that this infant, this tiny stranger who had joined her in the forest and ridden ever since on her back facing away from her, should not become such a part of her in this hazardous episode that its loss could break her spirit.

She returned to her contemplation of the tomahawks and blankets and provisions. Her body was feeling the pull of the long homeward river valleys. She was ready to rise, fill her arms and simply walk southward out of the Shawnee town, whether to home and freedom, or to death.

"Eh! La voila!"

It was LaPlante. He and Goulart had returned, with the Otter Girl following them.

There would be no walking away from the Shawnee town today. She had sat too long pondering it.

Mary reckoned by her calendar of knots that it was mid-September when Goulart announced the salt-making expedition. She would be in the party, he said.

Her heart began thudding. A salt-making expedition might well provide the opportunity to escape. But she hid her eagerness and said nothing.

"You. Me. LaPlante and his squaw. The old woman. And men from this town, twelve or twenty I would say, for the canoes and to escort us," Goulart said, stroking his beard and squinting into the treetops with the effort of speaking English. He was squatting on the earth beside her on his thick haunches as she sewed a final shirt from the exhausted supply of blue and white checked cloth.

Mary was beginning to be leery of Goulart. He showed signs of becoming familiar and proprietary toward her, as if he were beginning to consider her his squaw now that Wildcat was gone. He had not touched her, nor said anything ungentlemanly, but she had caught him contemplating her with a certain confident satisfaction showing in his face, and he would refer often, as he had just now, to *you* and *me*, as if they belonged together. After the division of the prisoners Mary had been moved from the hut she had shared with Bettie to the trading post, where she and Otter Girl and the two Frenchmen slept under the same roof. Goulart continued to call her Madame, and she had suggested several times that he should address her as Mrs. Ingles. Goulart was a virile man of big appetites, for whom it obviously was not easy to be patient, and sometimes she imagined she could smell his desire even through the sourness of his heavy, unwashed body and the leggings and loincloth he never changed, or that she could feel it emanating like heat. She did not know how long it would be until he would make some sort of advance. If he did, she had sworn to herself, she would kill him. He wore a sheath knife between his shoulder blades on a thong that passed under his left arm and over his right shoulder. She had seen him practice drawing it in idle moments. Acting as if he were merely scratching his scalp or tugging his earlobe, he would, quick as a striking snake, whip his right hand forward; the long knife would be in it. If he ever tries to embrace me, she had vowed, I will get that knife off his back and stick it between his ribs.

She had never contemplated killing before, except in that long-ago moment when the Indians killed Bettie's baby, but the abrupt and brutal events of the last two months had built up in her a readiness to strike back quickly at the next person who should try to encroach on her life. They had left her nothing but her own body and soul. She would brook no more insults on those.

"The old woman?" she asked, returning to what he had said.

"Oui. Madam Stumf. The great horse." He snickered.

"She is still in this town?"

"Oui. She works like two men. Who would give away such a one?"

Give away, she thought. Selling and trading us like cattle.

But a salt-making party! Not only a better chance to escape, she thought, but the salt lick is much closer to home! She reviewed her memory of the trek down, and recalled that they had reached the salt lick after less than two weeks' travel from Draper's Meadows.

Dear Lord, she thought, her heart beginning to fill up with hope again, they'll be taking us halfway home! If I can escape from them there, why, I can make it home, I know I can!

Mary watched the little whirlpools the paddles made alongside the canoe as the four vessels moved gracefully down the limpid green Scioto toward the O-y-o. The baby slept in its carrier on her lap, shadows of overhanging sycamore and willow leaves gliding silently over her eyelids. Mary felt as if the quick high pounding of her own heart might awaken the baby. She was going home! The Indians and the Frenchmen did not know it but they were helping her start her journey home! She had to lower her face from time to time to hide her sly smile. If they saw her eagerness, surely they would become suspicious of her intent.

It was a beautiful day: dry air, deep blue sky, profound green shadows under the great trees along the river banks. Patches of foliage were already yellowing or reddening in some places and their reflections mottled the blue-green surface of the river. Tassels of Indian maise and leaves of tobacco glowed yellow-green in the clearings. The paddles dipped and dribbled. Clouds of birds rose and settled along the shores as the canoes bore down on them. The birds seemed as free and cautious as Mary's own soul now. From time to time old Irish songs would rise in her mind, in her mother's sweet remembered voice. She thought of her mother talking as she always had with Tommy and Georgie, the buzz and lilt of their voices on a summer's day. And soon she found herself singing, voicelessly, with her lips only, to the tune of an old favorite ballad of her mother's:

> O ten times t—en times ten a—way,
> But I'll be home a—gain.
> O ten times t—en times ten a—way,
> I will O my Will, O my darrr—lin' . . .

"Ahhh," Goulart's voice growled behind her, where he sat wielding a paddle. "La Belle Riviere!"

Mary looked up. There it was now, a broad blue expanse across their way, the O-y-o. Her heart leaped again. She saw it as the highway to her freedom. She suppressed a smile, then looked back at him. "What did you say?"

"La Belle Riviere," he breathed, his voice almost an amorous croon. "All Indian names for thees mean 'The Beautiful River.' Iroquois say 'Oligen-Sipen.' Delawares say 'Kitonocepe.' Wyandottes say 'O-hee-zuh.' All mean 'The Beautiful River.'" He looked at her, after the poetic outburst, with such a strange expression, a sort of cow-eyed leer, that she realized he was feeling romantic, and she had to look forward again to keep him from seeing her mirth.

But he was right. It was a beautiful river. Its splendor had impressed her even through her terror on the way to the Shawnee town. And now that her heart was full of the promise of escape, this grand stream looked still more benevolent.

The shimmering vista widened slowly as the canoes moved down the mouth of the Scioto. Beyond the broad O-y-o, the dark bluffs of the south bank mounted up to loaf-shaped hills of lilac blue. A mere dot on the far shore she made out as the Indian hut where they had stopped to await the canoes.

Now the prows of the canoes sliced into the current of the great stream. The sense of spaciousness was thrilling. A strong, fresh breeze, sweeping up the river from the unknown lands in the west, nudged them as they emerged from the sheltering bluff at the Scioto's mouth. It whipped her hair about her face. She shifted herself slightly and bent forward to shade the baby's face from the sun and protect her from the wind, and looked upstream toward the east.

Now, ye bloodsoaked heathens, she thought in crafty, silent exultation, just turn left here and head me f'r home! I sh'll leave you at th' salt lick and make my own way thence, thank 'ee kindly . . .

The shoreline swung as the canoes began their slow turn.

And suddenly the smile froze on Mary's face, and then melted, and her blood drained out of her head.

No. No, wait, now . . . Not that way . . . NOT THAT WAY!

She turned a stricken face backward. Goulart was stroking over the canoe's left side with his paddle, looking quizzically at her bewildered expression.

"Q'est-que c'est?"

It was some time before she could speak. By then the canoes were clearly riding the current downstream toward the west. "I . . . I thought we were going to the salt lick . . . I thought . . . "

"Oui."

"But . . . " she moved her lips and found no words. She pointed back upstream. "Salt . . . "

He rested his paddle and pointed downstream. "La bas," he said. "*Much* salt. The Lick of the Giant Bones. You will see. *Incroyable!*"

The statement was nonsense to her. It did not matter. She had been foolish enough to hope again. And now they were not taking her closer to home after all. They were taking her father away.

She sat in the belly of the canoe feeling herself again grow small and hard inside as the paddles dipped and the water purled along the thin bark hull that supported her on the surface of the deep eternal water of the great river. After a while she turned halfway to Goulart and asked: "How far?"

He shrugged, looked skyward, translating distances into English in his mind. "Maybe," he said, "one hundred and fifty, maybe two hundred miles."

He heard her groan.

"Have no worry, Madame," he said. "You are in the care of Goulart."

They went swiftly with the current for four days, and every hour of the passage only tormented Mary, because each league they skimmed over with such ease was a league farther from home. She watched the magnificent wooded bluffs and cane-covered bottomlands glide by and estimated that the canoes were traveling down the river at least three or four times as swiftly as she would be able to walk up its banks. She did not even pretend to join in with the high holiday spirit of the expedition, with Goulart's clumsy, bearish attempts to be jolly and charming, with the Indians' peaceful good humor. They all seemed to be exhilarated by this effortless float down the beautiful river in the finest weather. But Mary was wrestling with her notions of the possible and the impossible. The summer was drawing to a close. Even if she could somehow manage to escape from this party, and keep herself alive in this steep and tangled wilderness, and find her way back by way of dubious landmarks along these rivers, surely such a trek would take as much as two months—into the raw and icy weeks of early winter. Her reason told her such a walk would be utterly impossible, even for a strong man, certainly for an unarmed woman. Reason told her that she must stay with the salt party, return with them when they were done, stay in the Shawnee town through the winter, and hope for a chance to escape the next spring.

But something as strong as her reason told her that she could not stay with the cruel Shawnees, could not become Goulart's squaw, could not forsake her existence as a Draper, as the wife of William Ingles. Their family had been devastated and scattered, and unless she and Will could find each other and rebuild the family, there was really no reason to go on living.

On the fourth day in the canoes, having traveled generally in a westerly direction, they passed the mouths of three rivers, one pouring into the O-y-o from the north, the next from the south, and the third from the north.

"This they call 'Pio-quo-nee,'" Goulart said, pointing to the first. "It mean, ah, river of high banks."

Mary made a note of its name and its appearance. She was studying landmarks again. He called the river mouth on the left bank the P-thu-thoi, which Mary remembered was the word for buffalo.

And the third river, which they passed in the afternoon, he called La Roque, or stony river. The Indians, he said, called it the Miami-zuh.

Mary saw these rivers as landmarks to remember, but also as further obstacles to any attempt she might make to escape.

They were obviously too wide and deep at their mouths to wade. If I was to follow the O-y-o shore, she thought, I sh'd have to turn up one side of these river mouths and go up that side till I found a shallow place to cross, then come back down t' other side.

That, she realized, would add an inestimable number of miles to a march already impossibly long, and her mind shrank from it.

Afternoon shadows were long when the canoes swung close to the left bank and curved into the narrow mouth of a creek. The O-y-o had turned southward during the afternoon, and now the ascent up this creek, whose waters had a strange tangy odor, was leading them eastward. The sinking sun at their backs laid a yellow pallor over a strange, desolate landscape before them as they moved up the stream.

It was a shallow, swampy valley, the ground on both sides of the creek treeless and bristling with yellow-gray reeds and clumps of thick scrub. The ground was mucky and full of stagnant puddles. In the shadows, rustlings and splashings told of the flight of many animals. The air grew acrid as the canoes slipped up the sluggish creek. Limbless tree trunks stood rotting at the fringes of the marsh. It looked, Mary thought, like a valley that had sickened and died.

About three miles up the valley the paddlers began talking rapidly. The setting sun's eerie light showed a basin of about ten acres looking more dead and bleached than any landscape Mary had ever seen. The flat ground was chalk-gray, pocked with thousands of hooofprints and footprints, and what appeared to be tree stumps and curved limbs jutted from the low ground. Smelly, murky water oozed up through the morass and dribbled down white rills into the water of the creek.

"Voyez!" cried LaPlante's voice from another canoe, "the Giant Bones!"

Mary shivered, realizing now that the bleached shapes littering the ground and protruding from the ooze were not stumps and dead branches, but huge skulls and ribs, tusks and bones. They were in a vast graveyard of fantastic beasts, beasts even bigger, surely, than the incredible elephant, of which Mary had seen a picture long ago in a bestiary. And now in the leaching twilight she saw that there were, mixed among these gigantic skeleton fragments, the bones and skulls of smaller animals. Near the edge of the creek where the canoes were now being run aground, an elk antler more than four feet long stuck up from the shallows.

The Indians quickly set up a camp as the dusk deepened. For Mary and the old woman they made a hasty open-faced shelter by tying buffalo hides to a great curved tusk. Mary lay under the shelter that night nursing her baby, while LaPlante and Goulart sat with the Indians around a roaring bonfire. Goulart was using some enormous skull as a chair.

The Frenchmen and the Indians talked long into the night, in strange, wondering tones that made her think they were talking of these enormous beasts that must have shaken the earth as they walked. She grew drowsy and pulled her blanket up to cover herself and the infant, and lay there watching the firelight gleam along the arch of the great tusk. She tried to fasten her thoughts to the matter of escape. Instead, her mind roamed back to this strange ghostly place and to the huge animals. Do they still come here? she wondered. It was curious that she had never heard anyone in her whole lifetime speak of giant animals, except the elephants, which were not on this continent. If they used to come here for the salt, she thought, surely they still do. What would the Indians do if such a beast came walking in during the night, likin' to crush us underfoot? she wondered.

Maybe that's why they build such a big fire to sit by, she thought.

She went to sleep listening for the tread of gigantic feet, anticipating the trembling of the swampy ground. She awoke once in the night from a dream of a bellowing bear thirty feet tall. She was shaking and covered with sweat. The roar from her dream was still trailing off through the real night, and she recognized it as the yowl of a wildcat somewhere in the distance. The fire had burned down to red coals. The night air was cold on her sweaty face. A patch of sky sparkled with icy-looking stars. One of the Indian bucks rose from his robe on the ground, stacked more wood on the fire, then lay back down. The wood caught and blazed up with a crackling and fluttering. She smelled its smoke and the rotten smell of the lick and the stale sweat of her own body. She shuddered again. To escape from this circle of firelight into that cold, black, rushing, howling wilderness was unthinkable.

At least it was unthinkable in the middle of the night in the middle of a haunted swamp.

To LaPlante and Goulart, salt making was business, and so it was obvious that they intended to make much salt. Mary and the widow Stumf were put to work at dawn the first morning at the big bone lick and they worked until the sun had set. They scooped out a shallow well at a place where the brine burbled vigorously out of the ground, and here they dipped pails to fill a row of kettles kept steaming over hardwood fires on a rise of firmer ground. They also gathered the wood for the fires, and scraped the salt from the bottom of the hot kettles when it was done. A miasma of unseasonal September heat lay over the dismal valley, and Mary found herself constantly sodden with sweat. LaPlante and Goulart occupied themselves with eating and overseeing; the Indian men usually were out hunting, or sitting in the camp playing a game with toss sticks on a deerhide painted with circles and symbols. Mary gritted her teeth in anger whenever she had to lift a heavy kettle, radiating iron heat, to the tune of the men's chatter and laughter. Ghetel would see the fury on her face, and would try to mollify her by making comical faces and gestures in imitation of the game-players' outburts. But Mary, though she had worked hard all her adult life as a pioneer wife, had never felt so much like a slave as she did in the operation of this salt factory. Even Otter Girl, who prepared the food and helped tend the fires and the baby, had a leisurely existence compared with that of the two white women. Mary again began to contemplate escape. As she poured brine into a kettle she would see in the steam a scene of poignant beauty: Will and herself, reunited, sitting hand in hand by the willow-shaded spring at Draper's Meadows. She began to bring up Will's strong, kindly, bearded face and his broad chest more than ever from her memory into her daydreams.

In these long and unclocked hours, everything evoked memories of their life so long ago, so far away. The grainy feel of new-made salt on her hands took her back to the previous autumn, when she and Will had worked shoulder to shoulder, salting a beef for winter.

It was hot now, and it had been cold then, but she could remember it as clearly as if she had stepped back into that season. Johnny Draper had brought the precious salt by horseback over the Blue Ridge to Draper's Meadows, along with a keg of gunpowder and Bettie his bride. Mary could remember the feel of rubbing the coarse salt into the cold, clammy surfaces of the raw beef, outdoors in the cabin yard on a gray day just a bit above freezing. She could remember the sting of salt in a splinter cut between her thumb and forefinger. She could remember laying the salt-encrusted slabs of meat into a hickory barrel, sprinkling salt over them, then laying on another layer of salted beef, then more salt, until the barrel was nearly full. And she could remember mixing cold springwater with salt into a strong brine the next day and pouring it into the barrel until the meat was covered. She remembered Will putting a big, flat, scrubbed piece of creekbed stone on top of the meat in the barrel to keep it sunk, and then covering the end of the barrel with a bigger flat stone to keep raccoons from raiding it, and leaving it all out there in the autumn cold to pickle for a month.

And the smell of the hickory smoke here under the salt kettles: It made her remember the little log smokehouse, where Will would then hang up the salt beef with ropes to cold-smoke for three or four days. Oh, all the happy autumn hours and days they had spent, after the harvests, working like one, putting food and firewood by for the winters! And every fall when they were done, Will would say the same thing:

"Mary darlin', five cords o' wood and a heap o' grain and a good cured beastie do make a man feel rich, O yea!"

And when they were in the smokehouse season, Will would always come to bed pungent with hickory smoke . . . Mary shut her eyes and smelled the smoke from the fires under the brine kettles and remembered Will lying next to her, breathing deep and easy in sleep, smelling for all the world like a smoked haunch. And she remembered him kissing her in the mornings and rolling onto her for what he called "a bit o' bawdry" before the children awoke . . . Sometimes just the smell of woodsmoke would make her want Will so badly she'd get loose in the knees. *I wonder how many a woman spends the time I do athinkin' on her husband . . .*

And the more she dreamed of Will, the greasier and uglier Goulart became, the more repulsive his patient and furtive scrutiny of her seemed.

The old woman's life before her capture had been centered on kitchens. She would tell Mary about the breads and strudels and snickerdoodles she had baked, the soufflés, the stews and pot pies, the roast lambs and fowl, the buttermilk pancakes she had made for her big family in the old country. She would describe, in all the detail her poor heavy English could convey, sauces and glazes made of cream and eggs and other things for which she had no English words but which sounded mouth-watering even in her own guttural language simply because of the loving way she spoke the strange words. Sweating over the steamy salt kettles, her rags and wattles gray with ashes, she would create visions of rich and various banquets, then act as if the thought of them were making her faintish, then would knit her brow and complain about the Indian men's appetite for roast meat. "Uakkkh," she exploded one afternoon. "We must get some good things for a cake, or I die!"

So she harangued the Frenchmen for a few minutes, making them roar with laughter, then came back to Mary. "Come," she said. "We gather things." She picked up her blanket and a pail. "To carry," she said. Mary hoisted the baby onto her back and followed.

They wandered out of the valley, onto the wooded slopes. Mary looked back from the brow of a hill and saw the Frenchmen and Indians loafing while Otter Girl stirred brine in the steam. Then she looked down the other slope. There was nothing but forest and meadow. To the west she caught a glimpse of shining water: the O-y-o. Her heartbeat sped up. It would be so simple to walk away now, she thought. There's no Shawnee town around us. There are no cornfields and bean-fields full of Indians to see me going and raise an alarm.

The thought stayed in her mind and grew. Her heart raced. The baby, as if sensing her agitation, began crying.

They found a stand of hickory trees. On the ground under them lay hundreds of nuts, their four-sided hulls falling off. Gray squirrels scattered as the women came under the trees to kneel, pry off hulls and toss the hard little yellow-brown nuts onto the blanket. They soon had about five pounds of them.

Then they discovered walnuts. They gathered perhaps ten pounds of those, picking up the green balls that had begun to deteriorate and blacken in places and would be easy to hull back in camp. Then they discovered a huge white oak.

"Acorns," Mary said. "Roast them and they're wonderful. And I know a way we can make acorn meal in the kettles." She was growing enthusiastic about their food-gathering now—not simply because she desired a variety in the camp menu, as the old woman did, but because she was beginning to see a possibility of staying alive on a long autumn journey through the wilderness.

The Frenchmen were delighted when Mary and Ghetel staggered back into camp with a pail of wild grapes and a blanket full of nuts, carried like a bag by its corners. They immediately sat down on giant skulls and bones and began cracking hickory nuts with their tomahawks, and picking out the meats with the points of their knives. They went at this with total absorption, munching and exclaiming over the nut-meats, until the Indian men were persuaded to join them.

The next day Mary made acorn meal. She shelled a large quantity of the acorns, ground them on a great concave bone, using a fist-sized tooth as a pestle. Then she boiled the mass in fresh water and squeezed it out through cloth to leach out the bitterness, and spread it to dry in the sun. That evening Mrs. Stumf used part of the meal to make a delicious pan bread, mixing it with cornmeal and chopped walnut meats and flavoring it with a paste made of the wild grapes. "Ach! For some sugar or honey," she groaned as she sampled a crumbly corner of the big cake. "I die for some sweet!"

That was the last she got of her cake. The men devoured it in two minutes. The rest of the evening Mrs. Stumf sulked around the camp with her mouth set tight and a hard edge on her eyelids.

In the next two weeks the Frenchmen encouraged Mary and Mrs. Stumf to forage in the countryside and experiment with what they brought in. The women would go out, each carrying a blanket now, and gather all they could carry. The baby cried almost constantly. It seemed to be bothered by the motions of walking and climbing and stooping.

"Hush," Mary said back over her shoulder one day. "Y're no man, t' be a-wanting to lay about the camp all the livelong day, good f'r nothin'; y're a woman!" But the baby still cried.

One cloudy evening, foraging on a hillside south of the camp, the women lost their way. They kept getting into thickets they had not encountered on the way out, and were almost frantic by dusk. Suddenly one of the braves appeared before them, so abruptly that Ghetel yelped and dropped her load of edibles. The Indian led them a short mile back to camp. He had come out to look for them when they didn't return. He had followed their trail southward out of the camp, then had found them by hearing the baby's cry. Mary, who was still contemplating escape and had been on the verge of enlisting the old woman to go with her, took note of those facts.

Goulart fussed at her that evening. He behaved as if it had been a severe imposition on the men to have to stop their loafing and game playing and nut cracking to go out and search for lost women.

The next afternoon, when the kettles were all boiling and the women were about to go into the woods, Goulart came to Mary and handed her a tomahawk. It had a thin hickory handle and a light, sharp steel blade, and a thong looped through a hole in its handle.

"Cut a mark on the trees en route," he said. "Then you find your way back, savez?"

She held the tomahawk and looked at it. Having it in her hand gave her many thoughts. She looked up. "Yes. I'll do that."

"Goulart does not want to lose Madame," he said, winking and grinning. He reached around and pinched her haunch.

He never suspected how close Mary came that moment to sinking the sharp blade between his eyes.

Ghetel!"

The old woman, stooping in the edge of a marsh pond to rake arrowleaf tubers out of the mud with clawed fingers, turned quickly at the intensity of Mary's voice. She stood there with muddy water dribbling from her fingers. The chill that went through her was caused not by the cold water she stood in but by the fierce blaze in the eyes of the slender young woman.

"Ghetel, listen to me."

"I listen. Wot?"

"I am going to leave. Will you come with me?"

"Hah! Nah, two more hours daylight. We just started. Help me dig, come. Plenty here. Very good, boiled and salted." She stooped again.

"Ghetel, listen to me!"

"Wot? I listen! You go back then. I busy."

"Not *back*, Ghetel! *Home!*"

The old woman straightened up quickly.

"You said wot?"

"Home." She pointed eastward. The old woman looked in that direction, then at Mary, then stopped again with a shake of her head.

"Not too funny," she said.

"No, I mean it."

This time when Ghetel stood up, her face was in a grimace. "You talk mad. Stop this."

"Look. We have blankets. This axe. Shoes. No Indians around. We could go. Just *go!*"

"Mein Gott! We would starf!"

"No! We feed a dozen lazy men on what we find in the woods."

"But they kill meat. This is only added."

"It would feed two of us."

"Mad talk, May-ry Inkles. I dun' want t' hear dis."

"I'll go alone, then. But two of us is better."

"Gott, I dun' wan' t' hear!"

"Don't holler!"

"Dun' talk mad, den!"

"I'm not talkin' mad! We could do it!"

"A crazy woman talks. Gott help me."

The baby began to cry. It was upset by their voices. A gust of cool wind blew Mary's hair across her face and brought a shower of yellow leaves down onto the pond. It was very strange, two white women standing here in the middle of the wilderness shouting at each other while a baby cried. Mary felt how strange it was. Ghetel was grubbing in the mud again, but absently. Her face was still working and she was muttering in her own language. She was thinking about it, Mary knew. She was upset by the notion.

"Think of it, Ghetel. You could go home to your kitchen and bake honeycakes."

It was a while before Ghetel said, "I haf no kitchen. No more home. All burn. Ev'rybody dead but me."

"Then come to my family. We have rich land and a good house." No, we don't, she reminded herself. It's all burnt too But she went on: "You could live with us and cook for us. We have a great, rich house," she lied. She had threatened to go alone but was deathly afraid of that, afraid of the nights, and would say anything to persuade her.

The baby was still crying.

"Her," Ghetel said, straightening again and pointing a mucky paw at the baby. "They would hear her and find you."

Mary shook her head. "We'd be miles a-gone before they knew. We could mark a trail one way and then go back another. I know the way home. By the rivers."

Ghetel was listening in spite of herself, and the admission of an argument was making her angry. Then she shook her head violently. "Nah. The baby would die. She would die first. And then me and then you."

Mary remembered: she had already told herself that.

"If we do, we do," she said. "Better than to live like this, isn't it?"

The old woman sighed. "I dun' know." She blew through her lips like a horse. "No. Maybe."

"Better than this."

"You say so, eh?"

"Aye, I say it. I'm no slave o' the heathen, by my Lord God I'm not!" She breathed deeply and shivered with the thrill of saying it.

"I have to think," Ghetel said. "Come back to the camp now. We will talk. We will make a plan."

"We canno' talk there. And there's not so much time left," Mary said. "They'll take us back to the town soon. We could never walk away from there, I'll vow."

"Such a choice I can only make when I wake up. I would know in the morning. We could each get a blanket. Some food from the camp. A knife, a flint."

"If we took things they would be suspicious." And then the word suddenly put Mary herself on guard. "Ghetel, if we go to the camp tonight, y'd not tell 'em what I mean t'do?"

Ghetel's mouth fell open. She looked as if Mary had slapped her. Then, scowling, she turned abruptly and with a muddy claw pulled open a gap in the back of her tattered dress to expose the ridged welts from her wounds of the gauntlet. Then she drew up into a stance of dignity. "May-ry Inkles, they haf done that to me." She strode out of the border of the pond, her feet sucking mud. She came close to Mary and stared into her eyes with a trembling chin. "Who we haf but each other? You are all my family now. Gott damns me if I would tell. You hurt me." Then tears spilled from under her drooping eyelids.

Something turned deep inside Mary's breast and her shrunken heart expanded so suddenly it seemed about to burst. She pulled the big old wretch to her bosom.

And now she was aware that this was stranger yet: two

ragged white women standing beside a pond in the wilderness, hugging and bawling as the infant bawled with them.

They stayed apart that evening, with the conspirator's instinct not to seem conspiratorial. The old woman boiled the arrowleaf tubers and served them with the venison. She had borrowed a knife from LaPlante to trim the tubers before cooking them, and only Mary saw her slip it under the edge of her blanket.

I believe, Mary thought, that she's going to wake up saying *yes*.

Mary was too excited to fall asleep. Her heart pounded interminably as the fires died down and the Indians one by one rolled into their blankets or hides and went to sleep in their lean-tos. LaPlante and Goulart were the last to retire. She heard them mumbling their bon soirs to each other by the last glow of the campfire, then saw them both rise and go their separate ways into the darkness. For a minute then she had to listen to one of them pissing copiously into a puddle nearby.

There was a sudden breath of movement directly in front of her; a dark shape blotted out the starlight and fireglow. Then she smelled the unmistakable rankness of Goulart's heavy body. He was spreading his blanket inches from where she lay.

Without moving, she flared into silent rage. So he had chosen this time and way to move in. Would God I'd decamped today when I was set to! she thought. If I have to stick this pig with his own knife I'll not even get a chance to leave.

So it was all up to Goulart now. The cool night creaked with late-season crickets, and Mary lay waiting to do whatever she would have to do.

Goulart was, to his own mind, an admirably patient gentleman. He believed that for a man of his limited physical attractiveness, patience and plenty of smiling must wear down what a more dashing man might try to break through at once. That had been his experience; in his years as a trader and *coureur du bois* along the riverways of New France, his rare successes with white and Creole women had been achieved that way. When they had become familiar with him, they had allowed him to edge closer until, usually, they would permit him. With Indian squaws, of course, it had been a different matter, depending on the cultural traditions of the village chiefs.

But Goulart had been even more patient than usual with this fair woman from the Virginia mountains. There was nothing in the least saucy about her, and she had showed no sign yet of needing or wanting any man. Surely she would eventually, he was sure, as she *was* a woman.

He had tired of waiting, though, and tonight he had made his first delicate advance. He had moved his bed next to hers. If she did not wake up tonight and respond, in whatever way, she would find him there in the morning, and would have to get accustomed to sleeping next to him. After that . . . *Eh bien!* he had bought her; she was his, and if nothing else, why then, when he was disposed to wait no longer, he could simply force his rights. But that was not a good way to start. He rolled off his back and lay on his left side facing her. He thought about laying his right arm over her, and then did that. He thought he felt her stiffen.

But she did not move, and her breathing did not change. He considered exploring her bosom.

But he was really very tired. And his left hip was bothering him. He was getting old-men's bones at an early age. After a while he rolled onto his back and then onto his right side, facing away from her.

At last he was snoring. Mary relaxed and went warm with a rush of relief. Thank God the man had not been bolder this night.

He'll not have a second night, little does he know.

She guessed this about Goulart:

He wanted the Indians to see that she was his squaw. He had moved his bedding next to hers so that they would see at daylight that he was sleeping beside her. After that they would expect him to sleep with her and it would not matter what she felt about it because she would seem to have allowed it now.

Then here is how we sh'll deal with Mister Goulart's presumption, she thought.

And in the pink-silver light before dawn while the camp was still asleep, Mary silently arose, gathered up her baby and blanket, stepped softly out of the lean-to and over Goulart's snoring bulk, and went to the high ground near the kettles, spread her blanket there, lay down and covered herself and shut her eyes.

Thank God this is the last night I sh'll have to outwit this swine, she thought. Such could become a very annoying game right soon.

She did not go back to sleep after moving her bedding. She had a decision to make.

CHAPTER
10

IT WAS THE MOST ENORMOUS DECISION SHE HAD EVER FACED IN her life. She had never even known of anyone who had had to make such a decision. To turn her mind directly to it created a great awful hollowness in her breast.

Either of her two alternatives was unthinkable, but she had to choose one. She had to choose one now. She had thought around and around it for weeks, and now there was no more time.

She knew that to take the baby with her would be to condemn it to a slow and wretched death.

It was not a question of whether or not she could carry the baby. She would gladly have borne its little weight the five or six hundred miles ahead—if there were any chance that it might survive. But there was no chance. It would starve while Mary starved. Ghetel had known that too.

And if its crying did thwart their escape, she and the baby surely would be put to death together. There was no question about that, either.

Only by being left in the camp, in the care of the Otter Girl, could the baby survive. The young squaw would adopt it and care for it. She already adored it with a full motherly passion.

She pined for it on the days Mary took it with her on foraging trips, and would rush to take it in her arms on their return.

To leave the baby with Otter Girl was the only humane choice. Yet it was as unthinkable as carrying it away to suffering and sure death. How could a mother ever say that she had abandoned her infant to savages? One could relate the circumstances and show why it had been the baby's only way to live, but the awful fact would remain in anyone's mind that here was a woman who had left her infant in the hands of heathens.

Her decision was that she would leave the baby here. Give it a chance for life. It could live a tolerable life as an Indian, never having known another kind of life. The Indian squaws, as far as Mary had been able to observe, were as content with their lives as most white women Mary had ever known, and more than some. You are happy or not happy insofar as you *belong*, she thought. The Shawnees know they belong and to them it is everything. I do not belong to the Indians because I know I do not. This babe would not know such a thing.

And so she would leave the baby. She had known, really, for weeks that she would leave it. That was why she had allowed herself recently to think of the baby only as *it* instead of as *she* or as *Bettie Elenor*. Mary had been preparing herself for something like this from the moment of the poor creature's birth on the forest floor.

There was, of course, a possibility that the baby might die even if Mary left it in the camp. If the Indians should guess that she was escaping deliberately, they likely would be angered to dash its brains out or throw it in a kettle of boiling brine.

So they must believe I just got lost, she thought. If they think I got lost while foraging, or that a bear or a panther got me, then they won't take it out on the baby.

I must make it appear that I did not flee, she thought. That's the best I can do for this little thing. Nay, it's the only thing I can do.

She looked down at the infant, whose eyes were open now, and had to look away. She could not permit herself to look at its eyes. She bared her breast and gave her nipple to it and the baby shut its eyes and sucked. Mary made her heart small and hard and cold again.

At midmorning, while they were gathering firewood, Mary had her opportunity to talk alone with the old widow. Before she could ask, Ghetel answered:

"Thank you I did not sleep an hour the night long. I think all night. I say, yes, no, yes, no. By the dawn time I am so weary I say, no, no, no!" Mary's heart slipped. The old woman went on: "Comes the sunrise, I look at you, I know you are going to go, and I say, *yes*. And that is it. *Yes!* Might be I hate you for it. But I go. Because I cannot eat Shawnee food all the rest of my life." She grinned. Then the grin melted and her eyes became intense. "And because I can not let May-ry Inkles go out there alone."

Mary told her why the Shawnees must believe they had gotten lost. And she told her of her decision about the baby. She felt as if she were exposing the most awful corner of her soul. She almost hoped the old woman would plead with her to bring the infant along. Then she waited for Ghetel's response, for an expected repugnance in her expression.

The old woman looked at her for a full minute, a succession of feelings reflecting in her face. Finally she put her hand on Mary's wrist.

"Yes," she said. "I would do this too. Even with mine own, I would do this."

"My knife!" LaPlante exclaimed suddenly. He and Goulart were sitting on mammoth bones next to each other, cracking walnuts with their tomahawks, and when LaPlante had reached for his knife to use as a nutpick he had found the sheath empty. A shiver went down Mary's back. She remembered that Ghetel had kept and hidden the knife the day before. LaPlante was on his feet, complaining in both French and Shawnee. It was a trivial incident but one that, Mary knew, might rouse suspicions in the camp and prevent them from going out foraging. Her heartbeat quickened and she threw a concealed glance to see what Ghetel was doing. The old woman appeared to be thinking very hard but was remaining calm.

What if they find the knife under her blanket? Mary thought. God, they'll watch us like buzzards if they do.

LaPlante asked something of Otter Girl, and she merely cocked her head and raised her eyebrows in innocent ignorance.

LaPlante moved around the camp in agitation, looking everywhere, turning things over with his foot. Now he was going toward the lean-to where the old woman's bedding was.

"Mister," Mary called. "Look by the cooking pots yonder. We were there cutting arrowleaf yesterday. Like as not it's right there on the ground."

"Ah, je me souviens," he muttered, and went toward the kettles. Goulart went back to his walnuts. Mrs. Stumf was trying to go, as unobtrusively as her big form would allow, toward her bedding. She moved with such exaggerated stealth that anyone seeing her would have known she was up to something devious, so Mary went to distract Goulart's attention. He looked up suddenly when he saw the elusive object of his desires approaching him. She smiled.

"For a favor," she said, holding out the tomahawk he had given her for blazing trees. "This is dull. It don' cut very well. But it's a good head f'r crackin' walnuts. What say y' to trade f'r the day? Why, maybe y' could sharpen this'n up f'r me while I'm gone. That'd be a nice favor." She tried to keep her voice pleasant but natural and not to glance at Ghetel. Inside she was quaking.

A cocky smile slowly established itself on Goulart's face, which had been sullen ever since he had awakened this morning to find Mary gone from his side. Obviously he now thought Mary was just being a *coquette*. "But of course, chere Madame!" he said gallantly, and gave her his tomahawk and took hers.

"Oh, thankee. Try that one on a walnut . . . it's nice and heavy . . . "

As he bent to place a walnut, Mary saw Ghetel sneaking toward the cookpots. The old woman dropped the knife on the ash-covered ground, stepped back and then walked about stooping as if searching the ground.

"Here, M'shoo!" Ghetel bellowed gaily, and when LaPlante looked her way she stooped and picked the knife up from where she had dropped it and held it up for him. He broke into smiles and went to her and took it, making pleased noises in his sinuses. Mary's heartbeat slowed and she had to hold her breath to keep from sighing out loud.

That was enough. She had a feeling that if they did not leave immediately, something else like this was going to come up and prevent them. "Mrs. Stumf," she said cheerfully, hoping not too cheerfully, "what say y' to goin' after that hickory grove we seen yonder . . . " She pointed southward. " . . . and I saw lots of sassafras. Mr. Goulart gimme a tommyhock sharp enough to cut sassafras root with!"

"'Eyyy! Gut!" Ghetel exclaimed, perhaps a little too eagerly.

"Well, then, let's be about it," Mary said. Her voice sounded strained and unnatural to her; her heartbeat seemed to be forcing all the air out of her lungs, and she hoped the Indians and Frenchmen would not notice the strain in her voice; surely they would sense that something was happening. She went, as usual, to roll up her blanket and sling it over her shoulder. Ghetel did the same. LaPlante and Goulart were still whacking away at walnuts, and most of the Indian men were playing their game or maintaining their guns.

Now, Mary thought. Just turn your back on it and go. Don't go look at the baby; y'll get all upset and they'll suspect something. Don't look at the baby!

But she went to look at the baby. There was no such thing as not going to look at the baby.

Fortunately, it was asleep. Its eyes were shut. Otter Girl sat beside it mending a moccasin, chewing the leather to soften it until she could ease the point of a bone needle into it and draw a rawhide thong through. She looked up, a smile of utter contentment on her round, bronze face. Mary knelt by the infant, her back to the Otter Girl. She lowered her face as close as she could without touching the baby and awakening it. Just an inch from it. She inhaled the baby smell and suddenly her heart clenched mightily and the baby's dark little eyelashes and tiny features blurred beyond a flood of tears and Mary's arms ached to grab up the little living bundle and run with it, run all the way back to Draper's Meadows without stopping.

Her hot tears were dropping on the baby's forehead and would awaken it; little frowns were disturbing its face and its little beak of an upper lip sucked in the soft red lower lip. Mary couldn't stop herself. She kissed the little mouth and then, with anguish that surely would kill her, she rose to her feet and stumbled, tearblinded, to the edge of the camp, her lungs quaking for release, her throat clamped to hold down the awful wail of despair that was trying to erupt. The old woman, who was the only one in the camp to see her livid, contorted face, was so stricken by its agony that she too had to force back a wail of misery.

Oh dear God help me! Mary's heart felt the way her loins had felt when the baby was being born. But ten times worse. Ten times ten times ten times worse. *Oh dear God help me! HELP ME! HELP ME!*

They were far into the woods before she could see or hear or feel anything, and what she became aware of first was the old woman's strong arm across her back helping her along, all but carrying her. She stopped her on a slope covered with tan dead leaves among gigantic beech and poplar trunks. She knelt and pulled her down and muffled her face with her blanket and started patting her back. "Now," she said. "Dey cannot hear you now. Cry up! Do it!"

It was an hour before Mary could get up and go on. She was empty and weak, even as bad as she had been on the day when they had taken Tommy and Georgie away from her.

She stood leaning against Ghetel, who was still patting her lightly on the back. "I thought I'd got myself ready for this," Mary strangled.

"Who could?" the old woman replied. "We could still go back."

"No. Don't even say it."

They wandered in no particular direction at first, barking trees with the tomahawk to leave a confusing trail. Then they came to a small clear brook and stepped into it barefoot, carrying their shoes, and went westward toward the O-y-o. The water was very cold.

After a mile the brook wandered into the salt valley and emptied into the salt creek, some distance below the camp. They waded to its other shore, dresses pulled up waist-high, then walked in the odorous muck at the creek's edge, the creek water dissolving their footprints as they stepped out of them. The sunlight was pale and the air had a chilly edge. Most of the foliage on the slopes nearby was still green, but a dry, yellowing green, and here and there were boughs and crowns of red and purple foliage.

"Ach. The riffer."

It opened up before them, ablaze with mirrored afternoon sunlight. The creek deepened and they had to climb out onto its bank to make the last hundred yards to the river. They stood and looked at it for a moment only. Its damp flowed around them on a breeze.

"So now?" Ghetel whispered.

Mary looked up the east bank of the O-y-o and dipped her head. Her sight was still fuzzy with tears and her eyes were red. She felt as if the first step would take the little strength left in her. "Along here," she said. "For a long, long way." She sighed, stooped to put on her shoes, then picked up the blanket and tomahawk and they started walking through the reeds and shrubbery, watching a few paces ahead for snakes. Long blades of grass whispered around their ragged skirts and slashed at their bare shins. The reflected sunlight from the river was hot on the left side of their faces. Huge dragonflies hovered and drifted away. The foliage of cottonwoods and willows and locusts shivered and hushed in the river breeze alongside their way. Birds rose, dipped, shrilled, skimmed close over the water. Mary looked at them now and then and gradually began to think of freedom. Through the deep lonely misery of her soul the thought came to her that for the first time in more than two months she was not a captive of the Indians—not a slave. Her legs overcame their heavy reluctance and began to like this walking.

She heard the old woman's heavy breathing and crashing, thumping footsteps behind her, and an occasional Dutchy oath.

"Step light, Ghetel. We must go far as we can afore night."

Mary felt a curious, soaring sensation in her breast as she said this.

It was a feeling strangely like happiness.

She was on her way to Will.

Just before sunset a towering line of grim clouds crawled up from the southwest. Thunder grumbled, lightning flickered on the horizon, and as the clouds climbed, a blast of damp air shivered the surface of the river and turned the leaves of the forest white side up. Soon the thunderheads dominated the whole sky above the river; they came gliding across, their undersides lowering and dragging gray veils of rain under them. Birds and insects fell silent.

In the moment of stillness as the rainfall came sweeping toward them across the river, Mary heard, or rather, felt, the stroke of a distant gunshot on the charged air. She stopped and raised a hand, and Ghetel almost blundered over her. They stood and listened for a moment, and she thought she detected another, then another, and one or two that were dubious because they were lost in the muttering of thunder.

"Eh?" Ghetel queried.

"Don't rightly know," Mary said. The reports had seemed to come from the direction of the camp. "Not hunting, surely, afore a storm like now." Were they killing the baby? Not likely with a lot of gunshots, she decided. "No, I'd reckon they think we're lost, and're tryin' to signal us the way back." It seemed the best explanation, and Mary smiled with a cunning satisfaction.

And then the sting of blown rain peppered them and hissed up the shore and into the trees.

"Ach! Nah!" Ghetel complained.

"No, it's good," Mary exclaimed. "Come. With this, we'll leave no trail f'r 'em to pick up come morning! They'll just think a bear got us, or lightnin' or sump'n, an' won't even try t' find us, I'll wager!" She was almost running now, feeling free, and cleansed of the degradation of her bondage by this pelting torrent. She could hear Ghetel huffing and slogging along behind her, muttering:

"Bears! Lightnink? Ach!" The forest and river turned white and the sky cracked open along a tortuous blue-white seam for an instant; a tree flashed and exploded a few yards ahead and a bolt of noise felled Mary to her knees. The tree smoked and a strange, fresh, exhilarating smell came through the air. Mary got to her feet again as the echoes of the bolt dwindled across the river.

"Lightnink *will!*" the old woman wailed.

They were drenched by the time the rain had passed and the thunder bumped away in the east. It was too dark by then to continue safely along the unknown terrain of the shore. The wool of their blankets was heavy with water, and their sodden dresses hung cold on their skin. Mary estimated they had come perhaps five miles since reaching the river. Now they had stopped in the dripping, dribbling gloom, the warmth of their exertions evaporated at once and their empty stomachs gave them no warmth. Mary remembered then that in the anxiety of the morning they had eaten nothing. It promised to be a grim and shivery night, and despite their exhaustion they likely would get no sleep at all.

They peered and groped until they found a level and relatively well-drained place under a natural bower, where the old leaves of the past years had drifted. They stood facing each other and twisted their blankets between them to squeeze out the water, then draped the blankets over themselves and squatted beside each other for a moment. Mary's teeth chattered and she trembled from end to end. Even the primitive salt camp seemed cozy and luxurious compared with this. "We've a hard night ahead, I fear. I'm sorry. We'll do as best we can, eh? Come daybreak we'll find us some nuts or pawpaws or sump'n, eh?"

"Take," Ghetel said.

"Eh?"

The old woman reached for Mary's hand and put something cold and mushy in it. She explained, "It vas bread, til the rain. I get it before we leaf."

They ate the pasty mass. Mary could taste hickory nuts and acorn meal in it with the corn. It was delicious. She licked her fingers and felt a degree warmer inside.

They shook and trembled in their wet blankets for an hour, listening to the flow of the river and the dripping foliage, the whippoorwills and crickets and each other's sighs. Mary was so wretched she could hardly even think of the absence of her baby.

"May-ry," the old woman croaked.

"Aye?"

"Come."

And when they lay body to body, even the damp blankets could not entirely douse the warmth they gave each other, and eventually they slept through a night they had expected to be sleepless.

CHAPTER
11

SOMETHING WAS HAPPENING.

Mary was jolted out of sleep by her own heartbeat, by the sound of rustling in the leaves mere inches from her head. The old widow was moving, rising, cautiously, lifting the blanket. Mary opened her eyes in the green dimness and groped for the tomahawk. But before she could gather herself to move, Ghetel surged behind her, grunted, dragged the blanket off and scrambled in the leafy thicket. Something scurried away through rustling leaves and the old woman expelled a breathy oath.

Heart walloping, Mary turned to see the widow on all fours, staring into the underbrush. The blanket hung from her hips and entangled her feet. Mary had to swallow her heart before she could ask what had happened.

"Almost got a meat for breakfast," sighed the old woman. "Almost in mine hands! Ach, for a gun!"

"We'd dare not shoot one if we had it. What kind of animal?"

They were both kneeling on the bottom blanket and the old woman was extricating herself from the clinging grasp of the other. She did not know what the animal was called, she said, but her efforts to describe it convinced Mary that she had nearly grabbed either a racoon or a gray fox, which had been sniffing curiously at them while they slept. "Then y' ought to thank heaven it got away," Mary exclaimed. "Such beasties as them would 'a' chawed y'r arm up 'fore I could 'a' put the tommyhawk on 'im! I swear, Ghetel, that appetite o' your'n will be the death of us!"

Ghetel seemed to understand now, and perhaps was relieved that the animal had escaped her clutches. "But I do like breakfast," she growled as they moved out of the thicket to the river bank, their blankets draped over their shoulders like capes.

They eventually did find a breakfast. Veering straight north inland to save distance at a place where the river elbowed, they found not only a good fall of hickory nuts, but a pair of paw-paw trees, small but heavily laden. They shook down all the firm yellow-green fruits they could dislodge, and bound them up in a blanket to bring along. On the ground under the trees they found a dozen that had fallen and turned brown with ripeness and gave up a heavy, sweet smell. They opened these eagerly and dredged out the soft, sweet yellow pulp with their fingers, moaning with pleasure as they worked it over their tongues and sucked it off the big brown seeds and swallowed it. In a few minutes they were full and sticky, and permeated with the cloying odor of the stuff. They washed their hands and faces at a cold brook and struck out to regain the bank of the O-y-o, bringing the paw-paw aroma with them.

The day was overcast and the ground remained soft from

the night's rain. Mary looked over her shoulder constantly as they moved along. Even though she was certain the rain had destroyed their traces near the camp, she knew they were leaving a spoor that would be easy to follow if the Indians had chanced onto it this morning.

They rested on a stone ledge at the riverside early in the afternoon, breaking and munching hickory nuts. Mary's breasts ached for the baby's lips, and to keep from thinking about it, she talked optimistically about their progress, and about their wisdom in leaving the salt camp. "We'd not ha' got away from the Shawnee town," she mused aloud. "All those people. And dogs. No dogs at the salt camp, thanks be t' God.

"But the best on't is, we're on th' right side o' the river. I don't know how ever we'd ha' crossed it, short of stealin' a canoe. And I f'r one deem the heathens handier at stealin' than bein' stole from."

Late that afternoon as they labored eastward along the bank of the O-y-o, Mary recognized on the opposite shore the mouth of the river that Goulart had called . . . she searched her memory for the French word, but remembered only that it mean "the stony river" and that the Indians called it the Miami-zuh. She recalled that they had passed it in the afternoon of their last day coming down, and thus reckoned that she and Ghetel had walked some fifteen or twenty miles up the O-y-o valley in this first full day of their liberation. Fifteen or twenty miles, she thought. It sounded good; they had done well indeed. But then she remembered all the days of coming down on horseback from Draper's Meadows—the *month* of days—when they had made perhaps fifteen or twenty miles a day mounted, and then the four swift days by canoe from the Shawnee Town to the salt creek; and suddenly the distance they had struggled today seemed but a tiny first step on the long way home. Why, they would have to walk this far every day for a month and a half or two months to get home! And this O-y-o valley, strenuous though it was, was gentle by comparison with the terrain they would meet along the New River through the Alleghenies.

But come now, she told herself. Y'll do no good thinkin'

discouragements o' this sort! A day is a day, and y'll take each as it comes. If 't requires two months o' days, that's little enough t' trade f'r a lifetime back among y'r own!

They were famished by nightfall, and ate three more of the paw-paws apiece. Their blankets had dried during the day, and the evening was mild, so they did not have to huddle together for warmth. Each rolled up in her own blanket—redolent of paw-paw now, almost sickeningly so—and lay in her private hopes and fears in the creaking, hushing, owl-hooting darkness above the murmuring river, letting the burning aches in her legs and back subside into an aching torpor of the flesh, then into numbness, and slid off into a sleep haunted by space and uncertainty.

They foraged for almost an hour the next morning, staying within sight of the river, but found nothing they recognized as edible. They had several pounds of paw-paws left, but by now their senses were so permeated by their over-sweet odor that the thought of eating one was nauseating. Ghetel wanted to range further inland, up the slopes into high ground where nut trees might be found, and Mary had to persuade her that their primary purpose was to cover distance upriver. Ghetel came along, a bit grimly; evidently she had meant it when she said she appreciated breakfast.

They slogged along through brushy bottomlands, wading small creeks and marshes, climbing slopes on all fours, struggling through brambles that ripped their tattered skirts and drew blood from their legs; by early afternoon they were gasping for breath and slapping at huge brown flies whose bites were fierce as bee-stings, and were so famished that the paw-paws were delectable again.

And suddenly, after perhaps twelve miles, they emerged from a densely wooded downslope to find their way blocked by the mouth of a river that flowed into the O-y-o. Mary remembered this one. The word for buffalo. This was the river Goulart had pointed out to her as the Buffalo River. It was far too wide and apparently too deep to try to cross here. Ghetel's face drooped in dismay and she sat down abruptly on

the ground in a slumping posture of defeat, sweat dripping off
the end of her shapeless nose. Mary looked at her and knew
how she felt. But she had, of course, already considered such
detours as this. "Eh, well," she said with a wan and uncon-
vincing smile, and pointed up the bank of the tributary with
her tomahawk, "let's us jus' stroll up this side a stretch till we
find a fordin' place." Mrs. Stumf just sat and gazed, slowly
shaking her head. Mary feared that if she sat there musing on
it too long, she might consider turning back to the relative
comfort and security of the salt camp. So she grabbed her
hand and, with false gaiety, tugged at her until the old woman
sighed and got to her feet. Mary sang softly as they went
along:

> O ten times te—en times ten a—way,
> But I'll be ho—ome a—gain . . .

But they spent the rest of that evening and all the next day
going up the shore of the tributary, farther and farther from
their guideway the O-y-o. It was depressing in the extreme to
be struggling five, ten, maybe twenty miles, for all they knew,
only for the purpose of returning to a point a stone's throw
away from where they had stood. It was almost as dishearten-
ing as going backwards. But there was nothing for it but to do
this; neither of them could swim.

They were exhausted, hungry, scratched and bruised when,
late on their fourth day out of the salt camp, they came to a
riffle that indicated a shallows. The branches of trees almost
met over the river here, producing such a deep green gloom
that they were unwilling to try a crossing before the next
morning—especially in their spent condition. They piled
leaves between two parallel fallen logs and spread their
blankets. They went down to the river's edge and forced
themselves to eat the rest of their paw-paws, which by now
were so ripe and familiar as to be almost revolting. And the
steady diet of paw-paws and more paw-paws and nothing else
had given them both a severe flux. Ghetel got up and stepped
a few feet away, squatted with the hem of her skirt drawn up
around her waist and discharged her bowels into the leaves

with a loud gushing, spurting noise and came back with a distasteful expression on her face. A few minutes later Mary felt the call and went away to do the same. She did not like this. It was her experience that the flux had a weakening effect, and they would need all the strength they could maintain.

Something with heavy footsteps and deep wet breathing snuffled and grunted around them for almost an hour after midnight, waking them and then leaving them in such a state of fright that they did not sleep again until almost dawn. They were sure it was a bear, and sat up, back to back, Mary gripping the tomahawk, ready to defend themselves blindly in the darkness. When Mary heard Ghetel snore, she at last gave in to her own weariness and they both dozed sitting up until they were awakened by the shrilling of some woodland bird and glimpsed a pearly-coral dawn showing through the trees on the other side of the river.

They wanted some strength for their attempt to ford the river, and so occupied themselves with searching for food until the light strengthened, pausing often to spew the scalding, fluid contents of their bowels onto the ground. The memory of their helpless fright during the long night caused Mary to think she should try to fashion some sort of weapons for them. Appreciating the properties of hickory, she found two arrow-straight saplings, about two inches in diameter at their bases, cut them down with the tomahawk, shaved off the bark, cut them to lengths of about seven feet and then whittled their heavy ends to spear sharpness. This arming somehow heartened them for the crossing of the river.

Mary led the way into the cold, swift water, feeling the slick, rounded stones with her bare feet, probing ahead for depth and bracing herself against the current with the blunt end of her hickory spear, while the old woman clung desperately to the back of her dress and grasped and mumbled, prayers probably, in her language. With every additional inch of depth they reached, her toes' traction on the slippery stones became more tenuous, and the certainty that they would be simply carried off their feet and swept into the

relentless stream to drown became more definite, more dizzy-
ing. The river, which she had estimated at fifty feet wide, now
seemed as broad as the O-y-o. The flow was generally only
thigh-deep, but when she would step into a muck-and-pebble
depression and feel the current tugging at her hips and waist,
the end of the whole ordeal would seem to lie inches away in
the watery void at her left.

She seemed to have been looking at the same exposed roots
on the far bank for hours when they suddenly were there in
her hand and then she was scrambling up the bank with river
water dribbling out of her skirt. "Ahhhhh HEEE!" Ghetel
roared with joyous relief. Unseen animals went rustling away
across the leafy floor of the woods. They had made it. They
were exhausted, trembling violently, but exultant. They
hugged, pounding each other on the back and laughing almost
hysterically in their triumph. They subsided eventually, and
paused to wring out their skirts and the ends of their
blankets, sighing and shuddering. Mary took note of her belt
then, and decided she should keep a calendar of the days of
their return, as she had of her descent. She counted back.
This was the fifth day since their flight from the salt camp, so
she tied a triple knot to mark the beginning of their trek and
then four more single knots. Ghetel, meanwhile, was express-
ing her familiar concern:

"Hungry," she said. "I need a breakfat."

So they made a brief excursion up the slopes to look for
food, being careful to keep the river in view. Mary was anxious to get back down the east bank of this river and rejoin the
O-y-o. She was worried about being out of sight of it.

High on the slope, where an old burn-over was covered
with scrub and second-growth timber, they found a profusion
of wild grape vines clinging to the small trees as if trying to
haul them down and strangle them. The grapes were small,
hardly bigger than peas, but were in such dense bunches that
it was only a few minutes' work to fill a blanket with them and
tie up its corners. Then they picked more and sat on the
ground nibbling the powerfully bittersweet grapes off their
stems. They chewed up the seeds too, finding the grapes
more filling this way. Thus filled, but left strangely half–
satisfied for lack of bread or meat, they scrambled back down

the slope to the river bottom and followed it northward toward the O-y-o.

At midday, the weather close and overcast, when they were perhaps a fourth of the way back down the shore of the tributary, they were dismayed to find still another obstacle before them: a deep, wide creek flowing across their path into the river. Mary sighed. They would have to make a detour from their detour. This was worse even than she had suspected. They had been fugitive for five days now and, though they probably had walked sixty or seventy miles, they had progressed no more than thirty miles toward home, because of these necessary digressions from their route.

In truth, she thought, because of these damnable side-trips, we're probably further from home now then when we escaped!

But no. Looking at it that way will only drive you mad.

This unexpected creek had added five or six miles to their trek by the time they had made their way up its south bank, crossed it on a fallen ash tree that had bridged it and then hiked and crawled back down its north shore to rejoin the Buffalo River. And thus by nightfall they still had not raised sight of the O-y-o. It was mid-morning of their sixth day of freedom before they stood, weary and weakened by their flux, on the banks of the O-y-o again, now above the mouth of the Buffalo river.

These last two and a half days, Mary thought, have brought us a hundred yards closer to home.

It was so grimly absurd it was almost like a joke. But it was a joke she decided not to tell Ghetel. The old woman was having enough trouble keeping heart as it was.

"Eh, now!" Mary exclaimed with a dreadful false jollity. "That wee diversion's done with. Now we've an easy road ahead f'r a good spell!"

CHAPTER
12

ALONG A RIDGE CREST DEEP IN THE TENNESSEE COUNTRY, FOUR horses picked their way over a stony game trail among dark pine trees.

On the lead horse was the half-breed guide, Gander Jack, who now was dressed in the Indian mode. Gander Jack spoke English and Cherokee and frequently in his forty-one years had passed between Roanoke and the Cherokee towns south of the Cumberland. He was one of the few men who knew the way to the towns of the Southern Nations, and so had been hired as a guide at considerable expense by Will Ingles, who rode on the horse immediately behind him. Johnny Draper was on the third horse, leading a pack horse that carried their provisions and several pounds of mirrors, glass beads, combs and small tools to be used as gifts and ransom. Gander Jack had suggested they bring rum, but Will had been opposed to it—first because he suspected it was prompted by Jack's own considerable thirst, and second because he did not believe that rum was conducive to levelheaded dealings with Indians. At length, though, Will had conceded and brought a few gallons of whiskey, which he guarded closely.

They reached the end of the ridge and began to descend through a copse of junipers, emerging then on a clear slope overlooking a vast and brilliant stand of mountain ash: a profusion of small yellow leaves and stark red berries. Cedar waxwings, bluejays and finches shot to and fro among the ashes, feasting on the berries. On the distant slopes, forests of dark evergreens stood among the fading hardwoods, while shadows of clouds slid slowly up the valleys.

The riders converged with a narrow mountain stream about

halfway down the slope, a gushing, roaring, leaping water-course among boulders. The descent was so steep that the horses all but slid down on their rumps. In half an hour then they rode out onto a gentle, U-shaped valley full of dry grass and pine growing in reddish earth. Here they could ride abreast. They went at a trot for an hour, their eyes shaded by their wide, three-cornered hats. Gander Jack wore a yellow bandana circled around his head. His hat hung behind his shoulder on a strap.

Jack pointed ahead, and Will noticed a haze of smoke hanging along a wall of dark pines a mile ahead. "Cherokee town there," Jack said. He reined in his horse; Will and John did the same, though uncertain why. After a full minute of listening and watching, Jack clucked his tongue and they moved forward again, but at a slow walk. Will had broken out in a sweat in the still heat and ominous quiet. And suddenly, in the corners of his eyes, he detected the movement of figures. Glancing about, his hand tensing involuntarily on the rifle that lay across his saddle, he saw that they were flanked by perhaps a dozen warriors on foot, some of them armed with bows and hide shields, others with guns. These were escorting them toward the town. It was eerie how they had materialized out here on this open space.

They rode in among pines and the smell of woodsmoke, and found themselves suddenly within a clean, orderly village of remarkably substantial log houses, some bigger than his own home in Draper's Meadows had been, roofed with split wood. Stick-and-clay chimneys showed that the dwellings even had fireplaces. Handsome, brown-skinned young women, naked from the waist up, working at grain mortars and kettles and looms in the pleasant shade alongside the road, paused and stood up to watch these white men ride in. Children wearing not a stitch paused in their play and looked in awe at what Will presumed were the first white men they had ever seen. A clear stream curved in toward the heart of the town, and it was full of naked children and women washing. Will was impressed by the air of peace and order. He turned to look aside at Johnny, who caught his eye at once and remarked:

"Nice town, ain't it?"

Looking back, Will saw now that much of the population had moved in behind them, following quietly and watching with great curiosity.

"Chief," Gander Jack said softly, and Will turned to see a well-formed old man with grizzled hair coming toward them down the sun-flecked street, carrying a long walking staff with white and yellow feathers at its tip. Jack raised his hand to him and reined in. The chief returned the salute, and Jack dismounted, stood before him and offered his hand. They clasped forearms and Jack began talking. The chief nodded, his quick eyes occasionally darting up to look at the white men. "Get down," Jack said. "He don't like you a-lookin' down on 'im." They slid off, eager to please.

Will and Johnny and Gander Jack went into the lodge, a spacious and cool structure with a high ceiling, and there they smoked a pipe with the chief and some leading men of the town. They ate a meal from a large bowl containing beans and squash flavored with strips of a meat they could not identify by taste. Gander Jack was canny enough to wait until they had finished before telling them it was dog. Will felt a twinge of nausea, then put it out of his mind and forgot about it.

The Cherokee chief was reserved but hospitable. He listened as Will described, with Jack translating, the massacre at Draper's Meadows and told of his hope that the hostages might be located in the Shawnee country and ransomed through the offices of the neutral Cherokees. He told of the gifts of great beauty that he could bestow upon both the Shawnees and the Cherokees if his beloved family were returned to him. The chief listened to all this with his eyes hooded, and if his soul was stirred at all by the mention of the presents, he did not show it. He spoke quickly to Gander Jack and then stood up.

"He's never had a chance to talk directly to Englishmen," Gander Jack said. "He has a few things on his mind and wants you to listen."

Johnny leaned close to Will, smiling with half his mouth. "What say y', Will? Shall we hear 'im out?"

"Can't say as I've got anything more pressing t'do. Tell

him," Will said to Gander Jack, "that we deem ourselves lucky to share his wisdom."

Gander Jack let the chief get a few seconds' head start talking, then stepped in at his first pause for breath and began translating:

"He says he's seen his cousins the Shawnees two times this year . . . and they've told him what's in their hearts . . .

"The Shawnees took up the tomahawk against the English white men because they've been drove from place to place by 'em. They used to live a good life but had to move away north to strange places when the English white men came close and made big farms and killed all the game . . .

"Then they had to move west and find new lands, on the O-y-o, because more white English came . . .

"He says he understands the hearts o' the Shawnees . . . that he himself got wary when he saw your white faces come today . . . He fears that the Cherokee nation may one day have to fight the white English too, to keep from being driven afore 'em . . .

"He says the Shawnees won't give up their captives easy. He wants you to understand that they take captives and adopt them into their families to replace people who been killed or died because of the white men coming . . ."

"Ask him if that means they're likely alive," said Will.

Jack exchanged words with the chief, then told Will:

"That's up to the families. They're given a captive to replace someone they've lost. If their anger's too strong, they might torture or kill that prisoner to have revenge. But if they believe that person is of good blood, they'll adopt him, or her, and give the same comfort and protection they gave their own."

Will and Johnny traded anxious glances. Then Will extended another question that had been bothering him. "Ask him why the Shawnee, if they hate white men so dang much, hire on with the French. They're just as white as we are."

The chief was not stumped for a second by that question. "He says," replied Jack, "that the French are different from you. They hunt and trap and fish, just like the Shawnee, and they make small villages like the Indians, and farm only for food to eat themselves . . . He says they don't try to drive the red man out and destroy his land and kill all the game. He says the French and the Indians can live side by side in a land and help each other. But not so with the English white men, and that's why the Shawnees use the help o' the French . . ."

At this point the chief sat down. A buck, at a signal, brought forth the pipe again, with coals to light it, and it was passed around. Then the chief began talking again, this time with a less pontifical demeanor.

"He says he's glad you come to see him. He thinks y're brave to come here alone and your reasons are kindly. The Cherokee, too, love their families, and would do as you do . . . He says he'd like to help you ransom your families, and he'll say good words for you to any Shawnees who come here. But he says it ain't likely any will. Wait . . ."

The chief talked again, and waved toward the southwest.

"He tells me there was a Cherokee named Snake Stick, from a village out yonder, came through here two days back, an' this 'ere Snake Stick told him he was going up to talk with the Shawnees afore winter. He says if Snake Stick ain't gone yet, y' might hire him as y'r go-between."

Will's eyes blazed with eagerness. "How far to this Snake Stick feller?"

"I know where his town is. Five days south an' west, barrin' floods or trouble."

Will pondered that a moment. They had ridden two weeks already into this strange country, and considered themselves lucky to have come so far unharmed. Five days deeper into the Cherokee lands would be risky indeed. He turned and glanced at Johnny.

"It's f'r Bettie an' Mary an' them," Johnny said. "I can't go back knowin' I hadn't done all I could."

"Nor me." He turned back to their guide. "Will y' take us there, Jack?"

The half-breed shrugged, a sickly smile on his face.

"I take it that means f'r a price," Will said.

The half-breed nodded. Then the Cherokee chief spoke again. Jack translated:

"He says y' oughter know that Snake Stick might not be inclined to do anythin' for a white English. He thinks like a Shawnee, talks like a Shawnee. His heart ain't 'xactly neutral. He goes up t' visit the Shawnee an' listens to 'em t' git his blood all hot. Th' chief warns us we oughter know that."

Will Ingles curved his forefinger over his upper lip and stared at the chief, thinking. Finally he said:

"I reckon this 'ere Snake Stick's like any other man. Like as not he'd do f'r us—f'r a price. Thank our chief here. Tell 'im I have some gifts for 'im, in pay f'r his hospitality. Then we'll be a-gettin' on, to go see this Snake Stick."

Gander Jack thought it would be a good idea to give the Cherokee chief and his friends some whiskey in return for their opinions and advice, but Will refused, knowing it was Jack's own thirst that had prompted the suggestion. "And don't you by God tell 'em we've got any, either," Will warned him. "This evenin's goin' smooth. No need to waste good liquor makin' good Cherokees bad. Now hear me, Jack: I'm a-sleepin' with these jugs, and with my gun, and if I wake up hearin' one squeak of a jug-stopper, I'm shootin'. D'ye get my drift?"

Nobody came into the hut that night to steal whiskey, but Will might as well have been standing sentry duty; sleep just would not come, even though he was bone-weary and the pallet was far softer and drier than anything he had slept on for weeks.

It might have been the sounds that kept him awake; it might have been the smells. Now and then he would hear sounds of soft movement go past the hut, like moccasins on soft earth, like legging brushing against legging. When he heard something like this, he would stare at the oblong patch of lesser dark that was the doorway of the hut and would put his thumb on the cold flintlock hammer of the rifle, which lay across his waist. He would stare at that black-gray oblong until it swam; then he would look a little way above it, realizing that he could see it more clearly in the edge of his vision. A child coughing in its sleep somewhere in a nearby shelter made Will jump in his blankets and his heart pound for five minutes.

The fact was, though Johnny Draper and Gander Jack had seen not a hint of it, that Will Ingles was scared halfway to death. It had been getting worse night by night during their long ride into the Cherokee country, but he'd been able to put it down. Now, lying in the dark in the middle of a Cherokee town, he was almost shrieking scared. And the thought of going a week deeper into tribe country, to parley with a nasty young Cherokee instead of a nice old one, made it worse. One minute he'd be thinking how scared he was now, and the next he'd be thinking how scared he was going to be next week.

Damnation, it's awful what a man's got to go through to keep people believin' he's got guts, Will thought.

Nobody had ever said Will Ingles didn't have guts. There had been too much evidence over the years that he did have. Anybody could say, and many did, "That Will Ingles, he's got no fear of man nor devil."

Well, it was true Will Ingles had guts. But there were times, like now, when it seemed the main item in those guts was a white liver.

I wonder if Johnny's scared as I am, he thought. I wonder if he's asleep or lyin' there havin' the gollywobbles like me. You can see it when Gander Jack's scared. You can't ever see such a thing on Johnny. Nor you can't on me, neither.

But I am. And I bet Johnny is, too.

He heard a whisper of a sound outside and his hair stood up. His eyes bulged and he raised his head and spread his ears. It had sounded something like the noise when a man half-whistles. Like a sneak-signal. Like an Indian imitating an owl, maybe.

Or maybe like an owl imitating an Indian, he thought, trying to smile it away.

He kept his neck craned, listening, till it ached, until his ears were ringing so hard that he couldn't have heard a hoot owl on his shoulder. Nothing happened. He let his head back down and stared at the invisible black ceiling, the gray of the smoke-hole in its peak, and he poured cold sweat and listened to his heart clomp around in his chest like a mule on a plank floor.

It's just from bein' in an Indian town, he thought. A white man don't belong in an Indian town.

Nor does a white woman, he thought. He had just thought of Mary.

That was why he was here in the middle of the night in the middle of an Indian town: because his Mary was somewhere else in the middle of the night in the middle of an Indian town.

I mean, he thought, if she's still alive, that's likely where she is.

He lay now, trying to pick up what she would be thinking. They had used to talk fanciful about being able to hear each other's minds and see through each other's eyes; that's how close they had been.

He imagined her thoughts as hard as he could, and came eventually to the conclusion that she was thinking about him.

What if she's doing this same thing and she hears how scared I am, he thought. I got to stop thinkin' scared. It wouldn't do her good to know.

That thought reminded him of something awful: It reminded him of the day of the massacre when he had seen her in captivity and had had to run away.

She may read what's in my heart about that, he thought. If she do, how could I ever look in her face again?

Pray God, she don't know that, he thought.

But he was afraid she did. When she started thinking about what he was thinking, she usually knew.

She might think I'm a poltroon, he thought.

But by God, it ain't what a man feels that counts, Mary, it's what he does.

And for you, Mary m'love, what I'm goin' to do is go on down and talk to this bad Cherokee Snake Stick.

I mean . . . Tears suddenly were running into his ears. *I mean, I love 'ee, Mary, more than I love my life. And here in the middle of this Indian town I got no more reason for scare than you do in that Indian town you're in. I mean, you're but a woman!*

CHAPTER
13

THE BIG CATFISH LAY ON THE SILTY CREEK BOTTOM ALONGSIDE A black sunken log, no more than ten inches down in crystal-clear water. It was the biggest catfish Mary had ever seen; surely it was three feet long. Its gray-green back was so close to the color of the creekbed that she never would have seen it but for the slight motion of its whiskers and the slow undulation of fins and tail as it held itself in place against the current.

Mary squatted on the bank above the fish. Moving as stealthily as possible, she braced herself on one knee and raised her sharpened hickory lance over her right shoulder. Ghetel was standing above and behind her, squirming with impatience and whispering what might have been prayers or advice.

"Hush!" Mary whispered. Her hand was trembling, both because of anxiety and because she was shaky from hunger. They had walked three days since their detour around the Buffalo River without finding so much as a blackberry to eat. Ghetel today had resorted to eating grass to keep something in her stomach, but Mary had heard men say that was not a good thing to do, and so she had not. When the hunger had become unbearable in the last two days, she had simply drunk water until her stomach could hold no more. Then she would feel the hunger not in her belly but in the fibers of her limbs.

And in her mind.

Now she held the tip of the lance, which she had whittled to a narrow, needle-sharp point with the tomahawk, about a foot above the surface of the water and aimed it at a spot just an inch below the catfish's undulating fin. She thought quickly

over the things she must and must not do when she struck:
she must not hit an inch too high or too low, or the point
would slip off the fish's slippery side. She must strike hard
enough that the point would penetrate the fish and not just
knock it aside. And, as the point of the lance was not barbed
to hold the fish, she must drive it all the way through the
creature and pin him to the bottom and hold him there despite
his thrashing, until they could plunge their hands into the
water and get a grip on him. She had never realized until now
that hunting was as much a thing of the mind as of the body.
And when one was starving, it was hard for the mind to make
the body wait until it was all figured out. She gathered the
ready strength in her right arm until it felt like the cocked
hammer of a gun. This was the first time in her experience
that her life had depended on her killing a creature; always
Will or her father had done whatever hunting or slaughtering
had been necessary. They, like the Indians, had thought it to
be man's work. Her heart pounded.

Now!

Her arm snapped down. The spear shaft swished into the
water. It seemed to bend upward under the surface and struck
into the creek bottom. Clouds of roiling silt marked the place
where the fish had been.

She groaned and the old woman wailed a curse in her
language.

Because of refraction in the water, the fish had seemed
higher than it actually had been. The lance had jabbed
through the water a good two inches above it.

It was a lesson she must remember the next time she had a
fish lying under her sight like this. If I ever do, she thought. It
had been so perfect. Too perfect. Big fish don't just lie down
where you can reach them every day, she thought.

The old woman was stamping along the creek bank, ranting
bitterly, yelling that *she* would do it next time. *She* would not
have missed it, she shouted. Mary stood up weakly, little
starlike dots swimming behind her eyes. The dots went away.
Water and mud dribbled off the end of her lance. She fixed a
hard gaze on Ghetel. The old woman's tantrum subsided like a
pan of boiling milk lifted off the fire.

"Y'do it next time, then," Mary muttered. "Tain't so easy as y'd think."

On the eleventh day of their freedom they had to walk five miles upstream and then five miles downstream to get around another creek that had barred their progress up the bank of the O-y-o. That evening they found a clump of tall, wilting yellow flowers growing at the edge of a natural meadow. Mary had seen fields of these flowers near the Shawnee town and thus guessed that they were somehow edible. She and Ghetel tried eating the flower heads, then the leaves, but they were unbearably vile-tasting. Then Ghetel grabbed one of the stalks and pulled with all her strength. The flower came out of the ground and they saw that it had a fleshy, knobby root. Mary chopped off sections of this root with the tomahawk and found it to be white and crisp, almost as palatable as a raw potato. They pulled up all the stalks and obtained about a pound of the tubers. They ate them that evening and then lay down on a bed of leaves in the lee of a fallen log. With the awful gnawing gone out of their stomachs for the time being, they had only the pain in their battered feet and legs to keep them awake. Those miseries soon were blanketed by their numbing exhaustion and they were asleep before midnight, under a huge sky full of chilly blue stars.

On the twelfth day they had to go around another small tributary. Near this one, shortly before nightfall, they found a large fall of acorns under a chestnut oak. They had no fire nor kettle with which to boil the tannin out of the acorns, and so had to shell them and eat them bitter-raw. The first few tasted good even though bitter; the rest they had to force themselves to chew and swallow. But again that night they slept with something in their stomachs and awoke with a bit of strength in their limbs to continue with the thirteenth day of their escape. That day, as if thirteen were indeed unlucky, they found absolutely nothing to eat and went to bed groaning with hunger and aching limbs. Mary lay looking up at the stars and listening to the river, and through the rents in her dress she examined her body with her fingers. Her pelvic bones under her skin felt like wooden furniture covered with cloth. There seemed to be no flesh. Her belly, which had been so swollen and turgid with child at the start of this ordeal—the massacre at Draper's Meadows now seemed years past, though it had been only three months—now sagged concave between her pelvis and her rib cage, and her breasts were hard and dry. They had stopped making milk.

She looked at the stars until her eyes burned, to keep from thinking about the baby. It was not terribly difficult, now that her body was forgetting. It was almost as if there had never been a baby, except when she would envision its eyes and mouth. Mary finally went to sleep lulled by the rhythm of Ghetel's snores, and dreamed of Tommy and Georgie and her mother.

They had been gone two weeks from the salt camp when, toward evening, Mary glanced over the O-y-o and saw a canoe moving northward across it. The canoe was at this distance a mere sliver of sunlit gray on the green water. Mary stopped and the old woman almost stumbled over her. Mary pointed at the faraway moving shape. They watched it head straight for the northern shore and then it disappeared.

She recognized the spot then. It was the mouth of the Scioto. Her heart thudded.

"Ghetel!" She found herself whispering. "There! There w'd be the Shawnee town! Up that river there!"

The old woman stared, eyes bulging, mouth hanging slack. "Gott," she exclaimed, "yesss!"

"Ghetel! That means . . . that means we've come along a hundred and fifty miles! Maybe more like two hundred, countin' all them go-arounds!"

"So, eh?" The old woman blew like a winded horse. "I'm feelink like *fife* hunder."

They rested lying concealed in high grass overlooking the river and discussed the dangers of being this close to the Shawnee town. They had come up to a place almost directly opposite the mouth of the Scioto and now in the ruddy-gold cross-light of the sunset they could see some of the fields and huts of the town on the far shore, and the haze of smoke from cooking fires. Now and then the bark of a dog or a wisp of human voice would carry to them across the wide river. They would have to move in concealment and as quietly as possible, Mary warned. She remembered the little Indian farm on this side of the river where she and her fellow captives had been held in wait for the canoes to come and ferry them across to the Shawnee town in August. Had it had dogs? She tried to remember. She seemed to remember that there had been a large yellow dog sleeping in the shade of a canoe. If it was a regular ferrying place, of course, there would likely be danger of considerable Indian traffic: war parties, hunting parties.

"We ought to lay here the night," she said, "then head away from the river at sunup, and go around."

The old woman was gazing wistfully at the smoke across the river. "Dey got food over there," she said, clutching her belly and rocking. "I could eat a dog or two. Ach. Dog, yet."

Mary's stomach too was an unrelieved silent scream of hunger. Then she remembered the cornfield at the little Indian homestead. It might not have been harvested yet.

The more she thought of corn, the less she wanted to lie here till morning. Sleep would be impossible anyway. She began to grow desperately brave. "Come," she whispered finally.

The sun had descended behind the bluffs downriver and it was twilight when Mary and the old woman crawled through weeds along a pole fence, watching the Indian hut for signs of light or movement, meanwhile making their way toward the cornfield. So far they had not heard a voice nor smelled a wisp of smoke nor seen a spark of fireglow. But Mary remembered the young boys she had seen here and knew that they would be as alert as watchdogs if they were about.

Sliding silent as snakes through the weeds along the fence, she and the old woman suddenly froze. Very close ahead they had heard a heavy footfall—or, rather, felt it through the soft ground on which they lay—and heard a heavy huff of breath like a sigh. As they flattened themselves further in the weeds with slamming heartbeats, they heard two more footfalls, followed by a dull metallic *clunk*. A large dark shape then moved beyond the screen of weeds not three yards in front of them, causing the metallic sound again. Mary turned her face against the ground and looked up into a dark brown eye, which was looking down at her.

A horse!

It was a roan horse with a bell on its neck. And at the moment she recognized what it was, the beast saw her in the weeds and shied. It half-reared, sidestepped, bell clanking loudly, then ran thumping and rustling into the scrub. Mary and Ghetel lay with their hearts pounding against the ground, covered with sudden cold sweat, now expecting the horse's flight to bring someone out of the hut, which was but a few feet away.

For five minutes they waited in the deepening twilight. There was not a sound or movement from the house. In the distance the horse's bell was still clunk-clunking.

"I do wonder, does this place be deserted," she whispered to Ghetel. "Wait now."

She arose as smoothly as her grinding leg joints would allow, and stood swaying for a moment. Her feet throbbed and stung as she put her weight on them again. She leaned on her hickory stick. When the dizziness was gone she looked over the fence, which was a sort of corral; two of its poles were down nearby, explaining why the belled horse was wandering about. She could see the entire hut and much of its setting now, and grew more certain that it was deserted. Gathering more daring than she had suspected she had, she crept up to the very wall of the hut and put her ear to it, then went around slowly to the front, raised a hide door-flap, stooped and looked into the dark interior, smelling the musty, smoky closeness inside. She trembled, ready to thrust with the sharp lance if anything moved.

Suddenly a twig snapped just behind her and a figure moved with a swish. Mary's scalp flushed with prickles and, her heart in her mouth, she spun and thrust the hickory lance with all her strength at a hulking human figure that was suddenly there in silhouette against the evening's hazy red afterglow.

"AIIII!"

The point of her spear dug into soft resistance at the moment Mary recognized the cry and the shape as Ghetel's and a shiver of horror cascaded down her flanks.

"Jesus in Heaven!" the old woman hissed, grabbing the shaft of the spear and yanking it out of the fabric of her dress. The point had missed Ghetel's neck by an inch and ripped through the right side of her collar.

Mary was in an uproar of confusion, of sinking relief and rising fury. The two stood staring at each other for long seconds. "How dare y' creep up on a body at a time like this?" Mary finally hissed.

"M'Gott! I t'ought you would *need* me!" The old woman's voice too was quavering with indignation. They sagged toward each other then with shuddering sighs and hugged each other's bones for support. The old woman patted Mary's shoulder, and then the hazards of their situation dawned on them again. They had been loud with their gasps and exclamations. They stooped at the door of the hut peering about in the chilly dusk and listening. On the far shore of the river now, points of campfire light gleamed. A fingernail moon hung above a bluff in the east. Two owls were fluting to each other from different horizons. Mary wondered whether they were real owls.

It was black inside the hut. The women had decided it was truly vacant. They felt around for things. They found only a broken clay pot, a strap of hide about a yard long and a bed of crushed boughs and leaves near the back wall. In the center of the hut was a circle of river stones around a pile of cold ashes. It was apparent that the Indian family had departed for some time, if not for good.

They went out into the cornfield and found to their joy that the ears were nearly ripe but had not been harvested yet. Mary said grace under the slice of moon. "Thankee, Heavenly Lord, for this manna." For a while then the only sounds were the rustling of cornstalks and the sounds of their gnawing and their little moans of pleasure.

Mary soon felt a rising queasiness replacing her terrible emptiness. She swallowed a mouthful of the moist, starchy mass, then warned: "Mustn't eat too much at once, Ghetel.

Might be we'll have a late supper too, eh?" They went down to the river and drank water out of cupped hands, then back to the fence where they had left their blankets. They sat there in the weeds with their blankets draped over their shoulders, the night air chilling their ears and scalps, listening to the burbling and stitching of frantic digestion in their distended stomachs. Occasionally they rocked to and fro, for warmth and to help the food work down. After a while Mary realized it would be hours before she would be able to eat again, but the old woman was still thinking of food as she had been for days, and she could not bear to ignore the cornfield before bedtime. She went among the stalks and gnawed the kernels off of two more ears before she would admit to herself that she was satiated.

"Da'st we slepp 'neath a roof?" Mary ventured. She was growing drowsy over her full stomach. "I think there be frost a-comin' on my head."

"O for a roof, yah. Why not, eh?"

They went in the hut and spread their blankets on the Indians' old bed-square, and rolled up in them, each with her spear lying at hand, after Mary had worked a bark shingle of the back wall loose to provide an escape-hole should anyone enter by the front door. It was fearsome to be sleeping in the home of savages who might or might not return, and the possibilities bothered her for an hour even as she grew cozy and less and less inclined to move. She decided to leave that chance in God's hands, and prayed so. Ghetel was not snoring yet, either, and late in the night Mary heard her chuckle.

"What?"

A sigh from the old woman. Then: "Vas I mad w'en you missed the fish! But vaz I happy this night you don't spear good!"

They laughed softly, and then they were able to sleep.

Mary woke with a gasp, the tense grip of a strong hand on her arm. Ghetel was clutching her, sitting up in her blanket and staring toward the grainy silver predawn light in the doorway. Somewhere out there, dry leaves were rustling loudly, as if many people were walking without concern for stealth.

The two women freed themselves from their warm blankets and snatched up their spears. In her waking panic, Mary recollected details of their situation; she remembered the escape door she had made in the back wall. On hands and knees she turned and lifted down the slab of bark and looked out into the nearby cornfield.

The noise was coming from there. She could see cornstalks jerking and moving. They dared not try to escape from this side. She watched, frozen, for Indians to emerge from the corn.

The first face poked out among the leathery stalks. But it was at knee-height. Then there was another. Mary suddenly went almost silly with mirth. She reached back and grabbed Ghetel's arm and pulled her down to the opening to show her the intruders.

The faces were looking toward the hut. They had comical black masks over their eyes, and busy little black noses. Then one of the raccoons rose on its hind legs, reached up with little hands and grasped an ear of corn. It shucked it skillfully and then started eating the tender kernels from the middle of the ear.

"Eh!" Ghetel cried. "It's *our* corn! GET!" She scrambled to her feet and ran toward the front door with her hickory lance, abandoning all caution. By the time she had plunged into the corn patch, flailing with her stick, the furry little bandits had vanished and Mary was almost helpless with laughter. It seemed the misery of ages dissolved and sloughed off with this release. She was wiping her eyes when Ghetel returned stooping, grumbling, through the door.

"Ah, Ghetel! You and your raccoons!"

In the pink light of dawn they picked as much corn as they could tie up in the blankets, breakfasting on plump ears as they worked. They watched over their shoulders toward the woods and thickets, and kept an eye on the river for canoes. Their laughter might have been heard across the river in this morning stillness. Sounds from the Shawnee town were drifting over clearly enough: snatches of voice; the faraway thump of some tool; the very distant gunshot of some hunter on the other side of the O-y-o. Mary was anxious to be well out of the vicinity of the town and this camp before broad daylight. They harvested rapidly the ears that the raccoons had not sampled. The little animals had done an amazing amount of sampling . . .

"Hush!" Mary whispered, listening.

It was the clunking of the horse's bell. Mary moved to the corral and saw the roan standing inside, looking at her. The animal appeared quite tame, evidently over its fright of the previous evening. Mary, her heart high with hope, quietly replaced the fallen rails of the corral and then went into the hut and returned with the hide strap. "How'd y' like us t' have a horse?" she said to Ghetel, who was knotting the corners of a blanket full of corn.

"Yah! For dinner, you say?"

"Nay, for ridin'!"

"Ah, 'at vould be acceptable also. My feets say so. Ha!"

Having won the horse's allegiance with a handful of corn and few syllables of sweet talk, Mary easily got the leather strap tied to the thong that supported its bell. The horse was a mare, docile, long in the tooth, and so complacent and easily led that Mary presumed she was accustomed to white people. Probably stolen from whites, she thought. With quick and surprising ingenuity and some strips of leatherwood bark, Ghetel retied the blankets in such a way that they could be slung over the horse's back with a bulging load of corn hanging at either flank, and by sunup they were ready to continue upriver. They were more cheerful than they had ever seen each other. They were strengthened by a supper and a breakfast of corn. They had enough food to last for several days, and a horse to carry it and themselves. They had already proven themselves by their first hundred and fifty miles, and with this food and this wonderful heaven-sent mare, the next three or four hundred miles loomed comparatively easy.

"You ride first, Mary," the old woman offered magnanimously. "I lead."

Mary suspected Ghetel was afraid to go first on an untried

horse, but of course did not venture that appraisal. "No," she said. "Till we're out o' this vicinity, let's us stay low. We'll both walk."

"Ah, yah."

They tried to keep themselves far enough inland that they could not be seen from across the river, but soon found that the cane and undergrowth were impenetrable everywhere but on the Indian trail along the river bank. So all they could do was stay along the trail most of the time and hope they would not meet any parties of Indians coming down.

It was a pleasant morning. Though they were in rags now, the walking and the food in them kept them warm, and the sun was pleasant on their faces when they were out of the shadows. The horse's hooves thudded softly, a reminder of this gift of Providence, and the little bell on its neck clanked, a sound musical and civilized to their ears after the rushings and roars and deep silences of the wilderness they had heard for so long, after the gunfire and tortured screams and sobbings of grief that had begun their wanderings in this savage purgatory. The bell was a dull bronze, old, and Mary wondered where it had come from. Civilized hands had made it, she was sure; bells were civilized things. Maybe it was part of the booty brought here by raiding Indians. The kind of thing LaPlante and Goulart traded for skins. Aye, it very well might have been through that very trading post sometime, she thought. The blue and white checked pattern of shirt cloth moved in her mind behind her eyes. It seemed ages since she had been engaged in that business. Even that, in a way, seemed like civilization compared with the elemental subsistence of these last weeks. But she smiled to herself. It was good not to be the bounden partner of those Frenchmen any more. She was free. With corn to eat and a companion who, though erratic and difficult, was a companion nonetheless, and with a good horse with a civilized bell.

But that bell, she thought suddenly. P'raps for safety it ought to be thrown away. She stopped the horse and reached to untie it.

"Vat you do here, eh?"

"Get rid o' this. Kind o' noisy f'r sneakin' by Indians . . ."

The old women grabbed her hands and jerked them down. Mary looked at her in astonishment.

"No," Ghetel said, shaking her head severely. "This bell is good luck. Haf to keep. I had dream, the bell is good luck for us."

"Nonsense. It could be the death of us . . ." She reached again; again Ghetel shoved her hands away, with real roughness. Then the old woman's face softened and brightened. She held a finger to her temple, indicating the source of an idea. She stooped and gathered a handful of leaves and stuffed them inside the bell, around the clapper. Then she tore off one of the rag tatters that had once been her dress, and bound up the bell to keep the leaves from falling out. "There," she said. "So ve keep the bell. Is luck."

Mary shrugged. The little conflict of the moment was gone.

And, in truth, she would have hated to throw the civilized little bell away into the wilderness anyway. Ghetel had done well, with her fond little superstition.

The horse was proving a great comfort to them. Late in the morning, Mary climbed onto a ledge of limestone and slipped a leg over the animal's broad back, tentatively, in case the mare was not accustomed to a rider. Gone are the days, she thought, when I could just spring on. The horse turned her ears and quivered her mane and tried to look back, but Ghetel held her firmly by the lead. Mary slid the rest of her weight onto the horse's back in the space in front of the bundles of corn. The mare blew softly but stood steady.

"Eh, now. Lead on, Ghetel, I think she's no objection whatever."

Mary was lulled by the motion of the horse's progress, and realized how weary she was. Her legs tingled and throbbed in waves. Having no underclothing, and scarcely any outer garments, she was directly against the horse's hide, could feel the friction against the insides of her thighs like a massage soothing away the stress, could feel the animal's flesh giving slightly over its ribs, could smell the wonderful remembered musk of horse. She went into fits of dozing, or rather trances

of oblivion, as she did not close her eyes; and faces and
scenes from Draper's Meadows—the faces of her mother and
the boys, Will sitting before the hearth luxuriating while she
washed and kneaded his feet after a strenuous day; the ticking of the old grandfather clock as she lay awake looking at
his sleeping profile after love while the pleasure of it in her
loins ebbed into the deepest sort of ease—such dreams of
their old hard but heavenly life drifted like smoke behind her
eyes. Will had often said that the kindest thing people could
do for each other was tend to each other's feet at day's end,
and he had "done" her feet almost as often as she had done
his; she could feel now Will's strong, warm hands kneading
her arches almost to the limit of bearability, sometimes making her legs twitch, and his loving fingers flexing her toes,
pulling them until their joints popped softly but surprisingly,
and then rotating her tense, resisting feet on their ankles until
her calves would relax—oh what a sweet good man was her
Will! Capable of the biggest and boldest efforts but kindly and
attentive to the smallest need, always having time to give to
anyone who needed him, however tired he was or how full of
tomorrow his mind might be . . .

*I'm a-comin' back t'y, William Ingles; oh I vow I'll reach
'ee . . .*

Suddenly a bolt of dread snapped her out of this reverie. In
her mind she had seen a looming of dark faces. She opened
her eyes onto the bright innocent yellow and crimson of
autumn foliage, seeing nothing ahead but the horse's neck and
ears and Ghetel's wild iron-gray hair and the gauntlet-stripe
scars on the sagging skin of her back. But the feeling would
not leave; it was the feeling which on that July Sunday morning had made her glance repeatedly at the cabin door. She
could not ignore it. "*Ghetel!* I'm a-gettin' off," she hissed.
The old woman's face turned to her, reflecting the alarm she
had detected in Mary's voice. She halted the mare and Mary
slid off to the ground. The pain of the sudden weight on her
half-rested feet and legs almost made her fall. "Listen," she
whispered, "something's a-tellin' me we ought to get off this
trail . . ."

At that moment the mare's ears pricked up and she gave a

low nicker, her head turned toward the shadows under a lofty wood.

From somewhere in those shadows came the muffled sound of a man's voice. They listened. A moment later it came again, louder.

Mary jabbed with a finger toward a thicket of sycamores and locusts lying down the slope at their left, close to the river bank, and both the women hauled at the neck-halter to bring the animal along. They made a din of rustling and crackling on the leaf-and-twig carpeted floor of the thicket, and had just halted the mare behind a head-high clump of scrub when Mary saw the Indians, a mere fifty feet away.

They were afoot, all warriors or hunters, going westward along the trail, toward the Shawnee town. They wore no war paint but carried their muskets at their sides. Several of the braves, in pairs, carried poles across their shoulders and there were dead animals and fowl hanging from these poles by their feet or necks. Mary counted thirteen men passing, then a brindled pack horse with the whole carcasses of two small deer over its back, then another horse, a large bay, carrying a black bear strapped across it, the bear's hanging head swaying and bobbing with the horse's movements. Ghetel watched them and kept crouching lower and lower, as if wishing the earth would swallow and hide her big pink and gray body. Mary watched under the mare's neck, stroking to keep her from starting or neighing.

The hunters took a long time in passing. They were casual and jovial, talking and sometimes grunting out short, cough-like bursts of laughter.

The two women remained still for a long time after the sounds of the hunters' passage had faded. They stood letting their heartbeats and breathing return to normal, watching the trail for any sign that the group might have been only part of a larger body. At last a horsy smile spread over Ghetel's face and she looked at Mary with some wonder. "I don't know how you know," she said, beginning to shake her head, "but I listen to you after now."

"Tell y' what I fear," Mary said. "That afore this day's done, them hunters will look down an' see our tracks a-comin' thisaway, an' send somebody back here t' see who we be. That's what I fear as much as meetin' more savages headlong."

Ghetel considered this, nodding and running her tongue thoughtfully over her back gums with elaborate ruminating movements of her lower jaw. Finally she announced: "Ven I vatch to th' back, you vatch to th' front. My turn to ride now, eh?"

"Aye."

"Get me a place to climb up, den."

And when Mary led the mare alongside a fallen log Ghetel could use as a mounting block, the old woman hoisted her broad bony rump onto the horse's back as if she were getting onto a sidesaddle. Then, to Mary's astonishment and amusement, she raised her left leg, instead of her right, and lowered it over the other side so that she was astraddle but backward, looking over the horse's rump. She turned and looked down at Mary. "Now ve go," she said, "and I see 'em if they follow."

Mary stared at her for a moment, mouth hanging open, then shook her head. "So be it!" She laughed. "Hang on!"

And so they continued, up an Indian trail through the blazing fall foliage in the valley of the beautiful river, keeping a vigil fore and aft.

CHAPTER
14

THEIR GREAT FORTUNE IN OBTAINING THE HORSE SEEMED ALSO to have extended to the weather. For three days they were blessed with mild, dry, southerly winds, sun-gilded, fleecy clouds cruising across a pearly blue sky. The wind soughed high in the trees above them, sent shivers across the surface of the river and stripped off the first loose leaves of autumn. A gust would boom in the crowns of the towering hardwoods; leaves would spill off and whirl away like yellow snowstorms. Deep drifts of ochre and orange and crimson leaves deepened on the forest floor, fragrant and crisp and easy underfoot. Docile wasps and weary flies stitched leisurely through slanting sunbeams. Mary and Ghetel went on through this dry, balmy weather, taking turns riding and leading the mare, wading and limping through the rustling leaves, carrying their homemade lançes upraised, like a pair of tatterdemalion remnants of some Amazonian cavalry. Mary sang her little homing ballad often as they went along. Ghetel had abandoned her retrospective mode of riding the first time the mare lunged roughly up a bluff and there was no mane to hang onto. The nights were dry and cool but not cold. Their supply of corn dwindled slowly, more slowly certainly than if they had dared to kindle a fire to cook it in any manner. Drying on the cob day by day, it made a gritty and starchy meal, almost like eating chalk, so they did not eat as much as they would have if it were more palatable. The few handfuls of berries, walnuts, wild grapes and persimmons they found each day were a wondeful relief. Because of her lack of molars, Ghetel had to find some way to crack and pulverize her corn, and usually smashed it with the blunt side of the tomahawk on a rock until she had a small dirty pile of yellow-white grit that she could wash down with water. She ingested a fair amount of dirt and stone dust to this primitive milling process. Mary's own teeth were beginning to ache and loosen because of their wretched diet, and she would have strange twinges and itches in her gums, and could suck a taste of rot from between her grinding-teeth. But at least the corn had bound up their flux, and both privately took satisfaction in the little hard stools they left behind every morning.

Mary estimated that they were covering twice as much distance each day as they had before acquiring the wonderful animal, partly because the horse could carry them both across creek mouths and shallow rivers they would have been afraid to wade on foot. The mare was a good forder, not skittish at entering water, and would with good footing make her way across a strong current as high as her withers, with the two women astride her, the water reaching their hips, Mary clutching the mane, Ghetel embracing Mary's scrawny waist. And when the mare would clamber out on the far bank, both the women would fuss over her, hug her neck, kiss her muzzle, stroke her throatlatch, hand-feed her a little corn and perhaps let her rest and graze if they were in grassy country. Mary had always loved horses, but never had she loved one with the same choking, tear-starting love she felt for this benevolent lovely beast that had appeared in her life when she had so desperately needed it. Sometimes she would look into the deep brown, soft-lashed eyes and would feel a rush of appreciation that felt almost like a prayer. "Ah, God," ,she exclaimed once, "would that people could be so good!"

But sometimes that kind of communion could devastate her soul, because into that same rich upwelling of emotion the images of her three lost children would rush, as if through a gate suddenly left unguarded.

On their third day with the horse, they came to a sandy-bottomed tributary that Mary distinctly remembered from the trip down in the captivity of Captain Wildcat. The Indians had crossed it in a canoe and had secreted the vessel in a canebrake on this shore. "Wait," she said, and leaving Ghetel with the horse, pushed her way into the tall, waving yellow-green stalks, holding her hickory lance in front of her, both to part the reeds and to be ready in case she should come upon a water moccasin—or an Indian. She waded through the muck searching for the outline of a canoe.

A loud splash a few feet in front of her made her recoil and break out in a cold sweat, and she stood with thudding heart until she decided that she had only startled a sunning bullfrog. She crept farther into this world of black mud and shimmering vertical lines, her shoes filling with cold water, but found no sign of a canoe. Eh, well, she thought. Likely some outbound party's left it on t'other shore. As she started to run back, her eye caught a glistening dark lump in the shallows almost at her feet; it was pulsating.

It was a huge bullfrog, half-submerged, gathering itself to leap away.

With a quick, desperate stab of her spear she impaled it. She turned her face from its sudden awful thrashing and squirming and waited until it was still.

"May-ry? *May-ry?*" the old woman had begun querying, when Mary emerged from the brake proudly holding up her stick with the limp frog on the end of it.

"Look, Ghetel. Look. Our first meat."

They twisted its big legs off and slid the slimy skin off as if pulling off stockings, and hunkered there on the river bank like a pair of aborigines, gnawing at the cold raw pink-white meat. Mary glanced up once from her own bone-picking and saw a string of slobber running from Ghetel's underlip as she threw away her frogleg bones and started examining the rest of the frog.

When Ghetel reached for it and began pulling off its tiny little arms, Mary had to look away.

Something about the look of Ghetel's hunger had sent a cold bolt of unnameable horror through her.

They went five miles up the west bank of that river, stumbling through ravines and forcing their way through thickets and brambles that cut and lashed their skin and further shredded their rags, before finding a shallows of sand and gravel bottom where they could ride the mare across. Then they returned down the east bank. Here they had to lead the horse and walk through a vast tangle of grapevines and thorny locusts. There were a few leathery, hard, wrinkled grapes within reach, but obviously their season was past and they were no pleasure to eat. Nonetheless, the women gathered a few bunches and slipped them into the blanket bundles with their remaining corn. They were certain that there would come a time when even these would taste good.

They were smeared with their own blood when they struggled at last out of the thorn ticket. They rinsed their limbs with river water, dug little black thorn-ends out of their wounds and continued downstream toward the O-y-o. Almost immediately they came to a creek mouth no more than knee-deep but strewn for yards with mossy, flat, sharp-edged rocks the size of dinner plates and tabletops, which tilted and slid and turned under their feet. By the time they had teetered and crashed across these to the other side, their rotten shoes had finished falling apart, and they were forced to abandon them and continue down the shore on bare, bloody feet that felt as if every bone in them had been fractured. They minced and winced at the stabs of twigs and stones in their soles, until their tender feet were at last so full of throbbing pains that new jabs could scarcely be felt. They took turns riding, but it seemed their feet hurt even worse hanging free beside the horse's ribs than when they were being walked on.

And, even more alarming, the mare herself was limping since the passage over the rocks. Mary examined her and found oozing abrasions, one on the pastern of her left foreleg and one under her right hind fetlock—very critical places, Mary knew, which could render her lame and useless if they were unlucky.

So the women both dismounted and walked. They stopped for the day at midafternoon when the O-y-o came in view.

Here they retied the neck halter into a hobble and set the mare to grazing. Mary limped about for a while looking for comfrey to make dressings for their feet and the mare's legs, but found none and presumed that the season for finding it was now past. With little certainty, then, she decided to dredge up some muck from the river's edge and put it on the mare's wounds, feeling that this would at least sooth them. While stooping there she saw a long dark shape lying among the reeds—a rotting log, she thought at first—which closer examination revealed to be a ruined Indian canoe, half-sunk in the shallows, with slabs of its bark cover fallen away from its hickory frame. This only reminded her that their entire route followed well-used Indian trails, and that there could be no carelessness or excessive noise. And though she yearned for the comfort of a campfire, for hot water to heal their feet, and she probably could have started one even without flint and steel—she had watched squaws at the Shawnee town ignite tinder with an easily made bow-and-drill device—it would be foolhardy in the extreme to do it.

She packed the cool black muck on the horse's fetlock and pastern while Ghetel sat nearby, watching with an approving

look while mashing corn and wild grapes together on a flat
rock with the tomahawk. They added a handful of water to
the meal later and made it into a purple paste that, while
strange and awful to the palate, was certain to be nourishing,
and did extend their little store of corn somewhat.

Each time they arose to move about their camp, flashes of
pain shot up from their battered feet. Mary remembered then
the thoughts she had had so recently about Will, about their
very personal attention to each other's feet. She looked at the
poor hag beside her, at her wrinkled, scratched skin hanging
like wattles off her arms, and suddenly was drawn out of
herself by a great tug of pity. "Come, Ghetel," she said.

And then for an hour as the late afternoon sun warmed
their faces, they sat at the river's edge, and Mary kneaded
and palpated the old woman's misshapen feet, those bundles
of bones and calluses and knobby joints, with the rich mud,
while Ghetel groaned deep with pain and delight. Mary talked
of Will as she tended the old woman's feet, and now and then
tears would run off the end of her nose.

Ghetel worked on Mary's feet then, and talked to her about
old Holland, whence she had come twenty years ago, "when I
vas gutluckink like you," and about great kitchens she had
known, with copper pots and ladles and sausages hanging
from the rafters, and cheeses maturing in cloth, and butter in
the churns, and big porcelain ovens fragrant with new bread,
until Mary was driven to exclaim:

"Have mercy! Y're caressin' me at one end an' torturin' me
at t'other!"

* * *

Their feet gave them agony the next morning when they
first put their weight on them, but as they limbered with the
walking, the pain lessened to a healthy ache and it became
apparent that they really were very much better.

Neither of them rode the horse that morning, but walked
and led her and studied her gait. She did not limp, and did not
start limping as the day wore on, so they presumed that the
mud had done as much good for her as for them. "We like as
not can ride 'er tomorrow," Mary said.

They went eastward all that morning, seeing no sign of
Indians and finding nothing but a fall of acorns to supplement
their dwindling corn. At midday their course began to veer
southeasterly, and Mary went back over the mental library of
landscapes. As she recollected, there were still three major
river mouths to be crossed before they would reach the great
northeasterly curve in the O-y-o's rivercourse and find the
place, that pleasant point, where the waters of the New River
flowed into the O-y-o. P'raps seventy or eighty miles to that
place, she thought. But it could add up to two hundred if them
three rivers 'twixt here and there detour as much.

Their good weather gave out at midday. A sudden chill
blasted over the river valley, sending millions of leaves spinning away in red and yellow whirlwinds, buffeting the treetops with an intimidating rush and moan. Iron-gray clouds
came scudding over low, dragging their dirty-looking skirts
over the hilltops, and in five minutes the river was flint-
colored and seething with whitecaps. Chilly gusts blew the
women's hair over their faces and flattened it against their
scalps, and the air around them was full of spinning leaves
and twigs. Their rags flapped and fluttered around them and
they inched along squinting, staying close in the lee of the
mare. And soon their skin—most of it exposed now by the
disintegration of their clothes—was being pelted by cold,
driven raindrops that stung like sleet. The wind increased, so
cold and powerful it seemed to suck out their breath. An
enormous dead beech tree gave up its foothold on the slope a
few yards above them and crashed to the ground, splitting
and splintering smaller trees as it bore them to earth. The
mare shied, reared and bolted. Mary hung onto its neck bridle
through ten awful seconds, her feet hardly touching the
ground, until she dragged the beast to a nervous, snorting
standstill fifty yards farther on. Ghetel, emitting little yelps
into the wind, came running to catch up, with that strange,
arm-pumping trot that had carried her through the gauntlet.
Steeling themselves against the wet cold and the shouting
wind, they walked the rest of the afternoon away, both hanging on to the mare as if they might otherwise be blown aside

into the river. Mary, though she had lived close to the edge of
the wilderness most of her adult life, had never felt quite this
way: like a weightless little speck of chaff lost in a universe of
tumultuous elements, shrieking trees and indifferent
mountains.

But finally, about sunset time, when the wet leaves were
cold and limp underfoot and the wet tatters of clothing stuck
to the pasty gooseflesh of their skin, a dull rose glow began to
burnish the bluffs across the seething river. Great horizontal
rents opened in the purple clouds above the western horizon
and glowed scarlet like bloody wounds. Soon a slice of setting
sun looked through these rents and glinted in every droplet on
every twig and every blade of grass. And finally the sun's
entire orb was freed from behind its bars of cloud; and the
storm receding across the river made a vast, bruise-colored
backdrop for a perfect rainbow that seemed to straddle the
river. Even through her misery, Mary felt she was seeing the
work of a God whom she had not thought much of for many
weeks. She and Ghetel rolled up together in a wet cocoon of
wool blankets that night, hugging, skin to skin, and shivered
until the feeble furnaces of their hearts warmed their blood.

While they slept, bold chipmunks and squirrels crept close
and nibbled at the little pile of musty corn they had emptied
out of their blankets.

Mary rode first the next morning. Ghetel, walking barefooted on sparkling frost, led the horse. The ground was
blanketed with wet leaves of every hue from livid crimson to
flame-yellow, all their colors intensified by the wet and frost
and wan morning sunlight. Ghetel was singing something to
herself in Dutch, just above a whisper, her breath and the
mare's breath condensing. Mary had her blanket over her
shoulders, Indian-style; there was little enough corn to tote in
one blanket now. They had agreed that the one riding would
enjoy the blanket, as the one walking would generate her own
heat. But if Ghetel was warm she did not show it. Her skin
was raised in bumps like a plucked turkey's, and every few
seconds a great tremor would shake her from one end to the
other.

God, but she is a rugged old thing, Mary thought. But I'd best trade places with her and give her the blanket right quick or she's like t' come down with a grippe ere this day is out.

She hugged herself inside the blanket.

In just a minute, she thought.

Gusty weather came again the next day. Dark clouds sped over the hilltops trailing veils of rain. The wind was so strong that a cloud would pass from horizon to horizon in a minute's time. Shrubbery shook and rattled as if being slapped to and fro by an invisible giant hand. The air was always full of flying yellow leaves; what little remained of the foliage clung and clung against the wind but invariably was picked off and swirled away, and the trees were almost bare now, bare and gray and brown, and their stark, desolate nakedness had a chilling effect on the spirit. Mary pondered on this as she walked along. I do believe the sight o' them autumn leaves, like the colors o' flame, kept my poor soul warm just like watchin' a fire will do f'r a body . . .

And she found herself thinking as she rode, looking down at Ghetel, who was at that moment walking and leading the mare:

If only these blankets was red, a nice hot red instead o' this cold gray, we'd be a sight warmer. . .

And then she smiled at her fancy.

Y're goin' a bit daft there, girl. Best y' get down an' let ol' Ghetel sit up here a-rockin' and a-daydreamin' a spell . . .

That day they came to another river mouth too wide and deep—and cold—to wade across. Ghetel gazed at the far shore and groaned. These detours seemed to frustrate her even more than they did Mary—perhaps because, unlike Mary, she did not know the lay of the land, and every new stream was just another unexpected obstacle, as if God were spitefully throwing down new rivers in their path every day to make their way longer.

So they turned and started up this latest river.

In skirting a marsh in this river's valley, they found a stand of browning arrowleaf stalks. They tied the horse nearby and spent an hour wading in the cold ooze, feeling with their toes for the tubers, stooping to pull them up when they found some. They gathered five or six pounds of them, put them in the bundle with the musty corn and continued upstream.

This river was wide and was running fast with brown water from the recent rains. It appeared they would have a long trek up its banks before finding a place to cross. And all the while they were aware, in the back of their minds, of the O-y-o River, their guide through the wilderness, dropping farther and farther behind them.

They tried to make a meal of the arrowhead tubers that evening, encamped under an overhanging ledge with the flooding river roaring noisily a few feet below. The raw tubers had an awful, woody, bitter taste. "If'n we had a pot t' bile 'em in," Mary grimaced, "I swear right now I'd risk buildin' a fire to do it."

But they *were* filling.

They had traveled perhaps twenty-five miles up this name-less river, when, the next day, Ghetel pointed down and cried, "Look! a britch!"

At a place where the river thundered down over a kind of rock step, a mass of driftwood had become lodged. It extended all the way across the river, a tangle of bleached logs and limbs and roots, and indeed was like a bridge. The brown water rushed through and under it, but it stayed, a great knot of debris.

"We can cross here, neh?" Ghetel urged with a happy, yellow-toothed grin.

But Mary looked at it dubiously. It seemed fine enough, but . . .

"Wait now," she said. "I'm getting a bad feeling about this. It don't look none too sure t' me, somehow."

Ghetel turned a darkening face on her, then pointed up-stream. "Eh, how far you vant to go up dis riffer, eh? Look!"

Above the driftwood bridge the river was still deep and swift. They might have to go another twenty-five miles before finding a fording place, maybe farther. And that would mean fifty or more back down the other bank to regain the O-y-o. That was an awful prospect.

And here was this bridge, as if put here by Providence to save them three or four days' travel.

But the bridge nonetheless gave her a premonition of dread. And she was learning to take her premonitions seriously.

"Vatch me," Ghetel was saying. She had gone down to the river's edge. She reached out, grasped a protruding limb for a handhold, put one foot on one of the logs. Then, cautiously, she lifted the other foot off the shore. She stood a moment on the end of the bridge, then began flexing her knees, rocking her weight on the lodgment, testing its solidity. Then she bounced more violently, crying, "Vatch! Vatch! It stays!"

Don't, Mary thought. It seemed too reckless a taunting of Fate.

But it held. Ghetel backed onto the shore, grinning. "Easy," she said. "See?"

"Aye, for us, p'raps. But a horse canno' walk logs, Ghetel."

"I t'ink she can do. It is like a britch, May-ry. Like a britch."

"I have this feeling. . ."

"Go to the deffil wit' a feelink!" Ghetel's face was growing stormy with impatience. "If you don' come over here, I do it alone! Yah, ve'll see! Who need you and your feelink!"

"No, Ghetel, please. . ."

"Yah, by damn! Or I go alone!"

"Then let's test it all the way across first."

"Yah! I do." The old woman, bent upon showing what a lark it would be, swung lightly up onto the driftwood again. She walked the logs lightly, and found a handhold every yard or so. In two minutes she stood on the opposite shore, holding her arms up gaily and grinning. Then she hopped onto the driftwood again and came back. "You see?"

"But the horse. . ."

"It is like a britch."

And so Mary gave in. She and Ghetel combined their strength to pull the horse down to the water's edge. It did not want to go. It dug its hooves in on the bank and refused to step onto the logs. Mary looked into its panicky brown eyes and her heart squeezed.

"Move, beast," Ghetel panted.

It would not.

"Eh, then, ve shall see," Ghetel growled. "You pull, May-ry. I put a stick up dis animal's hinder and she *vill* go, ve see."

She got one of the hickory lances and went around behind the mare. Gently at first, then harder as the horse continued to balk, she jabbed at its rump with the point. The abject terror and pain in the mare's eyes made Mary want to cry. But she talked to it and cajoled and encouraged and pulled at the neck-halter with one hand while hanging onto a limb with another. At last the mare yielded and took a step forward.

She got a good footing on the log jam with her forehooves and, finding something under her, resisted a little less. But she was still very skittish. The water roaring underfoot was frightening her and Mary did not blame her.

Ghetel roared a curse or command in Dutch and jabbed the hickory point straight into the animal's anus. With a terrible whinny, the mare gave up the shore and scrambled so suddenly onto the logjam that she almost knocked Mary off into the river.

Now Mary inched backward along the logs, reaching back for handholds, pulling at the halter, trying to ignore the rush of the water below, the swaying and trembling of the driftwood jam under the horse's weight.

The animal was surprisingly sure-footed, and was coming along now. Whenever she stopped or threatened to panic, Ghetel would prod her on with the now bloody lance, and she would lunge forward a step. These quick moves were dangerous, but obviously the mare was not going to progress without them.

They were midway across the jam now, with a mere fifteen feet to go.

Suddenly, both the mare's forefeet broke through the matted driftwood and into the water. She began neighing pitifully and throwing her head about. Her rump was high; her chest rested on the logs. She strained with her rear haunches, trying to lift her forelegs up and out. This futile thrashing lasted only seconds. A hind hoof slipped sideways off a log and poked through the debris, then the other hind leg plunged through on the other side of the log. A broken limb had penetrated her right side just behind the ribs; it was impossible to tell how far. The mare was screaming, her chest resting on the drift with her legs in the water. The water under the horse was running with red stain.

Mary cried encouragements to her, unconscious commands and entreaties, beginning to sob, hauling upward on the halter as if she could extricate the shrieking mare's legs by sheer force of lifting. Ghetel stood on the logs behind the horse, her ugly face working with disbelief and anguish. She began shouting in Dutch. She dropped her lance and grabbed the horse's tail and pulled up on it with all her might.

The log jam trembled with their exertions and the steady pressure of the river's flow. Limbs and logs shifted and groaned. "It's going to break!" Mary cried. The horse kept throwing its head about and screaming its piteous scream, and trying with futile spasms of movement to free itself. With each movement the wound in her side was torn wider and deeper.

And now the old woman was climbing past the horse, motioning frantically at Mary as she came toward her. "Get off! Get off!" Mary turned away from the beloved beast and scrambled on all fours to the shore. She stood shaking and crying as Ghetel jumped to the ground beside her. She couldn't look at the suffering beast now. She clapped her hands over her ears to shut out its pitiful cries. She looked at the ground and cried helplessly at this latest great loss. Ghetel stood making helpless gestures with her hands and looking back and forth between Mary and the horse. Finally she said, "Wait," and climbed back onto the logjam and crept toward the animal.

The mare suddenly fell still, as if trusting this person to come help her. She kept repeating a low, wet nickering deep in her chest.

Ghetel edged alongside her and lifted the blanket-bundle off the mare's back. Then she started forward again, pausing beside the horse's head to untie the halter and bell-rope.

She brought these things, all their belongings, ashore. She closed a big hand firmly over Mary's upper arm and started to propel her downstream away from the dying animal. Suddenly it began shrieking and tossing its head again.

"Oh, stop it, *stop it!*" Mary sobbed. "I can't bear it any more!"

They were a hundred yards down the east bank now but the horse's cries were still audible over the rush of the river. Mary felt as if she would hear them when she was a hundred miles away.

About an hour's walk downstream they stopped to rest. Mary felt ten times as weak as she had felt before. It was as if they had lost not only the horse's own strength but also an equal amount of strength the horse had given them just by being.

They sat on a black, rotting log. Mary had stopped crying. She sat with her face in her hand for a while and then turned a cold visage to Ghetel.

"You are a stupid old woman."

Ghetel winced and glanced down, but then raised her eyes to Mary's and reached over to pat her on the shoulder, saying:

"Eh, now. No. Ve could not do any help."

Mary pulled away from the extended hand. After a moment, she said:

"You told me you were going to listen to me when I feel something."

Ghetel nodded. "Yah."

"But you wouldn't listen."

"Eh, now, May-ry. Forget dis." Her voice was a little brusque now. She was sorry about the horse and she knew she was responsible and did not care to have the blame for that added to her present miseries.

"You said right after I felt them Indians a-comin' that you'd listen to me from that time on. . ."

Ghetel jumped up and stood before Mary with both fists raised over her head. "Eh?" she roared. "Eh, May-ry Inkles? I t'ink I listen to you too much already! If I did not listen to you I vould be in a varm Indian house! With a fire and a full belly!"

"Aye, y' would be, eh? A belly full o' squash an' dog meat, that's what full of!"

"A belly *full,* anyway! My stomach dun't care vhether the meat said 'roff, roff' or 'moooo' when it was alive!"

"Don't it now?" Mary snapped bitterly. "But it was 'ee complainin' about th' Indian victuals, not I. 'Twas 'ee blatherin' about all y'r fine kitchens an' y'r fine Dutchy dinners an' all. . ."

And while Mary was railing on this way, falling back, as she did when upset, into her mother's brogue, while she was pouring out all this grief and anger over the loss of the horse, the old woman had begun to pat her shoulder, and had sat down beside her on the log again.

And when Mary's invective had run down and some of the hurt had eased out of her breast, she became aware that her head was leaning on the old woman's shoulder, and Ghetel was gently stroking down her matted hair and saying, 'A gut girl now. A gut girl. And you're all I haf in dis vorld, May-ry Inkles. All I haf."

CHAPTER
15

THEY RAN OUT OF CORN. THEY ATE THE LAST OF IT ON THE O-Y-O River bank at a place where the river course came down from the north and went a long way west. Mary recognized the place, even though the foliage of summer was now gone and the evening sky was full of marching black clouds instead of sunset: It was the place where the Indians had stopped to gaze down the broad valley and she had caught Captain Wildcat staring at her in that strange and smug way as if she had been a good possession of his. She did not try to tell Ghetel about it. Ghetel cared about nothing now but that they had eaten the last of their corn.

They had detoured around two more rivers and two creeks since the one where they had lost the horse two days before.

Now they sat looking down the great, slate-gray river and held their blankets over their heads and clenched tight at their throats to keep them from being blown off by the relentless wind. Finally, unsettled by Ghetel's dark and lifeless stare, Mary ventured:

"I know where we are." She forced a smile. "We're just about exactly halfway home, accordin' to my reckonin'."

Ghetel said nothing for a while. Then: "Eh. Half."

"Y'd not've thought we could come this far, would 'ee?"

"Nor go farder."

"Oh, yes." She tried to be cheerful. She knew that Ghetel was now blaming her for their unspeakable circumstances, and she could see that the old woman was nurturing that resentment with every painful step they took and with every hollow twinge of hunger she felt, and that the resentment would surely only get worse from here on because food was getting to be almost impossible to find, and within a day or two they would be leaving the relatively easy terrain of the O-y-o valley and turning up into the steep and boulder-strewn valley where the waters of the New River twisted through the towering mountains of the Allegheny range. "I reckon we've walked all in all about three hundred fifty mile in less'n three weeks," she went on. "Don't that make 'ee feel some'at proud? It does me, I'll say as much!"

"Eh!"

"Come on, then. There's still an hour o' light. Then we'll find us a nice cozy place out o' this wind, an' we'll get all snug an' I'll do the kindness to y'r feet, eh? What say'ee t' that?" She rose, hurting in every joint but making herself smile. She stood leaning on her hickory spear. Under her blanket, in her knotted rope belt, hung the tomahawk. Its cold steel head against her naked flank made her shudder. But she did not want Ghetel to carry it. Since the loss of the horse, she had little faith in Ghetel. Ghetel would probably lose it, as she had lost her lance, and as she had lost them the horse. And they could not afford to lose the tomahawk. They simply would be out of all luck if they lost the tomahawk.

She reached down. "Up, now, dear," she said.

Reluctantly, the surly old woman took the hand and

groaned to her feet. Her gray face under the dark cowl of the blanket was full of hollows now, and in the gloom, with strands of wild, dirty white hair blowing over her face, she looked like a spectre, like a witch. The muffled bell hung on the strap around her neck.

Nay, Mary thought. She's but a poor crone thinkin' she's reached th' end of it all. A marvel that she can still get up. I'm a-goin' back t' Will. There's strength f'r me in that. But what's she got t' look to, other'n a fat hot Dutch supper someday?

"That's m' good darlin', it is," Mary encouraged, turning her and starting to lead her up the river bank. "Oh, I d'know what I sh'd do without 'ee!"

They had not found a bite of anything edible by the next evening and it was then that the old woman started talking about the horse.

The sun had at last broken through the cold dark cloud-cover, just in time to glow like a dying campfire between the river bluffs downstream. It reflected in Ghetel's eyes as she looked back down the river. She suddenly started spewing a stream of Dutch invective so bitter and unexpected that Mary stopped where she was and came back to stand in front of the old woman. With the red gleam in her eyes she looked like a madwoman. "What is this?" Mary demanded.

"Dat horse. How vas I so *stupid?*"

"Nah, nah, Ghetel. It's a past thing. I'm sorry too, but we tried and it failed. Don't blame y'self. . ."

The old woman was clenching her fist against her chin and the fist was trembling. "No! I mean the *meat!* The meat."

"What? What meat?"

"The horse! The *horse!*"

Mary blinked and stepped back. "Oh, no. Don' say. . ."

"Ve should haf meat! Dat horse dies. Ve should haf. . ." She made a sudden motion with her fist as if striking the poor beast between the eyes with a tomahawk. Then she turned to Mary with eyes ablaze. "Listen," she hissed, and her mouth worked into a ghastly smile. "Gif me the ax, and I go back and get us meat. Meat!"

Mary laid a hand on her wrist. The old woman's arm was

tense and trembling. Mary licked her lower lip and tried
to figure out how to talk to her. This was a new kind of thing
to deal with. "Dear," she said, in a soothing way as if trying
to teach something to a child, "now, we've come three days
a-walkin' since that sorry day. We've come along good, an' I
wager we've done fifty miles. Now, we're no such fools, you
an' me, as t' go back fifty miles f'r a poor nag. Th' buzzards
'as got 'er by now, anyway, if not a panther. . ."

"All dat *meat!* Gif me the little ax; I go back. . ." She
snatched suddenly at Mary's blanket, tried to claw it open
and get the tomahawk. Her hands were strong and she pulled
the blanket away and Mary was swept by the cold wind. She
spun away, and got her hickory lance between her and Ghetel,
stopping her.

"And besides," Mary continued, more firmly now, "we
loved that horse. She was our friend, give to us by God when
we needed 'er. That's why we never thought t' eat 'er. Never
even *thought* on't. . ."

Ghetel's face set in a strange, cunning resignation. Wherever her reason was, she could comprehend that at this moment, Mary was armed and she was not. But a shrewd little
smile stayed on her face as she seemed to acquiesce.

"Now if'n y' see my way o' thinkin'," Mary went on in a
level voice, "kindly hand me back m' blanket there, dear, as
I'm likin' t' freeze. . ."

Ghetel gave her the blanket and Mary draped herself in it
and smiled as if everything was nice and ordinary, but she
stayed on her guard and kept the spear at hand. They found a
bower carpeted thick with leaves in the lee of a rock outcropping, and Mary massaged the old woman's feet for a long
time. Then they rolled up in their separate blankets and about
an hour later Mary went to sleep waiting for Ghetel to go to
sleep.

When Mary woke the next morning before dawn, the old
woman was gone. She had taken her blanket and the
tomahawk and Mary knew she had set out to go back fifty
miles to butcher their old friend the horse.

Mary knelt in her blanket for a few minutes, trying to figure

out what to do. She was furious with the old woman, who had
let the misery in her guts overpower the reason in her head
and the nobility in her soul. For a moment Mary thought
about simply forgetting the crazy hag and pressing on alone
toward home. She still had her blanket and her spear. The
loss of the tomahawk was a serious matter. But not having the
old woman to feed and humor and contend with would give
her much greater freedom and probably much less trouble.
Ghetel was tough and magnificent, but she was erratic and
sometimes threatening, and could not be depended on to act
wisely.

But for those very reasons, the old woman would surely get
herself lost or killed or would go completely crazy running
around in circles desperately seeking food.

Mary imagined the old woman attacking a bear or something with the tomahawk to kill it for food and getting killed
herself instead; then she envisioned her getting lost and wandering alone in the forest screaming and mad.

And then, having imagined this, there was nothing to do
but get up and draw the blanket around herself and, using her
spear as a walking stick, go back down the river and try to
find Ghetel while there was still a chance of finding her. It
was terrible to go back even a step.

But the main reason she had to go back was because it was
unthinkable to proceed up into the dark mountains and roaring gorges and the cold, howling nights of the approaching
winter without a companion.

The sun was a white blot trying to look through the overcast, a quarter of the way up into the sky over the ridges,
when Mary heard a strange moaning and mumbling nearby at
her left. She had come perhaps three miles, and before her
was the mouth of a creek they had circumvented the day
before.

Mary paused and held her spear aslant before her, and
moved with stealth toward the sound. The leaves crushed
loudly under her feet. At the edge of the creek bank she
stopped and looked down.

In her drab blanket, Ghetel was as colorless as the sere

landscape and Mary would hardly have seen her but for the movement of her rocking.

The old woman sat on an exposed sycamore root at the creek's edge, rocking back and forth, groaning and talking to herself. The tomahawk lay on the ground a few feet away. Mary's pity flooded out to the old wretch.

Poor soul, she thought. Jus' couldn't face one o' these creek walkarounds alone.

Mary edged down the creek bank and picked up the tomahawk and put it in her belt. The old woman stopped crying and rocking and turned her face to Mary. It was wet with tears and snot and her nose was red. She showed no surprise at the sight of Mary. It was impossible to imagine where her mind was. Mary extended her hand. "Come, dear. Y' been goin' the wrong way."

However much or little the old woman comprehended, she apparently had forgotten about or given up hope of finding the horse. More important, she seemed to understand that she must follow Mary. Without Mary, the wilderness was utterly pathless and there was no such thing as direction. Mary was like a compass needle, steadily pointing toward somewhere, and if the old woman had learned anything in her morning alone it was the utter emptiness of having no guide. It was perhaps a worse emptiness than that of hunger. And so Ghetel was compliant and followed Mary, followed her and stayed close, as they continued northward along the winter-gray O-y-o and came at last to the place where the mountain river came down and emptied into it.

Mary recognized it at once, despite the change the season had wrought. There was that wide river mouth coming down through the narrow but lush bottomland, between those steep and dark-flanked mountains. There on the opposite side of the mouth was that spacious grove where they had camped, and where the medicine brave had made the hickory frame to carry the baby girl in . . .

She put that thought of the baby out of her mind quickly and led Ghetel southeastward to the place where the Indians had hidden the canoes after coming across. It would be good if we could find a canoe, she thought. It was not that she

wanted to cross the river here, particularly; this side of the
valley looked as easy to walk as the far side, and if they would
stay on this bank for a while, they would have the river
between themselves and the Indian road. But the river was
broad and slow here, and going up it in a canoe would be a
needed relief from walking, a chance perhaps for their
bruised and bleeding bare feet to rest and heal. Also she knew
that a canoe turned upside down on a river bank, with a deep
bed of leaves under it, would make a good shelter against cold
rains. November, according to her calendar of knots, was but
a week or so ahead, and she knew what November could be
like in the high and harsh Alleghenies.

But here again she found no canoes. If there were any
canoes at the mouth of this tributary, they were on the far
shore and it was useless to think of them.

She came back to the place where Ghetel squatted rocking
on her haunches and gazing forlornly across the river mouth.
"Eh, now, Ghetel. They's no canoes here, so it's time we get
on our shanks an' git."

The old woman shook her head slowly and extended a
gnarled hand toward the river. "Vat use? Ve nefer find a place
to cross dis big 'un."

"Ah! But y' forgot what I told 'ee! We don't have t' cross
this'n. We go up this'n all th' way t' home!"

Ghetel looked up at her as if this were beyond comprehension, or was perhaps just a ruse to get her on her feet.
"Home," she said low and flat, as if dismissing the word.

"Aye! *Home!* Trust me now, dear. I know the way."

I hope I know the way, she thought, remembering the
tortuous route along creeks and over ridges and game trails
and under cliffs by which the Indians had brought her down.
And interspersed among the memorized landmarks in her
mind there were those blank spaces: the hours, sometimes
whole days, when she had been so absorbed in grief and the
pain of coming childbirth that she had not been able to observe the route at all.

But I know the way. Far enough up this river, regardless of
the shortcuts th' savages carried me over, I'll come to places I
know.

"Aye," she repeated, fervently believing now that she was telling the truth, "I sure do know the way. Come along. *O ten times te—en times ten a—way. . ."*

And it made her voice sound so good that old Ghetel actually smiled as she unfolded her creaking bones and stood up.

CHAPTER
16

JOHNNY DRAPER LEANED CLOSE TO WILL INGLES AND SAID IN his ear: "This 'ere Snake Stick's sour as gooseberry vinegar. Reckon whiskey'd sweet 'im up a mite?"

Will looked at Snake Stick. The deep furrows in the Indian's cheeks ran down beside and then under the downturned corners of his mouth, and there were two deep vertical creases between his brows. A man would have to frown for forty years straight to get such a grouchy set to his face as that, Will thought. "I don't know," he murmured to Johnny. "It could just as likely craze 'im an' make 'im do what he'd like to do to us."

"English not make low-talk to each other," Snake Stick warned, his eyes looking even harder. "English talk straight to Snake Stick." He thumped himself on his massive hard chest. Then he leaned forward, his face lighted from below by the little smokeless council fire. Twenty men of the village sat behind him, making a semicircle in the lodge, looking as if they were competing among themselves to appear as grim as Snake Stick, who now asked:

"English say word whiskey?"

"Aye," Will replied, thinking: Lordy, but they got a keen ear f'r that word.

"English give Snake Stick whiskey." The chief seemed to

be very intrigued that Will Ingles' name sounded so much like "English," and had been addressing him disdainfully as "English" since the white men's arrival here this afternoon.

Will nodded and delved into the duffel pouch he carried slung by a strap over his shoulder, and brought out a pewter flask covered in leather. He pulled the stopper and handed the flask to Snake Stick. He could tell by the way the chief reached for it that he had quite a weakness for it; the Indian was trying to look casual but his cold eyes were suddenly blazing. He put it to his mouth and sucked hard on it, thus taking a lot of whiskey in what appeared to be a short swig. He might have been fooling his red comrades, but Will Ingles had watched men drink enough to know that Snake Stick had probably diminished the contents by a good third. The chief put the flask down on the floor in front of him and wiped his mouth on the back of his hand. His eyes were watering. He said:

"English have more whiskey on horse?"

"That I have."

"Snake Stick could take it from English and English could not do anything to stop him," the chief said with an arrogant half-smile.

"No," said Will. "Snake Stick could not."

The chief's eyes narrowed hard. "English say no?"

"I know the red man's honor will not let him rob a guest. I admire this in the red man."

The chief's eyes fell and then came back to Will's. "But English would give Snake Stick much whiskey, for his braves to drink." With two turns of his head he indicated those who sat around him.

"Yes, I'd do that . . . if Snake Stick would promise to try to help me in this matter with the Shawnee. If not, then no. I'll give whiskey to a Cherokee who'll be my friend."

The chief blew a breath so boozy that Will envisioned it bursting into flame over the council fire, then picked up the flask and took another powerful pull. Christ's good name, Will thought, I better get this heathen's word in five more minutes, or 'e won't be fit to give it. And he was not entirely sure he could hang anything on Snake Stick's honor anyway.

It had been Will's experience in life that a bitter man's word of honor was not as good as that of an amiable man.

"English will bring whiskey for my men," Snake Stick announced.

"Gander Jack," Will said to the guide without looking at him, "would y' trot out an' fetch me one o' them demijohns?" He felt the guide rise and leave behind him. He heard the shuffling of many moccasins as Jack left, and realized that the darkness in the lodge behind him had been filling with people. People coming in very stealthily. And he knew too that they would not be coming in unless Snake Stick was permitting it. He fought down a shudder. This Cherokee seemed a treacherous wretch indeed, and Will admitted the possibility that he and Johnny, and maybe even Gander Jack, might well be enjoying the final confabulation of their careers.

Jack returned with the demijohn. He put it on the ground in front of Will and looked at him with raised eyebrows, a signal whose particular significance Will could only guess at. Wish this dang Snake Stick didn't hear English, Will thought. I'd sure like to confer with Jack here an' see what 'e thinks.

Will thumbed the wax off the jug's neck and pulled the stopper. Snake Stick pointed to the jug and then to Will and Johnny and Jack. Will hoisted the demijohn with both hands and took a pull. Then Johnny took a long, gurgling drink, passed it to Jack and sighed, licking his lips. Jack then came forward and gave it to Snake Stick, who sampled it heartily and passed it to the brave on his right with some Cherokee talk that Will guessed to mean save some for me. The braves passed it around while Snake Stick's black eyes flashed with volatile thoughts.

The Cherokee's eyelids drooped a little now, making his malevolent gaze look shifty. Will's doubts about his trustworthiness increased.

"English listen: Snake Stick is not happy you come here and ask this thing." He swiped his hand downward. "Snake Stick will not be proud to go to his Shawnee brothers and speak for English. The Shawnee will say to Snake Stick, 'Why do you talk with English?' They will say, 'If you are so near English to talk, you should strike him.'"

"Then I reckon you would answer, 'Because the Cherokee are not at war with the English.'"

"They are not at this day," Snake Stick grumbled. "Tomorrow yes. Snake Stick this day is at war with the English in his heart."

Will's nostrils distended and he said: "I remind you that today I'm a guest in your lodge, and that y're a guest in my jug, big feller, an' I think we'd do well as each other's guest not to talk hostile." Will heard Gander Jack take a quick breath behind him, but he had borne about enough of Snake Stick's insolence and it was hard to remain diplomatic. "If my whiskey makes Snake Stick snap like a cur dog, maybe I'll just cut Snake Stick off from my whiskey, eh?"

The Indian's eyes flashed. But he was enough of a chief to understand the protocol of guests and hosts, and so contained himself. Gander Jack looked back and forth between them. He saw that Mr. Ingles had actually gotten away with that bold talk, and he looked at him with considerable respect. Still, the exchange had done anything but put him at ease. This was a formidable white man who could look and talk and act like one of those chiefs in the white man's Bible, but he was in a place where one could be too formidable for his own good.

Will Ingles said now: "Even if you're at war with English men in your heart, I hope you're not at war with English women and children. Your Shawnee brothers killed the mother of my woman, and they killed my brother's baby son. They took away my woman and my sons. I do not care what you feel in your heart about the English, but sure it's no brave deed t' murder and kidnap their women and children. Ask y'r Shawnee brothers if their Great Spirit would smile on them for this. Ask 'em if the Frenchmen are better people than the English if they hire red men to make war on those who cannot fight."

Snake Stick had glowered at Will Ingles through this, and now he put his hands on his thighs and took a deep breath and made ready to debate. He was gathering answers from back in his head, where the whiskey was working.

"The French men do not fear the Great Spirit. The French

men have medicine men of their Great Father. Wear black squaw-clothes. They forgive the Shawnee for what he must do in war."

"What in blue thunder is he talkin' about?" Johnny asked.

"Priests," Will said. "I heard Colonel Washington tell Jim Patton about 'em. The French make odd use of 'em. . ."

"English not make low-talk," the Cherokee warned again.

"I was just a-sayin' the French make ill use of their Great Spirit," Will said to Snake Stick. "You'd do better to stay with your own."

The chief thought on this and chose not to argue it. He picked up the jug and took another deep swig.

"You drink my whiskey," Will said, "so I reckon you're willin' to talk business with me."

"English talk."

"Good, then. When you go up to your Shawnee brethren, if y' please, ask after a woman named Mary Ingles—*Mary Ingles* —and her two little sons. And a woman named Bettie Draper. *Bettie Draper.* They were taken from a settlement near the upper—Jack, what is it they call the New River?"

"Chi-no-da-cc-pc."

"Chi-no-da-ce-pe," said Will. "Far up by Blue Ridge."

"Mer English," the chief said. "Mer English with two sons. And other woman. . ."

"Bettie Draper. Can you remember those? And there was a man took with 'em: Henry Lenard. I would buy him back too."

Snake Stick shook his head. "Not buy English man back. Shawnee at war with English men."

"Ask anyway. Henry Lenard was not a soldier. He was a hunter."

"A hunter can be a soldier. Not sell back."

"Let the Shawnee decide who they'll sell back. I'm only askin' you to carry my offer," Will said, trying to mask his impatience.

"How much is English offer?"

"I'll show you." Will leaned forward on his crossed legs and stood up. "Jack, m'lad, help me bring in the packs." They went out through the crowd of Indians, who parted to let them reach the door. The sky was starry and the air was crisp outside the lodge where the horses were tied. "How're we doin', Jack?" Will asked. He had been so scared at first that he'd thought he'd mess himself, but getting mad at that god-damned mean Indian had braved him up. He was almost having fun.

"If he don't kill us, we're doin' better than I'd a' thought," Jack muttered.

They unstrapped the packs and carried them into the lodge, and spread their goods out where Snake Stick could see them all. His warriors and chieftains crowded close around and admired the treasures. Their eyes were covetous but their faces remained closed. Will tried to look at the stuff from their point of view. He had invested everything he had in this junk.

After a while the chief raised his eyes, and Will was sure he had memorized every item, the brown liquor jugs in particular. "How much for Snake Stick to do this?" he said.

Will thought quickly. "All that lays on this blanket," he said. "Or, all the whiskey in these."

"Snake Stick could take all this from English, not go to Shawnee." Again he was taunting.

"I have to have faith in the honor of Snake Stick. And if you betrayed me thataway, all the Cherokee septs would soon know. 'Cause I'd tell 'em of my disappointment."

"Dead English could tell no stories to Cherokees."

"I am your guest."

"After you leave Snake Stick's town, you not guest. My braves could silence you."

"I reckon they could. But some of your braves would have to die to silence me. And the rest would know you lacked honor. You could never silence *that*." Will was sweating inside his clothes. He knew such talk was dangerous, but he felt that boldness, not timidity, was the only answer to Snake Stick's taunts, or threats, or whatever they were. He doesn't intend to do such a thing anyway, or he'd be a fool to talk about it, Will thought. He's just a-testin' my resolve and my wits.

"If Snake Stick take all this to his Shawnee brothers, and they say is not enough for Mer English and Bettie Dra-pah?"

"Then you bring it all back here and send for me, and we'll talk again." He was banking on the hope that this Cherokee would be persuasive on his behalf, rather than haul all this up to the O-y-o country and back in vain, or simply do nothing and make himself a rich man. However well or badly Snake Stick might do, Will could see that this transaction would take until next summer at least. His dear ones well might have been killed or lost or ruined by then.

They might be lost beyond all findin' already, he thought. Or changed beyond all redemption.

But y' can't let yourself think like that, he told himself. Y' can't do a thing without faith.

Even if havin' faith is just a matter of foolin' y'rself as long as y'can.

CHAPTER 17

MARY SAT ON FROSTY GROUND AND STARED AT THE BRIGHT COLors of her toes. They were the only colorful things she had seen for two days in the grim and shadowy valley. The colorful toes glowed through her lassitude and held her attention.

They were gray-blue with bruises and there was bright red blood oozing out around her toenails.

Ghetel's feet were the same.

Now that they had entered this valley, the luxury of walking through the level, grassy, leaf-strewn O-y-o bottomlands was a memory. Here every mile they walked was a gauntlet designed to bruise and abrade their heels and ankles and cut their soles and stave their toe-bones. The bottomlands and creekbeds were littered with boulders and splintered logs, jumbled stones and pebbles, the rock debris and forest trash that had been sliding down the mountainsides since Creation.

They had not eaten anything for four days except a handful of acorns they had found under an oak at the top of a bluff they had climbed to shortcut a bend in the river.

They had made several such shortcuts. Perhaps they had saved themselves as much as five miles altogether, but in their weakened condition it seemed that they had added five vertical miles. They would pull themselves up the steep hillsides by roots and rocks and shrubs, pausing every twenty feet or so to hug the slopes and breathe against the ground until they could raise the strength to go on a few more feet. Then, after resting a few minutes on the ridges with the raw wind whipping them, they would start down the opposite slopes, more sliding than walking, slamming into tree trunks and stone outcrops, slashing and bruising their flesh and tearing their dresses. Now even their precious blankets were growing tattered at the edges, and had snag-holes in them.

Ghetel had fallen into a profound and gloomy silence in these last two days, speaking only to answer direct questions and sometimes not even then. Now Mary looked up from her own pulsating, stinging, aching feet and glanced over at the old woman, who was contemplating her own. Suddenly Ghetel turned her head and caught Mary's eyes with a malevolent stare and there was a trembling grimace contorting her mouth.

"I listened to *you*," she said.

Ah, Lord above, Mary thought, give me a little miracle, for I've got to try to cheer the old thing up yet again.

"Aye, dear," she said, forcing a benign smile. "Y've listened to me, an' we've come more'n three hundred miles with no hurt t' speak of, eh?"

"*I* hurt."

"Eh, well. I feel same as you, not m' very best ever. But I'm whole, an' y're the same. An' damn'ee, we're no squaws. Keep in mind, Ghetel m' darlin', we're free as birds!"

Ghetel looked incredulous at this cheery lecture. Finally she said, indignantly:

"Free as *birds?* Eheh! You know how free is a bird? Alvays a bird goes here for a seed, and he goes dere for a gnat. And dat's *all* he does in his whole day! And he nefer yet gets enough. So dere for your freedom of a bird! Hah!"

Mary was delighted by this outburst. So the old woman's brain was still alive after all! She grinned into Ghetel's wrinkled scowl. "Well, y'see then! We really *are* as free as birds, then, ain't we?"

And Ghetel, after scowling for a moment, actually laughed. It *was* a little miracle.

They had come to recognize hickory, walnut and oak trees from a distance, and would go to them if they were accessible. The season for berries and wild grapes was past, but there were still nuts to be found—sometimes.

Now they were toiling up a steep, rock-studded slope toward a pair of likely looking hickories, a few yards above the river, whose shaggy bark made them conspicuous. Mary had given Ghetel her pointed lance to use as a walking-staff, as the old woman seemed to need its support more than she did. As they climbed, their breath was shallow and harsh and their feet dragged through the rustling leaves on the slope. It was a dry morning, without wind for a change, and except for the sounds of their progress and the wet murmur of the river below, a vast silence filled the valley. The winter-stripped trees were stark, and without foliage to screen it, the hard angularity of the terrain was forbidding: mountainsides tilting skyward, V-shaped ravines full of mossy boulders and detritus, huge fallen tree trunks strewn like jackstraws on the slopes and in the gullies or sometimes leaning half-fallen, hung in the branches of other trees. Some of the mountain ridges ended abruptly in sheer gray rock cliffs facing over the river. From some of these rock faces, water seeped and dribbled and darkened the rock, and in places, mountain springs and freshets would simply spew over the ramparts of such cliffs into space, disintegrating to mist before reaching the valley floor.

When Mary and Ghetel reached the hickories they found that squirrels had been working there before them. The ground below the trees was covered with husk-quarters and a few broken, yellow-brown nutshells, but most of the nuts were gone and the few that remained were marked by the dark little pinholes that meant worms had already invaded the nutmeats. The two women scratched over the leafy slope for fifteen minutes for a yield of a dozen good nuts. Like most of their recent disappointments, this gave Ghetel an excuse to glower in silent accusation at Mary.

They sighed and sat down on a lichen-mottled slab of limestone, to break the nutshells and get to the tiny breakfast within. Mary pulled the tomahawk from her belt and, before she could crack the first nut, Ghetel said:

"Gif me the ax."

"Mmm? Well, wait, I will. . ."

"Now. Me first."

Mary shrugged, and started to hand it to her, to humor her as she had done so often recently, when a sudden caution turned in the back of her mind. Ghetel already had the hickory spear, and if Mary gave her the tomahawk too, the unhappy old woman would be in possession of both their weapons.

Mary hesitated. She was surprised by the thought, by what seemed an unwarranted suspicion. Surely Ghetel would not hurt her. And yet she could not shake off that strange whisper of dread.

"Gif me," Ghetel said.

"Ahm, would y'give me the spear there first?" Mary asked, as nonchalantly as she could.

"W'y vant dat?"

"Because I, uhm, I want t' poke about in the leaves and see if I can find a few more nuts. This is scarce enough t' keep a bird alive." She offered the little bird joke to try to gauge Ghetel's frame of mind. But the old woman's eyes only narrowed and she held out her hand for the tomahawk. Mary held out her hand for the spear, and for a moment they sat there like that, the tentative uneasiness hanging between them, until Mary began to fancy that, even if this dread were only a product of her imagination, Ghetel could surely read it and *get* the idea of having both weapons, even if she had not been thinking of it before.

"Give me the stick, please," Mary said through such a tight throat it almost came out a whisper. She chose to call it the stick, not the spear, lest she betray her fears.

"Ach! Like a child!" Ghetel sighed, and picked up the stick and extended it to Mary. Point first, Mary noticed. And when she closed her hand around the stick, Ghetel closed her hand around the tomahawk handle. They exchanged them simultaneously.

Am I imagining all this? Mary wondered. If so, then indeed I must seem childish to 'er.

And as Ghetel bent over her hickory nuts with the tomahawk, Mary, with the familiar spear shaft in her hand, remembered the strange ghastly feeling she had had watching Ghetel tear off the little arms of the frog.

I'm a-gettin' too spooky, she thought. I'm a-gettin' feelings I needn't.

All the same, she resolved as she scratched among the leaves with the stick, looking for more nuts while keeping Ghetel in the corner of her eye, when she gives me back that tommyhock, I'm a-gonna cut me one o' these hickory saplin's hereabout an' make another spear.

The overcast sky that afternoon was swept a shimmering blue by a northerly breeze. The last rags of the sun-washed clouds disappeared up the valley, and the towering landscape, ridge after ridge, brightened from the colors of lead and pig-iron to silver and brass. The leafless trees were engraved in clarity: white and tan limbs, blue-black shadows. Cliff faces a mile away showed their flinty details as if they were close enough to touch.

The women were picking their way over the shingle at a river bend, gingerly placing each step of their bleeding feet among the rocks, when they heard a small clatter off to their left toward the river's edge and looked up and saw the fawn.

He was a little white-tail, a few months old, no bigger than a large dog but walking high on his stilt legs away from them, looking back over his shoulder at them, as much in curiosity as fear. He was out on the end of the shingle, almost at the water's edge. Both women at once seemed to realize that they had him cornered on the point, being between him and the woods; they heard each other gasp and whisper and each saw the other turn the point of her spear toward him. Mary could actually feel her little reserves of strength rushing to readiness in her breast and arms. Her hurting feet were nothing now as she turned toward the creature, staring unblinking at him.

This was their greatest stroke of fortune yet. A hundred times more wonderful than a cold catfish lying on a creekbed. This creature could feed them red meat for a week or more. His hide could make moccasins. In her mind Mary was already building a fire, risk or no risk, to cook their first meal, to cure the rest of the flesh for food to eat along the way. She held the spear-pole with both hands, angling it forward from her right hip. Instinctively, she and Ghetel were moving in concert, slowly closing the space between themselves and the animal, leaving no space for it to flee between them or around them.

The fawn stopped at the water's edge now, and turned its left flank to them, its face toward them as if it were watching one of them with each limpid brown eye. Its glistening black nose trembled as it tried to identify them by scent. Doubtless they were the first human beings it had ever seen. It still did not seem to have become afraid; it stretched its neck toward Ghetel, who was now ten feet from it. Mary was closing in on its flank. Another yard, she thought, and I can strike. Her hands were shaking and she was almost nauseated by her desire to feel the lance plunge into that soft hide of brown and black.

She heard a clatter of rock behind her, and at the same instant the fawn looked in that direction, seemed to comprehend its danger. It contracted an inch suddenly as its legs tensed for flight.

Mary lunged desperately at the fawn with her spear, falling forward, aware as she fell forward that something big and alive was running past her toward the fawn. Pain slammed through her knees and hip and arms as she fell on the rocky shingle. Hooves were clicking in the stones a few feet away and Ghetel was roaring something, and then the hooves rattled up the shore and away and something hard skittered along the rocks in that direction. Mary opened her eyes and looked back over her shoulder to see the fawn and a doe, its mother, springing like jackrabbits down the shore and then out of sight up a wooded slope. Ghetel's thrown spear slid to a stop among the rocks behind them.

Mary put her face against the pebbles and winced and sobbed and waited for the physical pain to go away.

She knew from her cold and empty feeling and from Ghetel's abandoned howls of frustration that the pain of their failure would be with them much longer than this of the stone bruises.

"Ah, Ghetel, this looks t'be a lovely, fat an' juicy 'un!"

"Eh, May-ry! And here! This one makes a feast for a kink!"

Mary was holding up a brown stalk she had pulled from the mud at the water's edge. Mud-clots and water dribbled from the gray root. Ghetel had just torn some nameless scrub-plant from between two rocks and was brushing dirt off its reddish-brown taproot.

They had been acting this way, desperately silly, since their failure to kill the fawn. For a few hours after its escape they had wailed and prayed and fallen into silent rages of frustration. Then, as if freed from any more hope of getting meat to eat, they had been swept with a wave of giddy cheerfulness—even Ghetel—and had returned to foraging for anything that grew within reach, whether they knew it was edible or not.

They had stopped at every bush that had large winter buds, and had picked off handfuls of the buds and eaten them like nuts as they stumbled along. It was like eating wood, though often more bitter. Some of the buds were too hard and fibrous to chew with their loosening teeth, so they would soften a mouthful of them in their saliva until they could chew them apart and swallow them. And they would pretend to each other this way that they were indescribably succulent and delicious. It was a dismal joke, but it was a joke and they would repeat it and repeat it and break out in high, wild laughter, the steep mountainsides echoing the laughter.

Then there had come a time when they could not bear to

chew another dry, tough bud, and they had remembered arrowleaf tubers. They could not find any arrowleaf stalks along these swift waters, but they began to see every sedge and cattail as a banner signaling the location of some succulent root or tuber below. They began pulling up whatever the ground would let loose of, and chopping out stubborn roots with the tomahawk. Then they would wash the dirt off the roots and rhizomes they had gathered, and continue upstream, mincing on their bruised and lacerated feet, making desperately high-spirited remarks about the delicacy of what they were eating.

Some of the roots really were not too bad. Some were crisp and could be snapped between the fingers like turnip flesh, and easily chewed, tasteless or bitter or spicy in flavor. Others, no matter how promising their shape or color, were nothing but wood. Some of these woody ones, however, had soft and palatable bark that could be gnawed off before the root was thrown away.

And others, they found, had tough and stringy bark that was bitter and inedible, but inside the bark there would be a whitish or yellowish core with the consistency of a potato or onion. The tomahawk was indispensable to the task of digging these and getting to the flesh of them. The women were spending perhaps two hours of every day on their hands and knees, going nowhere, digging and chopping and peeling roots and snapping off buds. The tomahawk blade grew nicked and blunt and less useful. Mary experimented with different kinds of stone and finally learned to identify the kinds that would whet steel. And so she was able to keep an edge on the weapon—nay, she thought, it's no more a weapon, it's a tool—despite its rough usage.

Every time she would pull up a new root or pull down a withered berry and start to put it in her mouth, she would think fleetingly: pray this'n's not poisonous. She had heard the menfolk talk about poisonous plants and berries and leaves, and she herself knew precious little about them. She would simply look at one a moment, and if she got no forebodings, she would try to eat it. She had learned to trust her forebodings.

And anyhow, she would think, the big poison of all is to have nothin', nothin', nothin' whatsoever in th' belly.

Poison or no, this diet included many things not intended for human innards, and the women were afflicted by a succession of fluxes and blockages, nauseas and intoxications they had never experienced before. One day both of them began vomiting helplessly, spewing up green fluid and undigested plant fiber, until they were empty, then continued to heave up nothing until they were too weak to get to their feet. They hardly slept at all that night, a night of cold moon and shimmering frost on the ground, owl-hoots fluting among the mountaintops, disturbed every few minutes by the sudden explosive spasms of their own retchings. By the next morning they were feverish and yellow-faced and covered with cold sweat, but the spasms had moved deeper, now clutching at their bowels until they would double over in agony and pray to die. By that afternoon they were stopping every few yards to excrete scalding gray waters. Then even that went dry while the need continued. Mary would stop, not hearing Ghetel's footsteps behind her, and would look back to see the old woman squatting on the trail redfaced, groaning as if in childbirth, trying to pass something that would not move. Then it would be Mary's turn to squat and strain without success.

And then there came the trouble with seeing. The river would suddenly turn black; cliffs would turn yellow. Mary would see two Ghetels, Ghetel two Marys. Once a huge blob of darkness with blazing white edges ballooned out of the ground in front of Mary and swallowed her with a rush of noise—hissing and voices—and then left her standing, weaving, in a landscape piercing white and shadowless as if illuminated by lightning.

And then these things, or some of these things, would cure themselves, and the women would be lucid and even-tempered again for a while, and would try to determine which of the roots or berries or buds had poisoned them, so that they could avoid them next time. But of course they had no way of knowing, as they had tried anything they could chew and swallow, so they were doomed to be overcome every few days by the same afflictions.

Despite all these miseries, Ghetel seemed to be having a resurgence of that brave good humor that had first incited Mary's admiration on the day of the running of the gauntlet.

Mary studied her from time to time and marveled. It's almost more than I can bear at my age, she thought. And she's two times my years at least.

Once the old woman must have been quite fat. Mary had noticed, when first seeing her at the Shawnee town, that her frame was massive and her flesh was loose as if she had lost perhaps thirty or forty pounds of fat between the time of her capture and the time of her arrival at the Indian village. Now there was nothing massive about her any more. She was burning her flesh up from inside. She was a framework of heavy bones draped with a hide that once had been full and now was empty. Wrinkled folds of flesh hung from her arms like thrums on the sleeve of a hunting coat. Her breasts drooped like empty wallets and the skin of her legs bagged and wrinkled at the knees and ankles like hose ten sizes too big. Her shanks were covered with running sores. Her nails were split and broken and caked with black dirt. Her unruly white hair was matted with twigs and leaves and filth, and much of it was coming out. There were sores around her ears and scalp where she had scratched constantly at lice, and from the end of her nose there perpetually hung a string of snot. Her eyes were sunk in wrinkled red pouches and her face was cadaverous. Somewhere once quite long ago, Mary had seen a face that looked like this, and she had been trying to remember where, and now suddenly with an awful jolt she remembered: In Philadelphia when she was a little girl, in the cellar of a house nearby, neighbors had discovered the body of a derelict woman who had crawled in there and died as much as a month before. Mary, with other children of the neighborhood, had had a horrified glimpse of the corpse as it was brought out to the dead wagon. It could have passed for Ghetel's twin.

Yet here was this wretch, looking fully like a cadaver that would not lie down; here in this roaring huge wilderness, in this valley where surely no white human had ever been before, except Mary and her fellow captives last summer, here was Ghetel, refusing to die yet, sitting here at this moment on a boulder tearing strips of cloth from the rags of her dress to wrap around her feet, still trying to take care of herself. The old muffled horse-bell still hung useless from her neck like a pendant.

"Ah," the old woman said, looking at her new footgear and then turning to smile at Mary. "Now I make a pair for you, eh?"

Mary choked back a sudden swollen ache in her throat, and the old hag-face shimmered beyond a film of tears. "Thankee, yes, Ghetel. Yes, God lov'ee!"

Mary stopped, aghast. She stood there leaning on her spear, an awful panic of confusion building up in her.

In their way lay a river mouth. It came out from between two mountains swift and deep, and swirled into the river they had been following. It was not just another river course to be detoured; worse, it was a river that did not exist among the succession of landmarks in her memory.

For days she had been watching the opposite bank for that whitish beach that would be the salt lick where she and Bettie and Henry had camped and worked on the way down. That salt lick was supposed to be her next landmark. She had not noted a river here.

"Vat?" asked Ghetel, who had stopped beside her.

I can't tell 'er. I mustn't tell 'er I think I've got us lost. She'd kill me sure.

"Vat?" Ghetel repeated.

"Oh, m'dear. Just another tiresome walk-around, is all." She forced herself to smile. "But we sh'll make quick work of it, shan't we? Shan't we, old friend? By now we sure know what t' do aboot rivers in our way, don't we?"

And so they turned south and west, though the compass in her head said south and east. And as they climbed over cold mossy boulders and snarls of driftwood, she ransacked her memory; she tried to remember where they might have taken a wrong turn; she tried to keep from lying down and giving up.

The dark swift water rushed by, almost beneath their feet. Mary looked down into it with a dreadful longing.

She was thinking how simple and quiet it would be, how easy it would be to terminate this infinity of miseries, to find eternal rest from this struggle, to take one step sideways off this rock, into this nameless river.

CHAPTER
18

AS IF REFLECTING HER SOMBER DOUBT, THIS CANYON BLACK-ened as they climbed, crawled and hobbled up its twisting course among the mountains. Much of the rock debris under-food was black, and there were wide strata of gleaming black rock along the cliff faces. A heavy overcast had ended the spell of bright cold weather, deepening the gloom of the valley, dulling the details of the forests. The water looked like ink. Ghetel's brief period of good humor seemed to be gutter-ing out like a candle under the influence of this hellish gorge and Mary's own dark preoccupation. They went along in grim, laborious silence, hearing only their rasping breath, the sliding and grinding of shale and rock underfoot, the ominous, hollow rushing of the dark river and the moan of the wind in the trees high on the hillsides. The leaves had fallen out of Ghetel's beloved bell, and now it clunked dismally as they struggled along.

I just don't remember this black valley, Mary told herself time after time. If I'd come by it once I'd not have forgot it. I remember a valley farther up where the stone was blue. But I don't remember this black valley. I'm sure I've never been by this black valley!

She kept watching the opposite shore for sight of the salt spring.

Surely we'd ha' come to th' salt spring by now. Surely. If'n we were on the proper river.

Once her heart leaped when she saw a line of white at the shoreline in a riverbend ahead. There, she thought, wanting to shout it, there's the salt spring!

But when they drew abreast of it, she saw that it was not a white beach, but the swift white water of a riffle. The shores were relentless black and gray. She sank to the ground and re-tied on her feet the strips of cloth, which had grown pitch black. "What a bleedin' dirty place," she muttered, looking up at the crumbling black cliff at their backs. "Have y' ever seen th' like?"

"Yah. Coal, is all."

"Oh, aye! But it is, ain't it?" She had seen coal in Phila-delphia, but only in wagons, on the way to hearths. She had never thought of it making up mountains.

"But you cannot eat coal," Ghetel said.

"Ghetel, leave me be awhile. I have t' think. Go look f'r victuals. Something. But leave me be."

Mary sat for a long time on the rock, pondering. She shut her eyes and made herself concentrate. She had never thought this hard. She would concentrate on landmarks and their sequence as she remembered them, and tried to separate from them all the disorientation she had been suffering since entering this valley of coal. She put her mind far back to the day of the massacre at Draper's Meadows and came day by day through her memory down the New River, the fording places the Indians had used, the burning spring, the salt lick, to the O-y-o, past its tributaries to the Shawnee town, on down to the salt lick of the big bones, and then started back up. She studied on each landmark until her head ached, trying to imagine where she could have made a mistake that would have lost the New River. She would think until she was dizzy, then would breathe deep and think some more.

And finally, after more than an hour, she opened her eyes. There was only one explanation, and it calmed her and made her peaceful inside:

There was no way they could be lost. The river they had been following *was* the New River. It could not be anything else. This coal river was just another tributary. The only reason she could not remember it was that somehow she had not seen it as the Indians were bringing her down. Somehow she had failed to notice it, and that was why it had appeared so shockingly, so unexpectedly, today, and thrown her into such a whirl of confusion. It was just another tributary that, like the others, they must cross when they could and then descend on the other side to regain the New River.

She saw Ghetel sitting on a log nearby, rocking back and forth with her arms folded over her belly, looking at her.

"You prayed?"

"Aye, after a fashion," said Mary.

"I too prayed."

"Good. Now let's us cross this river."

They went in gasping with the shock of the cold, there at the riffle. It was the only shallow place they had seen, and although the water was alarmingly fast, the day was growing old and Mary was very impatient to get across it and back down to what she was now sure was the New River. She was beginning to feel that if she slept a night up in this black valley she would never get her sense of direction straightened out thereafter.

The spear-poles helped. With them, they sounded the rocky bottom that they could not see, and they leaned on them when the current pushed hard against their bodies.

They prayed all the way across.

They got back down to the river mouth before dark. Mary guessed they had walked some eight miles up and eight miles down that gloomy gorge. Those miles, and the strain and effort of wading the cold river, had so weakened them that they were forced to sit and rest every ten minutes or so by the day's end.

There was no light left by which to search for food. Their blankets were still damp from the crossing and from two or three brief rain showers that had fallen during their descent through the canyon. The rags on their feet had been worn or torn through by the stony passage of the day. Both women were further weakened by the scouring bowels that had been draining their vigor for days. And now with dusk came a slow, steady rain that promised to continue much of the night. Mary hurt in every joint, and her heart seemed to be fluttering more than beating.

A few feet above the river mouth they found the hulk of a great beech tree that had long since fallen. Its center was rotted out, leaving a cavity some three feet wide, floored with the soft punk of decay and drifted leaves. Mary jabbed into the cavity several times with her spear, both fearing and hoping that it might be serving as some animal's lair. Then they dragged themselves in, rolled into each other's arms for warmth with the blankets wound around them and passed out to the hiss of rain.

In the night a pair of gray foxes, one carrying a dead partridge, trotted to the log, smelled the intruders, bristled, skulked a few minutes, put their quivering noses into the musty opening, then turned and left to find other quarters, their damp bushy tails low over the ground, taking their partridge with them.

Oh, heavenly God, she's dead.

"Ghetel. Ghetel!"

She shook the old bony shoulder violently. The old woman did not respond. In the snug worm-eaten hollow of the log, enveloped by the smell of decay, it was too much like being in a coffin. Then Ghetel rolled onto her back and groaned, and exhaled a rank breath into Mary's face. She began to stir, then sank back into torpor. Mary hugged her. She's not dead. But she's ready to lie here and die.

Mary raised herself painfully onto an elbow. Daylight outside the end of the log showed only a stretch of ground covered with wet dead leaves. But she could hear, in the hiss of rain and the drumming of the rivers, all that hopeless wild inhospitable space out there. And within the fastness of this log it was soft and warm. They had not slept so profound a sleep before. It would be so nice just to lie here and not wake up, ever, she thought. One could die quite nice here. She closed her eyes and listened to the hush.

But then she opened her eyes. She needed to make water.

And besides, she couldn't just up and die. Will was waiting for her to come home.

She couldn't make Ghetel move. So she strained and pulled and dragged her own blanket free and wriggled out into the dank, rainy air, drew her blanket over her head, and stood shivering, legs apart, pissing, looking around. The dark river was high and fast. It had risen to a level within a few feet of the log.

We might well 'a' been swept into th' river, she thought with a strange, bemused indifference, an' back down to th' O-y-o. An' lost all that ground we've gained so hard. But o' course we'd not 'a' knowed. Or cared.

She staggered listlessly down to the bank of the New River, her feet chilled by the wet leaves, the filthy rags of her footcloths dragging, and stood there looking upriver for landmarks. The river was gray-green, more than half a mile wide, sizzling with rainspatters, rushing down the V-shaped valley. The iron-gray mountainsides slanted up, their summits out of sight in the rainclouds. The whole valley looked as forbidding and hellish as the coal valley had seemed yesterday. And what nagged her was that it looked no more familiar.

Surely we'd have come to the salt lick by now, she thought, if we was really on the right river.

No, damn 'ee! Don't admit them doubts again.

She closed her eyes and swayed. She heard the horse bell. Ghetel was up and moving, then.

God, I'm empty. She reached inside the blanket and ran her hand over her belly. For the first few weeks of this hungry trek it had been flat, even hollow. Now it was so full of emptiness that it was bloated.

What is that smell?

It grew stronger as she went toward the river's edge.

"May-ry." Ghetel came alongside, waddling and staggering, clutching her filthy blanket about her and carrying her spear.

And then Mary saw it. The river had cast it up amid the shore drift: a doe's head, considerably decomposed, its eyes milky, tongue gray. It had been neatly cut off just behind the skull, cast away, perhaps, by Indian hunters upstream. Shuddering, Mary bent and picked it up by grasping one of its cold, wet ears, and carried it up toward the beech log. Ghetel walked beside her, staring at it. Mary put it on top of the log, as if setting a table, and drew the tomahawk out of her belt.

"It's putrid," she said.

"Yah."

"Hope it don't sicken us."

"Just cut. Hurry!"

The skin slid off the slimy meat easily. There was flesh on the jaw muscles. It was pasty white, a little blue, even, and they almost gagged as they chewed it.

There wasn't much else but the tongue. Mary got it loose and threw away the rest of the head so she wouldn't have to see the eyes. She split the stinking tongue lengthwise and gave half of it to Ghetel. They sat down on opposite sides of the log to eat, as neither could stand to watch the other eating offal.

The stench of the rotten head was still in their nostrils and hands and clothing that afternoon when they passed opposite the mouth of another large river that flowed into the New from the east. It looked familiar, though Mary was beginning to suspect that winter had changed the aspect of everything so completely that she might never recognize another landmark against the ones she had engraved in her memory.

And if so, she thought, then we sh'll just have to travel largely on faith alone.

Ghetel coughed loudly several times behind her, and Mary felt a rush of sympathy for her.

On faith alone, she thought. That's all poor Ghetel's been a-travelin' on this whole way.

"Dem deers," Ghetel said at twilight as they were inching their way over rain-slick rock slabs at the river's edge. "Oh, all dem deers! I want 'em!"

"Eh?" Mary stopped and looked back. Ghetel was pointing toward the opposite shore. There at the river's edge a quarter of a mile away there were three white-tail bucks and two does, their heads down as if grazing. Mary felt her hand tighten instinctively on the shaft of her spear-stick and wished she could be on that side of the river. I'd get one, she thought. I swear I'd get one and we'd make a fire an' roast it so nice . . .

And then she noticed something.

The deer were all licking at the beach. And the beach was pale, a strip of gray-white, as if snow had fallen there.

"Ghetel!" she whispered intensely. "It's th' salt lick!" Her heart frolicked inside her ribs.

"Vat's?"

"The salt lick! Ghetel! I know just where we be!"

"I t'ought you alvays know dat."

"Aye, but . . . "

Two of the bucks had raised their heads and were looking across the river. They had heard the voices. They were alert, beautiful, tiny at this distance, the enormous dark mountainside rising a thousand feet into the clouds behind them.

Ghetel raised her spear over her head and shouted:

"You! I could eat you raw!"

"You raw! You raw!" the mountainside echoed.

They found shelter under a shelf of rock stratum twenty feet above the river that night. It was not quite a cave; it was perhaps three feet from floor to ceiling at its entrance and six feet deep into the cliff. The dry floor was littered with sticks and leaves, and animal and bird droppings, and there was a fragment of a clay pot near the back. A charred flat stone on the floor and soot on the ceiling showed that somebody, however long ago, had enjoyed a fire. At one end, Mary found a scattering of cracked turkey or duck bones and some flakes of flint, including two sharp but broken arrowheads. Dast we try a fire? Oh, she thought, how I should love t' look in a fire after all this lonesome cold an' gray!

She shaved a fistful of tinder from a stick with the edge of the tomahawk, stacked twigs near at hand, and knelt, shivering, over it with the tomahawk in her left hand and a piece of flint in her right. She struck several sharp, glancing blows against the steel with the flint. But the flint was so small and light that she could produce only a spark or two. She exchanged it for another scrap of flint but it was even smaller.

The sparks flew like little stars in the darkening cave, but were too feeble to ignite the tinger. After a while, breathing hard, cursing, knuckle and thumb smarting and bleeding, she gave up and sat back on her haunches, all but crying with frustration. "Well, I reckon we're just not meant . . . "

"Hssssst!" Ghetel was peering out into the twilight, listening.

And then Mary heard it: a syllable in human voice from across the river through the hush of rain, and shortly after, another and another, and the clatter of hooves. Words were indistinguishable, but the inflections of the voices left no doubt that Indians were passing on the opposite shore. Maybe her imagination was tricking her, but in the murky gloom over there she thought she saw figures moving downstream among the tree trunks. After a while the sounds were swallowed up by the rain and the river but the two women huddled motionless for some time longer.

And when they rolled into their blankets, she gave a prayer of thanks to the same Providence she had been cursing a moment before for the same reason: her failure to ignite a fire.

They left the cave early the next morning, too cold and hungry to sleep past dawn. They went flinching along the stony river bank for five minutes, their aching-cold feet punished unbearably by each step, their stiff toes seeming to stub on every rock. Finally Ghetel stopped and sat on a log, saying, "No, no, no. Gif me de ax." Mary hesitated. "Come, come. Gif," Ghetel insisted, putting her palm up and waggling her fingers for it.

She took it and bent down to a leatherwood shrub and deftly scored a branch and stripped off several strands of bark.

Then she tore four large rectangles of cloth from the remains of her skirt. Mary sat and looked on, curious. The old woman worked, talking to herself, her breath condensing in the bitter air. Every few minutes she had to stop and put her stiffened fingers between her thighs to warm them. Mary sat with her hands between her own legs. With the constant hunger, her blood seemed more and more sluggish, her heartbeats more feeble and uneven, and her extremities seemed to be getting no blood at all to warm them. It was, she thought, as if her heart were trying to pump cold sorghum instead of blood.

Ghetel raked a pile of dry leaves onto each of the pieces of cloth. Then she placed her right foot on one of the piles, drew the edges of the cloth up around her ankle, and tied a strip of bark around the ankle. She did the same then with the other foot, so that she now had, in effect, a bag of leaves bound around each foot. "Now you," she said.

Mary was touched; her eyes brimmed as she watched the miserable old creature kneel at her feet and struggle with her gnarled and benumbed fingers to knot the stubborn bark. She helped her rise, and smiled at her. The old woman grinned broadly, quite pleased with herself. And they set off again up the river bank. They had to walk carefully to keep from snagging or loosening the makeshift shoes, and had to stoop and retie them often, and replace the crushed leaves, but the warmth and cushioning were luxurious, and Mary turned often to Ghetel with smiles and sighs and happy headshakes to express how much she appreciated them. This in turn kept the old woman much more genial than she might have been otherwise.

Mary saw the flames first. For a moment she was baffled by the sight of yellow-orange fire billowing out of the riverbed a mile ahead. Then she remembered. She stopped and pointed at it. Ghetel looked up from her careful negotiation of the rocky shore and her eyes bugged. Delight and then fear passed rapidly over her features, then she hung onto Mary's arm and looked to her for explanation. Mary told her about the odorous air that bubbled from the mud, and how the Indians had ignited it. "Must be them Indians we heard last night thrown a brand into it," she speculated. "What sport, eh?"

They found a rock ledge directly across the river from the burning spring, and brushed up a thick pile of leaves under it. Then they foraged up and down a nearby ravine for two hours. They were uncommonly lucky, and brought in half a pound of acorns, eight walnuts and a handful of wildflower bulbs that looked something like wild onion. Almost gleeful, they huddled in their blankets against the biting cold, gazed across the broad river at the cavorting pillar of flame and its reflection on the water and ate their variety of victuals as a purple dusk gathered. "Odd. We wanted a fire so last night. Now here we jus' wait a day an', I be blessed, we got one. Hum?"

It was too far away for them to feel any of its heat, of course. But as the nourishment of their repast stole out into their limbs and owls hooted and wolves wailed among the mountains, they gazed at the flames long into the night and thought of their respective hearths, and their souls at least were warmed by the sight of the distant fire.

CHAPTER 19

SOMETIME IN THE LONG, COLD HOURS AFTER MIDNIGHT, THE wind strengthened and backed into the northwest. It began moaning up the valley, rattling the millions of bare branches. Then it gusted suddenly to a gale strength, shrieking along the steep mountainsides, sweeping leaves off the ground, flinging a hail of broken twigs through the forest and blowing down shallow-rooted trees. Mary and Ghetel were jolted awake by the ripping and snapping and thudding of great limbs and tree trunks, and in terror clutched at their blankets, which the icy wind threatened to tear from their bodies as it scoured all the leaves of their bedding out of their alcove and pelted them with flying debris. They huddled together, squinting. Across the river, their friendly pillar of flame from the burning spring leaped and ducked and fluttered horizontally over the

water before the force of the wind, then with a *pouf* was
blown out.

They sat clinging to each other in the howling darkness the
rest of the night, their backs to the rock, trying to keep their
blankets tight around their shoulders and anchored under
their feet. There was no such thing as sleep now, just shivering and waiting, clutching each other when some huge splintering, slamming weight would thump to earth above or below
them. The wind sang through a range of demon voices, now
harsh as a wildcat's yowl, now lowing, now shrill as a man
whistling through his teeth, sometimes all those at once.
Toward dawn a fierce hissing joined in and the women
lowered their faces to their knees to protect them from the
needle-stings of sleet.

It was maddening. It seemed to Mary that this pitiless cold
lashing had gone on for a year. She clenched her jaws to keep
from screaming because to scream would be to become a part
of the wild-devil's soul of the storm itself and she knew there
would be no coming back from that. Mary had some confidence that she could anchor her own soul against the storm
until daybreak, but she feared for Ghetel's soul, which, since
that morning she had tried to go back for the horse, Mary had
suspected was unstable and at times on the very brink.

A woman in her state c'd easy go stark mad this night, Mary
thought.

And so from time to time she would reach over and find
Ghetel's hand and squeeze it reassuringly, hoping to keep her
in touch with her reason.

They crawled from cold water into colder air, out of still
another creek. They lodged themselves in a crevice between
two boulders, to keep themselves from slipping back into the
cold swift water if they should faint. They were shuddering
and gasping, unable to stand up without support. It was the
second creek they had waded this day. It had been breast-
deep. The first one had only come to their hips.

They stayed there pressed between the boulders and tried
to recover their breath, but after five minutes, Mary felt she
would die of chill or shake her brittle-cold body to pieces with

shivering if she did not start moving. "Come," she muttered through chattering teeth. "Must get along."

"No. No farder."

"Come now."

The old woman glowered and shook her head, her slack lower lip wobbling to and fro as she did. It was chapped and split and bleeding. In these last two days, Mary had seen Ghetel eat the flaking skin off her lips and chew it as if it were food. They had not found anything truly edible since they had left the place of the burning spring. They had been chewing buds and slippery elm bark and the hairy, hard, sour berry clusters they had found on a small stand of red sumac. None of this seemed to be giving them any strength that they could feel. It filled and stretched their shrunken stomachs, but the exhausted fibers of their flesh still clamored for nutrients with a hunger of their own.

Ghetel embraced the cold boulder and put the side of her face against it and closed her eyes.

"Y' must come, Ghetel." A powerful spasm of shivering broke Mary's voice as she said it.

"No. I do not have to do vat you say."

"Oh, but y' do."

"No. I die from doink vat you say."

"You'll die *here*."

"Because I listent to you!"

"Come." She stretched out a gray, cold hand and grasped Ghetel's wrist. The old woman jerked free and struck at the hand. Feeble though the blow was, it hurt Mary's bones.

"No!"

"Ghetel . . ."

"No! Damn, damn! Don't touch again or I kill you!"

"Ghetel!" Mary was stunned. She reached to her face to pull back a rope of wet hair that hung over her eye, as if to see this rebellious outburst better.

"I kill you," Ghetel muttered. This new thought seemed to have fixed itself in her desperate brain. "Kill you."

Mary tried to smile, feeling that the old wretch was merely venting her misery with a meaningless, pitiful outburt. But her smile crumbled when she saw Ghetel cast a sidelong glance at the tomahawk, which still hung in a loop of Mary's belt. She remembered suddenly the premonition she had had days ago about giving Ghetel the tomahawk to crack hickory nuts. She inched back, bracing herself against the boulder, to get out of Ghetel's reach. She lowered the point of her hickory spear between them defensively. Ghetel turned painfully and leaned now with her right shoulder against the rock, and in turn held her spear-point directed at Mary.

They stood like this for minutes. Mary's heartbeat was skipping and fluttering. The old woman's eyes were terrible, watering with the cold but burning with naked hate. Her filthy white hair, matted and snarled with leaf crumbs and moss and pieces of scab, was plastered wetly against the right side of her face.

Mary began shaking her head in disbelief and backing around the rock to get out of this creek gorge, to get away from that treacherous stare.

She had kept this old woman alive. She had led her safely out of captivity. She could not comprehend how Ghetel could now turn on her. Unless she had truly lost her reason. Sometimes on this trek—during the storm at the burning spring, especially—Mary herself had barely managed to cling to her own reason. But never even then had she harbored any notion to hurt Ghetel. Dear God, she thought, what have we got but each other?

She hauled herself painfully up a slope among leafless shrubs, looking back constantly for fear that Ghetel would come at her from behind with her spear. When she reached the high ground where the hill sloped off toward the river, she stood looking back with her spear in her hand, looking back at the boulders at the edge of the creek, watching to see Ghetel come out, come out smiling and contrite, she hoped, ready to go on. Oh, I can't bear it, she thought. To have come this far together and then to lose her. She can't just stay here and *die*. She doesn't know where to go, without me.

Maybe she'll get herself together and come along and we'll be all right as we were before . . .

Ghetel, gray as a ghost, came slowly out from behind the boulder, stopped there holding her spear and peering around like a hunter until she saw Mary standing above her. Mary felt a surge of compassion. "Good," she called down. "Come along now, dear. I knew y'could . . . "

The old woman began laboring up the slope toward her, her mouth working as if she were counting her steps or telling her feet to go. The old bell clunked and clanked. When at last she had approached within four yards, she stopped and stood gasping. But now again she lowered her lance tip threateningly toward Mary.

She's still half daft, Mary thought. Lord, give me the wit to talk 'er back to 'er senses.

"Ghetel! Imagine this! I recognize this place. Darlin', we're no more'n a hundred or hundred-twenty mile from home! Oh, I reckon that sounds a lot, but we've come five or six hundred already, and we're quite all right, aren't we now? Another hundred will be easy for such as us, now, won't it?"

But at the same time she was asking herself: A hundred miles? Can I really even go a hundred more yards?

Nothing changed in the old woman's face. She shuffled forward a step, still holding the sharpened stake and glaring like a soldier on attack. Mary moved on a few steps along the river bank, side-stepping more than walking so that she might keep a wary eye on Ghetel. In the meantime, she cajoled: "Good! Why, y're a-comin' right along. Didn't think y' could, now did 'ee? Oh, that's a fine lady, that is. I knew y' weren't th' kind as 'd give up. Nay, Ghetel. Y're my friend, an' I need a friend I can count on . . . " The old woman was getting alarmingly close. Mary feigned a burst of gaiety and fairly danced away, as quickly as her aching, exhausted limbs would allow, putting another fifteen feet of safe distance between them. "Come along, dear! Oh, I feel just so fine about 'em last two cricks, how we just crossed 'em right where we come to 'em, eh? And didn't have to do a walk-around? Oh, I feel it, this is a fine day for gettin' along! Just a *fine* day! Why, another week o' days like this'n an' surely we'll be almost home, home to a big ol' table covered with hot bread, an' quail pot pies, an' a great pitcher o' milk—an' Ghetel, I promise 'ee, I sh'll make 'ee one o' my huckleberry cobblers, that are a legend in Virginny . . . "

Thus chattering away, creating hopes and strengths and

mouth-watering images out of a mind that had almost gone barren during their weeks in the wilderness, Mary coaxed Ghetel along for another two miles through a cold sifting rain that afternoon, around the bases of steep hills, over ledges and screes and knots of roots, and through tangles of driftwood, coaxed her along, staying a safe distance ahead of her, fearing her and pitying her and never knowing what was going on in the brain behind that hideously wrinkled and mottled face, that strange, menacing silence.

Until, with about an hour's daylight left, they came to another torrential, steep-sided creek, this one far too wide and fast to wade at its mouth.

Mary stopped and looked at it, aghast. She looked up the awful chasm through which it poured, and there was no shallows within sight before it curved away into the mountains. Her little strength, which she had talked into a high state by cajoling Ghetel, suddenly drained out of her with a rush, and she nearly fell down.

And suddenly with a bolt of terror she heard the old bell and felt a hand clutch her blanket.

The crazy old woman had closed the gap between them while Mary stood stunned by this obstacle.

CHAPTER
20

MARY TRIED TO SNATCH HER BLANKET OUT OF GHETEL'S GRASP and hurry out of her reach. But she had too little strength. Her sudden movement simply threw her off balance and she fell with bruising impact on the rocky slope. Ghetel, hardly any stronger, was pulled down with her and fell on her with a grunt and a clattering of the bell. Mary tried to wriggle out from under her and push her back. They grunted and breathed harshly, and stirred leaves and dislodged rocks. Ghetel clutched Mary's blanket and pulled, as if trying to climb on her and crush her. She had dropped her spear and was clawing at the blanket with both hands. Mary tried to squirm out from under the stinking, desperate, persistent embrace. Their weight on the rocks under her was grinding her flesh against her bones. Mary's heart was pounding with fright and fury but seemed to pump no strength to her exhausted muscles.

Mary at last got a leg free and pressed her knee into the old woman's throat. The old woman squeezed out a gurgling groan and twisted her head aside, and her yellow teeth clamped down on the naked flesh of Mary's thigh. She seesawed her jaws as if to bite out a mouthful of flesh. One of her big front teeth worked loose and fell out. Mary made a fist and struck several times at Ghetel's temple. With her aching cold fingers and swollen joints, every blow was as painful as striking a rock. But one last blow did cause Ghetel to open her mouth to yowl in pain. Blood was oozing from her toothmarks in Mary's thigh.

Now Mary's blanket was almost pulled off her, and she was naked on the cold ground except for her belt and the few remaining tatters of her dress. She felt the icy steel blade of the tomahawk turning against the flesh of her waist and realized that Ghetel had grasped its handle and was trying to twist it from its loop in her belt.

She grew truly desperate now, overcoming even her physical lethargy and reaching down to grasp the steel head of the weapon and to try to pull it away from Ghetel. For several seconds they strained against each other and wheezed and grunted. Then the loop of yarn broke and the painful bite of the steel edges on Mary's fingers was too much to bear, and the old woman had the tomahawk.

On gaining possession of it, Ghetel began to rise, as if to be in a better position to strike with it. Freed of her opponent's weight, Mary quickly scrambled aside and got onto all fours. Her right hand found the worn shaft of one of the spears and she picked it up as she rose to her feet.

The old woman now was standing, a few feet away and up the slope above Mary, raising the tomahawk to strike. Mary swung the end of the lance in a swift arc at the moment when Ghetel brought the tomahawk down at her. Ghetel's knuckles whacked against the hickory and the tomahawk flew out of her hand. She roared in pain as the weapon sailed through the air, swishing through bare twigs, struck a stone ledge several yards down the slope, clattered down a scree of loose shale, ricocheted off a mossy rock at the river's edge and splashed into the deep, fast, dark water of the tributary.

Ghetel's yelp of pain echoed away into the rush of water and space as the two women watched this precious tool of their survival vanish forever. Even Ghetel, a moment ago seemingly so crazy and bent on destruction, now appeared to comprehend the awfulness of this loss. She stood, gaping down at the place where it had disappeared, slowly and unconsciously folding her barked fingers into the comfort of her other hand, something like fear or shame dawning in her face, transforming her face from a Fury's mask to that of a guilty child.

It was as if the rage leaving her were filling Mary, like some scalding liquid being poured from one cup into another. Mary slowly came around on her, eyes blazing, her scrawny naked limbs shaking with outrage, trembling lips shaping words of damnation.

"Oh. Oh, ye . . . great . . . dull . . . *sow!* Oh, thou *demon* of stupidness! D'you *know* what y've done to us now? Eh? Do you? Oh, you hateful *blunderer!* I'd ha' better left 'ee with y'r terrible big appetites back there wi' the' *savages* t' be their *squaw!* Aye, that's th' full measure of 'ee, damn y'r greedy, whining soul to th' Infernal blazes!" Her voice rose to a shriek as she poured this out, and she began advancing on Ghetel holding her spear like a long club. And Ghetel began backing away, blinking, raising her hands to protect herself. "Aye! Now y've got your wits back, haven't 'ee, now th' damage is done? Oh, tha' reechy . . . Dutch . . . *lump!*"

And with that, she laid on with the long stick, pounding the old bony flanks and shoulders as if beating dust out of a carpet, the stick whistling and whacking, the old woman

howling and shrilling, the bell clanking. Now there was none
of the brave dignity that had carried Ghetel through the
gauntlet. She stumbled backward a few steps and then fell on
her rump and sat with her hands laced over her head, begging
for mercy.

By then Mary had expended all the strength of her outburst, and she dropped the end of the stick to the ground and
stood leaning on it, hauling in deep, rasping breaths, exhala-
tions steaming in the chilly air, her ribs rising and falling
under her gray, bruised skin, the nipples of her little hard-
dried breasts puckered in the cold.

And all was still again in a moment, except for Mary's
strenuous breathing and Ghetel's low, whimpering lamentations in Dutch.

Mary was chilling quickly after the heat of her outburst.
The cold, raw air penetrated her naked skin and made her
bones ache. She eased herself down the slope and picked her
ragged blanket up from the ground and wrapped it around
herself like a hooded cloak. She took up her spear, and then
also the one Ghetel had dropped, set her jaw and turned up
the course of the tributary to seek a place to cross it. She did
not look back to see whether Ghetel was following or not. She
was still too angry, and too full of trepidation about being in
the wilderness without a cutting tool, to concern herself with
Ghetel.

She's been as much bother as a stubborn mule anyhow,
Mary thought indignantly. Glad t' be shed of 'er, truly. And
she's so miserable, I reckon she'd be better off dead. She
thinks so too, or acts like it. Well, by heaven, 'tis a relief,
withal, and I sh'll enjoy light goin' the rest o' the way home.
Reckon it's easier to find edibles f'r one than two, at that.

So she thought as she advanced along the steep and rock-
strewn slope, placing her numb and bleeding feet carefully,
hauling herself over ledges and root snarls, dragging the
spears with one hand while with the other she fought to keep
snagging branches from stripping her of her precious blanket.

But she had not progressed a quarter of a mile before she
was aware of a terrible aching knot in her throat, so thick and
aching that it forced out little strangling noises and made her

mutter the name of God over and over, and squeezed out
unexpected curtains of tears that she had to wipe away so she
could see to continue. It was growing dark now, the dull grays
and greens of moss and sycamore dimming to dark gray, and
the other tree trunks and the water almost black, and the day
cold slid down to evening cold. She heard a rustle of leaves a
few yards ahead and looked up to glimpse a wolf trotting
ahead of her with its tail low to the ground, pausing now and
then to turn its gaze on her before going on. Mary stopped
then, propping herself against a fallen tree trunk as thick as
she was tall, where she caught her breath and tried to keep
from calling Ghetel's name back down the valley. She busied
herself for a few minutes by untying the yarn rope from her
waist. She swept off the blanket and stood for a moment
shaking it out and rearranging it, finaly draping it around
herself in a fashion that allowed her to rope it at the waist,
pull two corners of it forward over her shoulders and tie them
down in front, thus in effect making a wool dress that left her
hands free for the business of carrying the spears and grasping handholds. It was not as warm as before, as her hands and
head were bare, but it would be better for moving through
tangled brush. And while she was thus dressing herself, she
kept glancing back down the chasm. Tears stung her eyelids
and her bosom ached, and the lack of her companion spread
like a stain over the whole wild landscape. She was beginning
to have the surprising comprehension that she *needed*
Ghetel—probably as much as Ghetel needed her.

But Ghetel did not appear, and when Mary had stalled for
ten minutes at the fallen log she told herself that she must get
along and try to find a fording place before dark, and that she
must not retrace her steps to go back and fetch Ghetel or she
would not manage to get herself home.

The old thing's naught but trouble, she reminded herself.
She's like an anchor and she's gone daft and wants to kill you,
as you've just seen. You'd be the worst kind of a fool to go
back and get her. If you plan ever to get the last hundred miles
up this canyon, y've got to forget about her just as you forgot
about the baby, and put her behind forever. That thought,
which she had forbidden herself for so many weeks, sank in

on her loneliness and remorse so heavily that she leaned back
against the fallen tree trunk and squeezed her eyes shut and
bit the inside of her lip until the worst part of the anguish had
passed. She faced up the gorge and, holding a spear in each
hand as walking-sticks, her bone joints grinding in their sockets, the rock bruises of her fight with Ghetel making her
wince with every step, she limped forward.

Sometimes under the rustle of her footsteps and the rasp of
her breathing she would imagine that she heard a voice, and
would stop and listen, and would strain to listen through the
pulse-poundings in her head and the rush of wind and water,
but was never certain she heard a voice, though one seemed
to be there, just under the hiss of space and the whiffing of
wind, a hair-thin suggestion of a human voice. It made her
spine tingle and her heart ache.

It was the most utterly lonesome sound she had ever heard,
even though she was not sure she was hearing it.

Objects—tree trunks, rocks, hanging vines—were losing
their outlines, receding into the deep gray of dusk. Mary
eased herself down on a flat rock the size of a table to study a
place that might provide a crossing. The river fell rapidly
here, riffling and spilling over and around slabs and shelves of
rock. From here as far as she could see up the stream there
were ghostly lines across the watercourse, showing where the
water spilled white and foaming over ledges, as if pouring
down a flight of rugged stairs.

Aye, here I could cross, she thought. Come daylight. Must
find a place to lie down and wait out the night, sleep if I can.
It'll take strength I don't have left now to cross here.

Something moved in the corner of her eye, something on
the shore a little way upstream, on her side of the stream. She
tried to look directly at it, but saw nothing at first in the half-
light. She turned back to the stream, then detected movement
again. This time she saw it.

A wolf was standing among the boulders looking at her,
perhaps forty feet away. Then she detected another blur of
motion coming down to the river's edge. They stood together
for a moment, then began slinking cautiously toward where

she stood. They moved with an eerie silence, or seemed to, as
nothing could be heard over the burbling and shushing of the
stream. Sometimes they would stop and then she would lose
sight of them. Their dull markings blended them into the
leafless undergrowth and leaves and rockfall of the mountainside and they were invisible now, except when they moved. A
few feet at a time, they were approaching her, coming close
down along the water's edge, weaving among the rocks, close
enough to be visible now against the darker wet mass of rock,
now stopping to sniff the air, raising and lowering their heads
to peer at her, in much the same manner as shortsighted old
men will squint and move their heads to make out someone
who has entered their room.

Mary held her lances pointed toward the wolves. Her heart
was whamming but seemed to be pumping ice-cold blood.
She sidled away from the wolves, closer to the water's edge,
feeling the cold, wet, sharp-edged rock with her bare feet.

What do wolves do? she thought. She had heard them howl
many nights among the mountains, but far away; none, as far
as she knew, had come this close. Unless maybe when we
were sleeping, she thought. What do they do? Jump on you?
Or do they wait till you lie down? Likely they have their ways
o' knowin' whether you're weak, she thought. Once she had
heard Henry Lenard tell Will that a wolf can sense dying.
They're not too cowardly to attack, he had said, but they're
smart enough not to risk throwing themselves at something
that might be stronger than themselves. Like Indians, Will
had observed. Aye, Henry had nodded, like Indians. Mary
remembered this old conversation, and she made a decision
then that she would have to cross the rapids now, as she dared
not lie down on this side of the river in the darkness. Under
the roar of the water she thought she still heard the keening of
that voice but now she suspected that what she had been
hearing, or imagining she had heard, were the warnings of her
own fears.

Her blanket was reasonably dry and she wanted to keep it
that way so she could get warm when she reached the other
side of the stream. She laid the spears down within reach,
pointed toward the wolves and, keeping an eye on them,

began fumbling with numb fingers to untie the knots with which she had fashioned her blanket-dress. She took off the blanket and rolled it into a bundle and tied the bundle with the rope of yarn. All that remained of her dress was a few rags of cloth hanging from her shoulders. The dank cold searched over all her body, and she shuddered, knowing that the swift water would be even colder.

The wolves, though she had not really seen them moving, were a mere ten or twelve feet away, still watching her. One opened its mouth and she saw the curved line of its white teeth. Then it licked its muzzle and peered at her.

Mary put the blanket bundle on her shoulder and slipped the yarn-rope over her head so she could carry the bundle high on her shoulder while keeping both hands free. She gave the wolves one last long look, then with a sudden sense of exhilaration, told them, "Bye now, lads, I got t' be a-leavin'."

At the sound of her voice, one cocked its head quizzically and the other side-stepped a few feet in retreat. Then Mary picked up her hickory sticks and turned her back on the wolves and put one leg down into the strong and icy current. The shock of the cold went up her leg, making her hip-joint ache and sending a cascade of shudders from her scalp down to her knees. She lowered her other foot into the water and leaned against the current. She felt ahead for footing with her toes and thus went out an inch at a time into the roaring water. Again she thought she heard a voice, and then a moment later she was *sure* she heard a voice. She was concentrating with all her attention on footing and balance, staring down into the blackness of the stream as if she could penetrate it and see where footholds and dropoffs were, and afraid to look up from this concentration, but now she could hear a voice and it was calling her name. She braced the lances against the bottom and leaned on them and slowly turned her head to look around for the source of the sound.

Ten yards downstream there was Ghetel, creeping along the bank, banging onto rocks with one hand. Her drained face and white hair were like a faint, pale lantern against the deep twilight grays of the gorge. Here she came now, that stubborn, cranky, half-mad, hostile old crone who had complicated the flight, and Mary had never in her life been so glad to see anyone.

"Here!" she hallowed back.

And then she remembered the wolves.

They had seen and heard the old woman's approach and Mary saw them retreating slowly up the slope, looking over their backs at her. They were not scared, and were not going to run away, but were backing off to appraise this newly arrived creature, perhaps to determine whether she had death on her.

And as Ghetel saw Mary, and began moving more purposefully toward her, crying something incomprehensible over the noise of the rapids, the wolves stopped and turned and began moving toward her, somehow emboldened.

"Ghetel! Look 'ee up!" Mary raised one of the sticks and pointed it toward the predators. "Wolves!"

The old woman paid no attention. She was busy crying her greetings or pleadings or apologies or whatever they were, and climbing over and tottering around the boulder heaps and slabs of rock toward the fording place.

"Wolves!" Mary cried again. The old woman was almost opposite Mary now, still jabbering her words, her bell just audible, and the shadowy wolves had come down within ten feet of her, their gray legs tensed and bent as if coiled to spring at or away from her. The roar of the river was a maddening barrier of sound, baffling their efforts to make their urgent words understood. Mary pointed repeatedly and violently toward the stalking beasts, but Ghetel, perhaps thinking she was shaking the stick threateningly at her, kept coming toward Mary, talking, and then in a moment she was at the water's edge, pleading and gesturing, a mere arm's length from the larger of the two wolves, which crouched on a rock ledge at the level of Ghetel's shoulders and seemed to be aiming his muzzle directly at her throat.

"Ghetel!" Mary screamed hoarsely, and then in desperation, forgetting how precarious was her balance in the current, she shifted her grip on the spear in her right hand, cocked it over her shoulder and threw it at the wolf.

The moment exploded into confusion and movement. Mary

lost her balance and fell forward into the fast water. The wolf, struck in the shoulder by the pointed stick, gave a fierce, snarling yap of pain right at Ghetel's ear and sprang almost straight up; and Ghetel, startled by the explosion of savage sound and motion, lunged forward off the bank and plunged into the icy water.

The wolves scrambled and bounded away in the rocks, yelping with fright and rage. Mary and Ghetel were on hands and knees in the swift, shallow water now, trying to get handholds and kneeholds on the rocks of the bottom and keep their faces above water. The current tugged at Mary's blanket bundle, pulling the strap of yarn tightly across her throat. The icy water swirled and pressed around them, threatening to lift and carry the women away into the deep pool below the ford. Ghetel, now totally occupied with hanging on for her life, had released her hold on her blanket, and the water carried it off of her and away.

Mary at last got a foot under herself and teetered to a standing position. She shouted Ghetel's name and extended to her one end of the lance she still held in her left hand. The old woman felt it touching her shoulder and had just enough presence of mind to grab for it. With the last of her waning strength, hardly able to draw breath because of the stunning coldness of the water, Mary pulled on the staff until Ghetel could get her feet under her. And now, all but naked, gasping, quaking and moaning, the two women stumbled and floundered in near-darkness through the roaring rapids, each holding one end of the hickory spear, one or the other usually falling and trying to rise, until Mary's outstretched right hand encountered something solid and rough above the waterline in front of her: a root.

She clung to it, crying, "Ghetel, we're over! Hold tight!" She pulled herself toward the bank with the dwindling strength of her right arm and with the other pulled on the staff to drag Ghetel the last few feet.

The root was part of the exposed, gnarled root of a big sycamore that had been almost undermined by the flow of the stream. It provided a profusion of handholds as well as stepping places for their benumbed and bruised feet, but they were so spent and stiff with cold that their climb out of the creek occupied some five minutes, during which they were in danger of falling back in. It was almost totally dark now. Mary staggered onto the steep bank, trying to support herself with the staff, but fell among stones and driftwood debris, and lay there sucking for breath and enduring waves of shuddering that swept from one end of her aching frame to the other. Ghetel was somewhere nearby in the deep dusk, gasping and voicing long, pitiful, quavering moans.

Mary felt that the cold had gone into the marrow of her bones and through her innards, and that the remaining warmth of her heart itself was about to wink out like a candle.

To bend a finger hurt, and so it took her a long time to remove the blanket bundle that was slung around her neck and untie the knots that had held it together. As she worked on it, teeth chattering, nose running, fingers stiff and clumsy and powerless as twigs, she remembered Ghetel's blanket sliding away into the stream. What an incalculable loss that seemed now. Two women, one blanket. Surely it could be the difference between surviving or not surviving.

And something else had been lost this awful day, she seemed to remember; yes: as if it had happened twenty years ago and just now returned as a memory from childhood, she saw the tomahawk skittering down the slope and disappearing into the river . . .

Ye God but this day has cost us dear, she thought.

And there had been still something else. Her mind was almost too numb to remember, but then she did recollect: the spear she had thrown at the wolves. Aye! That was gone too! In the benumbing traversal of the stream even the frightful encounter with the wolves had slipped out of her mind.

There. A knot loosened and she drew the end out and groped for the other knot.

A tomahawk and a spear and a blanket, she thought. Almost everything of the little we had to keep us alive is gone. We could make another spear, she thought. Oh, no, we can't! Without the tomahawk we can make nothing. God help us.

And we'd ha' lost none of it but for the folly o' that great antic bitch of a Dutchwife lyin' over there . . .

The indignation made her heart glow a bit stronger. She thought, defiance flaming up in her breast and warming her blood: Well, by heaven, old Ghetel, we shall see just how long I'll put up with a troublesome piece o' baggage th' like of you . . .

But then she remembered the unbearable aching emptiness, the loneliness, when Ghetel had been out of sight behind her.

"Come, dear," she said, rising with agony to her feet and letting the partially wet blanket fall open and advancing toward the sounds of Ghetel's misery, "let's us bundle now in this blessed blanket, or . . . or we're goners for certain . . ."

Sleep was impossible, of course. They had blundered weakly about in the darkness, every stinging cold raindrop and every touch of their sodden rags provoking a bone-rattling shudder, seeking some overhang or hollow log under which to roll up, finally getting under a huge log that had fallen across a fissured outcropping; they had raked enough fallen leaves into the fissure to insulate their cocoon against the clammy earth under them and the dank air above, and had burrowed into the leaf pile and pulled the blanket around themselves and lain skin on skin in an embrace, waiting for their bodies to produce some faint warmth for each other. But each found the other cold as death; Mary remembered her father ice-fishing once, and two fish lying in a snowbank; their contact now was like that. Their heartbeats were weak flutters and skips. Each felt the other's tremors as well as her own. They lay breast to breast and belly to belly, each one's arms full of the other's bones. No warmth came, for a black, hissing eternity; instead, just a gradual numbing of the senses and a dulling of minds, a slowing and thickening of dreams, as if thought itself were congealing; and Mary's last nameable thought was that this nothingness was the relief of death. She waited and listened inside her head for familiar voices and watched behind her eyes for light or familiar faces or other hints of heaven.

The rain stopped. For a while water drops dribbled and pattered off the twigs to the leaves of the forest floor and the clouds above the trees dissolved to let starlight through, and after a while there was a sliver of a moon over the mountain, and after it had ridden for two hours into the sky above the gorge, all the leaves on the ground looked like silver flakes in their sheen of moonlit new frost. Across the river, from high on a ridge, spun the eerie tremolo of a wolf's howl. Moonlight flickered like cold flame on the fast black water. In the blanket covered with leaves under a slanting tree trunk, nothing moved. The women's wretched shivering and shifting had fallen still.

Mary lay in total darkness remembering dying; before the blankness had come she had been thinking that that was the experience of dying, but now she knew that she had not died, but had only gone unconscious, because now she was alive, had just now been awakened by a dream of wolves and could hear them now outside, far away, howling in the cold. And in a way she was disappointed that she had not died, because death had seemed like a rather fair place after all, certainly better than what she had been enduring for the last four or five weeks and had yet to endure for another week or two.

But no, she thought now, I don't really want to die so far away from Will, I don't want to die without Will knowing whether I'm alive or not or where I am. I don't really want to die at all while Will's still alive because I'm his wife and he counts on me. Nay, she thought with a long sigh, I don't really want to die at all because I'm young and Will's young and we have to beget us another family to go on in place of our three tads them bloody savages has cost us; Will wouldn't be happy atall if they was no Ingles children t' reap what he's sown.

He might find another wife if I was to perish here, she thought. Now I don't like the thought o' that hardly atall, so let's just not have any more thoughts of this dyin' business . . .

Mary's breathing was slow and steady now and her heartbeat was thumping along steadily, not fluttering like a candle in a draft as it had been, and she could hear that Ghetel's breathing was all right too.

Oh, Dear God, but we come near enough t' have a peek at you this night, I swear we did. Ghetel and me both.

She remembered that after the crossing of the cold fast stream they had been too chilled and exhausted, desperately hurting all over, to say anything to each other. Ghetel had simply followed her and they had hollowed out and padded up this crevice they were in, and Ghetel had crawled in beside her, and maybe Ghetel had thought she was dead, too.

Old Ghetel got sane again after that crossing, Mary thought. Guess she was just too miserable t' think any more about killin' me. An' now here we are sleepin' close as a man and wife do. After her takin' after me with th' tomahawk and me thrashin' her with that hickory pole. Oh, God, don't it beat all!

Somehow during the night, after they had gone unconscious, instead of their hearts stopping, instead of the cold creeping the rest of the way in and snuffing out their hearts, their hearts had driven the cold back, driven it back out of their torsos and their limbs and finally even out of their feet, and the warmth of their blood had eventually reached to their skin; then the warmth of Mary's skin had reached the warmth of Ghetel's and Ghetel's had reached Mary's and they had been heating each other the way a hot stone warms your feet when you step off the cold floor and slip into bed. They had warmed each other so well that even the damp blanket felt dry now. The utter numbness had gone out of Mary's feet and they ached in a dull way now, even, from time to time, felt as if they were being struck with thousands of little needles, which would make her legs twitch, and she was glad she could feel them. It was not truly what one could call warm here in this blanket, but it was not terribly cold, and where the two women's bare skin touched, there actually was warmth.

It's a miracle what's happened while we slept, Mary thought. Thank 'ee, O Lord in Heaven, for another little miracle. I reckon I've thought some unworthy thoughts your way from time to time since last July; still don't quite know why y've done me th' way you have, but y' do seem to come around an' look after us now and then after your fashion, so I must guess you haven't forgot us altogether.

Now I admit Will and me often forgot our prayers, some-times for days at a time, as they's so much t' do when you live out here this side o' th' mountains and have to make and do everything, just *everything,* for yourself, so we often forgot, it's true, and maybe that's why' y' brung th' Shawnee savages down on us. As that horseback preacher said last spring, might be y're a jealous an' wrathful God, and need reg'lar devotions from us thy mortal children—like Will hisself needed it a lot from Tommy an' Georgie—but Lord, Lord it don't seem fair what y've done to us.

Or maybe all this misery is just random, she thought then, and God has nothin' t' do with it. It seemed for a moment a more charitable way to consider God, but soon she was ashamed of herself for having thought that anything could happen without God's intervention.

I wonder me what Ghetel will be like on th' morrow, Mary thought. Back to herself, I pray. I figger there's a hundred mile more to go, provided we don't lose our way, an' more if we do, and I surely can't go a hundred mile while a-fightin' a crazy woman every step, now can I?

Mary was drowsy again and her limbs were buzzing with the sleep feeling, but she wanted to run the succession of landmarks up out of her memory one more time, because the difficulties of the last few days had rather befogged them.

There weren't many landmarks left. They had come back past most of them. The next one she could recall was the big creek where the Indians had washed the paint off of them-selves and had painted the trees. That was the creek where they had made a camp and the chieftain Captain Wildcat had playacted the birth of a Shawnee baby. Let's see, she thought. We was ten or twelve days—twelve, if I remember correct—down from Draper's Meadows when we come down out o' that crick, an' I remember we crossed th' New River there at a shallows to th' other bank there.

She could remember that, and was sure she would recog-nize it, but beyond that the prospect became quite bewilder-ing, with hardly a landmark. She could remember that they had ridden for several days north along a high-level ridge without a glimpse of the New River. Lordy, she thought, a shiver of awe running down her flanks, I can't guide us up that crick and up that ridge because I was half out o' my head when we come down it and it's all either blank or dreamy. I couldn't find our way back the way we come those few days; I got to keep us right along the New River. I das'n't get us away from the New River.

She wondered, as she had wondered before, why the Indians had left the New River and gone up that mountain ridge. The only reason they take a way, she thought, is 'cause it's most passable. That'd likely mean we came down over the mountain way because the New River for some stretch in there was too rough f'r good travel.

Her heart sank and she felt even more hollow than she had been feeling all these hungry, tiring weeks. God knows what we're a-gonna find the valley like after we get above that painted-tree creek, she thought. God help us. Lord, she thought, I hope y've had your fill o' punishin' me, for I've a feelin' I'll need all y'r kind aid and guidance to get through this next week or two.

And then Ghetel groaned and shifted in her sleep, one of her legs drawing away from one of Mary's, leaving it cold where it had been almost warm, and Mary lay there in the blackness in the old woman's stink and her own, hugging her still with one arm, this old woman who had tried to kill her, and it was strange, the strangest thing ever, because after trying to kill and beat each other they had needed each other so much that Mary had lingered waiting for Ghetel to come along and Ghetel had come along the ravine crying for Mary. They had needed each other because it was more than one could bear to be out here in this land alone.

But Mary knew, even as she held the sleeping hag for the warmth of life, that she would have to be on guard every minute Ghetel was awake, and that she must never sleep while Ghetel was awake.

I'd better just stay awake now till morning so's she won't wake up afore me, Mary thought.

And that was what she was thinking when the wooliness move into her head and she went to sleep.

CHAPTER
21

IN PHILADELPHIA WHEN SHE WAS A LITTLE GIRL, MARY HAD taken pity on a pariah dog she had seen sniffing for slops in the gutter; there had been something wordlessly good in its dark brown eyes when it had looked up at her, and she had gone into the house and taken a blood pudding from the pantry, stolen it out past her parents and given it to the pariah dog. Then she had gone back in the house thinking about the dog, and that night the dog had scratched at the door. Mary awoke now to a sound of scratching, dreaming about the dog.

She started awake. It was early dawn. Ghetel was sitting up, half out of the blanket, her legs still covered, doing something that made that scratching sound, and Mary was instantly defensive, angry at herself for not staying awake. Stealthily, she extricated her arm from the blanket and reached behind her to grasp the handle of the pointed pole which she had placed in her side of the hollow the night before.

Ghetel was clawing at the rotten bark on the underside of the big fallen tree that sheltered them. Bark debris and wood-punk kept falling on the blanket. Ghetel, a silhouette against the half-light, would scrabble in the decaying wood for a moment, then pause and put something to her mouth.

Th' poor thing's eatin' punk, Mary thought. She's a-goin' to kill herself yet to fill 'er guts. Mary herself was nothing but a tremendous craving hollowness; the blood pudding of her dream was still tantalizing the back of her mind, even though she had never liked blood pudding.

"Enough o' that, dear," Mary said wearily, and at the sound of her voice Ghetel jerked around like a child caught stealing. But then she said, in a voice that sounded actually cheerful:

"Nah, May-ry. All's well."

"Please don' eat wood. Y' make me ill." Hauling against an enormous weariness, Mary crept out of the blanket and stood up outside the shelter in a frost-covered world, squatted on pain-wracked legs to make steamy water, shivering and surveying the weather and trying to get her bearings. It was still gloomy in the ravine, and the fast stream they had crossed last evening rushed and gurgled nearby. The sky above the ravine was pinkish-blue and the leafless trees on a ridge far downstream caught the early-morning sunlight and gleamed a soft rosy yellow. Promise of a fair day but cold. It would be hours before the sun could mount high enough to light these deep valleys.

And us with one blanket a-tween us now, Mary thought. One and t'other of us'll have to go naked in turn.

Nay, she thought then, angrily: She lost *her* blanket. *She'll* go naked.

Forgive me, she thought then. Of course we'll take our turns. If the old thing'll cooperate we will. I think she be a-needin' a lecture.

She heard footsteps above; over the noise of the stream she heard leaves crushing. She stood and turned, hoisting the spear.

A deer came down between two mossy ledges of rock, going toward the creek. It was a buck with fine antlers. It sensed her presence, paused to look at her, then went on down to the stream. It was too far away for her to throw the spear at it. She took a few cautious, wobbly steps toward it, her skin in gooseflesh, frost biting her bare feet, her breath condensing. The buck raised its head from drinking and bounded away up the bank. The white under its tail disappeared in the brush.

Ah well, Mary thought. Nothing lost. No expectations for that'n.

She went back and peered under the log. Ghetel was sitting in the dim cranny, the blanket up over her shoulders, a mass of wood-rot in her upturned palm. She was probing in it and putting things in her mouth. She was too intent to see Mary loom over her. Mary bent down and looked closely, then shuddered violently. Ghetel was picking little dark beetles out of wood dust and eating them.

Ghetel became aware of Mary, raised her eyes and suddenly hid her hands in the blanket. She looked angry. "Not enough for both us. You find a tree."

Mary's mouth gaped. She saw a blaze of red behind her eyes. She reached in and grabbed the edge of the blanket and jerked it with all her might, dragging it off Ghetel and dumping her over. "*You* find a *blanket*," she snapped. She flung the blanket around her shoulders, took one hard last glance at the awful-looking bundle of baggy gray skin and protruding bones floundering to sit up under the log, then stalked away down the creek bank. About thirty yards farther on she stopped, stood looking at the cliffs, took a deep breath and sighed it out, and waited until she heard Ghetel's neck-bell and querulous mutterings coming along behind her. She turned and watched her catch up, meandering as if drunk, kicking up leaves as she stumbled forward, her baggy skin flapping as loose as the rags of her dress, holding something forward in her palm.

"Forgif?" she said plaintively, drawing near. "Here. I bring you some . . . "

"I'll not eat bugs! Ghetel, hear me, I must tell you how it's to be if we go on together . . . Listen!" Ghetel stood there twitching and trembling with the cold, eating the rest of the beetles, then dusted the wood punk off her palms, and waited, ruminating on her revolting cud, staring ingenuously at Mary with her bleared hazel eyes, waiting for admonitions she perhaps understood were deserved.

Older'n my mother, Mary thought, yet I must now scold 'er down like a nose-pickin' child.

"Ghetel, I come away 'cause I got a pinin' for a faraway place and my husband who needs me. That, dear, is why I'm not t' be stopped, by starvin', nor sickness, nor any kind o' hurt. Nor'll I be stopped by a woman who grudges me my purpose.

"I know your purpose is weaker, as you're goin' t' no one. And Lord knows y'r gut rules ye more'n mine does me . . . Mercy! One who'd eat bugs!

"Many ways, I know, y're stronger'n me. Oh, aye! How you took that whuppin' at the Shawnee town! Now, I'd've died I'm sure! I admired that more'n you could know.

"But now, dear, having purpose, *I'm* the stronger one. And though I need 'ee quite some, why, I sh'll just go on alone if 'ee ever serve me as bad as 'ee did yesterday! Aye, leave 'ee back, and a good riddance, too! Now, are we agreed, eh?"

The old woman had swallowed her bugs. She nodded and stood hugging her bosom and shaking. "Aye, aye. Vat I done yesterday I don't remember. But I don't hurt you again, Mayry. Oh, I am *cold!*"

"We must get a-movin' or we'll seize up frozen. Now, listen, Ghetel, I sh'll give 'ee this blanket now and then, in turn, but only if 'ee promise to give me it back when I say. A promise?"

"Yah, a promise."

"I mean your true word, God as your witness."

"Yah. Gott I swear."

"So be it. Now come."

They reached the mouth of the roaring creek and turned southeastward late in the morning. The descent had taken them hours because they had had to cross two great, precarious rockslides where any misstep sent stones and boulders tilting out from under their feet and rattling and crashing down into the creek. They had also been slowed by Ghetel's new taste for bugs. She had picked up a sharp-edged piece of flat rock, and at virtually every downed tree she had lagged behind to hew rotten bark away with the stone and look for such beetles as she had enjoyed for breakfast. Mary grew impatient, and was constantly coaxing her on. But in a way it was better; as long as Ghetel had hopes of finding food and was preoccupied with it, she seemed less desperate, less sullen toward Mary, less dangerous. Ghetel had found no more bugs despite all her stalling and hacking, but she seemed certain that she would, and was comparatively happy.

Crossing the rockslides had done awful damage to their feet. The skin was off most of their toes and ankles and they left little red smudges of blood wherever they stepped. Mary had a deep gash in the arch of her right foot and a puncture in the sole of her left where a locust-thorn had gone in at least an inch. She had pulled it out but a part of the point had broken off and was deep in the flesh. Ghetel had caught her left foot between two jagged rocks, and in trying to lift one off had badly ground up the flesh of her little toe. But, as the white bone was visible, they had been able to inspect it and see that the toe was not broken. Every part of their feet had been stubbed and jammed and scraped countless times, so often that each time it happened it was a surprise that the new pain could be felt through the old pain. And so when they reached the narrow strip of bottomland in the New River gorge, they sat down on a drift log in the weak November sunlight and, despite the chill of it, made plasters of the icy mud and caked each other's feet in them. They spent an hour there, sitting side by side on the log, the blanket across both their backs, facing the sun, all the weight off their feet, letting the mud dry and pull the sharp pains out of their feet. "Notice?" Mary said. "Y'can count your heartbeat by th' throbbin's in your feet." They did that for a while as the sun shone on their faces and closed eyelids. Ghetel jerked awake suddenly, saving herself from falling backward off the log.

They sat in the hush of the river valley and waited for the courage to put their weight back on their feet and go. A flash of intense scarlet shot through their vision and stopped on a bush ten feet away: a cardinal. He sat on a swaying twig looking about with abrupt little turns of his crested head, his bead-black eyes almost invisible in the band of black around the base of his beak. Mary was seeing him with an intense clarity of vision brought on by her utter emptiness, a kind of seeing in which he was not just a bright red bird in a wintry landscape of browns and grays and dying greens, but was a flying vehicle designed to carry the vibrancy of its life from place to barren place and thus to keep all places from being without the beauty of life. Mary had never had such a thought before, and she was staring at the bird the way she had stared at the burning spring several nights before, warming her soul at it, when Ghetel moved abruptly beside her and flung the rock she had been carrying. The toss was feeble and inaccurate; the rock struck low in the bush, shaking it, and the cardinal fluttered away untouched. Mary turned and looked at her, incredulous. "Why?" she demanded.

Ghetel's eyes were blazing, happily. "I just t'ink: There are alvays birds, here, dere . . . and a bird is not much to eat, but it is more den a *bug!* We carry rocks, eh? And one time now and den, ven ve trow ve don' miss, eh? And ve vill eat a bird dat day, eh?"

Mary shook her head. Ghetel and her gut.

But when they put their weight on their feet, groaning with the returning pain and then getting used to it, and started to move on, Mary stooped alongside Ghetel and gathered rocks of good throwing size, enough of them to carry at the ready in one hand. It was true, there were always many birds darting about, even in this stark season, and one bird, one cardinal or mockingbird, even one small oriole or robin or a tiny sparrow, would be more nourishment than they had taken in the last week.

Maybe, Mary thought, still working things out in the light-headedness of hunger, maybe that is what the redbird was telling us, all bright red and full of life like that.

Early in the afternoon they reached the creek of the painted trees. By that time they had gathered and thrown several handfuls of stones, but had come nowhere near bringing down a bird, and Mary was beginning to understand that if they ever did hit one of the swift little creatures with their feebly-thrown missiles, it would be more by chance than by aim. She had resigned herself to that. Still, there was a chance, and so they carried rocks and they stalked birds and threw at them as they went along.

But somehow as they progressed they saw fewer birds, and Mary sensed that somehow the birds were warning each other.

The river and the paint-tree creek both were higher and faster than they had been in July. They could not wade across the New River at the shoal; it would have been too high and fast now even if they had been on horseback. And it appeared that they would have to do still another walk-around to get across the paint-tree creek. So they turned up through the brushy, narrow canyon.

The narrow bottomland where they had camped on the way down was under water now, just saplings and bushes sticking up out of the water, and where the sides of the gorge were too steep to walk on the two women waded in the cold water up to their knees and held to a bush, a tree, a root, a vine. They were extremely weak now and did not trust their benumbed legs to support them even in this shallow water, so they would not let go of one handhold until they had a new one. This creek twisted like a snake around the base of steep mountains whose sides seemed to mount to the very center of the sky, and the sun was down from sight early in the afternoon so there was not even that faint warmth to bless their skin. The ravine was so narrow that Mary sometimes had to hang onto a tree and look up and around to assure herself that the mountainsides were not moving together to crush her.

They went about five miles up the west side of this creek before they found a place of riffles and decided they could cross there. Mary decided. The old woman was simply following along now, moaning with hunger or pain or both, stopping now and then to heave a rock weakly at some bird. They waded across the creek easily, simply clenching their teeth and letting the egg- and fist-sized pebbles of the bottom torture their feet as they would; that did not matter any more; they just had to get across this creek and back down to the river before dark.

Mary had assumed a similar attitude about her stomach. It was simply going to gnaw and hurt and give her that awful, weakening hollowness, and that was the way it was. She did not try to find just any old thing to put into it anymore; she simply was not as desperate as Ghetel to have something in it for the sake of having something in it. She thought it probably was better to have nothing in it at all than to have it half full of such trash as Ghetel was continually picking up and gnawing and swallowing: bark and seed pods and husks, fungus off the dead trees, dead moss full of dirt, and now, even beetles and grubworms.

But as dusk came down and they returned to the valley of

the river, Mary's hunger made her so faint that the world
around her began humming and swooping, and she realized
that even though she could stand the misery of starving, her
body would not keep going much longer on nothingness. It
really had exhausted all the residue of roots and sumac berries and slippery-elm bark she had eaten days before and was
now consuming itself, and will or no, or Will or no, her body
would simply stop here. The truth was that she could not
ignore her hunger any longer; she could not just rise above it.

And so in the last light of this day she hunted food alongside Ghetel with an equal urgency. They pulled up and
gnawed roots. They ate buds. They found a few acorns,
cracked them with rocks and ate the dried-up, leathery, bitter
meats. They threw rocks in vain at a few sparrows. They
threw the spear at a raccoon and missed. And when Ghetel at
last barked an old log that yielded a few squirming grubs,
Mary did take a few in her palm and, trying to think of
faraway things, threw them into her mouth and swallowed
them, unable to bear the thought of chewing them. When they
were down she gave a great shudder. And she had a grim
thought then that made her smile:

If you don' eat worms, they'll be eatin' you.

She felt a little stronger in the morning. Clouds had come
up from the southwest, again dulling the colors of the valley
but warming the air a bit. There was no frost this morning and
the ground was soft and moist, squishy with cold damp.
Ghetel was reasonably cheerful, being warmer and not quite
so famished as she had been on previous days, and even gave
Mary a grand, spontaneous hug.

We'll do all right mostly, Mary thought. But when times are
at their worst, I must watch 'er.

To keep Ghetel complacent, Mary decided to devote a
while to feeding before they started up the gorge this
morning.

They found a quantity of the sour, fuzzy sumac berries in
an old burnt-over draw, but could eat only a handful as they
were brown and dusty dry and disintegrating. They flaked old
shelf funguses off dead trees, gray, leathery and foul-tasting,

but filling, and pulled a few water's-edge stalks and ate their bitter bulbs. Still queasy about the eating of worms, though now resigned to it, Mary helped Ghetel hunt for grubs. They found none. But Mary remembered how Henry Lenard had used to turn up rocks to find earthworms for fishbait. And somehow the thought of healthy pink earthworms this morning seemed less revolting than that of the white grubs, which reminded her too strongly of maggots. So, in the humus-rich, leaf-covered soil at the base of the mountainside, Mary began turning rocks over, and in fifteen minutes had a palm full of glistening, reddish-pink crawlers. Ghetel, delighted, fell to the same work and soon had a good handful.

All right now, Mary told herself, don't think, just do it. Just like a bird. She shut her eyes and put three or four in her mouth and chewed them quickly and swallowed them. They were tough and slimy and cold and strangely sourish, and left her teeth gritty. But there was no doubt: it was meat. It would strengthen her fibers and enrich her blood. She ate the rest, and, under the influence of those thoughts, they tasted more palatable each mouthful. "Eh well, dear," she said to Ghetel, who was beaming now, "truly that was the best breakfast we've had in an age, say what? Y' ready to walk now? Here, you wear the blanket a while first." Ghetel nodded and flung it over her shoulders. Mary had noticed that Ghetel talked little to her now; since their fight, she had hardly said a dozen sentences, but would often discourse with herself in Dutch as they struggled along.

Within a few hours of walking, Mary began to notice a change in the aspect of the valley above the painted-tree creek. The mountainsides were steeper and more forbidding, and were footed right on the river's edge. There was no level bottomland to walk on. The river tumbled furiously, glassy green and white, among boulders as big as houses, which lay at the bases of the cliffs from which they had fallen. The mountainsides soared steeply a thousand feet or more up from the roaring riverbed, darkly forested all the way from the water's edge to their crests. Huge, water-weathered gray trees, undermined by the river's force, lay jammed among the boulders, their gnarled roots upended, their branches in the

tugging river, sometimes entangling great masses of dead
bushes and reeds that had been swept into their clutches by
old floods.

There were places where whole mountainsides seemed to
have sloughed off and fallen into the river, leaving stark blue-
gray cliff faces as precipitous as walls, hundreds of feet high,
topped with full-size forest trees which, from this distance,
looked tiny as blades of grass.

Ahead stood a mountainside whose entire slope from the
crest to the base was covered by the scar and scree of an
avalanche: an enormous slide of boulders and dirt leaning a
third of the way up the mountainside, full of splintered trees
and jutting root-boles, massive ash and walnut trees bent
double or twisted open like segments of frayed rope by the
weight and force of the rockfall; above was the bald face of
new rock from which it all had come, slanting a thousand feet
into the sky.

We'll have to cross all that rubble, Mary thought. Pray it's
done all the fallin' it's going to do.

Inured though they were by now to the power and indifference of the wilderness, the two women felt the grim force
of this gorge pressing on their senses and squeezing their
hearts. To be enclosed by the walls of this gloomy, craggy,
roaring canyon was like being on the floor of the den of a
giant, who might step on them at any moment without notic-
ing or caring. Mary felt as tiny as any one of the lice now
making their way through the folds of her own flesh. It's no
wonder the Indians take the ridge road around it, she thought.
For a moment she considered turning back to the paint-tree
creek and going that way.

Nay, she thought. I'd get us lost in the mountains for sure.
At least I know this awful gorge leads to home.

There was nothing so simple as walking now; it was now
mostly a business of climbing, scooting, crawling and sliding
over and around the gigantic rubble of the riverbed. To skirt a
square-cornered rock chunk the size of a barn they would
have to climb over two or three as large as cabins. Often they
would find their way barred by a huge snarl of fallen trees or
drifted brush, and would snake through or under these, scrap-

ing their skin, spraining joints, taking thorns and splinters, snagging and losing still more of their skimpy rags, forever afraid that their efforts would dislodge some key log and cause the whole jam to rend itself apart and crush them or drop them into the torrent below.

By midafternoon, they were in a trance of exhaustion. Mary lay face down on a huge tilted slab of gray rock. Blue-green splotches of lichen grew dim, then sharp, then dim again, an inch before her eyes, while the river drummed loud and faint and loud in her ears. She might have slept. She was not sure. But after an indefinite time she became aware that she was very cold and it was time to move.

Looking up the raging stream, between the V-shaped canyon walls, they could see range after range of such steep-edged mountains sitting with their feet in the river, each mountain a degree higher and hazier than the one in front of it, a progression of fading grays marching into the distance until they were indistinct in river mist. In the gloomy, furrowed valleys slanting up from either side of the river, ragged wraiths of mist curled and shifted upward, like a slow dance of ghosts. Now Mary began to suspect that the Indians' avoidance of this gorge was as much from a fear of evil spirits as of terrain.

They crossed the debris of the avalanche late that afternoon. It took them an hour to climb through the boulders and rubble and dead wood. Several times, rocks loosened under their feet and bounced and crashed down into the river; worse, they heard stones clattering and bumping above them once, and hugged themselves against a jutting log, expecting to be buried in a rockfall.

The wind was cold, the stones were cold, the water, when they had to step into it and wade around the bases of bluffs, was very cold. Their skin was clammy and white and usually covered in gooseflesh. They would get hot and winded while climbing, and when they had to stop to rest, the wind would chill them immediately. They took turns wearing the blanket as they climbed; neither would wear it while they were wading; and when they dropped down to rest they would huddle together in it.

They finally found a place where a finger of land sloped gently enough that they could walk in the woods, on a cushion of dead leaves. Here they found another hollow log lying on its side and decided this would be their camp for the night. They had to shout to make themselves heard over the roar of the river. Mary wondered how they would be able to sleep in such noise. Sometimes during the day the noise had pressed so hard on her soul that she had thought she would scream and go mad. It was as constant and loud as the windstorm the night they had spent across from the burning spring. Mary thought it was making her heart beat faster. Under this constant drumming of wilderness, the faint metallic sounds of the bell were welcome, like delicate music, a civilized sound.

Here in the woods they turned over rocks and found a few more worms. They had spent so much energy climbing that Mary was hungrier than she had been yet. There had been periods downriver when they had not eaten anything for four or five days, but even then she had not been as famished as she was now. So she ate the worms this time with no thought except how good they were.

Ghetel was behaving rather well. She seemed distant and distracted, but she was not giving Mary those hostile looks, and she had been following well. Really, very well, Mary thought. I may not be havin' any more trouble with 'er. I mean if I can keep 'er full of worms.

Let's hope there won't be a hard freeze where the worms go deep, she thought. It's nice to be able just to turn over a few rocks and find meat.

She was beginning to think of the worms in terms of meat now instead of as worms. That was good.

They filled the hollow log with leaves and burrowed in with the blanket. With the leaves and the blanket up around their heads, the roar of the river was muffled a bit and it was not so intimidating. As they lay together skin on skin they grew warmer, and as they grew warmer, their aches and bruises eased a little and they grew sleepy. Mary appreciated Ghetel's body heat, and she thought a great deal about her and tried to imagine what must be in her mind. She's truly stalwart, Mary thought. She really is something out of the ordinary.

She felt tears sting her eyes as she held the old bones close. Thou'rt close as family, she thought to the old woman. Like family, a great botheration sometimes. But what we two've been through'd bind folks closer'n family.

She remembered the uneasiness she had had that day so long ago, when she had been afraid to give Ghetel the tomahawk. She had been right about that. The old woman really had wanted to hurt her; she'd been out of her noggin. It wasn't hard to understand, really. But now Mary seemed to understand that the reason she had been able to read Ghetel's intentions was because the two of them had become so close through this ordeal. It was almost like what she had heard about twins. There was some bridge between them. We're close as twins, you and me, because we been dependin' on each other so long out here in these valleys where there ain't anything else but you and me, she thought.

Aye, old thing. You're family. And when we get home, I'll have Will see to't that y'have anything your heart desires, I will.

She wondered how far they had come today. Surely not more'n ten or fifteen miles, she thought, though it seemed more like fifty, all that climbin' an' scootin'. She smiled at the thought: Been days since I had any skin on my feet. Now my knees and my hindy end's likewise.

Ghetel's breathing was gurgly. She coughed in her sleep, jerking violently, enveloping Mary's face with rancid breath and spraying it with spittle. Mary patted her gently, rhythmically on the back, as if soothing her baby.

Her baby.

For a moment she pictured her baby. Or, rather, a little shape. She could not see its face. She had been careful not to know its face. Now she could not have remembered its face if she had tried to.

She envisioned a little shape, nursing at the breast of Otter Girl.

She was slipping into sleep. She saw Will. She saw herself with Will. He was asking her where the baby was, their baby that he had never seen. There was a blank space in her mind when she fell asleep because she did not know how she would answer that when he asked her.

The valley seemed to widen as they went on the next morning. The river was about a quarter of a mile wide, running shallow, its surface roiled. The noise of its flow was less overwhelming here in this wider space. There were broad flat tables of rock to walk on and not so much climbing to do. They progressed without great difficulty for three or four miles. The sun was trying to break through the gray clouds that hid the mountaintops. They could see it as a pale smear in the dark sky, but sometimes the mist in the draws would swirl over it like smoke and blot it out again.

Something was drumming on Mary's ears. She grew aware of it little by little, some deep rumble beyond the rushing of the river. They rounded a bend and it became louder.

"Look'ee, Ghetel!" Mary pointed. A mile ahead there was a line of greenish-white extending from bank to bank. Beyond that was a great dark mountainside topped with clouds. "A waterfall, ain't it?"

Ghetel peered up the river, her mouth hanging open. Her lower front teeth were yellow and there was gray matter against her gums. Her lower lip was a rim of bleeding sores and scabs. She nodded and looked at Mary with a question in her eyes. Mary knew what the question was: Would the falls be another obstacle?

As they went up, the falls became more distinct, louder, more formidable. They were like a giant's stairsteps, over which the gray-green water fell roaring five or ten feet at a drop, seething white at the foot of each cascade. The falls extended from shore to shore, broken only by a small wooded island that lay in the great pool below them.

The shore here was sand and shingle. Trees stood high out of the sand, their gnarled, grotesque root boles three or four feet above the ground where the soil had washed out from under them. As the women moved along and came opposite the island, they saw that there was a smaller island at the top of the falls, with brush growing on it. The dark water seethed with foam here in the pool. The air was wet with the fall's mist.

Mary kept studying the falls at the right shore, where they would have to pass, to see whether there would be a dry place to climb. They could not climb where the water gushed down; they would be swept away.

It looked bad. There was no sloping ground to ascend. The falls roared over their rock shelves right at the base of a perpendicular bluff of striated rock.

No, she thought. Oh, no. We just can't come up blocked here. Not after all this. Let's go closer. Must be we can find a way up.

The narrow shore of shingle and sand dwindled to nothing as they crept under the bluff. Soon they were standing right in the falls' spray, on a narrow ledge of wet rock with the foamy water swirling a few inches below their feet. They held onto the sheer rockface and stared, nearly hypnotized, at the glassy curtain of water falling beside them. Mary clung with her fingertips to the cold, wet rock, squinting up the cliff looking for a way up, her heart tripping, her skin and rags growing damp. The hissing, rumbling force of the plunging river was pounding her senses into a state of disorientation. She felt that the very cliff they were clinging to was moving, tilting with them on it. She swallowed rapidly against panic. Her mouth was dry.

"Go back!" she cried. She turned her face toward Ghetel and shouted it again. "GO BACK!"

The old woman's face was a mask of cringing terror. She clung to the rock, frozen, afraid to move a muscle. There was no room for Mary to go around her and lead her back to safety; the ledge was too narrow. Mary was trapped on the lip of rock, her legs beginning to twitch and quiver uncontrollably, and Ghetel was frozen between her and the route back to the shore. And that awful notion of giving up, of stepping so easily off into the water and putting an end to all this suffering, was beginning to insinuate itself in her head again.

What's it matter? she thought again.

And somehow that thought calmed her. Her legs stopped quaking.

She grinned at Ghetel. It was meant to be a reassuring smile but it was ghastly as a death's head; she could feel her mouth corners drawn back and down against her teeth, and the strain around her eyes.

Got to move her, Mary thought. Got to. We're both going to fall in a minute if we don't get back.

Leaning her precious spear against her left arm, she freed her right hand to reach over and touch Ghetel's left hand, which was locked, rigid as a root, in a tiny crevice at eye level. She patted the hand gently for a moment, then closed her hand over it and gently tried to pull it loose, to move it over a few inches and make Ghetel understand that they were to go back. But the old hand grew even harder; the fingers dug in like talons. A terrified, keening wail started coming from Ghetel's open mouth and she pressed her face against the rock. Her eyes were wild.

Dear God, she thinks I'm trying to throw her in, Mary thought. She'll never budge if she thinks that.

Or she'll try to throw *me* in.

She took her hand off Ghetel's. The old woman stopped wailing.

Mary searched her mind for something to say. Then:

"Ghetel, hon," she yelled, "I know an easier way! I know a way around!" She forced another squinting smile, and looked past Ghetel toward the way they had come, and nodded.

The look in Ghetel's eyes changed a bit. She shut her mouth and looked suspiciously at Mary's face for a moment, as if not sure she should turn her attention away from her for even an instant. Mary nodded and looked downstream again, nodding emphatically.

At last Ghetel began turning her head, but kept her eyes on Mary as long as she could. Finally she was looking the other way.

Now, Mary thought. She's lookin' the way of safety; maybe now she'll go. Slowly, she moved her hand toward Ghetel's again, and lightly patted it.

At the touch, Ghetel's head spun around and the scream started, and in the same instant she released the rock to fling Mary's hand away. The motion nearly dislodged Mary from

the face of the cliff, and Ghetel herself tottered for a moment
before hooking her talons into the crevice again. An enervat-
ing shiver sizzled through Mary's body and her heart seemed
to be twitching in her neck. She clung to the cliff with both
hands herself now, face pressed against the rock, the water
still roaring ominously beside her. That had been too close.
She breathed deeply until she could think.

Eh well. No gentle coaxing was going to do it, she realized.
Sometimes there's but one way to get through that thick
Dutch head. She locked her own left hand more firmly into its
fingerhold. With her right she took the shaft of the hickory
stock and swung it out behind her over the water, then yelled:

"God damn'ee, Ghetel! MOVE!" And she swung the stick
to whack across the bony old rump. It was not much of a
blow; her balance was too precarious for that. But she struck
her again, then again, yelling like a banshee: "MOVE,
Y'CLOD! GET THAT REECHY CARCASS O' YOUR'N
OUT OF MY PATH! MOVE, DAMN 'EE!"

Ghetel looked at her, flinching, and she seemed suddenly
more afraid of Mary than of moving; she began to move. She
inched back along the cliff. Mary followed her.

In a minute they were back on the beach. They were so
weak they sank to the ground. Mary moved close to Ghetel
and drew the blanket over them both. They sat there for a
long time, trembling, while Ghetel moaned to herself and said
things in Dutch.

When they had calmed themselves, Mary got up and went a
few yards down the shore, pausing now and then to peer up
the mountainside. After a while she found a gap in the cliff
where they could climb up by holding roots and ledges and
get onto the slope above the cliff, and thus bypass the falls in
the woods far above.

The climb took two hours, and they became dizzy when
they paused and looked down through the bare trees onto the
huge jagged waterfall far below them, the relentless gray-
green water and swirls of white foam. The mountain slope
they were on curved to their right, following a bend in the
river above the falls. They had gone a mile around the mountain, a hundred feet above the water, when they saw below

them a juncture of two rivers, one coming toward them from
the east, the other from the south. These two rivers joined at
the base of this mountain to make the river they had been
following; it was their combined waters that they could still
hear rushing over the falls a mile behind them. But the sight
of this wide fork of rivers stopped Mary in her tracks and
threw her into confusion.

One of these two forks, she thought, is the New River. But
which one?

There were no landmarks in her memory to answer that
question, because she had never been through this place
before.

Ghetel was hovering at her shoulder, waiting, as ever, for
her to lead on. Mary knew she must choose one fork or the
other immediately, because if the old woman sensed that she
was uncertain of the way, she might well grow rebellious
again.

Mary chose the fork leading right, toward the south, for
two reasons. First, it looked to be just a little wider and thus
probably was the main rivercourse. Second, because there
was no way to get to that other river without crossing this one.

And so she led Ghetel down the slope closer to the river
bank. She proceeded as if she were absolutely certain they
were on the New River. But she knew there would always be a
doubt in her mind as to whether that other stream had been
the New River, her highway to home.

And if I ever find out it was, she thought, it'll be too late by
then.

That doubt became a burden, as heavy as if she were
carrying another person on her shoulders. In a way, she was:
that other person she was carrying was the Mary Ingles who
believed that the stream not taken was the right stream.

Her footsteps, heavy and painful enough already, were
dragged down with reluctance.

And the gorge up which they were moving now was even
more gigantic and ominous. Now every ridge they could see
came directly to the river's edge and ended in a sheer cliff
dropping fifty to a hundred feet to the river, where the current

over the centuries had cut under the mountainsides. Ten feet offshore from where Mary and Ghetel now slid and crawled, there were three or four rock chunks in the river, big as ships, with trees growing on top of them. The women were passing under a steep gray cliff now, a hundred feet high, from which those huge monoliths evidently had fallen into the river. Across the river in a shadowy, narrow ravine, a creek poured over a stone ledge and cascaded in twenty-foot leaps down the picturesque, narrow notch it had carved for itself. It was the kind of place Mary would have lingered hours to gaze at under any other circumstances. Now, in her frightened and doubtful state of mind, things of great beauty saddened her.

Ghetel was coming along automatically now, stumbling a few yards, sitting down to rest and rub her feet, talking to herself. She had not said a word about the pounding Mary had given her with the stick at the falls. She seemed to be retreating into herself, drawing a cloak of resistance around herself to shut out the miserable realities of their plight.

I could do that too, Mary thought, if I had but to follow; if I needn't think.

That other river back there, she thought. Oh, that haunts me!

CHAPTER
22

IN THE THREE DAYS SINCE THEY HAD PASSED THE FALLS, THEY had found nothing to eat.

They had seen hickory trees and walnut trees and oaks high on the slopes above, but invariably, on climbing to them, they found nothing but a few broken shells. Squirrels and other animals had harvested everything.

There were no swamp plants with succulent roots up here in this stony gorge because there was no still water anywhere. All the rain that fell and all the sleet that melted poured down steep rivulets into creeks, raced over shallow brown rock-and-pebble streambeds and plunged over ledges into this river, which hurried recklessly down its zigzag course as if desperate to get out of these high Alleghenies and down into the stately O-y-o, now more than a hundred miles behind.

There were not even any worms now. There was no soil at the river's edge, only rock. And up the slopes; the ground had hardened with cold; if there were earthworms in it, they had burrowed deep.

There were fish in the river and the creeks: big, swift, beautiful fast-water fish, but they were not like a catfish, to lie lazily on a shallow bottom inviting a spear; they were darters, seen in a flash and gone deep; and Mary had nothing with which to make a serviceable fishhook. Even if she had had a fishhook, there would have been nothing for bait. And even if she had had a fishhook and bait, she probably would have had no patience to sit and fish. She was driven and tormented by her uncertainty about this river. She could not rest in this thundering gorge, not knowing whether it was the New River or not. She had decided to give herself six days to turn up a landmark, any landmark she would remember having seen before the Indians had set off overland. If she did not see anything she recognized by then, she would contrive some means to get across this river—floating on a log or something, whatever the risk—and would go back down to that river that had led up to the east and follow *it* until she recognized something. She had grown that desperate. She was sure they had walked six hundred miles or more since they had fled from the Indians. To have come six hundred miles through a hostile wilderness and suffered such hardships, all in vain, would prove a God too mocking and cruel to abide. As it was now, she would scowl at the wintry sky several times a day and demand to know why a decent woman like herself had been thrown into this dank and thundering hell-pit.

There were not even birds in this gorge, it seemed. She

could remember seeing no small woodland birds since passing the falls; this was a craggy land fit only for hawks and eagles and vultures, all of which she had seen diving from cliff-tops or wheeling over the gorge. You could not throw a rock up there and knock one down to eat. Likely you could not even bring one down with a rifle. She had seen wild turkeys at a distance, but they were nervous and impossible to approach.

And the forest animals were simply too wary and agile to kill for food without a gun. In these three days above the falls they had glimpsed a fox, three wolves, or one wolf three times, a blazing-eyed lynx crouched on a bluff looking down at them from twenty feet above, an elk on the far shore. And in one startling instant just after dawn, they had glimpsed the face of some cat-creature, as big as the face of a man, in a clump of bushes five feet ahead of them, before it disappeared with a swish and a rustle. They had not seen any bears for weeks, which was all right with her. The cold weather had also retired the snakes.

That's just as well for the snakes, Mary thought, as I'd stone one and eat 'im now if I could find one.

Ghetel had groaned all night; neither of them had slept. The night had seemed a year long. Mary, herself eaten up inside with cramps and gnawings, had fallen into spells from time to time, in which she would be looking at the cold stars glittering above the cliff-tops, then would be awakened, by a shudder or a fibrillation of her heart, to the realization that she was still looking at the cold stars but that she had not been seeing them for a while. And Ghetel would still be groaning. Sometimes the old woman would twitch violently, or would suddenly jerk her knees up and curl herself into a ball, hugging herself, her bony knees slamming into Mary's side. And then the blanket, which had been arranged so carefully over them to keep all their limbs covered, would be pulled askew and Mary would have to sit up, shivering, to rearrange it and tuck in its edges. During those hours, she would think of virtually nothing but the tragic loss of Ghetel's blanket. In those early morning hours with the frost seeming to fall on them directly from the bitter blue-white stars, the loss of that blanket would grow in her mind to be the greatest of their misfortunes, greater than the loss of the tomahawk, greater than their want of food, greater than their need of shoes. In the daytime her great preoccupation would be that awful growing certainty that they were on the wrong river, and that they would perish before having a chance to verify and correct their mistake.

It must be a simple matter to be Ghetel, she thought. To her, our greatest misfortune is always the same: that we're starved nigh to death.

Mary felt, as she had been feeling all night, the pebbles of the narrow beach grinding against her fleshless bones, even through the crushed bed of moss and drift leaves they had laid down, and she thought:

William might well not even know me if he saw me now. Surely I scarce weigh six stone anymore.

Her stomach gripped. She drew her legs up and squinted against the pain and drew cold air through her clenched teeth, and the cold air on her teeth sent needles of pain through her face, into her eyeballs. Her gums were rotting and her teeth were loose and sensitive to cold, even to biting. It was an agony to drink water, and chew a root.

And another strange thing had happened to her, something she had realized one long, sleepless, thoughtful night somewhere along the way, one night when she had been going one by one over the effects of the ordeal: by her count of the days on the knotted belt, she ought to have had her monthlies by now. She had gone through them once since the baby's birth, while she was still in captivity, but she should have had them once again, just a few days ago. It was good not to have the bother of them, of course, but still they were something her body always had done when it was supposed to, and now it was, she suspected, a sign, along with the loose teeth and the swollen joints and the constant coldness and the periods of distorted vision and unclear thinking, a sign that she was truly starving—not just desperately hungry, but starving.

She thought about these things and waited for the daylight, though she now felt such an overwhelming lassitude that she didn't know whether she could even get to her feet, come morning—or why she should.

It was doubly hard to think about getting up and moving now that she suspected she was following the wrong river—and perhaps going farther from home.

The stars had faded out and the sky had turned peach-colored above the walls of the chasm. Now Mary could see the rivercourse again, could see the boulders and shrubs gradually set themselves out from the massive silhouettes of the cliffs, and the hopelessness of the night receded into the back of her mind again as it did every morning when she could look up the river and see their way.

It took her five minutes to stand up. First she would sit up with a groan. Then she would fold a leg a little at a time, wincing, then the other leg, until both feet were flat on the ground. Then she would push her weight forward or pull on a limb until her weight was on her feet. Then she would squat there a while, resting, moaning at the stabs of pain in her knees and feet and hips, until she was ready to haul herself to a standing position.

Some mornings, if there was nothing to hold onto and lift herself, she would turn over onto her stomach and get onto all fours and then stand up.

It was as if her leg and ankle and hip joints froze in the night. It was like breaking them loose every morning. Then after she had helped Ghetel get up, and had walked gasping a few hundred feet, the joints would stop grinding and shooting their pains through her, and she would be ready for another day's going.

The desultory clunking of Ghetel's bell bothered Mary now. Now that her head was in a fuddle over this dubious maze of rivers, the bell seemed a silly thing, a stupid indulgence.

But she ought to wear a bell, Mary joked grimly to herself sometimes; she is, after all, such a mule.

This morning they came to a place where the river curved away to their left. Along the outside of its curve, where they were now limping along, the river had carved its way into the base of a high cliff. There was a stretch of several hundred feet ahead of them where the water swirled along right at the

base of the cliff. There was no place between the roiling water
and the stone wall to walk.

Mary stopped and studied it. They had come to such places
every day since the falls. There were only two ways, sometimes only one, to get past these places. Either was horrible in
its particular way.

She tried the direct way first. Steeling herself against the
cold and clutching at handholds in the sheer stone, she
probed the water with the hickory pole in her left hand. She
felt a rock bottom. It was shallow enough here for a first step.
She stepped down into the water; she felt the shock of it shoot
up into her chest and make her heart skip. Then she probed
ahead with the pole again and found another solid place. She
put her left foot on it and then brought her right foot over. The
icy water was swirling around her hips now, and she moved
her right hand from one crevice to another, then reached out
again with the pole.

It found no bottom this time. She pushed it further down
into the water. Nothing. She shifted her grip to the upper end
of the pole and shoved it farther down until her hand was in
the river. The whole length of the pole was underwater and
was touching nothing. That meant it was over her head and
they could not wade along the base of the cliff and would
therefore have to do it the other way. The cold water was
seizing up her joints again. She turned her face back along the
cliff and started inching her way back across the distance she
had come. Ghetel was sitting there in the blanket, as if in a
stupor, just waiting to be told what to do. Mary climbed back
onto the bank, shaking violently. She had to struggle briefly
with Ghetel to get the blanket, and wrapped herself in it.
"Let's go back a ways," she said. "We've got to climb this'n,
I'm afraid."

Ghetel got up and followed without question, her bell clunking dismally; she did not really seem to know anymore
whether they were going one way or the other.

They went back beyond the place where they had slept.
Every step back was twice as hard as any step in the right
direction, and Mary would almost despair whenever she

had to expend her waning strength backtracking from a dead end.

Mary found a place at last where they could start up the slope, a place where there were roots and rocks to haul themselves up by, to climb the mountain and pass over above the cliff.

They spent the rest of the morning on this passage. They could go only a few feet before stopping to slump against a tree trunk or to lie face down against the slope hanging by roots to get their breath while their legs twitched and trembled from the strain. They would stop when the dizziness came, when the huge rampart they were ascending would seem to waver and tilt and threatened to dump them off into the dark river below.

Then they moved across the lip of the cliff, scooting and sliding rather than walking, afraid to stand up above the yawning chasm, afraid they would faint and fall off through space.

There were evergreen trees up here, dark green, carpeting the scrabbly soil with their fallen needles. The women sat for a while on this carpet, warmed by the sun, and seemed to be able to breathe more deeply up here than down in the confining, shadowy valley with its dank air. Up here the noise of the river was a whisper instead of a roar, and the sky was like new blue steel and seemed almost close enough to reach up and touch. Mary felt a strange lightness, almost an elation, and pressed herself tighter to earth against the feeling that she might simply float off in the wind. Strands of her hair blew across her face. She was startled by a voice.

It was Ghetel. It was the first thing Ghetel had said in days without first being spoken to. She said:

"I vant to be an iggle."

Mary was pleased. Ghetel's mind seemed somehow to have surfaced. "An eagle, eh?" she said, turning to her with a smile. "Aye. Likewise."

Ghetel was grinning a strange, wild grin. "I vould fly down," she said, in a crackling voice, holding her hands curved like talons; then she added, clamping the talons suddenly, very hard, on Mary's upper arm: "and GET YOU!"

She grinned crazily and clutched and shook Mary's arm,
tugging and shoving at it with those bony, unbelievably strong
fingers. The bell clanked with her motions. Mary was
alarmed. The grip hurt, but Mary was afraid to struggle, on
this high place, with a grinning, fierce-eyed woman who possibly believed herself to be an eagle. Mary forced a smile.

"And why would you *get* me?"

"Because . . . I am *hungry!*" She nodded violently, still
wide-eyed, still clutching the arm.

"But I'm your friend."

Ghetel shook the arm to and fro a moment, then said:

"You are bad."

That surprised Mary. "Why am I bad?"

"Bad voman," Ghetel said, squeezing the arm harder, "you
ate your baby."

Mary's mouth fell agape. "What say you?"

Ghetel stuck her jaw forward so that her lower teeth were in
front of the upper, and seesawed her jaw from side to side,
wrinkling her nose. "You ate your baby. You had a baby. I
know. Now it is all gone."

Mary jerked her arm out of the clutch. "I did NOT!"

The hands grabbed her again. Mary pulled, shouting:

"I did no such a thing, madwoman!"

"Den *I* ate your baby." She let go of Mary's arm suddenly
and looked sad. Mary tightened her other hand on the hickory
stick to be ready, but hoped to talk Ghetel out of this spell.
"Why'd you do that?" she asked.

"Hungry."

"Eh, well." Mary was frightened, but she was hurt and
angry. She made her own left hand hard like an eagle's
claws and grabbed Ghetel's arm and squeezed as tightly as
she could, digging her broken, jagged fingernails in hard. "I
am hungry, too," she said in a harsh voice. "Remember
that!"

Ghetel's eyes suddenly went shrewd. She looked at Mary's
eyes until stared down, then looked down at Mary's hand on
her arm. "It hurts," she said.

"Well I know."

Ghetel winced, then put her hand on Mary's hand and tried

to remove it. After a moment, Mary let go, and sat looking at Ghetel, alert.

The old woman seemed to have been subdued. She would not look in Mary's eyes.

"So now," Mary said. "Let's get off this mountain and go on."

And they did. But Mary could not shake the old woman's crazed and awful words out of her mind.

Yesterday Mary had inquired why God had sent her, a decent woman, into hell.

And today Ghetel, speaking in unearthly tones on a mountaintop, had said Mary was a bad woman.

Because of the baby, she had said.

The old woman was tetched, of course.

But it is said that the tetched know God.

For a mile or so after coming down from the mountain that afternoon, they had comparatively easy going. They were in the inside of a bend in the river now, and the river had deposited a few hundred yards of silt and gravel along the base of a mountain. The other side of the river was another undercut cliff.

The curving beach was overgrown with shrubs and there was a low place where the mouth of a backwater had silted up; in this stale pool they found a stand of reeds, and hobbled over to pull them up and muck about for their roots. The yield, after they had all but turned the slough upside down, was a dozen black-skinned, finger-sized tubers which, when snapped in two, revealed white centers. They scraped off as much of the repulsive dark covering as they could, and then, teeth aching, they masticated the crunchy, tasteless flesh as if it were the finest delicacy. Two more of Ghetel's front teeth came out in the mass, and she picked them out and put them on the ground. The longer they chewed the pulp, the bigger it became. Soon their shrunken stomachs were turgid with the mass they had swallowed; a few minutes of near-nausea followed, and they kept swallowing it back until it subsided. Mary had been unable to eat the last one of the tubers, and she secreted it in her hand for later as they left, smeared with

cold mud but almost happy, and continued up the bank toward the next bend in the river. Mary was singing, but just
above a whisper.

Over the hush of wind and water they began detecting a low
rumble.

It was a familiar sound, a dreaded sound. Ghetel looked
terrified, and stopped where she stood on the narrow spit of
land, shaking her head.

"Aye, another waterfall," Mary said. "No fear. Likely we
can climb right past this'n." She was not going to make the
mistake of getting wedged in as she had at the other falls,
even if she had to climb a mile-high mountain to get around it.

As they worked their way into the bend of the river, they
saw an enormous black bird swoop low over the shore a few
yards ahead and disappear on the other side of a huge rock.

Eagle, Mary thought at first.

But then a shadow flickered over their path. Looking up,
she saw another great dark bird, descending on graceful outstretched wings turned up at the tips. A buzzard.

It was a moment before she remembered the meaning of
buzzards: there would be something dead up there.

"Hurry," she said.

There were three buzzards there, hunched over something
small, working on it, now and then pushing one another aside,
beating each other with their wings, hobbling awkwardly on
the flat rock. Beyond them, silhouetting them, was a vast,
seething, churning pool of water and the right edge of a
waterfall visible around the bend. Sunlight striking the rising
mist made a fragment of rainbow at the river's edge.

Mary plucked up her courage and hobbled over the rock
shouting, "Hey, hey!" at the buzzards and swinging her stick.
The birds arched their wings and stumbled about, then beat
the air and rose off, one at a time.

The object of their attention lay near the edge of a slanting
table of rock where it had been washed up: a little mass of
dark fur, torn open to show tattered pale flesh and white
bone. It appeared to have been a muskrat or some such thing,
probably killed by a plunge over the waterfall. It was not

fresh, and the buzzards had been at it for a while, leaving little. It was tainted with the contents of its own shredded bowels. Mary squatted at the water's edge and washed the little wreck of a carcass, and then with the sharp edge of a broken rock, extracted the little flesh the buzzards had left. This amounted to two or three ounces of flesh and organs for Ghetel and a like amount for herself.

There are some things I shan't want to tell back home when I get there, Mary thought. Leaving my babe with a squaw, for one. And eating after buzzards.

But truly I'm not a bad woman, Heavenly Lord. Or thou'd not have give me meat.

Thank'ee, O Lord, she thought, remembering to give grace only after she had eaten.

This waterfall was as beautiful as the other had been fearsome. Perhaps it was the sunny day, the shaft of rainbow leaning above it. Perhaps it was that they were looking at it with a little something in their stomachs.

The river was wide here, came flowing broad and smooth down from a curve between gently sloping hills and then spilled twenty or thirty feet over the great crooked stone sill of the falls, foaming and misting and thundering onto the huge chunks of stone that had broken away and fallen in the pool at its base.

And this cascade would be easier to bypass. A heap of boulders lay where the falls swept past the shore, and these could be climbed to put the women on the upper level of the river. They lifted and pulled themselves up these and in ten minutes were above the falls.

The mountainside they were traversing now was steep but not precipitous, and they were able to walk upright most of the time, not having to hang on with their hands. They were passing through a magnificent forest of beech, hickory, oak and ash now, on a floor of dead leaves, now and then veering to skirt some massive outcropping of solid rock, green with moss and splotched with blue-green lichen.

They were shuffling through dry leaves on that forest floor, alongside just such a subtly colored bluff, when the strange sweating started. Mary felt her skin prickling all over. Her

vision blurred as sweat ran into her eyes. When she wiped her
hand across her brow it came away wet. Cold drops were
coursing down her flanks. Her face felt hot just under the
skin but icy on the surface. And the hues of the mottled rocks
faded suddenly, everything going white and shadowless. Her
heartbeat was racing. Suddenly her knees went limber and
she sat down abruptly. Her stomach hurt—no more than it
had been hurting for weeks, but differently. It was as if someone were inside it stabbing outward with a sharp object. Her
stomach contracted hard with each pain, making her bend
forward. Ghetel had stopped beside her, and was looking
down at her, but her face was not clear; it was as if in
silhouette.

"Ghetel! I . . . I think we shouldn't've et those roots. Ah!
Ah! Share me th' blanket, would y' please? Oh! oh, dear
heaven. You feel it too? Oh! OH!" She doubled over and her
forehead touched her knees. Ghetel knelt by Mary and saw
that she was shivering visibly. Her skin was white but
splotched red, and covered with gooseflesh and a sheen of
perspiration.

Ghetel knelt beside her, confused, and drew her inside the
blanket with her. She held her there and looked around her at
the trackless woods, the ranks of dark mountains stretching
away up the rivercourse. When Mary was not moving ahead,
Ghetel had no notion of where to go or what to do.

She knelt there and hugged the convulsing young woman to
her, while the sun descended behind a ridge and left them in
chilly blue shadows. The other shore of the river was bathed
in a creamy, rosy glow of winter sunlight, and that glow
dimished upward as the sun descended. It was during this
time that Ghetel too began to wince with stomach pains and
feel dizzy and wet. She slowly keeled over, drawing Mary to
the ground with her, and they lay there on the leafy slope for a
measureless time as the valley darkened. After a while they
began feeling a powerful backing-up of pressure in their
chests. Mary began heaving first, then Ghetel. Nothing was
coming up, but their bodies were trying to get rid of the alien
matter in their stomachs.

They retched dryly for a long time, retched and moaned,

shivering and drooling uncontrollably. Night came, un-
noticed. There were blank spaces in time, then moments of
feverish, shuddering wakefulness, then more cold blank
spaces. Sometimes Mary would come to and be aware of
Ghetel writhing beside her, of her own tripping heartbeat and
stomach spasms, of the profuse watering from her mouth and
nose, of the darkness and the cold, the sound of the river, the
tilt of her body as she lay on the slope. Once she saw, or
imagined she saw, the face of a wolf in the starlight a few feet
away. Then she would dream of falling—soaring, rather—
from high, bright places.

Her head ached. The stars were brilliant. There was a hard,
heavy knot in her stomach, as if she had swallowed a stone,
but she was no longer heaving. Her throat was raw and there
was a dryness in her mouth, feeling like wool and tasting like
soap. She had never in her life felt so weak and shaky. Her
lower body felt as if it were full of hot water.
The poison of the roots, whatever they were, seemed to
have spent itself, and she presumed that she would be all right
now—though the bowels had yet to be heard from before she
could say it was all over. Ghetel was sleeping, breathing
heavily beside her, sometimes murmuring incoherent words.
The blanket was in disarray. The ground was sparkling with
frost and Mary's legs were uncovered, stinging with cold. She
tugged at the blanket until she and Ghetel both were covered
as well as they could be, and the next awareness she had was
of pale pink light over the mountain on the other side of the
river. She could feel the damp cold coming up from the
ground, permeating her flesh, making her bones ache. She lay
there shivering, waiting for sufficient daylight to move by, and
thought, trying to gather her understanding back to the place
where it had been before the poisoning had dispersed her
senses.
This, she remembered, was to have been the day when, if
she had not yet seen a familiar landmark, she was going to try
to cross this river and go back down the other bank to that
other river that had beckoned so strongly to her premonitions, the river just above the first falls.

But how am I to do that when I'm doubtful I can even get me up off the ground? she thought. How can I cross the river here? It's still wide and wild and I've not the strength to ride a log across. And we're too close to the falls. We'd be dashed in the falls afore we'd get halfway across.

Maybe we could go back below the falls and put in a log and hang on it, she thought.

Nay, she argued. We'd be beat to death on the rapids. We might even get carried all the way down to the lower falls and over them. Put a log in this river and y'd have to go where the river takes it. It was some days to get from that falls to this one but I reckon if you were floatin' a log y'd be swept back down to 'em in a few hours.

She felt the worst wave of helpless frustration she had experienced at any step along this endless, aching, soul-crushing journey.

There's just nought to do but go on up this one and find a ford, she thought. It's just another o' these eternal walk-arounds, and from the looks o' this river it could well be a hundred-mile walk-around.

The night's sickness had left them so weak and cold and shaky that they had to support each other when they finally arose with the dawn and started on up the river bank. They trudged awkwardly along, the blanket drawn over their shoulders, leaning on each other, their legs limber and wobbly, hands palsied, and sometimes when one started to cave in, the other could hold her up, but as often as they held each other up, they brought each other down.

The toil of moving eventually worked out the shaky hollowness left by the poison and replaced it with the old familiar aches. About midmorning Mary's bowels got out of control and she squatted moaning by the wayside every few minutes, groaning and spewing out the scouring fluid, while wave after wave of shivers ran down from her temples to her thighs.

As if following Mary's leadership even in this, Ghetel was soon having to stop every hundred yards to suffer the same miserable scouring. Each such stop left them feeling colder and more exhausted. There was an eerie kind of lightheaded-ness now, and a distortion of time, as if the roots had drugged them. Mary would look at an object, a tree or a chunk of rock, a few hundred feet ahead; then she would walk, her mind full of thoughts as light and formless as clouds, for what seemed an hour, and then when she became aware of the object again it would seem to be no closer. Thus when afternoon found them too exhausted to go another step, Mary had no notion of how far they had come. They sat down in leaves with their backs against the sunny side of a rock that sheltered them from the cold breeze. In minutes they were warm and lethargic, and slumped into a dazed sleep. When Mary awoke, the sun had slid low into the valley downriver. Most of the queasiness and disequilibrium was gone now and Mary saw every detail of the landscape with knife-keen clarity. Her heart had ceased its dreadful racing and tolled slowly, solemnly in her breast now like a muffled bell.

When she stood up it was not as if she were stronger—she was too empty to feel stronger—but was as if her body had become as light as a summer garment. The pain in her feet and her joints was still there, but it seemed to be coming from a greater distance and thus, like a faraway sound, diminished.

"I'd say this. That partic'lar root's one delicacy I can do without, from this day on." Her voice sounded strange after all the silence, a clear, thin wisp of a voice that was absorbed by the vast outdoor hush. She looked over at Ghetel, who was beginning to stir, awakened perhaps by Mary's voice. Ghetel looked at her, blinking rapidly in the light, smiled weakly, raised her eyebrows and shut her eyes again and lowered her chin onto her chest. "Nay," Mary said. "Y're awake now; it's up we go." Ghetel grumbled. Mary took her hand and coaxed her to her feet and they continued up the shore, two women under one blanket, looking rather like a misshapen gray little four-legged creature almost invisibly tiny between the high canyon wall and the turbid river, its little dull bell faintly chiming.

But if they had by now become as one suffering creature, it was a two-headed creature, one head thinking they were going up the wrong river, the other presuming that the first knew the way.

CHAPTER
23

TWO DAYS HAD PASSED SINCE THEIR SICKNESS, AND THEY HAD found neither food nor a place to cross the river and go back down the other side. They had found fallen logs along the shore, and each of these Mary had contemplated as a possible raft to float them over, but each time the thought of the rapids and riverbed boulders below convinced her that it would be suicide to put themselves into the grasp of that fast current.

In these two days they had passed under or over or around half a dozen towering cliffs that reared themselves up from the water's edge, some of them perpendicular, some actually jutting out over the water. They had crossed the screes of two more avalanches, and their legs and arms were marked with abrasions suffered in those passages.

Ghetel had become gradually more sullen and troublesome. She had not spoken more than ten words to Mary in English for these two days, even to answer Mary's questions; she had grown more balky at every rest stop, needing to be threatened to get up and move or needing to be left behind for a few minutes until fear of loneliness moved her to follow along; and she had been watching Mary with that cunning hostility in her eyes again, as if waiting to catch her off her guard.

The eternal *clink-clank* of Ghetel's bell had become almost unbearable. Mary turned on Ghetel with gritting teeth once and grabbed it. "Lord 'a' mercy!" she cried. "Why couldn't y'a lost this cussed jingle jangle, 'stead o' tommyhocks an' blankets?"

But the outburst threw Ghetel into such a slump that Mary let go of the bell and decided not to mention it again—unless it became insufferable.

*   *   *

This morning Mary had been awakened by Ghetel's movements, in a tiny, hard-floored cave they had found for shelter, and had found the old woman trying to reach the hickory spear, which Mary always kept under one arm as she slept. Mary had grabbed it and sat up quickly, her heart pounding in alarm, and had pushed Ghetel back with it and demanded an explanation.

"I need stick to help valk," Ghetel had complained then. "You alvays use it."

"I could make you one," Mary snapped back, "if'n you hadn't flang away our tommyhock back yonder like a perfect fool."

Ghetel hadn't answered, only scowled in the dawn light, and that was how they had started this day.

As for the spear, it would have been of little use as a weapon now anyway. It had been thrown in vain at so many animals, and its point bumped inadvertently against so many boulders and cliffs during its use as a sounding-pole, that it had become as blunt as a finger, and without the tomahawk to sharpen it, it was in truth now little more than a walking staff. Ghetel could have armed herself just as well as Mary by picking up any straight limb or sapling from the ground, but she kept a covetous eye on Mary's lance instead of thinking to do so, and Mary was not about to suggest it to her. As long as Mary was the only one carrying a stick that had the reputation of a spear, she had a semblance of command. She was strangely amused by this, by the absurdity of it, and when she considered it she smiled for the first time in many days.

At one point this afternoon, when Ghetel had sat on a log, three-quarters naked in the cold, stupidly refusing to come along, Mary had a devilish idea. She stood beside a cliff, glowering back at Ghetel, and whetted the blunt point of the staff against the stone, as if sharpening the spear. It worked. Ghetel rose and came following.

And Mary was pleasantly surprised to see that this whetting actually had sharpened the point somewhat. She stayed there for another minute and rubbed it against the stone until it was almost as sharp as it had been when she had manufactured it with the tomahawk.

* * *

Mary was thinking that they would die before reaching a fording place; she was almost crushed with the weary frustration of this long detour, when they straggled around a cliff that led to the right, and her heart fell so heavily in her that she dropped to her knees with a groan.

They had come to the mouth of another river.

It flowed straight across their path, deep and wide, the kind of river she knew would twist for miles back among the mountains before growing narrow and shallow enough to permit them to cross. Another walk-around just to get back onto this walk-around they had been ascending so painfully for a week! Oh, cruel God, she prayed in angry despair, who would fling two poor sufferers down in this maze of rivers and canyons! Why? *"WHY?"*

Ghetel, who had stopped and stood dumbly behind her, was alarmed by this wailed question. She scurried to Mary's side and bent down, exclaiming, "Vat? Vat?" Then she seemed to notice the river before them, and through her torpor finally seemed to recognize it as still another obstacle, and she fell to her knees and began to howl, letting the blanket drop from her shoulders and clutching Mary's arm in that same hard, two-handed grip she had used on the cliff, her eagle's grip.

After a minute, the pain of that grip on Mary's bony arm became worse then the anguish in her soul, and she transferred her anger from God to the hysterical hag beside her. She wrenched her arm free with a violent jerk and then swung it back hard and hit Ghetel across the mouth with the back of her hand.

The howl stopped with the blow. Ghetel blinked repeatedly, eyes streaming tears, mouth gaping and closing, gaping and closing, a trickle of blood tracing from her lip-corner. She raised her hand slowly, as if waking to some strange reality, touched her mouth, looked at the blood on her fingers and said in quiet disbelief: "Why you hit me for, May-ry?"

Mary shook her head and gritted her teeth and said something she would never have thought she could say:

"'Cause God's out o' reach, I reckon."

And so they turned reluctant steps up another nameless river.

It was going to be a hard one. There was little room for a path among the fallen rocks; the blue stone cliffs seemed to close in closer with each turn in the river.

Mary was talking to herself as they limped along this river-course. It was the first time she had done this—as far as she knew. She was simply running out of dignity and control. This last diversion from the long way home had simply broken something down inside her. She was not sure she even cared anymore. She had a strange, resigned sense, a notion that she might just die on her feet and her body would keep going up rivers that divided into smaller rivers, and those into creeks, and those into smaller creeks, until she would come to a place in the heart of the wilderness where there were no more creeks reaching up, and there she would stand, dead, and rot, and her bones would stand there forever to mark the source of all rivers.

And someday Will might come along exploring, she thought, coming up rivers and creeks lookin' for land and rememberin' me, and he'd find m' bones a-standin' here, and he'd be startled at first, but then he'd get bold and come close and he'd recognize this marriage band—it would still be here on me on account of I can't get it off over my knucklebone— Ah, Will, darlin', old sturdy, furry Will, best man in Virginia, O believe me I tried to come back to you. O how I tried only God could tell you and only He could tell you I loved you so much I left my baby with the savages so's I could come to you . . . I don't know if you'd ever understand and forgive me that, Will darlin', but the Lord could tell you why.

I just wanted to come back to you and start new, new sons, new daughters, start new and have again the kind o' life we was havin' before the heathens come down on that Sunday and ruined everything . . .

She stumbled and hurt her knee on a stone, a sharp bone-pain that made a sunflash behind her eyes. She grimaced and rose, dizzy with weakness and that shaft of pain, cursed under her breath and limped on.

The fall had jolted the reverie out of her head and the canyon was clear and specific before her eyes, and it seemed, for a moment, as if she had been in this very place before, alongside this blue-stone cliff, going up along this limpid river; there where that sycamore grew with its roots in a split boulder—she had seen that before, hadn't she, in some other time, or . . .

Yes. She had seen it before.

She stopped.

She looked at the sycamore, at the cliffs.

Blue stone.

O heavens.

O yes I know this place.

A hot shiver poured out of the top of her head and raced down over all the skin of her body.

"O Lord God thank 'ee!"

It was the tributary they had turned into on the way down. On the fifth day after the massacre, her memory told her.

We been on the New River all this time after all!

"Ghetel!" She turned and hugged the old woman. They sagged in each other's arms, Ghetel's face showing only confusion and a little fright at this outburst, as if she would be struck again. "Ghetel! We're but five days from home!"

CHAPTER
24

GHETEL'S MOOD DARKENED AS MARY'S BRIGHTENED. WHENever Mary would sing, Ghetel would howl at her to shut up. The old woman began stalling at every resting place, and she walked stooped, moaning and clutching her abdomen, as they moved up the river along the blue-stone cliff. She wailed at every little sort of hurt that she had long ago learned to absorb without complaint.

It was as if she were trying to destroy the first exuberance Mary had felt in weeks. But Mary understood it.

I been coaxin' her on with promises and singin' and false cheer so long, she like as not thinks this's just another sham to keep 'er going, Mary thought.

Ghetel's surliness and whining could not bring down Mary's high heart now. Five days it had taken the Indians to bring her down this far from Draper's Meadows in July; if she and Ghetel could keep going enough hours a day, they should be able to reach the Meadows on foot in that same amount of time, or a week at most.

We can keep going for a week more, she assured herself. I feel stronger now than I've felt in a month, just a-knowin' where we are.

She could not recall just where the Indians had crossed this river. That particular day she had been so miserable and faintish from the childbearing that she had noticed little. Somewhere they had ridden across a river; she could remember its blessed coolness on that hot day; she could envision the blood washing from her thighs and reddening the water. But it seemed that that crossing had been on some other stream. She could not recollect the experience of crossing this one.

And there had been a crossing by canoe somewhere around here, too, she remembered. That was farther up, she thought. We crossed to this side of the New River by canoe, before we got to this river. I'm sure of that. Aye. O but I'm glad I started glancing back and memorizing the look of places. Lord in Heaven, thank'ee for givin' me the sense to do that, even amidst my torments of that day.

She was feeling very expansive toward the Lord now; she was thanking him for every little thing. It had become easier to believe in him after her discovery that they were on the right river after all. He did not seem quite so cruel and devious a God now; it was possible to forgive him for the forty days and forty nights of obstructions and sufferings he had put them through.

But if he had had them on the wrong river all that time, he likely would have lost a believer.

Poor Ghetel, she thought. If there was but a way to make her understand we truly *are* close to the end of it.

She had told Ghetel, had tried to explain, three or four times, that this river was within a few days' walk of their destination. But it had been as futile as trying to cheer up a costive mule. Ghetel was either not hearing her words or was just refusing to believe them anymore.

Eh well, Mary thought. I could drag 'er the rest of the way by 'er heels, kicking and squalling, if I had to. I could stand anything these next few days, now't I know.

I'll be with 'ee soon now, Will, she thought, trying to remember what he looked like.

She couldn't remember. She just couldn't. When she tried to remember how her man looked, standing close to her, she could remember only the look of another man standing close to her: Captain Wildcat with his smooth, oiled skin and the silver bands around his arms; Captain Wildcat, the man who had brought her down this river into these months of purgatory.

All she could remember of Will was warmth.

Remembering Will now was like remembering not a person but a time. It was like remembering a summer.

By twilight they had come perhaps two leagues up this river, and reached a place where white riffles indicated a shallows that seemed to extend all the way across the stream.

Mary wanted to cross immediately, to gain the other side so they could start their return down the other bank at first light the next day. The sky was clear and cold and there was a nearly full moon sighting down the valley. They could cross now, perhaps even walk a few miles down the other side by moonlight. Every mile now is a mile less tomorrow, she thought.

But Ghetel had come as far as she was going to come this day, as Mary realized after a long spell of cajoling and scolding. The old woman was absorbed in her suffering, sitting on the ground rocking back and forth with her forearms folded across her abdomen, shaking her head and crying, but she was not too flummoxed to see that she was being urged to wade into cold water again, this time in near darkness. Mary would have had to beat her unconscious and carry her bodily to get her across this river tonight. So she gave in on the point, and raked leaves into a niche under the cliff to make a place where they could roll into the blanket and sleep.

Probably best thisaway, she admitted to herself. The night air was snapping cold. Exhausted and empty as they were, getting wet tonight and then crawling out into this air might well bring on the finish of them.

Even though she had gotten her way, Ghetel kept up her woeful carryings-on. She let herself be led into the shelter and stretched out in the leaves, but kept whining and sobbing, curling up and hugging her waist, like a child having a bedtime bellyache tantrum.

Goin' to have to smack 'er again if she don't pipe down soon, Mary thought. She didn't want to do that. She had done it today in her desperate rage, but she did not like to remember that she had so lost control of herself as to strike a poor dying wretch.

And it is true we are a-dyin', Mary thought. She could feel it going on inside herself, could feel her body eating itself, burning its little remaining flesh as logs on a hearth are consumed by their own embers. She knew that Ghetel was genuinely suffering, as badly as she herself was suffering, and that they had been dying bit by bit for weeks, and surely would never be the same again even if they did manage to rescue themselves. They *were* dying; they had come within a breath of it many times in these weeks in the mountains.

But I won't finish dyin' while there's still a mile to go, she vowed. If I got a week o'dyin' left to do, then I got six days left to travel.

When she was at last warm enough to feel drowsy, she prayed, looking at the moon above the trees as if it were God's face, thanking him still another time for showing her the sycamore in the rock and the blue-stone cliff; and then she thought of Will Ingles, looking at the now fuzzy, warm moon as if it were Will's face, and promised herself that she would be lying next to him, instead of next to this writhing old woman, before the week was out.

Suddenly her eyes started open and the moon was sharp and cold and clear again because she had had a thought that

she had never allowed to enter her mind during this journey:
She really did not know whether her husband was still alive.
She hadn't seen a sign of him after the massacre. Likely he
and Johnny had been killed down in the fields that long-ago
Sunday.

But that thought was too dreadful to keep in her mind for
more than a few minutes.

O' course he's still alive, she thought.

I couldn't have come all this way if he wa'n't.

Then even with the coming of morning, Ghetel was not
ready to wade into the water. She stood hunched in the cold,
looking at the purling shallows, hugging herself and shuddering and making a low, undulating moan in her throat and
shaking her head in refusal. It was not hard to understand.
Just looking at the crinkling, ice-blue water, while standing
barefooted on the frosty bank as a moon-cold winter sun rose
between the upstream mountains, made Mary herself quake
in anticipation of the chilly shock.

"Well, then, Ghetel, I'm sorry, but I canno' leave you a
choice in the matter." She lowered the tip of her hickory
spear and jabbed it hard against the baggy flesh of Ghetel's
buttock. Ghetel yelped and spun on her, her face wide open in
pained astonishment. Mary was now crouched, pointing the
stick at her face. "Git," she snapped. "GIT!" She thrust the
stick, this reputed spear, toward her face two or three times,
then motioned toward the water. "GO ON, DAMN 'EE!
YOU'VE SLOWN ME DOWN ENOUGH, BY HEAVEN!"

Ghetel backstepped toward the river's edge, glancing up
and down between the spear-point and Mary's demonic expression, and, with a high sob, squatted and wrapped her
arms around her head. Another fierce jab with the stick
brought her to her feet more quickly than one would have
thought she could move, and she stepped knee-deep into the
stream with a terrible gasp. Mary stepped in right at her
heels, still poking her in the rump with the stick-point, and
they floundered toward the opposite bank, sucking air in
deep, involuntary gasps.

The water reached halfway up their thighs at midstream,

and seemed to have frozen the marrow of their bones, but they stepped streaming onto the other bank within two minutes. It had been their coldest but their easiest crossing.

They were back down to the New River by midday, and turned southeastward along its right bank. There was a narrow fringe of bottomland here between the river and the mountainside. It was brushy and cluttered with fallen rock, but at least it was relatively flat.

"Level feels good, don't it, hon?" she said to Ghetel, still trying to break through that black curtain of suffering and resentment that Ghetel had drawn between them. Mary tried to joke. "I bet my one leg's shorter'n t' other, I been a-walkin' on right-handed mountainsides so long. You too, eh, Ghetel?" The old woman did not answer. She hulked along ahead, with the filthy, tattered blanket over her hunched shoulders, and did not turn or even shrug to acknowledge Mary's words. She just kept stumbling and mincing along, muttering in her private tongue, howling when rocks hurt her feet. "Hi, what say'ee to that?" Mary called, still trying to arouse a response. Now Ghetel turned her head just far enough to show Mary one baleful eye, looking not at Mary but at the spear-point, and then turned forward again, and shambled on.

"By th' Eternal!" Mary exclaimed, now joyously indignant. "If'ee don't make me feel like a red savage m'self, and you my white captive woman . . ."

Shouldn't 've said that, she thought. Might be terrible close to what *she* feels; too close to seem a joke.

But hey. I don' think she hears *anything* I say anymore.

By dusk they had made many miles, and were now so fatigued and weak with hunger that they were sitting down to rest more than they were moving. The place looked vaguely familiar; it seemed to have been somewhere hereabouts that she had been ferried across the New River in a bark canoe.

Must find something to gnaw on, Mary thought, or we'll not make it even another day.

The good spirits she had been using as fuel the last full day were no longer enough. Another frigid night was falling and Mary could feel her soul flickering weakly like the wick in a used-up candle.

She got to her knees and tried to turn over a rock. It was embedded in the frozen soil. She crawled to a smaller one and strained until she managed to dislodge it and tumble it over.

There were no worms under it. The ground was black and frozen. Ice crystals delicate as snowflakes lay in tiny patterns on the iron-hard earth.

She turned over another rock and it was the same. The small effort had left her winded.

Ghetel, a few feet away, had noticed this activity, and she began turning over stones, panting, cursing in Dutch each time she found nothing.

They now began trying to pull up shrubs to look for roots. Neither of them, alone, had enough strength to budge even the smallest bush. Ghetel's voice grew more desperate with each failure, keening up and down a wavering scale so pitiful that Mary forgot all her annoying and stubborn behavior and felt a tug of pity toward her, and warm tears started from her eyes and ran down her nose in cold trickles.

"Come on now, hon," she groaned through a tightening throat. "I bet th' two of us together can pull an ol' root." She hauled herself to her feet with the aid of the hickory stick and hobbled to her. She laid the stick on the ground and with both hands grasped the shrub Ghetel was straining at, and put her whole aching body into it, wheezing and groaning, her hands and finger joints aching and popping, her shoulder pressing Ghetel's.

Suddenly that pressure was gone. Ghetel had released the bush; at once Mary heard her emit a shriek of triumph and lunge behind her.

And even before she could turn to look, she knew that Ghetel had snatched up their weapon.

Mary turned slowly to face the most demented cackling she had ever heard.

CHAPTER
25

THE WORST OF IT WAS, HER TEARS OF PITY FOR THE CUNNING hag were still wet and cold on her face.

The treacherous Ghetel now had everything: the blanket and the spear. Mary had nothing, nothing but a rope of knotted yarn around her waist and a few rags of what once had been her summer dress, these hanging from her shoulders and collar.

Mary stepped backward. Her heart was beating fast in her throat. She could not tell by looking at Ghetel's crazed eyes whether she was going to stab her with the lance now or enjoy for awhile the power of having Mary at her mercy. Mary wanted, in either case, to get far enough from her that she would have to throw the spear if she chose to attack.

If she throws it, Mary thought, she could miss and then I'd have it again.

She kept stepping backward, feeling with her feet for rocks that might trip her. Ghetel came on, grinning, her laughter now voiceless, a kind of quaking whisper. Ghetel's conception of the hickory stick as a true, fearful weapon, that conception Mary had tried so hard to nurture to keep the old coot under control, seemed to remain now that it was in her hands. Now Mary had to keep telling herself that it was only a stick after all. She had to keep telling herself that, to keep from growing panicky. Just a stick, she thought. Just an ol' *stick*.

Talk to her, she thought. Talk. Surely even a crack-brain can't try to kill somebody who's talking to her. "Well, now, hon," her voice came out, strained, "looks like you got th' old walkin'-stick you wanted so bad. Well, that's good, hon . . . y' should have it awhile; I know the walkin's been hard, and that'll make it easier for you . . ." Ghetel came on, still with that hissing laugh.

"Well, now, hon, don't know 'bout you, but I'm just tuckered," Mary continued, "an' I think we walked fur enough for one day, don't you? We ought t' find a nice holler place t' roll in an' go beddie bye-lo, eh? or maybe, uh, maybe . . . I 'spect there's 'nough light yet we could . . . grub up some nice roots 'round here . . . I reckon we could pull up that shrub back yonder, if . . . we's to tug on it together a mite more, eh? Why don't we do . . ."

"I eat no roots anymore," Ghetel said, then laughed that strange breath-laughter again and kept coming on.

"Aye. Well, y'know, I'm kind o' tired o' roots, too, now't you mention it . . . 'specially after those a few days ago, made us so sick . . ." Her retreat was backing her up against the bluff, where she would be cornered, so she began veering up along the bank. " . . . Maybe we could find some nice buds, then . . . or maybe there's nuts th' squirrels've not got yet . . ."

"Those too I dun eat."

Mary had backed away from the cliff now and was retreating toward the open shingle along the river bank to keep from getting trapped in the shrubbery and driftwood she could glimpse out of the corner of her eyes. She was more afraid of Ghetel's strange, sudden coherence and purpose than of her possession of the "weapon." The old woman had been bothersome when she was whining, bawling and helpless, but now she was sinister. Had her capture of the spear transformed her so abruptly, or had she been feigning helplessness all this time with her eye on obtaining it? Mary had heard people speak of the cunning of the crazy, and now it was something she could comprehend. She sighed now and smiled and tried again to molify her with chatter. "Well, then, might be we could try our hand at, uh, spearin' a fish with that thing . . . if'n it ain't too dark . . . Been a long while since we tried to get us a nice big fish t' eat . . ."

"Dun' eat fish, too."

Mary forced a gay little laugh. "Well, dearie, that's about all th' choices we got on our bill o'fare . . . Not a whole lot, as y' well know by now . . ."

"I can eat May-ry!"

The words came with a jolt. Mary realized this was no jest. She remembered suddenly the awful bite-mark Ghetel had left in her thigh when they had fought for the tomahawk.

Mary was unable to move for a moment, as this appalling comprehension rooted itself in her. Ghetel had continued closing the gap between them and was near enough to strike.

Fear suddenly shot a bolt of energy through Mary's exhausted muscles. She spun, crouched and ran along the river bank.

Her legs and lungs gave out within fifty yards, and she fell sprawling on the shore gravel. She lay panting, hearing Ghetel coming along, saying cheerfully:

"Dun't run! Dun't run! I get you!"

She hauled herself to her feet, breath rasping, heart pounding, and stumbled ahead, to keep distance between them. It would be dark soon; shapes were receding into the gloom; if she could stay out of reach for a little longer she might lose Ghetel.

If she could.

She tripped over a rock and fell in the gravel again. She took two breaths, rose painfully once more, looking back at the approaching figure, staggered a few more steps, and tripped on a root and took a fall among rocks, a flash of pain bursting behind her eyes. Ghetel gained several yards on her while she was down. When Mary got up again, the old woman was within fifteen feet of her.

But now Ghetel was flagging and stumbling, too. This was a pursuit neither had the strength to maintain for long.

A thicket grew down toward the river's edge here. Mary plunged into it, hoping to lose Ghetel. Twigs and limbs slashed at her and held her back. She fought through them with flailing arms, and in minutes was again fully spent. She hung in the bushes by her arms to keep from falling, and sucked for air. Over the sounds of her own rattling breath she could hear twigs snapping and swishing a few feet back, and Ghetel's terrible chuckling and the ringing of her crazy bell.

A few more breaths and then Mary lunged forward again, hands in front of her face to protect her eyes. Once she glanced back, and could not see Ghetel, only the gray and black tracery of bare branches, but she could still hear Ghetel crashing and clanking through after her.

If she couldn't hear me maybe she couldn't find me, Mary thought. She darted aside and stopped still.

The crushing and crackling of the old woman's progress came very close, then fell still.

It seemed now that Ghetel would be able to hear her heartbeats and grating inhalations.

She's stopped and's listenin' for me, Mary thought. *Lord God, how can 'ee permit such a wickedness?*

"Oh, ho ho, ho *ho!*" The old woman's voice, laughing, panting, taunting all at once, was coming from a few feet away in the thicket, somewhere between Mary and the hillside. "I get you, May-ry!"

Mary began edging toward the river, as quietly as she could move. But silence was impossible. The thicket crackled and rustled with every movement.

"I hear you! I get you, May-ry!" Now she too was again moving through the brush.

It was all too crazy. It demanded an explanation. Mary had helped her through every imaginable suffering and now was being hunted like an animal. Her face contorted; she could feel it twisting all up as it would when, as a child, she could not keep from crying. Tears trickled down her face, and she cried out: *"Why?"*

And Ghetel's voice, so recently full of madcap glee, now came through the thicket a pitiful, strained, half-weeping cry:

"Becauss! I'm *hung*-ry!"

Then she was moving again, sobbing, but coming after Mary relentlessly all the same. Mary crouched low and moved as swiftly through the deep dusk as she could, going toward the open space at the river's edge. And Ghetel's voice followed her, still sobbing and whining like a heartbroken child's: "I can't stand it any more, Mary-ry! I *can't* any more! I . . . I . . . I'm *hunnng*-ry!"

Mary imagined now that if she could get back out of the thicket a few seconds before Ghetel, she could move quickly and quietly enough to hide herself somewhere along the river bank. Branches whipped her face: she turned her ankles and stumbled repeatedly among the roots and fallen wood and rocks in the thicket. A prayer of deperation backed up in her throat but there was nowhere to send it now; it seemed that a God that would permit such an evil as this was not a God worth praying to. No, she thought. Forget a god. There's none.

It outraged her, and she gained a spurt of strength from the anger. She shoved her way out of the thicket and stumbled along the rock shore, grimacing, often having to touch the ground with her hands to keep from pitching face-forward.

"MAY-RY!" Ghetel's voice was such a desperate wail now that Mary glanced back over her shoulder, shuddering at the sound of it, and saw the old woman burst from the thicket only twenty feet behind. She saw her stop and raise her arm, saw her lunge forward, saw the slim hickory spear come arcing through the air toward her. She shut her eyes and, too late, tried to raise her hands to ward it off.

It whiffed past her ear. She heard a soft *slurp!* as it plunged point first into the river.

And now neither had a weapon. The two women stood twenty feet from each other, heaving for breath, looking at each other, each trying to comprehend just how the situation had changed so suddenly again. Mary's heart was thudding and her emotions were in an uproar of relief, hatred, love, despair and fear. Ghetel seemed to find herself suddenly powerless again: she was blinking, looking down at her empty hands. The blanket, which she had somehow managed to hang onto in her plunge through the thicket, was now at her feet, having slipped off her shoulders when she threw the spear. Their faces looked ghostly gray in the deepening twilight and everything else around them was a deeper, violet-tinged gray. The river, full of dull silver evening sky, burbled and sighed a few feet away.

Mary hauled in a deep breath at last and looked at Ghetel and tried to imagine what she should do. There seemed to be no answer. She wondered whether she should simply pick up a fist-sized rock and cave in her skull and be rid of her once and for all. Of what worth was the old bedlamite anyway?

Or should she simply walk away and let her find her own way? She had tried that once, and had found the loneliness unbearable. This valley, she knew, would crush the soul of one alone.

She's like t' die any hour now and I'll be alone anyways, she thought. Or if she don't die, I shall.

Mary's mind could not seem to come back to the horror that had filled it only moments ago: that this witch, this Ghetel who by their suffering had become bonded to her as close as her own mother ever was, had been studying and stalking her for she knew not how many days as a piece of food. Mary still knew this, but as she stood here lightheaded and swaying with weakness, looking at Ghetel who was in the same condition, she could not really believe what she knew.

Or maybe *I'm* the madcap, Mary thought for the first time. Maybe this's only happening in my head.

"Ghetel, can 'ee hear me? I think we need t' talk," she said, in the quiet, sad tone of a mother deeply disappointed in a child. "Ghetel, people don't just *eat* each other *up*. D'you understand? I don't want t' be et up. You try it, an' I'm a-going' to stop 'ee." Her voice cracked and quavered.

The old woman was still looking at her hands, slowly moving her head from side to side, and making snuffling sounds that might or might not have been weeping. It was growing too dark to see. Mary went on, hoping somehow, even though she was almost too tired and hungry to think, that she could penetrate Ghetel's miserable confusion with a tiny gleam of reason:

"I mean t' say . . . if one of us is to eat t' other . . . if one of us sh'd die so t' other won't, well, then, tell me why it shouldn't just as fair be *me* that eats *you*? Eh? Tell me *that*. Why, I could o' stuck that spear through you *any* time and ate you up. Didn't, though. Y'ever think, I'm as hungry as you are? And . . ." She paused, feeling her chin crumple up and a knot ledge in her throat because of the thought she was about to say:

"Y'ever think I got somebody t' live for, an' you ain't?" It was the cruelest thing she had ever said and she started crying immediately. And her crying precipitated a new outburst of abject howling from Ghetel. They stood there in the darkening valley twenty feet apart with their souls caving in and their knees sagging, and bawled.

"So . . . so . . . what then d'you propose t'do?" Mary spoke out of her profound emptiness after the crying stoped. "Goin' to come along, or . . ." Come along, she thought. But I can't go another step myself.

"I said . . . I haf to eat you, May-ry."

There it was again. That which Mary had begun to doubt she had really heard. Ghetel was serious about it. It was fixed in her mind; even if it was the only thing fixed there, it was there. Mary had no strength left to act in any way. She could only stand here feeling the cold seep back into her flesh and try to talk, try to temporize. She feared that Ghetel was likely still physically stronger than she—she could remember the clutching power of her big hands—and expected that if Ghetel were to come at her again, even barehanded, that would be the end of it and this hellish journey would have been in vain. But what could one say to someone gone cannibal?

Then Mary remembered something she had said, something that might yet penetrate the utter darkness of Ghetel's soul:

"Well, fair's only fair. If one's to eat t' other, then only chance can say which. I say we draw cuts. Who gets the short lot gets et. How say 'ee?" The river gurgled nearby in the gloomy silence. Mary wondered after a while if Ghetel had heard her. Then Ghetel replied:

"Aye."

"That's fair, y' say?"

"Aye. Fair."

"It means like as not I eat you."

"I don' care. I eat or I die now anyvay."

It was said so flatly, so finally, so realistically, that Mary could believe the old woman had regained her senses. Or maybe she had had her senses all along, knowing that in this extremity the only true insanity would be in their both dying when one could have lived on the other.

Mary felt around on the ground and found a dry twig. She

snapped it into two pieces, one four inches long, the other six, and put them inside her fist. She placed the short one in a way that it extended a little higher than the long one.

It would be proper to cheat a little, as she had no intention of eating Ghetel if Ghetel took the short one.

Ghetel had come close, and, strangely, Mary had no fear that she would be attacked now; the old woman seemed past deceit and betrayal now, ready to abide by the dictum of the straws.

There was just enough light for them to see what they were doing at these close quarters. Mary watched Ghetel studying the two twig ends and could smell her fetid breath. She found herself looking at the old woman's slack mouth, the big, discolored teeth; she had a sudden chilling notion of herself disappearing whole into the awful mouth . . .

Ghetel studied the twigs for a long time and then slowly raised her hand toward them. She touched the short one, looked up and saw something in Mary's face, then touched the long one. Despite the fear climbing in her heart, Mary smiled and held the smile until Ghetel saw it and moved her fingers back to the short one.

But she still did not take it. She took a long breath, exhaled it stinking into Mary's face and then, as if she had received a sudden divination from something besides Mary's expression, she went back to the long one and put her fingers on it.

She may say she didn't care, but she wants to win, Mary thought.

Still Ghetel didn't draw. She moved her fingers back to the short twig and very slightly lifted at it, as if to test Mary's hold on it.

I see, Mary thought. She guesses I'll hold the long one tighter.

So she squeezed her hand to resist Ghetel's pull on the short stick.

And it worked; Ghetel then touched the long one again, tugging ever so lightly on it, and Mary loosened her hand so Ghetel would think it was the short one.

But still Ghetel did not draw. She looked at the two sticks and concentrated, her face showing all the shrewdest sort of calculation, and Mary thought, suddenly chilled by dread again:

Did th' old loon read my mind just then?

"Dis one," Ghetel pronounced.

And she took one of the sticks between her thumb and forefinger and drew it out of Mary's hand. Mary's heart plummeted. She was left holding the short lot.

"Show me yours," Ghetel said, smiling. She seemed to know she had the longer one.

Mary opened her hand, but not until she had found footing behind her and prepared herself to flee. She drew back slowly, almost imperceptibly, in the gathering darkness, trying to get out of reach.

Ghetel laughed. "I vin it!"

"Now, wait, darlin'. It's but a game, right? Why, who'd really harm a dear friend over a drawed lot?" She tried to force a chuckle. It choked in her dry throat.

"I vin it!" Ghetel began moving forward.

"If *I'd* won it, I'd not 'a' hurt y' anyhow," Mary said, still stepping backward. "Listen, Ghetel, 'twas but a game. Listen, we're nigh home now. My husband's O so rich . . . why, we'll give 'ee banquets—O, roast duck, and . . . and mince pie, and frumenty . . . and stewed hares . . . and marchpane . . . then when 'ee can hold no more, why, we'll give'ee gold money, and a coach an' driver to carry'ee aboot . . ."

Ghetel lunged. Mary recoiled, and the old woman's claws caught the rags of Mary's dress. The rotten cloth gave way. A loose rock turned under Mary's foot and her leg buckled, and she fell, twisting. She landed prone. She heard the horse bell clank and suddenly Ghetel's weight was on her back and her hand was in her hair, pulling her head back; then Ghetel's other arm came snaking around, striving to encircle her throat. Both were grunting like pigs with the effort. Mary pulled against the grip in her hair and managed to get her chin down a few inches, so that the strangling arm was across her chin instead of her throat. Straining against the old woman's unbelievable strength, she managed at last to get the bony wrist between her teeth, and bit down with all the power of her jaws until her loose teeth and spongy gums sparked with pain and she tasted blood and Ghetel's grunts rose into a gurgling growl. The old woman began thrashing her legs and let go of Mary's hair but stayed on top of her. Mary heard a scrabbling beside her head and saw that with her left hand Ghetel was trying to pry up a rock from the frozen ground. If she gets one I'm dead, Mary thought. She bit harder, and stretched out her left arm to clutch Ghetel's groping hand. She got it, dug her fingernails in and held on for life, and for most of a minute they lay straining against each other on the river bank, pulling and biting but scarcely moving; then Mary began trying to buck Ghetel off and Ghetel started jerking with pain, and they struggled and twitched on the rocky beach like some insect in its death throes.

Mary was reaching the limits of her strength now. But she could feel Ghetel weakening too. Mary had the fleeting notion that if she could swallow some of Ghetel's blood she would gain strength from it. But she could not swallow; she could only bite, her tongue dry, her jaws burning with fatigue.

And then Ghetel, with a desperate howl, pressed her face against the back of Mary's neck and nuzzled about for a tooth-hold, finally getting a fold of flesh and the rope of shoulder muscle at the base of Mary's neck and clamping her big horse-teeth on it so hard that Mary saw a sunflash and almost passed out, and released her bite on Ghetel's wrist.

Ghetel seesawed her jaw, really trying to tear the flesh out. With a desperate lurch, terrified that she would faint from the pain, Mary managed to turn onto her side and roll Ghetel off. She was out from under her weight now but Ghetel was still attached to her shoulder like some great leech and Mary's heart faltered under the onslaught of that agony. The only sounds were their strenuous breathing, the scrabble of gravel, the metallic grate of the bell, the hush of the river.

Mary reached back around her head with both hands and found Ghetel's face with her fingers. She got one thumb into the hollow cheek and pressed frantically against the jaw muscle; her other thumb found an eye socket and she began gouging, feeling the eyeball behind the lid sliding like a grape. Three seconds of that and Ghetel loosened her mastiff-bite on Mary's shoulder, sprawling back and trying to tear Mary's hands from her face.

Then they were separate from each other. Mary realized

that she no longer had hands on Ghetel and Ghetel no longer had hands on her. Pain was receding; the darkness was full of bright golden sparkles; Ghetel was lying close by on the ground, moaning and gasping, stirring gravel as she moved. Mary at once snaked away over the rocks, downslope toward the water's edge. After thus crawling for a few feet, she rose into a crouch and, groping with her hands in the darkness for obstacles, she crept upstream. Behind her she heard Ghetel's groans trail off, and then heard her calling, in a weak, quizzical voice:

"Vhere are you? Ma-ry? Vhere are you?"

Through the ringings and roarings and throbbings in her head, Mary could not tell whether she was moving silently or not. But as Ghetel's voice grew fainter behind her, she knew she was getting wonderful, safe distance between them. She paused and looked back. All the shadows were almost black now, and she could distinguish only the inky-looking river, off which an early star occasionally glinted.

When she could no longer hear a sound from Ghetel, she slipped under a lip of the river bank, at the very edge of the water, crouched there hanging onto roots, and waited, fighting off a strange precipitous drowsiness which she felt must be the brink of dying.

It was while she crouched here, now stark naked but for her rope of yarn, winter night air numbing her skin, that Mary began to think about the canoe. It was a wildly improbable notion. Surely it would not still be around here. She had been able to find no canoes at any of the other crossing-places along the war road. And she knew nothing about steering a canoe if she did find it; she had never been alone in one. Nor could she expect to continue up the New River in one. The current was too strong and she was too weak.

But now she knew she must have this river between her and Ghetel. With a canoe, maybe she could at least get across the river.

Mary finally knew without a doubt that Ghetel had become an implacable hunter, as single-minded as a panther or a stalking Indian, and that she was Ghetel's prey. Traveling along the same narrow river bank, they would without a

doubt encounter each other again. And surely one more encounter would be fatal.

To one or the both of us, she thought. Most likely to me.

A faint sound nearby caught her ear and she put everything
out of her mind to listen. There was a voice, very faint, then
the sound of rock grating on rock, and the clangor of the
bronze bell.

She pressed herself further under the narrow overhang and
breathed slowly. The noises grew louder.

Ghetel was passing just above her. Mary could hear her
footsteps among leaves and rocks now, and the snap of a twig.

Ghetel was muttering softly to herself, and among the unintelligible syllables Mary thought she detected her own name.

Then the mumbling changed slightly and became almost
sing-song. There was no tune, but Mary realized, with a
squeeze of her heart, that Ghetel was trying to sing:

Ten times ten times ten a—way
But I'll be home a—gain.
Hm—hm hm, da da, da da . . .

Ghetel was moving very slowly, and it was some minutes
before she had passed and her pitiful noises were absorbed by
the wet whispers of the river.

The moon was up over the mountain and shining brightly
when Mary came out from her concealment. It was too cold
for a naked woman to remain immobile any longer. And now
that the valley was flooded with moon-silver, its shadows
inked in, she could see to look for the canoe. After a minute's
hesitation, she decided to turn upstream to seek it, although
she realized there was a possibility that it might have been
hidden in the thicket through which she had been pursued.

I'll go up just a ways, she thought; then if I don't find it, I'll
come back down and search the thicket.

Now you know better than that, she told herself. If y' go
upstream y'll never come back down. Best go back and look
in the thicket first.

About a hundred yards back she came to the place where

they had emerged from the thicket and fought. A little beyond that, the thicket grew still closer to the river's edge, and here seemed to be a logical place for hiding a canoe. The winter scene by moonlight was so much different from the summer scene by sunlight that she could find nothing really familiar.

She searched among the leafless bushes at the water's edge for perhaps ten minutes, trembling ever more violently with the cold, stopping now and then to listen for Ghetel, who might well return down the bank to look for her.

She saw a long, low silhouette, one end in the water, the other among the bushes. Dear heaven, could it really be? she thought, and hobbled to it.

It was only a log, a water-soaked, frozen driftwood log.

But beyond it was a similar shape. She hauled herself over the log and went there.

O it is!

It was the canoe, half-sunk and blown full of dead leaves. It would take much work even to determine whether it was whole, and to launch it and see if it would float. It might require more strength than she had. But, strengthened by hope, she set to work.

A half hour of scooping and raking emptied it of its cargo of ice and sodden, half-frozen leaves.

Now, she thought: the hard part.

She would have to raise it on its side to spill out the water.

She grasped the gunwale with both hands and lifted. It was fast, frozen to the shore or wedged in the brush. She strained upward until she was faint and gasping for breath. She squatted in the moonlight and hugged her icy skin and rested. Then she went to the stern, bent down, put her shoulder to the rough bark, got a footing on the pebbles and pressed. It remained unmoved until she thought her bones would crack.

She had to rest again. Then she put her shoulder to it once more, strained to the point that a groan burst from her throat—and then it budged with a creak and a grind.

Now she could rock it slightly; the water sloshed and broken ice rattled inside. She rested another five minutes, then again lifted at the gunwale.

It was terribly heavy, but it moved. It tried to settle back;

she panted and lifted. It rose slowly. She had to shift her grip, moving one hand down to the underside, and soon she could hear water spilling over the far gunwale. It grew lighter as the water poured out. Soon she had it all the way up on its edge and the last of the water was out. She was so exhausted she barely kept it from falling back to its upright position.

Another five minutes' rest and she was ready to launch it. But wait, she thought. Must find the paddle.

There was no paddle. She crawled in the thicket and scrabbled on the beach and under the canoe bottom but found no paddle.

The moon was higher now. She had spent an hour or two getting the canoe ready and now there was nothing with which to steer it.

Almost crying with frustration, she started moving down the beach looking for a pole or anything with which to control the vessel. It would be fatal to shove off into this fast river and be at the mercy of its current. She thought of the countless rapids and falls they had passed.

After almost an hour of wandering, during which she became so confused and lightheaded that she forgot several times what she was searching for, she noticed a length of something lying on the beach, almost white in the moonlight.

A tree lay along the shore, broken, apparently shivered and shattered by lightening or windstorm, and she found an almost-flat slab of the trunk, hanging white, attached by only a few fibers. It was about three feet long and four inches wide. It would serve as a paddle, if she could detach it from the tree. She twisted it around and around, and finally, using the edge of a flat rock, managed to pulverize the fibers until she could yank the slab free.

Now she had a paddle of sorts.

It was almost enough to make her believe in God again.

She had never before been in a boat or canoe by herself. She was thankful for the moonlight.

She shoved the end of the vessel out into the stream, then flung herself over the prow into the canoe before it could float away. Her weight, little as it was, grounded the bow, and the canoe hung to the shore. By her touch on the bark of the hull and the hickory framework, she cold feel the river moving.

She remembered how the Indians had done it. She held both gunwales and walked along the center toward the stern. As her weight moved to that end, the bow lifted and released the shore, and she was moving. Her heart was beating high. This was a harrowing business for a non-swimmer, especially one all but too weakened to move.

She turned and knelt in the stern. The shore was slipping by, silvery by moonlight. The broken and distorted reflection of the moon swung by as the canoe turned on the current.

She dipped the end of the slab into the water alongside and tried to steer. She managed to make the canoe stop turning, but now it was drifting sideways, even faster. It was not nearing the other shore.

She felt icy water under her knees. It was running in somewhere. The canoe was filling with water.

With her flagging strength, she began stroking the end of the slab in the water. The canoe turned. It was moving toward midstream. She stroked more. Now it was pointing upstream, but being carried backward downstream. This was worse yet. And the water now was perhaps two inches deep in the bottom of the canoe, streaming by her knees, first this way, then that.

She put the wood slab over the other side and stroked, straining, her fingers being torn by the jagged splinters. She strained against the water's resistance, sucking breaths of cold air that made her teeth stab with pain.

But at last the prow began swinging back toward the far shore.

She understood it now. A stroke on this side, then a stroke on that side, and she could keep the vessel moving aslant downstream, toward the opposite shore. She remembered that somehow the Indians had been able to steer without switching sides. Maybe you can with a paddle, she thought. With this stick, I better just do what I know to work.

Her course was erratic; several times she got sideways in the flow, or found herself racing backward, but now she was near the other shore. The water in the canoe was four inches deep now and the vessel responded sluggishly. Her arms were burning with exhaustion; her fingers were bloody and full of splinters.

And then she felt the soft *bump bump* as the bottom scraped over rocks. The prow nuzzled against the shore and the stern, with her in it, swung downstream. There was a dull crunch as it hit a rock; the rotten bark yielded and gapped and water came pouring in.

Mary stumbled and crawled toward the prow and threw a leg over. In a moment she was standing knee-deep in the cold river and the canoe was slipping away from shore, half sunk. She watched its curved black lines for a moment as it swerved slowly through the shivering path of moonlight on the water, and then saw it no more.

She dragged herself out of the water, chilled to the bone and scarcely able to stand. But a feeble, sobbing, almost hysterical laughter shook out of her, as she stumbled up the shore, hugging herself in her bony arms, tears running down both sides of her nose: She had made it! She had crossed the river! Ghetel could not get to her now.

There was really a river between them now. They were no longer together, after forty days and nights of the most crucial interdependence. They were separate in the wilderness.

The laughter coagulated into a huge knot in her chest and she was blinded with crying.

CHAPTER 26

IT SEEMED THAT THE MOON RADIATED COLD AS THE SUN RADIated heat. Now there was no blanket. And there was no Ghetel, no fellow human warmth, to draw close to in the night. Mary felt that nothing could keep her from freezing to death now except to keep moving. But after this calamitous night of mortal terror and fury, struggle and flight, she had no strength left to keep moving. She kept sinking to the ground with dizziness after every few yards of progress up the left bank of the river.

She was on her hands and knees on frozen mud. Somewhere an owl was repeating its one forlorn syllable. Mary listened to it with a strange, fascinated attention, sensing somehow that it would be the last life-sound she would hear and wondering if there might be some reason why God would give her this as her death song. She thought the word "God," but it was just a word now, cold and distant as that moon and as meaningless as that owl-hoot, too remote now to stir anything in her heart. To pray now was useless and she did not have the strength of mind even to formulate a prayer. The finding of the canoe and her successful escape across the river had been a miracle, an answer to prayers, and she had no reason to expect any more miracles. She did not want any more such deliverances as this one, which in effect had only placed her where she could die alone instead of with somebody.

She trembled as the last of her warmth seemed to die down inside her, and crumpled from her position on hands and knees into a curled, trembling ball, her knees under her and her arms hugging her chest and her forehead on the ground, the cold moonlight seeming to penetrate deeper and deeper into her back.

But really shouldn't leave without praying, she thought. What if Mother and Tommy and Georgie was a-waiting for me over there and I went across and couldn't reach them because I'd left here without a prayer . . .

She raised her head from the ground and looked at the wavering silvery lights and shadows. Her eyes fastened on something a few yards up the slope, something that looked like a house. It would be, she thought without wonder, just a mirage. I'm through with silly hoping, she thought. It's just something I think I see and I can blink it away . . .

But it was still there.

Well, I need to know, she thought, and she started crawling toward it over the frozen ground, expecting it to retreat or fade before her like the mirage it was.

And eventually she was there. She had crawled to it through what she realized was a patch of corn-stubble, and she reached out and touched a wall. It really was a wall, a wall of bark. She found a door.

It was some sort of a hut, whether made by Indians or by white people from the settlements above she could not tell. There was not much of it. It was dilapidated and the moon showed through cracks in the walls and there was nothing on the dirt floor but drifted leaves. But it was a roof to protect her from the stabbing cold of moonlight. It was the first building she had been in since . . . since that hut where they had stayed on the O-y-o and had found the belled horse and the corn. A *building*, she thought. I'm in a *building*.

She raked leaves into a pile along the base of the back wall and burrowed in among them, covered herself with more of them, and now that her bare skin was no longer in the light of the piercing moon-bright sky, even dead leaves seemed like a blanket. She shivered for a while, her mind wandering back and forth between nothingness and the awareness of shelter, and then she was dreaming of turning over on her own rustling corn-shuck mattress to roll closer to Will. She opened her eyes in the dream and there was some sort of a great cat standing in the doorway, in the morning sunlight looking at her, a cat as big as a person, and when it saw her eyes it turned and darted away from the doorway.

When morning truly came, she sat outside against the sun-warmed east wall of the hut for a few minutes until her skin was dry and almost warm, and her heartbeat strengthened from flutters to a weak rhythm, and she was able to think and remember things and even anticipate that she might yet live another day.

She did not remember having seen this place on the way down. Perhaps it had not been built yet then—though it seemed old, abandoned. No, she realized then. We'd have been on the other side of the river when we passed it. That was the explanation.

She got to her feet and stood, weaving, spots drifting across her vision, and had to lean against the wall until she could see again; then she went down into the corn-patch and searched it for dry ears or stray grains that might have fallen to the ground.

But there was little left of the corn-patch, other than trampled stubble and the prints of wild animals, and they seemed to have gleaned it thoroughly, leaving her not a grain.

Alongside the corn-patch there was another small plot of cultivated ground, once a vegetable garden, with some withered stalks of something lying along it, mostly eaten. Mary found a stick and poked and grubbed in the hard ground. She saw something violet and white just below the surface. "Oh, my," she said aloud, dropping to her knees and clawing at the frozen earth.

A half an hour spent digging up the whole garden yielded two small turnips which the animals had failed to find. Trembling with anticipation, Mary took them down to the river's edge, knelt with sunlight glancing up from the water into her face and carefully washed them, taking her time as if she were in the luxury of her own kitchen, prolonging the anticipation, enjoying the knowledge that here was food, real domestic food, not worms or buds or buzzard-leavings, but turnips, real turnips, and furthermore that she would not have to wolf down her share of them before Ghetel got them.

Careful now, she thought. Slow; must no' sicken yourself.

She could not have eaten them fast if she had wanted to. Her teeth were so loose that she could gnaw through the tough skin and firm flesh only with care and difficulty, wincing and squinting. As she chewed, a molar came out into the mass of turnip pulp. It was the first tooth she had ever lost. She worked it forward in her mouth as one does a fishbone, took it out and looked wistfully as it as she chewed and savored the mouthful of turnip. She chewed and chewed that first bite, almost in a state of bliss, and it softened in her mouth and tasted heavenly, and her stomach clamored for it. What I like about a turnip, she thought, the longer y' chew it, the bigger it gets. And y' want it big, don't 'ee, my belly? She smiled at the thought of talking with her belly. Then she swallowed and shut her eyes and smiled and felt it go down. "There, how'ee like 'at, my belly?" she said aloud. Her stomach clutched up and hurt for a moment at first, but she did not get nauseated, and she got up and went back to the hut and sat against its sunny side again and carefully began working her teeth through the second bite, and carefully chewed it, her gums itching and aching with the pressure of chewing, and she ruminated on this mouthful, dreamily, ecstatically, soaking in the weak dry sunlight, shivering now and then when a cold breeze would touch her, and she believed she had never, never been quite so happy.

She used up about an hour, eating the first turnip, which had provided four bites, and when it was gone she sat and gazed at the other one. She was full now, and she wished Ghetel could be here to eat the second turnip. O but wouldn't she be in heaven, the poor thing, her and her appetites, Mary thought.

She lay there in the sunshine for perhaps another hour, her mind drifting like fog, blank and light, looking at but not really seeing the river, while her innards burbled and grumbled over the unaccustomed task of digestion. She was too blissful and lethargic to move.

When she woke up, the sun had moved around to the south side of the hut; it was about midday; she felt drugged. The whole bright gray-yellow landscape pulsated with each heartbeat.

Must get on, she thought. Now't I got the wherewithal.

She yawned and groaned and hoisted herself to her feet. "G'bye," she said, looking back at the hut and garden. "It's been a nice visit. I sh'll surely come back sometime." I shall, she thought. Sometime I'll come back down here with Will and have another look at a place where I ought to've died but didn't, thank the Lord.

She carried the remaining turnip in her left hand and hobbled along the narrow bottomland. With her immediate agonies of starvation allayed a bit, she was more aware of her other discomforts: the feet and legs with their hundred aches and stabs, the silent grinding of her swollen joints, the various twinges around her kidneys, the gurgle of phlegm in her chest and the wintery air on her nakedness. But now at least she felt she could bear these things and keep going. Having a little strength was everything; having pain was nothing.

She had lost a few hundred yards during the canoe crossing and she had walked for half an hour before she saw on the opposite bank the thicket where she had fought Ghetel and later found the canoe. A little farther on she saw the low bank under which she had crouched and waited for Ghetel to pass.

The New River here continued its twisting course among mountains of awesome height and mass, mountains that seemed to be the backbone of the world, but for some miles now there had been flat bottomland to walk on, though occasionally it was necessary to clamber through windfalls and tangled drift. These obstacles tired her and demanded all her attention while she was in them, but during most of her progress she would look up every few minutes from her footing and search the opposite shore for a sign of Ghetel. O it's strange after all that's happened, she thought, but 'twould be a lovely thing to see her over yonder.

It was midafternoon and the sun was already dipping behind the high ridges, whose shadows crept up the mountainsides opposite, when Mary noticed something she had been seeing for several minutes without heeding: Circling in the wedge of blue sky in the valley ahead, silently and gracefully winding a course downward toward the riverbank, there were buzzards.

Something dead, she thought, remembering the muskrat remnants she had pirated from a flock of buzzards back at the waterfall. Pray it's on this side of the river . . .

And then she thought:

Ghetel.

O, pray not . . .

Heavy brush impeded her way as she went with dread curiosity toward the place upon which the buzzards were descending. She plunged and wove through it in the greatest haste she could manage, ignoring the scratches and the stinging slaps of the branches on her cold skin.

At last she broke out of the thicket and found herself looking almost directly across the river at the sight she had dreaded to see.

There on a flat rock shelf next to the river bank, out in the open, lay a gray and white shape, which was Ghetel half-draped in the old blanket. She lay sprawled, inert, on her side, one arm extended stiffly beyond her head, the other lying limp over her waist, as if she had died while trying to claw her way one last inch forward across the rock surface.

The buzzards were almost upon her old carcass now; one had landed on a bare limb a few feet above her and was watching her; the shadows of the others drifted back and forth over the blanket as they rode the air down to her. Mary sank to the ground, her heart squeezing, her face crumpling up, and moaned. The whole pitiful scene blurred beyond her tears. She felt as crushed as when she had watched the Indians come down with the scalp of her mother.

O God, to have come this far together, Mary prayed. O dear God, if she'd only behaved, we'd still be together and I could've kept her alive, I know I could've; I did for weeks and weeks and weeks.

She wiped the tears away and looked at the dreary, final tableau of that brave old woman's eventful life. She thought about throwing rocks across the river to drive the buzzards away. At least I could do that for 'er.

But that would be futile. She could hardly lift a rock. She could not possibly throw one even halfway across this river. And even if she could, how long could she stay here throwing rocks to keep hungry buzzards off that pitiful old carcass? One thing she knew about buzzards was that they had the patience that outlasts all other patience; theirs is the final hunger to be satisfied.

Eh well, then. The next best thing I can do for 'er, I guess, is not to watch 'em. When they do it to me I'd not want anyone t' see it.

So . . . Ghetel, old dear . . . I'll say bye now . . . an' get along . . . leave 'ee in privacy . . .

She took one last look, rising to go on. Tears were trickling down her nose, and she saw that the buzzard on the limb had half-spread his wings and was dropping toward the carcass, and one of the flying ones was just settling on the blanket and folding his wings. From this distance she could just see the ugly red nakedness of their heads.

"HAH!"

The scene burst into a flurry of motion: black wings beating the air; Ghetel's form suddenly lurching; Ghetel's outcry and the clanking horsebell echoing faintly over the river. Mary had to blink to see it.

Ghetel was trying to scramble to her feet. She had a buzzard by the leg and it was beating frantically to escape, losing wing feathers. "I got you! I got you!" Ghetel was cackling. Mary stood with her mouth agape, shivers of awe running down her flanks, and then with a jolt of gleeful comprehension, she whooped.

The cunning old devil had finally got hungry enough to ambush buzzards!

Mary was doing an exuberant dance now, screaming with laughter, cheering Ghetel, having the time of her life. It was simply the most wonderful thing she had ever seen. Even though this was the same desperate visceral cunning that Ghetel had used to attack and hurt Mary, Mary cheered it and thought Ghetel was surely the most marvelous madwoman who had ever come round the mountain. Her heart leaped the wide river to her.

The ambush didn't quite work. Ghetel's feet got tangled in the blanket, and when she fell the buzzard tore itself free and blundered along the ground until it could gain the air, surely having learned never to approach a carcass in a blanket again. And Ghetel stood there in her scanty rags, a skeleton in wattles of loose skin, shaking her fist and hurling a screeching stream of Dutch profanity skyward after the climbing carrion birds.

But what heart it had given Mary!

Ghetel was stooping to gather up the blanket when she seemed to realize that she was not alone. She straightened up and looked quizzically about, simmering down from her rage and disappointment, until her gaze finally came across the river and she saw Mary rocking back and forth and waving to her.

Ghetel raised both hands and called Mary's name. It came faintly across the river. It was very strange, hearing her name come from that distance and then echo along the hills.

Ghetel, white in the winter sunlight against the enormous gray and brown backdrop of the wintery landscape, pulled the blanket up around her shoulders. "I am sorry!" she called.

"So, then," Mary called back. "I'm glad to see you!"

"Ya, ya, me also! May-ry, you come back now, heh?"

"I can't!"

"Please! You come! Ve be friends like before!"

"No!"

"I like better to be with you! Please you, come back!"

Mary shook her head. "This is my side! That's your side!"

Ghetel cupped her ear. "Vat you said?"

"Better we stay apart!"

It was impossible to see the old woman's expression from this distance, but her postures and hesitations and gestures showed her to be very cast down and full of remorse. "I am sor-ry!" she called out in drawn-out syllables and pitiful tones. She paused for a long time, extending her arms toward Mary again and standing that way with her head tilted. Finally she called: "I vill not hurt you, I promise! I found a root to eat!"

"Good! I found two turnips!" She held up her hand with the turnip in it.

Ghetel was silent for a minute. "Turnips! O, I vant!"

"Sorry!" But Mary yearned, for an instant, for the strength to throw this turnip across the river to Ghetel. She wondered at herself for having that impulse, after all that had happened the night before.

She wished she could go across to Ghetel and give her the turnip and put her arms around her and make things be the way they had been before Ghetel had lost control of herself. Because they had had each other close, those had been good days, despite everything. She now remembered their easy passage along the beautiful O-y-o in the warm autumn sunshine as if recalling a balmy holiday with a dear friend.

Now the valley was in shadow and the air was becoming bitter cold again and it was time to move or freeze. She started up the bank.

"*Pleeeeease!*" Ghetel was wailing now. She got down on

one knee and wrung her hands, far over there. "I vant us together!"

"I can't come over anyway!" Mary called back. "Now, come on! We'll walk now, shan't we?" In a way it would be like being together, she thought, if they could keep each other in sight. They would still be together. There would just be a nice safe river's breadth between them. It would be just fine. She was a long way from the blanket, of course, and from the warmth of a fellow body to sleep alongside in the cold of night. But she was an equally long way from that murderous craziness that came over Ghetel when her belly was truly, truly empty.

"Come along," she called again, waving her arm. "We're still together, dear!"

And at last, slumping, chin on her chest and head wobbling from side to side in dejection, Ghetel clutched the bedraggled blanket around her and began trudging up the other side of the river.

So they were together again, in this new and necessary manner of being together, with a river between them, and they resumed their upriver journey which had been interrupted by that hour of utter terror the night before.

Mary lay shuddering with cold in a deep drift of leaves and waited for dawn to lighten the way enough so that she could rise and go on. Because of the cold, she had not slept at all during the night. The leaves had not kept her warm, as she had been when sharing the blanket with Ghetel; they only slowed her heat loss enough to keep her from freezing to death as she lay still during the interminable night.

The sky gradually grayed. She rustled the leaves around her head and raised herself far enough to peer around. It was perhaps light enough now to make her way along the cluttered shore. It was easy enough to see the path and the obstacles now; they were outlined with a heavy frost.

When she rose, the cold pressed on her naked skin like steel. She was painfully hungry. The two turnips had fed her momentarily yesterday, but they had also taught her stomach again to have expectations.

She shivered and peered across the steaming river to its dim frosted shore and tried to see where Ghetel lay. She would have slept well, doubtless, with the blanket, and probably was still asleep. Mary called her name, her breath making a frosty cloud, then called it again and again. She did not want to lose sight of the old woman, but knew she could not wait here in this frigid air while Ghetel slept late.

"Yaaaàh!" Ghetel's voice answered across the river, a grouchy wail that made Mary smile in fond amusement.

Mary trembled and rubbed her forearms up and down over the gooseflesh of her bosom, and bawled back in high spirits: "Roust the old bones, slug-a-bed!" There was no answer for more than a minute. "Up, dearie," she called again, "if y're a-goin' t' walk with me!" She tried to press her thighs together to warm each other but they were so wasted that only her knees touched. While she waited for a sign of life from the other shore she remembered to tie another knot in the yarn rope that was now not only her only garment but her only possession. And her history. She was wracked with a painful spasm of coughing and her nose was running like a spring. She could scarcely move her swollen fingers or control their trembling to knot the yarn.

She had reckoned it all out during the sleepless night; according to her count of days and her perception of terrain, she was sure they were not much more than thirty miles from home. She was not in the least inclined to waste a minute of daylight waiting for Ghetel to get her sleep out. But, on the other hand, she had dragged and prodded and coerced the old crab more than seven hundred miles and was determined not to lose her this close to salvation.

They were able to keep each other in sight most of the day as they climbed and stumbled and crawled up the dark, wild valley with the seething gray river between them. The sight of Ghetel over there, looking as insignificant as an insect at the base of an enormous, mist-shrouded mountain, made Mary aware of how small and weak she herself was in this immense, indifferent wilderness.

Nought but a couple o' bugs, she thought. O how mighty

stupendous this world is, and how feeble we, and O how far we've creeped over it! Ten times ten times ten. Aye, it's no surprise if the Lord overlooks us entirely, as I fear He has done.

They called to each other often across the water, to keep in touch and to keep their spirits up. Mary sang, and Ghetel would sing *da da, da, da, da, da* . . . They were past worrying whether Indians might hear them. Anyways, if Ghetel met a Shawnee now, Mary thought with a grim smile, she'd doubtless kill and devour 'im.

At every resting place, Ghetel would come to squat at the water's edge, huddle there with the blanket drawn cowl-like over her head and plead with Mary for one chance to rejoin her. She professed penitence, and made elaborate and contrite promises, which Mary could barely hear over the rush of the water and the rising wind in the forest, and implored forgiveness, and begged to resume their old companionship. Mary could not seem to make her understand that she could not have recrossed the river if she had wanted to. Mary yelled to her about the canoe, about its sinking, but Ghetel seemed not to understand a word of that. Maybe she did not recognize the word *canoe*, or maybe she could not hear Mary's words. Or perhaps she was still, or again, in that condition of mind she had so frequently been in, when she simply *would not* hear anything but her own plaints.

Rain started, then turned to sleet, stinging their skin, driving them onward and increasing their lamentations.

Withal, our witchy wailin' ought to haunt this Devil's valley, Mary thought, f'r many a generation t' come.

CHAPTER
27

WILL INGLES, JOHNNY DRAPER AND GANDER JACK RODE SLOUCH-
ing in the cold rain. Water dribbled off the drooping edges of
their hat brims. Each had his rifle lying across his loins,
protected by their deerskin capes. The skins were sodden and
clammy but the men were warm inside the pungent wool
clothes they wore under the hides.

They were not in good spirits. Their trek down among the
Cherokees in the Tennessee and Georgia country seemed to
have been a waste of weeks and expense. Snake Stick had
given them no sense of confidence. He had not only remained
reluctant to carry their ransom offer to the Shawnees, he had
also, as his parting words, told them that he might not even go
up to the O-y-o country until next spring, instead of this fall.
That pronouncement had been almost the last straw for
Johnny, who had been simmering under Snake Stick's insolence, and Johnny had boiled over. Eyes flashing, he had
demanded that Snake Stick return the ransom goods. "I'm
damned if we give you all this if y're just a-gonna sit here in
your hutch an' count it all winter!" But Will had managed to
cool Johnny down before he could make a real scene, which
might have been fatal. In the end, the chief had shrugged and
said only, "Snake Stick might go now and he might not go
now. Snake Stick does not live to please English."

Their return from the Cherokee lands had been uneasy.
Gander Jack had sworn a hundred times on the way back that
he saw Indians in the corners of his eyes, though he had never
managed to get a fixed glimpse of any.

And so autumn had muted into winter gray on their disconsolate trip back toward Virginia. They had ridden up an

endless series of rocky creeks between somber, hazy mountains, joined the Tennessee River and followed it past the Nolichucky and then the Watauga, finally crossing a high range to reach the headwaters of the New River, which flowed in exactly the opposite direction, here running north and east toward Draper's Meadows and Ingles' Ferry. Now they would stay generally in this valley for the next few days, following the New River downstream, to reach the settlements. Their journey was nearly over. That it might have been futile was uppermost in all their minds, but they had never said so to each other.

Gander Jack was in advance about twenty feet; he slumped so low in his saddle that he might have been thought asleep, but Will knew from their long weeks of travel with him that his downcast eyes were scanning every inch of ground for signs of Indian passage. Johnny was bringing up the rear, leading the now lightly burdened pack animal. The horses' coats were dark and shiny with rain.

Will and Johnny had acquired scout's eyes, too, and from under their half-closed eyelids they scanned the trails and mountainsides before, alongside and behind them constantly for that little displaced something, that half-hidden motion, that unnatural shadow, that unlikely sound, that skittish behavior of animals and birds, which might indicate the proximity of Indians.

But both were at the same time preoccupied with thoughts of their wives. They were trying to get themselves accustomed to the likelihood that they would never see them again. On the way out to the Cherokee country, they had dared to hope for Mary and Bettie. If ransom negotiations could have begun now before winter, there would have been a decent chance to trace the women and children and bring them back still physically and spiritually whole. But since their encounter with Snake Stick, they had come to believe that the trail would be too cold by next year, that life among the Indians would have ruined them. Will burned continuously inside with chagrin, heated by his imagination, in the knowledge that his young wife's body, so sacred to him—his wife's body that he considered *his*—was at the mercy of

savages who would have no respect for it or for his sacred
conjugal right to it. True, he had heard that the Indians did
not practice rape on their female victims, but he found that
impossible to believe. Surely no man who lived the wild and
sensuous and naked life of a heathen, who could so abandon
himself as to dash out a baby's brains and scalp an old
woman, would have the discipline to honor the desirable temple of a young woman's body.

Why, even a white man wouldn't have the discipline to mind
his morals in such an opportunity, Will thought over and over.
Surely not a heathen.

Though he tried to keep it out of his imagination, a disgust-
ing image would appear and reappear during these long periods when there was nothing to do but ride and think.

In his mind there would be his beautiful, lithe Mary, always
in a council lodge like that of Snake Stick, and she would be
staked down naked, spread-eagled on a buffalo hide, lit by
flickering fireglow, biting her lips and tossing her head from
side to side, her auburn hair spilling and tangled, her precious
breasts red and bloody with bite-marks, while one naked,
shining, slavering, drunken Indian after another—all looking
like Snake Stick— would kneel between her lean white thighs
and then throw his weight upon her and thrust his filthy dark
stiff unimaginable profanity of a lewdness into that sacred
secret place of hers, and pump his heathen seed into her,
yipping with lust while she screamed Will's name—or
God's—with no one to hear her but the other savages who had
finished with her or were waiting their turns . . .

Or sometimes, even worse, he would see her face change
from pain to pleasure and hear her screams turn to moans,
and she would begin raising and moving her hips the way he
remembered . . .

And when he saw these pictures in his mind in all their
pitiful and revolting details, his heart would swell with rage
and then shrink down cold and sick, and a pall of hatred and
disgust would darken his emotions so that he would not want
to see or converse with Gander Jack or even with his own
brother-in-law. He would stay in this mood sometimes for
hours, thinking and rethinking the repugnant but somehow

fascinating scene, until he could not bear the notion any longer and he would take a deep breath and squeeze the nightmare out of his mind.

Often Will would turn and see Johnny, hot-tempered Johnny, wrapped in just such black moods, his mouth drawn so thin the lips would look gray, and would presume that Johnny was thinking like thoughts about Bettie.

Will had even wondered—even while exhausting his every resource and risking his neck to repatriate her—whether this same lewd image would be his first thought upon seeing her again, and whether he would be charitable enough and tolerant enough in his soul ever to draw her close to him again if he did think it.

The three men had reached a place where they had to decide which of two paths they would take. One would lead them overland along the shadow of the Blue Ridge to their ruined settlement at Draper's Meadows, where a little restoration had been started after the raid in July; the other would lead them across the New River to the little fort at Dunkard's Bottom, where most of the neighbors in the region had congregated for protection earlier in the fall after getting their crops in.

"What say'ee, brother?" Johnny inquired, looking tiredly at Will from under the dribbling brim of his hat. They both felt so much let down after the apparent failure of their long mission that nothing seemed worth doing, and no choice worth more than the flip of a coin. "Want to ride up to th' Meadows and put in a few days o' work on th' roofs?"

Will peered up at the rainy skies. "There's y'r answer," he said. "This is no roof-mendin' weather. Partick'ly if this turns t' snow."

Johnny shrugged. "Dunkard's it is then, Jack."

"Yep," Will said. "I would like t' look in on th' ferry, too."

The guide nodded, looking relieved. They had been out long enough. He would like to sleep behind a stockade for a change, as it had been a long time since he had enjoyed the luxury of sleeping with both eyes shut. It would take them three or four days yet to get to Dunkard's Bottom. When they

did, he was going to get a jug with some of the money Will and
Johnny had paid him, and he was going to drink it and go to
sleep in a real bed, with his moccasins off.

CHAPTER
28

THIS GRAY AND SLEETY MORNING THE TWO WOMEN REACHED A
place Mary distinctly remembered, where the river narrowed
and seemed to have carved its way straight through the solid
rock of a high mountain. As they inched around the bases of
the cliffs on their respective sides of the river, they glanced
across at each other frequently, keeping track of each other's
progress. "You're a-goin' just fine," Mary called across, and
above the murmur of the river over the rocks, her voice
bounced back and forth between the cliffs as if she had
shouted in a big room. Often Mary could hear the faint *dink-
dink* of Ghetel's bell. It was a pretty sound again.

There were stretches along the bases of the cliffs where the
fringe of river bank simply ran out, and in these places they
would have to wade down into the cold, tugging water and
search for underwater passages with cold-benumbed feet,
clinging with aching-cold fingers to fissures in the rock for
support. Ghetel wailed her dismay constantly while making
these passages, but she made them. She would stop at each
such obstacle as if afraid to wade in, but then, on seeing Mary
moving ahead, she would brave the water. Her one night all
alone in the wilderness had convinced her that anything was
better than losing Mary.

It seemed to Mary that they now must be in the very
backbone of the great mountain range through which they had
been laboring for so many weeks. Towering straight above

her, she was certain, were some of the same great peaks she had been able to see, all purple-hazy and majestic, from the high ground at Draper's Meadows. Doubtless that great smooth-topped mountain six or seven miles ahead, which she could glimpse now and again from turns in the rivercourse, was one of those her mother had pointed at in the distant west when talking to the boys about "ten times ten times ten."

Her mother. The boys. They seemed so vague in memory now, like somebody she had known in another lifetime. Before this lifetime. It seemed that she had been born and had spent all this present life ascending this maze of roaring canyons: blue-gray rock jutting into the heavens, green water, howling wind, caves, dead leaves, buzzards and eagles wheeling far overhead, wild animals lurking out of reach, tributaries and avalanches thwarting her progress, and the relentless cold, the merciless grinding and regrinding of the flesh of her feet, the endless wheedling and cajoling and pampering with Ghetel. And *hunger.* It was always there, sometimes clarifying thought, sometimes muddling it down to the simple incoherence of instinct and nightmare. This seemed like a life in which she had never known the warmth or the nurture of a mother's bosom, but had, rather, been spawned and left like a frog egg in a slough or a turtle egg on a river beach, never to know anything in life but creeping and cold blood.

But vague and distant though most of her memories were, there was one that could still come through: the strong hairy warmth of Will Ingles. It was like a ruddy-gold hearth beckoning at the end of every gray valley; it was like the gleaming reward at the end of purgatory. The bearded face of Saint Peter at the heavenly gate would glow like the bearded face of Will Ingles at the cabin door, she fancied.

And, holding to that warm light, she could drag one bloody, blue foot up over the icy rocks and place it before the other, and do that again, and then do it again.

It was afternoon. She was going northeastward toward that great flat-top mountain. She had passed by a low island in the river, for a while losing sight of Ghetel, who was inching along the base of a cliff on the opposite shore and was hidden by the leafless brush on the island. Then Ghetel appeared beyond the upper end of the island, stooped so far she appeared almost to be on all fours. But she raised a hand and waved and her horse-bell clinked and they went on.

Now the river bent like a horseshoe to the right, around the base of a smooth curved wall of sheer stone three hundred feet high. As she crept into the curve under this precipice, more and more wall revealed itself to her, and it began to appear that it might sweep around for a mile or more, broken only by steep notches carved back into it by falling brooks. It was the kind of wall she had learned to dread, where there might or might not be ledges to cling to, where there might or might not be a riverbottom shallow enough to wade.

Across the river, on the inside of the curve, the slope was gentler and there was an alluvial beach. Ghetel would have much easier going around this river bend. If I was her, Mary thought, I reckon I might try to go over that hill and shortcut the bend. God, I wish I was over there. I'd do that, I would. "Ghetel!" she called. She raised her hands and cupped them beside her mouth. "GHETEL!" The old woman looked. Mary pointed up a gentle draw that seemed to lead to the hilltop above Ghetel. "Go over!" Mary shouted. "Go up and over!"

The old woman looked up the draw, then back to Mary. Mary pointed to herself and made a sweeping motion to indicate that she would be going around the outside of the bend, then pointed to Ghetel and then up the draw. Ghetel shrugged, nodded, then turned up the draw.

Mary moved on for a few hundred feet. The narrow ledge she had been following dwindled to nothing. Eh well, she thought. It's into the river again. She waded in, up to her thighs, clutching at irregularities on the cliff-face. The water was really not much colder than the air, but it seemed to wash away what little warmth her skin had generated, and she was shaken through and through by uncontrollable spasms.

Then she went on, over the uneven rock bottom. Sometimes the water was to her knees, sometimes to her ribs. She hugged herself close to the wall from time to time when she grew faintish. Her vision grew uncertain. She would be looking up at the gray curve of sky above the dark blue curve of stone and would get the sensation that she was floating on her back under a stone bridge. Sometimes the cliff would be like a black curtain; sometimes it would be brilliant with details of texture. Sometimes it would seem an hour had elapsed during the taking of a single step.

At last she came to a resting place, a rocky niche where one of the springs had worn its way back into the stone wall, and she got out of the river there and drew herself into a ball, her skin cold and wet and fish-belly white. But the spray from the falling spring in the winter air was even more chilling than immersion in the river. She hugged herself, trembling violently, squinting, and tried to recover her breath. Every inhalation was a spasm of gasping. Her heart seemed to be not beating now, but quaking.

She heard a voice through the hiss of falling water. She looked around, looked across the river. There near the brow of the hill inside the bend, a quarter of a mile away and two or three hundred feet above the river, Ghetel was waving down at her, a tiny gray speck of a person. It was good to see that she had managed the climb.

Mary could see down the east arm of the bend now. She had perhaps another half-mile to go along the base of the cliff before the slope eased off, and beyond that, the river took a sharp bend to her left. In that bend, the sheer wall of the river was on Ghetel's side. She'd better stay above it, Mary thought. If she comes down from right there, she'll have a wall just like this'n ahead of her. She tried to shout that warning to Ghetel. A noise, half-croak, half-squeak, came out of her throat. It hurt her throat and made tears sting her eyes. The days of stark exposure to the elements of late November had taken their toll. Her voice was gone.

With an exhausted wave, she gestured for Ghetel to stay high on the hill. She had no way of knowing whether the old woman understood it or not. Then she uncurled, groped for crevices in the wet rock, and let herself back down into the river at the base of the cliff, and continued upstream.

It was dusk when she felt the slope rising and growing

sandy under her feet, and soon she was on a gentle, brushy beach ranging from fifty to a hundred feet wide and extending down to the next bend of the river. Opposite her now was a sheer, fluted cliff rising five hundred feet out of the river like ribs of rock. Somewhere up there Ghetel should be traversing high along the brink, unless she had been stupid enough to come down to the river. Mary dropped to the ground on her knees and embraced herself, teeth chattering, and searched the enormous craggy wall from end to end and from top to bottom for a sight of that bent old figure.

No. She's up top somewhere, or she's fell, or she's found a place to crawl into. Too dark now.

Got to find a place myself ere I perish.

She crawled toward the base of the hill. A narrow creek came out of a ravine and poured into the river. Turning left up the ravine, she found a depression between a boulder and a log, drifted full of dead leaves, and burrowed deep into them, shivered and gasped voicelessly, feeling the cold creep closer and closer to her erratically skipping heart. She lay there considering, almost indifferently, that the heart itself would likely slow down and congeal with cold and finally stop before she should ever see daylight again.

The sound, long and thin as a hair, came coiling into the gray misery of her stupor. It continued for some time before she paid any attention to it and realized that it was a voice. A long, high, wailing voice, repeating itself from a distance and harmonizing with its own echoes.

Then she also became aware of the liquid syllables of the nearby creek running over its stones down toward the whispering river, and of the stab of cold and the buzz of numbness in her body, and realized that she was somehow still alive, and that the voice was Ghetel's, coming down the canyon from somewhere, calling for her. She opened her eyes and saw flecks of gray daylight showing through the dead leaves that covered her face.

It was perhaps ten minutes before she could overcome the paralysis of chill enough to move her limbs and raise herself out of the leaves. The river was steaming in the colder air,

faint wisps of mist rising against the dark blue of the cliff on
the far side. The clouds were crawling over the mountaintops,
dark and ragged and slow, looking pregnant with snow.
Mary's vision was blurred this morning by the swelling and
the matter in her eyelids. Ghetel's voice had faded away and
Mary could not hear it now.

There was moss on the boulder. It was winter-dead, turned
to a dull greenish-brown. She clawed some off with her broken fingernails into the palm of her hand and ate it. It was
half dirt, and gritted between her teeth. But she kept clawing
it off and eating it until she had the illusion that there was
something nourishing in her belly. The illusion itself gave her
some warmth. She could tell that her blood was reaching her
limbs now because the numbness was dissolving and impulses
of pain were coming from everywhere.

What hurts, she thought, y' know's alive.

It was difficult to think, but she put her mind to reckoning.
There's maybe ten miles more o' this canyon, she thought,
before I'll find that gunpowder spring where we stopped on
our first day out. Then I'll turn east off the river and a day or
two's walk would bring me up Sinking Creek to Draper's
Meadows.

I'm that close! she thought. I can't be more'n fifteen-twenty
miles from home! Oh, Will! Oh, darlin' Will! Wait, hon! Two
days more an' I'll be a-warmin' m'self at your side, y' great
hearth of a man!

She loved that thought. It seemed marvelously tender and
funny. She threw her head back, eyes teary, and tried to roar
with laughter. But there was no voice, only a wheeze, which
quickly caved in and became a debilitating fit of coughing.
She hacked up great gobs of brown mucus.

But fifteen miles! I swear I've come nigh eight hundred. I
c'd go fifteen more on a pair o' broken legs if I had 'em. Up,
now!

A quarter of a mile brought her to the abrupt left turn of the
river, and she was no sooner around that bend than her beach
ran out and she was again inching along an almost perpendicular cliff, some two or three hundred feet high, going hand
over hand, hanging onto roots and cracks and shrubs, a few
feet above the river. This cliff seemed to extend a mile east-

ward before curving southward under the very shoulder of that great, level-topped mountain she had been seeing in the distance for so long.

Most of the time she heard only the gurgly rasp of her own breathing and the wet murmur of the river below, but sometimes she would sense again that distant howl of a human voice. Most of the time she would see only the next root, the next fingerhold in the vertical rock, but sometimes she would hug the cliff and turn to search the opposite wall of the canyon from end to end and top to bottom for the source of that voice.

I know she's still alive, Mary thought, but not that I'll ever see 'er again.

This place is just so big, and we're so little.

After two hours she had traversed the wall of that cliff and begun working her way southward again. Here the canyon made a long, slight curve and she could see about two miles down to the next eastward bend. There was a narrow lip of shoreline along the base of the cliff most of this distance, so she could progress like a human instead of a spider. With her hands free, she was able to pick up any shred or bit of chewable material to put into her mouth—white filaments of root, bits of inner bark from driftwood, winter buds, the pith of reeds, a stinking, half-frozen fragment of a dead fish left at the water's edge by some feeding animal, and some little cold, squishy gray globule that could have been anything from a turtle egg to a fish eye, for all she knew or cared—for she would eat anything she could swallow now; she was as desperate in her hunger as Ghetel had been, now that her task was to keep going a mere twelve or fourteen miles. At midmorning she squatted, covered with gooseflesh, and strained to pass a small, hard knot of stool. She turned then to study it, for the possibility that it contained something undigested that might be eaten again.

Nay, she thought, with a sudden violent shudder of disgust. Never that. I sh'll never be brought so low. I'd lie down an' decoy buzzards first.

But yet, she thought in queasy amazement, I did get to th' point where I gave it a thought. God forgi' me.

"AAAAAYYY!"

Ghetel's bawling voice spilled down the valley so loudly that Mary started. It sounded as if she were only a few feet away. Mary scanned the curving opposite shore and, despite the filmy vagueness of her vision, spotted her almost at once, directly across the river but perhaps a hundred feet up the slope of a scrabbly knoll. She was as gray as the slate itself, but easy to locate by her vigorous waving and raucous yells. She was a heartening sight after this latest night of solitude. Mary returned her wave, and tried to answer her calls but found herself still voiceless.

Now Ghetel was shouting something else, which Mary couldn't make out at once. She cupped her hand behind her ear. Ghetel shouted between her hands:

"Can't go! Can't go!" Then she pointed down the slope to her right with emphatic jabs of her finger. Mary followed the slope down with her eyes and saw what she meant: at the base of the knoll there was the mouth of a creek, pouring its waters into that side of the river. It was not a wide creek—little more than fifty feet, Mary estimated—but steep-sided and likely quite deep, really a formidable obstacle to Ghetel's progress, the sort of obstacle that had added countless miles already to their odyssey.

Mary simply shook her head. "Walk around," she whispered, and to try to convey those words to the distant Ghetel, she pointed up the creek's ravine and then brought her hand back toward her. "Walk around," she whispered again, and thought: Lord-a-God, she must know *walk around* by now.

Ghetel understood it, all right. She turned and looked down at the offending creek, crouched, made fists and slammed them down against her thighs, having a tantrum, her unintelligible Dutch curses rolling in the hollows of the canyon. That apparently being insufficient, she squatted on the slope and picked up slabs of rock and hurled them down the hillside at the creek.

Save thy strength, Mary thought to her. Y're sure not scarin' the creek much at all.

Then Ghetel, as if reading that thought, stopped throwing stones, and jammed her chin down into her fists and squatted there in this disconsolate pose, rocking herself and looking down into the ravine. Mary waved at her, but could not get her attention now. Ghetel obviously was locked into a battle of resentment with indifferent Nature, and had forgotten Mary again.

Well, nothin' I can do for 'er, Mary thought. Just pray she don't sit there whupped till it's too late t' move on. As for me, I *got* to move on.

She hobbled along the narrow bank as it curved left around the mountain. As the newest view up the river unrolled itself before her, her heart sank.

Both walls of the river canyon, running straight eastward for at least two miles before bending again, were almost sheer cliff. It was a steep cut straight through a mountain. A colder wind was picking up, beginning to moan in the leafless trees high on the mountainsides. And it was a wind now unmistakably sharp with the feel of snow.

Give me strength, she prayed, teetering along a crumbly ledge inches above the slate-gray river; give me strength, for once again I'm a spider on a wall.

All the way along this cliff, Mary was in view of the knoll on which she had last seen Ghetel. She would look back and see the knoll there beside the creek mouth on the other side of the river. The first three or four times she looked back, she could still see Ghetel slumped, a tiny speck in the stupendous landscape. The next time she looked back, having come perhaps half a mile, she could still see the place but could not tell certainly whether Ghetel was there or not. If she was, she had become just another atom of gray in this great, ageless river-sculpture. Mary blinked constantly against the smarting and tearing of her swollen eyes, to combat the blur and distortion.

If I can't see, I'll die for sure on this selfsame wall, she thought. She squeezed her eyelids shut and felt the warm tears grow cold on her nose, and felt the mucus from her nose cold on her lip, then opened her eyes and ran her right hand out along the rock until it found a crevice. Then she looked down and found a little lip of stone, within reach of her right foot, moved her weight onto it, then hung there, thigh quaking maddeningly, brought her left foot alongside the right and, having added another eighteen inches to her eight hundred miles, reached out with her right hand for another fingerhold to anchor on.

As she did so, she saw a snowflake touch her arm, felt its tiny cold kiss. And then more, spitting cold against her shoulders, her back, her thighs, her face.

And more.

And then, after a measureless age of such tedious going, her skinned fingers and feet leaving crimson spots in the snow dust on the rocks, Mary ran out of cliff and found herself on a gentle slope beside a spectacular loop in the river.

Dazed, she walked away from the steep blue cliff with its thin white etchings of snow, and looked back along it and realized that she had actually done it; she had come those two miles along that vertical wall, inch by inch, almost in a trance of concentration, and it was behind her now.

She was dizzy, and staggered, barefoot and naked, along the wide, curving beach, going southward now. The beach seemed to have been deposited by two small creeks, each about ten feet wide, which emptied into the river about three hundred feet apart, one coming down from either side of a cone-shaped crag. These creeks were but knee-deep and she waded through them as if they were not there, and followed the easy shore. This appeared to be another great horseshoe bend, perhaps two miles around, but she was on the inside shore, where ages of silting had created a wide fringe of gentle, wooded bottomland. The other shore was a curving stone bluff four or five hundred feet straight up, undercut by the river, and so obviously impassable at its base that Mary, despite her torpor, knew she was fortunate to be on this side rather than that. Thanks be to God, she thought.

And pray there's no such a cliff ahead on my side o' th' river, she added.

Within an hour it looked as if there would be.

She had gone down the west arc of the bend and was proceeding up the east when she saw through the veil of falling snow ahead that the river made another sharp loop. The wide bottomland she was walking on seemed to narrow abruptly to nothing a few hundred feet ahead, and there was another one of those curved stone parapets dropping straight to the water's edge.

She was too numb and lethargic now to think of any approach to the obstacle. The notion of going two miles back around the horseshoe and finding a gentle slope to climb over was simply more than her mind could handle. There could be no such thing as retracing steps, after all these hundreds of leagues; it was as if she had been allotted some predestined quota of footsteps and heartbeats, exactly enough to carry her to Draper's Meadows and no more, and to backtrack a thousand steps or a thousand heartbeats would subtract them from the end of the odyssey and leave her to die a thousand steps, a thousand heartbeats short of home.

And she had too little strength left to climb hills anyway. There was nothing to do but plod straight for the base of the cliff and, as she had done so often already, traverse it like a spider or try to wade under it.

And if she could do neither, there was nothing but to perish in the attempt.

The cliff had been polished smooth by the river. There was no footledge to be found.

Fatalistically, numbly, hair and skin now totally wet and clammy from the snow, Mary waded into the river at the base of the cliff. Blood from her feet stained the water as she went in. The bottom was a jumble of small rock shards and pebbles, sand and silt. She hugged herself against the cold stone of the cliff and pressed against the river's current. The cliff leaned out over her, seeming to topple against the drab sky. Snowflakes whirled down to the gray water and vanished. The water rose to her waist, to her ribs, to her breasts, to her shoulders.

She clawed at the cliff with her fingernails as the current tried to lift her feet from under her and pull her down into its cold, gentle, final embrace. She tried to grip the bottom with her toes, but they were as rigid and numb as wood. She stood there for an immeasurable time, afraid to move, the cold again penetrating inward toward the feeble lamp of her heart.

Then she thought of will.

She moved her right foot a few inches forward, and stayed upright. She brought her left foot up after it. Then moved the right foot forward again.

The bottom was sloping upward slightly now. Her shoulders were out of the water. She moved three more steps. The water was under her breasts now. A little further and she was only waist-deep. Her upper body was covered with gooseflesh and the snowflakes were dissolving against her skin with icy little kisses. But now she could see a little lip of beach under the cliff. A few more steps and she would be out of the river.

Dusk had descended while she was in the river. She was at the very elbow of the bend now. She stood on the narrow shore leaning back against the cliff and looked down both sides of the bend. The river had virtually doubled upon itself. It had come around a long craggy neck of land scarcely a hundred yards across. Now she started down the strip of bottomland along its eastern side. She was gasping, shaking so hard it seemed as if her brittle frame would break apart. She went faintish. The mountain at her left seemed to reel in the sky and a sizzling flood of white light poured through her head.

She was lying on the snowy ground. The dusk was deeper. She gathered her limbs under her and stood up slowly. The white light rushed through her head again and more time passed before she gathered enough strength to stand up again. This time she stayed up.

She was moving automatically now. There was still a little light. She walked on and on through the swirling, sifting haze of snowflakes, feeling nothing but the ache of bone sockets and the agonizing reduction of distance. It was beyond her mental powers now to try to calculate how far she had come today or how much distance remained. It was even beyond her mental powers to think of finding a place to stop. It was simply easier to keep dragging one bloody, frigid lump of a foot ahead of the other, and suck in one icy, rasping breath after another, and watch the landscape twitch with every new heartbeat.

The canyon veered gradually to the left as she staggered along in this fashion. Again the beach narrowed and grew steeper, and here brush and saplings grew down almost to the river's edge, and she wove her way through these. She tripped over a root and lay in the snow. When she got up she remembered to gnaw some leaf buds off and try to grind them between her teeth. A back tooth came out of the gum and she swallowed it with the woody pulp of the buds, and stumbled on through the thickets. She almost blundered into a massive, gray pillar at the water's edge, which at first she took to be the trunk of an immense beech tree. But she put her hands against it and it was rock. A pillar of crumbly rock, standing directly in her way. She stood against it, panting, and tried to think what this could mean. It seemed like some trick of nature, to put such an unlikely thing in her way, after she had learned to know and surmount every other kind of obstacle Nature had ever invented.

No, really, now, she thought, as if explaining her plight to God; no, really, now. I can't have anything else put in my way. I'm almost home. I've almost run out of everything I am. There's not much time. I mustn't have any more stops. No. *Please*. No more stops.

She tried to go around it to the left, but found an almost vertical slope of snow and rock and roots. She turned and tried to go around it to the right, slipped in snow and mud, fell slamming among tree trunks and brush and floundered into the edge of the river, thigh-deep, holding herself upright with one arm hooked over a rough-barked branch.

She hung there for a moment, gasping for breath, the current swirling very strong around her legs.

And being now in the edge of the river, out of the thicket, she could see what this obstacle was.

The river flowed by, wide and dark. Just in front of her, rising straight up from the river's edge, stood what first appeared to be a row of gray stone pillars, rough-edged, towering perhaps three hundred feet above her, their tops actually overhanging the river, so high they were vague in the snow-swirl. It was a cliff, a gigantic, fluted cliff of eroding stone shafts.

Her mind worked at this. She struggled to gather her scattered faculties and concentrate on what such an obstacle could mean, and whether it could be circumvented somehow. What could this be, she thought. It was familiar, in a strange, disturbing sort of way . . .

And then she recognized it.

It came back to her in a rush: that terrible first night after their capture, when she and Bettie and Tommy and Georgie and Henry Lenard had been carried to the top of a cliff by the Shawnees and then herded out onto the precipitous cap of a stone pillar to spend their first night.

O God, she thought in awe, looking up and up and up to the top of the cliff: up there is where we were! Up there is where we made a splint for poor Bet's arm in the dark! Up there's where we slept clinging together, afraid of falling off into this river here below . . .

Her soul, so benumbed for so long that she had nearly forgotten what it was to experience an emotion, became a turmoil of memories, joys, regrets, fears, a bittersweet flood of gratitude and despair.

She was at the end of the river journey. Beyond this cliff was the gunpowder spring that marked the overland trail up to Draper's Meadows by way of Sinking Creek. Here was where they had joined the New River and started this incredible lifetime river journey down to the O-y-o and back, this journey that had cost her her three children, her sister-in-law, and every last shred of her comfort and security . . .

And that now threatened to close it all by costing her her very life.

Between her and her Will Ingles stood this sheer cold stone wall.

It would be too incredibly awful a joke, to be stopped here, a mere day's walk from home, after six weeks' toil through an untracked wilderness. Surely, she felt, God would not mean it to end this way, not God in whom she and her people had always believed.

She hauled herself out of the edge of the river. She was angry now. Her resolve was returning, and it once again rekindled energy where she had thought there was none left.

I've waded under many a cliff, she thought. This is nothing I haven't done before.

She found a dead sapling on the ground, a section about eight or nine feet long. She carried it back to the river. She clung to shrubbery and waded back down in the river at the cliff's edge and probed for depth with the pole. It did not touch bottom. Suddenly the pole was gone.

It was as if some great unseen fish had snatched the pole out of her hand and taken it under. It was simply gone. She clung to her handhold, mystified.

Then, a few feet out and downstream, the stick popped through the surface like a leaping fish and floated away.

Mary understood. There was some sort of powerful whirlpool under the base of this cliff, caused apparently by a great depth and by the doubling back of the river under this precipice.

There was this dangerous undercurrent. There were no ledges or shelves by which to traverse the face of the palisade. She was thwarted.

And now it was dark. Only the snow kept the scene from being obscured in pitch blackness. She was wet, and colder than she had ever been. She had come some eight or ten miles up the canyon this day, much of the distance under the effort and tension of creeping along cliffs or wading in strong, cold river currents. Now there was nothing left to sustain her. Even the inspiration she had drawn all day from knowing she was close to the end of the trail had deserted her now, in the face of this impassable wall of craggy rock.

As if her spine had crumbled, she quit resisting the great desire to give up. She slid to the ground. She sat in the snow for a minute, gazing dumbly at the dark lines of the trees against the snow, her mouth hanging open, too defeated even to scold at God. After a few minutes she keeled over onto her left side and rolled into a ball with her hands between her scrawny thighs. As the snow sifted down on her and her heartbeats weakened, she dreamed of voices—a low, dolorous babble of incoherent voices seeming to come down the corridors of time, now and then a man's voice, familiar, almost recognizable, rising above the mutter, and then subsiding back into it.

After midnight the snow stopped falling and the clouds scudded out from under the moon, and the palisade towered silent and dark among the silvery mountains.

CHAPTER
29

SHE KNEW SHE SHOULD HAVE DIED DURING THAT LONG NIGHT, but there in the east the sky was pale and she was looking at it and seeing it. The snow was pale blue and the last of the stars had winked out, and low in the west over the far shore of the river, looking thin and translucent against the fading sky, was a shaving of moon. Steam was rising off the river. Mary was shaking continuously now. Her arms and legs felt paralyzed.

The eastern sky warmed to the hues of a peach. Mary heard a tiny buffeting sound and opened her eyes to see a tiny black bird with a white breast swaying on a slender twig a few inches above her face, looking at her. Mary tried to grab it but could not raise her arm. The bird darted away and snow dust fell off the disturbed twig.

How do they stay alive? Mary wondered.

She had been seeing without thinking. But now she was thinking. She had wondered how birds stay alive in the winter, and she had noticed that she herself was still alive when she should not have been.

She remembered something her mother had said once, once at the breakfast table on a Sunday morning, when they would all try to talk a little like preachers because real preachers had seldom come over the Blue Ridge to Draper's Meadows. Her mother had said, in her brogue, with a cheerful glow in her face:

"Any marnin' th' good Lord lets'ee open your eyes, that's a day he's got somethin' f'r ye t' do."

Do what? Mary wondered. There was that cold river; at the base of the cliff its surface was dimpled with turbulence, and she remembered the force with which it had tugged the sounding-pole out of her hand last night. Even in morning light the cliff above looked as ominous and insuperable as it had in the night; it looked now, silhouetted against the chilling dawn, like the walls and crenels and battlements of a storybook castle. What, she wondered, has th' Lord for me t' do?

She peered up at the craggy rampart against the sky and once again remembered the night the captives had spent up there, almost five months ago, that miserable and terrifying night which since had been eclipsed by a hundred nights more miserable and terrible. She remembered how the land below had looked from that high brink: the land dark with summer foliage, the depths below shrouded in river fog; the mountain range dwindling away eastward toward Draper's Meadows . . .

That, of course, was the only recourse. The Indians had brought them *over* the cliff because there was no other way to pass it.

The only possible way to get home to Will, then, was to climb around and over this gigantic obstacle.

O that's mad, she thought; I've not th' strength to lift an arm.

But any day th' good Lord lets'ee open your eyes, that's a day he's got somethin' f'r ye t' do.

"All right, then; so be it," she whispered, as if replying to her mother. She tried to straighten her limbs, to rise out of the snow. They were swollen huge, and as cold and stiff as the limbs of a corpse. She looked at her right hand as she tried to open it. The fingers felt as if they were breaking rather than bending. The fingertips were brown with dried blood and the hand was swollen to twice its normal size. When she tried to lift her head from the ground it felt as if her neck would snap. Snow fell from her cheek and from her hair.

It was half an hour before she could uncurl her body. Her hips and knees were the most agonizing.

I'm like a whole set o' rusted hinges, she thought. She imagined her joints squealing as she moved them, and the thought was nearly funny.

It'll be funny someday when I can tell it t' folks, she thought.

To folks!

O what a lovely idee! she thought. To *talk* to folks! It had dawned on her then, for the first time in months, that there were *folks* in the world, people who spoke her language and knew her name, people of her own kind, with whom one could sit by a fire or in the sungold of a summer eve, just . . . just talkin' ordinary . . . just *palaverin'* about the twaddle and the piffle of the day . . .

Because for most people, for most of their lives, she thought, there's lesser things on mind day by day than stark survivance.

Oh, dear heaven, yes, I'd nigh forgot th' happy time ordinary folk pass in trifles and flummadiddle . . .

O, *get home!* she thought. *Get home!* Y'been too long on th' bare edge o' livin' . . .

And after a while she was up, standing unsteady, leaning on a rock to keep from falling. Her feet were huge and blue and puffy, and as her blood flowed down into them they felt full of sparks, almost unbearable sparks.

She forced herself to move. She went back a few painful paces, looking up the palisades for a place to begin her climb.

In the daylight now she could study the strange formation of the cliff. The stone of the cliff was rotten and crumbling. Between the columns of stone there were eroded gaps, full of dirt and rock debris, scrub and roots, saplings and gnarled black grapevines. It appeared that the only way to the top of the cliff would be up through these gaps. While steep, they were not quite vertical, as were the rock columns themselves.

Raising her arm to reach the first handhold caused such a stab of pain in her shoulder that she almost swooned. She shut her eyes and took a deep breath and reached up again and hooked her stiff fingers over a root. Sharp twinges and prickles went down the arm. She winced against the grind of her hip socket and got her left foot up onto a lichen-spotted chunk of rock jutting from the slope. With this handhold and foothold she drew herself a few inches up the slope. She was on her way. She hung there for a moment, saw a little leafless dogwood sapling two feet above her head. She got her numb left hand up to it and around it, forced the fingers to close, and pulled herself, panting and squinting, a little further up, her naked abdomen and thighs scraping over snow and rock and frozen soil, her cold-petrified toes trying awkwardly to gain traction.

The next handhold was another root. Then a snarl of rough, black grapevines. Then a chunk of rock, slick with ice and snow. Then the rotting stump of a broken-off sapling. Then a dead branch wedged between two rocks.

Every four or five feet she had to stop and press against the slope to recover breath, coughing up gobs of phlegm.

The effort of climbing was gradually thawing her cold-stiffened body, but it was all at the cost of renewed sorenesses and stabbing pains. Gasping the cold morning air was searing her throat; her eyes watered constantly and her nose drained.

She was perhaps forty feet up, clinging for life to an ice-coated chunk of rock, when the first ray from the rising sun burnished the top of a great, tooth-shaped stone pillar a hundred feet above her. It struck her as being so beautiful, so enchantingly God-given beautiful, that she went all weepy inside with sentiment and could scarcely gather the strength to go on.

Half an hour later she was only ten feet further up. She realized that she was expending more of her waning energy in shivering and clinging desperately than in climbing. That same sun-gilded pinnacle seemed as distant as it had been.

If only that sun would touch *me,* she thought. It'd do me good! She remembered long-ago times when she had sat on the cabin stoop at Draper's Meadows, leaning back against the sun-warmed log wall while the sun had eased the aching

weariness of field work out of her muscles. And she remembered that recent morning when, having escaped across the
river by canoe and slept in the hunter's hut, she had leaned
against the hut wall in the wintry sunlight breakfasting on a
turnip. O, she thought, but that was a happy time! A little
sunlight now would double my strength, she thought.

She was not likely to get any sun here on this palisade,
though, not for a while. She was in the cold shadows between
two enormous shafts of stone and at this rate it would be
hours before she could attain the summit and rest in the
sunlight.

She pulled herself up five feet more and lay gasping against
the slope with a quaking arm hooked around a sapling. And
then she went away somewhere in her head. She returned
with a shock to find herself sliding down the slope toward the
river below, pulling a small avalanche of dirt and snow and
shale fragments with her, rocks and roots scraping and lac-
erating her skin. She jolted to a stop against a small shrub,
her heart slamming, and hung there, gasping and shaking and
hurting, listening to the dislodged debris scrabble on down
the cliff-face into the river.

She had lost about thirty feet of ground—an hour or two of
climbing—and for a while was too shaken to move. She
courted the notion of climbing back down to the shore and
quitting. Or just letting go. She looked down longingly
through the trees to the glassy river, that river now reflecting
the blue of the sky.

Rivers. She had come so far along rivers. And so often she
had looked deep into them, seeing permanent peace under
their waters. It would be over in moments, and surely would
not hurt much—not as much as to continue living.

But then she thought of Will, waiting for her to come home;
she thought again of sitting on a stoop in the sunlight with
people of her own kind, just *folks talking*.

And with a sob she started climbing again.

This time she rested every five feet or so and concentrated
on the next five and did not let her mind slip away to yearning
or daydreaming.

It was midday when she hauled herself the last few inches

up the slope and onto a saddle of earth that ran like a bridge between two pinnacles. She lay heaving for breath with her fingers entwined in the prickly dry foliage of a cedar shrub to keep from falling.

I made it, she thought. I made it to the top o' this devil cliff. Her nose leaked onto the ground and coughing wracked her body. After a while she opened her eyes and looked down and she was looking down onto treetops with blue-shadowed snow under them, and the river going under. Now, she thought. Now I can go across the top of this devil cliff and down the other side.

She looked over the saddle of ground and her heart sank. She was *not* at the top of the cliff.

The pinnacles she had reached were separated from the rest of the cliff by a deep, eroded chasm.

And the pinnacles she had reached were not the tallest ones of the cliff; they had weathered far down. She was a little more than a hundred feet above the river.

The other palisades stood nearly two hundred feet higher.

She would have to go over the saddle and down into the chasm and then up through another eroded crevice to get to the top of that higher rampart.

"O God I know thee now as a one for mean tricks," she whispered through clenched teeth and tears.

She stayed there for a few minutes feeling the weak sun and trying to believe it was strengthening her. Then she started down the other side.

Going down into the chasm was more frightening than climbing up. She could not see where she was going. Her toes, bleeding, brittle as ice, groped for projections that might support her weight. The only way to know a projection would not support her was to feel it crumble underfoot and hear it rattle and crash down below, leaving her to hang by her hands until her foot could find another surface to test. And the ones that were strong enough to hold her were icy. Countless terrifying times a hand or a foot would slip off and she would be hanging by a single pain-wracked hand, trying by the sheer friction of skin against hillside to keep from losing her purchase and slithering down the steep chute toward the river.

Her face and the skin on the front of her body were scraped and bleeding, splinters and dirt-grains embedded in the wounds, when she reached the bottom of the chasm and started climbing up the eroded gap between two of the taller stone columns.

She had seen a chimney sweep go up the dark hearth-flue of her parents' house in Philadelphia, when she was a little girl, and she had had nightmares about it for years afterward: of human legs disappearing up a dark stone shaft. And now this was terribly like a chimney, a dark passage up through stained and crumbly stone to a mouth of light at the top. She braced her arms and elbows out against the sides and strained toward that distant top. There was only the noise of her harsh breathing, and, now and then, coughing spasms and the sifting and dribbling of dislodged dirt and rock down through the passage.

After about thirty feet, the passage widened, and with a deep sigh of relief she found herself above the oppressive tunnel; now it was more like a steep trench between the two pillars, whose tops were still more than a hundred feet above.

She had to rest here. Her arms were trembling uncontrollably from tension and fatigue, and all her innards were queasy and quivering. The bits of moss and bark and buds she had eaten the day before—was it a mere day? she wondered— had been digested long since, and any nutrition from them had been burned away by a night of shivering naked in the snow, and she was as empty as if she had not had a bite for a month. Her body was still consuming its own fiber and there was little left. And there was nothing here on this crag she could even put in her mouth and pretend was food. There was not even any moss on the rocks.

She clung to the stony wall of the trench with her feet on a jutting slab of rock and looked down past her bloody, mangled toes through the crevice, then out and down onto the tops of the pillars she had surmounted earlier, and then up at the anvil-shaped tops of the columns above.

There was blood oozing and drying on the pads of her fingers. She put one finger at a time into her mouth and sucked to ease the throbbing and stinging, and she salivated as she tasted her own blood and she wondered if it could nourish her. Nay, it's prob'ly thin as sassafras tea, she thought.

Then she was thinking of sassafras tea, and remembering how she and her mother would go up to the sassafras clump above the settlement with the little boys after the spring thaw had softened the ground, and pull and grub up the aromatic roots—ague tree, her mother called it— and shave them into the tea kettle to boil for a spring tonic to thin winter blood, and flavor it with maple or cane syrup . . . O she could smell it now, the steam off it . . .

Oh! Hold, now! No more o' that barmy-headness or y'll fall off the mountain . . .

Go now, she thought.

She looked at a rock lip just above her head. Then she looked at her right hand, and willed it to reach up and grip the rock. Then she looked up at a little crack in the pillar at her left side, then looked at her left hand and willed it to stretch up and take hold. She hauled herself up half a yard with trembling arms and dug in her toes and looked above for another handhold, and forced herself to reach up and get it. Then another. Then she had to rest again, and then she had to force herself again to continue.

She went on, three or four feet with each renewal of effort, for two hours that seemed like a lifetime. The sun had moved across and now was behind the pillar at her left and there was no more of its feeble warmth. She inched upward through a chute of frozen dirt and rock between gray monoliths flecked with snow in blue shadow.

The pain was good for her now. It had become so severe and total that it would not allow her to drift off in woolgathering. She could not daydream now, nor think of anything but bloody fingers and feet and sharp fragments of stone, of ice against skin, of the shock of cold inhalations against her bad teeth, of the fetid smell of her breath and the sores in her mouth, of the sounds of rock shards clicking and rustling down behind her, of the brilliant jabs of pain in her bone sockets, of the spells of white dizziness that would sweep like blizzards through her head. The whole world was this steep and flinty gouge in a cliffside and the salvo of agonies she was expending against it. She was more intimate with this jagged square yard of earth and stone within reach of her tortured senses than she had ever been with Will; this climbing was a process as immediate and personal and critical as giving birth. It *was* like giving birth: If she could survive it there would be life beyond this cliff; if she could not, there would be nothing.

At each pause for rest she would look down at the treetops and the river below them, and each time she looked down, the more enchanting she would find that world below. She seemed to belong to the riverbed. It was familiar; she had been down there looking up for so long that it seemed terrible and wrong to be up here looking down. She would look down almost with longing. All one would have to do, she thought, without thinking it in words, would be to let go—open these cramped and bloody hands—and fall away to eternal rest.

For a long time she looked up at her hands and played with the notion. At last she smiled a little smile and willed them to loosen their grip.

But they would not do it.

It was deep in the afternoon when she ran out of cliff. She clutched at the trunk of a small cedar and drew herself up onto a level table of stone and dirt and snow and realized that she was now on the summit.

There was a forest here on top of the cliff. There were the tables of snow-covered rock that were the tops of the stone pinnacles.

She had no spirit left to rejoice. But in her mind she knew she had done it. She lay with her face against the frozen dirt and had her say with God.

Lord, I'll thank'ee never to give me another day like this if I grow to be eighty.

No one deserves a day like this.

This is the most terrible day I've had in a hell of terrible days and I'm no' grateful for it.

Now give me the strength to make my way across and down

this devil's scarp. Do that and then maybe I can make peace with'ee.

She was too weak and shaky to walk. She went on all fours or crawled along the brink. There were places where erosion had cut far back into the summit, and she had to detour around these crumbling clefts. She stopped at one place and leaned against a tree and looked out at a narrow precipice that was covered with leafless scrub and she became certain that this was the one on which they had spent that fearful night under the eye of a Shawnee sentry. Aye, there was the very rock he'd sat on with his musket across his knees . . .

She really had not intended to crawl out on that eagle's nest of a place now; it was too near the edge; it was out of her way.

And yet it was, in a way, a kind of sacred place, where Bettie had bled from her wound, and where they had labored together in the darkness to help each other. And to recross this cliff now on her return, without going out on that precipice to touch that place, would be a sacrilege, somehow. So she crept out on it.

It was different now. There were no leaves on the shrubs; the ground was covered with snow and ice. Far below there was that hard earth in the bend of the river, snowy ground etched with black bare trees, range after range of naked white hills stretching away to the southeast and finally the Blue Ridge as the last horizon. Aye, here were the fragments of rock that had tortured their sleep. There was no trace of Bettie's blood now.

I was so full of child then, and so full of fear.

Now I am empty of everything. I am even empty of fear, finally.

She looked down over the brink. The river was three hundred feet straight down. To her right there stood pillars that were entirely independent, detached from the cliff itself; they stood like gigantic stone tree trunks on the edge of the river. And to her left was the way down, the way home. She could see from here the gunpowder spring. And somewhere above it there should be the Harmons' camp hut . . .

She could not quite see it, and strained far forward on the ledge to look for it.

A shower of pebbles tore loose under her hand and dropped silently through space for many seconds, then plipped into the cold river far below with tiny white splashes.

Aye, there it is, she thought. The little hut. It was a tiny dark rectangle among the etched trees, at the mouth of a ravine above the spring. There was a sere cornpatch below it.

My, she thought. It looks cozy. That's the place to lodge tonight when I get down off this accursed scarp. Swear I can see smoke comin' off that . . .

No, she thought. Y're daydreamin' again.

No. It was no mirage. She knew chimney smoke when she saw it. And there was chimney smoke above that little hut down there. No more than a half a mile away. Her heart tripped.

It could be Indians, she thought.

Or it could be Adam Harmon.

It didn't make much difference. She would have gone to Indians now. Even an Indian would have fed and warmed someone in her condition. Maybe he would kill her later but he would feed her first.

She opened her mouth and tried to call out. But she was still without voice.

While there's still daylight, she thought, get down off here to that lovely cabin.

She felt giddy, wonderfully giddy.

I could spread my arms, she thought, and just sail down there like any old buzzard.

CHAPTER
30

Adam Harmon laid in the poles to close the cow pen behind the hut. Two brown cows and a calf moved close together for warmth and stood looking at him, their breath clouding in the twilight.

Adam bent his stocky old body and gathered the last armload of the pea-vine fodder from under the eave of the hut and dumped it over the fence to them. Then he brushed chaff off the front of his shaggy bearhide weskit with his huge hands, while scanning the valley with quick, keen brown eyes. The squint-lines showed them to be merry eyes, but they were serious and suspicious now. He ran his tongue back and forth between his lower teeth and lower lip as he searched the valley shadows, and smoothed down his grizzled beard with the palm of his right hand. "Hank Boy, come 'round 'ere."

Adam Harmon's elder son, even taller and thicker than his father, came around the corner of the hut with a greasy, bloody knife in his hand. His sleeves were turned up and his hands were slick with animal fat. He had been flensing an elk hide that was stretched over poles at the front of the hut. "Aye, Pa?"

"Quit that f'r now. We'd best go down, he'p Junior with th' corn while there's still light. I got me a spookish sense we oughter light out f'r Dunkard's Bottom come mornin'."

"Gettin' t' you too now, eh?"

"Mhm," Adam Harmon admitted.

Hank threw the knife at the hut and it stuck in a corner log and quivered. He wiped his hands on the thighs of his breeches and turned down his sleeves. They picked up their rifles, which had been leaning against the side of the hut, and went down toward the corn patch. Passing Indian bands evidently had taken much of it; wild animals had destroyed some, and the rest was dry and hard. They had been late getting down to this New River camp of theirs from the settlement because of Indian alarms. They had come down only three weeks before, and had spent much of the time hunting in the hills across the river. Only yesterday, Adam Junior had hastily abandoned a little hunting camp about two leagues down, spooked out by Indian signs. He had fled in such a hurry that he had left a kettle of stewing meat over a fire, a pair of leather breeches, and a hobbled old pack mare that had wandered out of sight of the camp. He had been a little ashamed of himself since, and had not said much, and had worked by himself, sullen, away from his father and brother. A couple of times he had said he might go back down there and retrieve the horse. "No, forget 'er," Adam Senior had said. "She's no' worth th' risk o' goin' back there alone. If they was savages there, they got 'er by now anyhoo."

Adam Junior looked up from his picking when they walked into the cornpatch, then back down. "'Bout t' quit," he said. "Light's gone." He picked up the bag of corn he had gathered and moved a few feet away, set it down and twisted an ear of corn off its dead stalk with a quick rustle.

"Let's get all we can find," the old man said. "We're a-gonna pack out o' here t'morra, first light."

Junior looked up, surprised. "Why, Pa?"

Mr. Harmon grunted, shrugged. "I just feel it in m' little finger."

Junior nodded. He felt better now; he was not alone in his uneasiness about Indians. Old Mr. Harmon was a bold man, as only a bold man would have built an outback camp this far from neighbors and right along a main Indian trace. And when Harmon said he felt something in his little finger, it usually meant something real was in the air. "Me too," Junior said. "Never felt it so strong as I done yester . . . "

"*Husht!*" young Hank cautioned suddenly, laying a hand on Junior's arm, crouching, and raising his rifle.

The other two turned, holding their breath and listening,

and brought their rifles up and around, to point at the thicket at the far edge of the cornpatch.

They all heard it now: a rustling; something either in the thicket or among the dry stalks of the corn. In the dusk they could see nothing yet. But they understood that it was not any wild animal. Wild animals simply did not approach talking men they could smell and hear. Therefore, they all understood, it could be only one or another of two things: a domestic animal, or Indians. The only domestic animals hereabouts were their own: the cows and calf in the pen, and their horses in the corral.

Mister Harmon and his two sons stood now with all their senses focused on a place at the edge of the field where brush was being moved and a strange, hoarse, intense whisper was being repeated: human whisperings, they were certain; Indians passing information to each other, most likely. The three men knelt now, each on one knee, to lower their visibility and steady themselves for shooting, checked the powder in the flashpans of their guns and slowly pulled back the flintlock hammers. They aimed the long weapons at the sounds of approach and waited for their target to appear.

"*Help me, help, help me,*" Mary was trying to cry out. "*Help me, Mister Harmon!*" But the words only came as a raspy whisper.

She stopped and listened. She could not hear the men's voices now, and was afraid they had left the cornfield.

She had seen Mister Harmon and his sons as she crawled down the slope from the palisade cliff. She had seen the one youth working in the cornpatch and then she had seen old Adam Harmon and the other son start down from the hut. She had tried to walk down to the cornpatch where they were but her legs finally had failed her entirely, and she had dragged herself through the thicket toward the edge of the corn, trying to yell for their attention through her ghostly husk of a voice.

She tried to rise to her feet again but her legs were simply gone. She crawled into the snowy stubble of the cornfield now.

She saw dim shapes ahead of her through the cornstalks. There they are, she thought.

She shouldered past a stand of cornstalks and suddenly she was face to face with them. Her heart plunged.

They were all aiming rifles at her face.

"NO!" she whispered.

Powder flashed orange in the flashpan of Junior Harmon's rifle when he squeezed the trigger. But at that instant his father's hand came up under the rifle and knocked it off target. The ball whickered off through the foliage and Mr. Harmon's voice roared:

"It's a woman!"

He and Hank kept their rifles cocked. They were still not sure of this situation. They knew only that there was a gaunt white face of a woman there in the corn a few feet in front of them. But the thought of Indians had not left their minds and Mister Harmon wondered for a moment whether this emaciated creature crawling toward them might be a decoy, backed by Indians.

Mary raised herself onto her knees and reached toward the three Harmons with her hand. She could not understand why they had shot at her and did not come to her. Then she heard Mister Harmon say:

"Damnation! Can that be Missus Ingles?"

And at the sound of her name, everything wheeled and there was another one of those blizzards of dizziness, and this time she could not fight it and her mind blew away.

They stood over her, speechless, for minutes. They had never seen a human being in this condition. She was a skeleton covered with bruised and lacerated skin. Her hands and feet were bloody and swollen to a grotesque hugeness. Her knees were worn through to bone.

Her hair, though matted and dirty, was white as snow.

"Take this," Mister Harmon said in a choked voice, handing his rifle to his son. He knelt beside the unconscious bundle of bones. He turned her onto her back and slipped one hand under her knees and one under her back and stood up.

When he felt how light she was his throat closed up, and he

carried her toward the hut blinded by tears. His sons were crying too.

CHAPTER
31

"Go kill th' calf," Mr. Harmon said to Adam Junior. The youth looked at his father, at the broad, bewhiskered face, the old, strong face so sad in the light of the hearth fire and a tallow wick.

"Why that, Pa?"

"Your Ma always said beef tea's the best thing f'r a gone body. Butcher th' calf an' bring me a chunk o' loin."

"We got three hundred pound o' venison and bear already, Pa," said Hank. "Wouldn't that do?"

"Beef tea," Mr. Harmon repeated, looking down at the unconscious skeleton lying under a bearskin blanket on a pallet in the corner. "An' be quick about it, boy. You, Hank: Stoke up that fire an' boil water."

They didn't argue. That pitful hag in the corner was for them, as well as for their father, the center of the world now. They were thinking of Will Ingles, who was about the finest man they knew. If he came back from the Cherokee country and found out they'd let her die, that would be a disgrace on them.

The fire roared.

There was some grievous commotion outside in the night as Junior caught the calf and strung it up by its hocks and slaughtered it. He came in with blood up to his elbows and put a fat piece of meat in one of the kettles. In the other kettle, Mr. Harmon was boiling rags. He would lift them out steaming on sticks and apply them to the little woman's swollen feet and hands.

Late in the night the beef tea was ready, and Mr. Harmon dipped some up in a gourd and knelt by the pallet and put his hand under the pitiful knob of a skull and raised her head and put the gourd to her lips. She mumbled something and reached out from under the bear robe with her misshapen paws and held onto the gourd and sipped over its edge. Mr. Harmon had the sense to limit her to a few sips at a time.

After a few hours, she slipped off into a slumber so deep that he had to put his ear to her mouth to determine that she was asleep rather than dead.

Young Adam and Hank took turns standing sentry under the stars. When Hank came out to relieve his brother, they stood for a while together. Junior said:

"I been wonderin'. Where d'y reckon she been, five months?"

"Lost out yonder, I guess," Hank said, waving a hand up toward the palisade cliff and Butte Mountain beyond it. "Not far, d' reckon. Y' know a woman. Git lost twenty yards off th' doorstoop."

"Yeah," said Adam Junior. "Poor thang. Five month! Jesus God!"

She was warm. For the first time in many weeks, she was not shivering. All her body felt hot and sweaty. A jumble of bad dreams was dissolving like smoke as she remembered where she was. She heard a fire crackling and someone snoring. She could smell the musky bearskin robe under which she had slept, and the smell of meat stewing. Her mouth was full of saliva and kept filling with saliva as fast as she could swallow it.

She opened her eyes as far as their swelling would allow. They were gummy and everything she saw was blurry-edged. There was firelight flickering on the pole-and-bark ceiling, but she could also see a thin, fuzzy-edged angle of gray light and knew it was daylight outlining a chink of door-crack.

She had a very important question to ask. *"Mister Harmon?"* Still no voice. Her whisper gurgled with saliva and phlegm. The snoring nearby stopped and she saw dark bulks moving above her.

"'Mornin', ma'am," rumbled Mr. Harmon's deep, soft voice, a music so profound and comforting that her eyes unexpectedly washed with tears. Oh, my, she thought. Her miraculous deliverance had left her on the edge of such a deep, wide sea of sentiment that, she realized, anything and everything—from food to voices to fireglow—likely would drown her in weepiness.

"*Mister Harmon,*" she whispered, then swallowed, then whispered: "*what d'y know o' Will an' Johnny?*" The saying of their names nearly strangled her with bittersweetness.

He cleared his throat. "Ah, well. They be fine, I reckon."

"*Can 'ee take me to 'm?*"

"You eat an' sleep a day 'r two. Then we'll talk about movin'." Mr. Harmon and his son whispered something to each other that she could not hear. She hissed:

"*Then maybe fetch 'em here?*" They could ride down here from Draper's Meadows in half a day, she thought. "*O, sir, I must see Will this very day!*" Again the tears poured.

"Hank, dip 'er up some o' that bear chowder," Mister Harmon said. He wanted to get some more nourishment in her *before* telling her about Will and Johnny. "Now, sip this, Missus Ingles, an' we'll talk about what we're going to do."

He spooned the savory broth to her lips. There was very tender meat in it, in tiny bits, and corn. It was the best food she had ever eaten and she appreciated it so much that she had to stop eating for a while to cry. The food churned and burbled in her shrunken stomach and made her burp with almost every breath. It was so rich that it made her drowsy and she slipped away again. When she awoke the Harmons were sitting in a circle, working on their rifles and talking low. " . . . an' till we can leave," Mr. Harmon was saying, "we'll one at a time stand picket outside."

"Aye," one of the boys said. Then it was quiet for a while, until the same voice said: "I saw 'er prints. She come down off the cliff."

"Th' deuce y' say!"

"Yup."

"*Sh-sh! She's awake, boys.*"

Mister Harmon moved close to her and squatted by the

pallet. He put his big rough but gentle hand on her forehead and smoothed back her hair. "Hullo. How goes't?" She burped, nodded, then whispered:

"*Please send f'r Will.*"

He inhaled a long breath through his nostrils. "Well, mum, y'see, y'r husband ain't hereabouts, nor 's y'r brother John . . ." He saw the look of sheer dismay strike through her wasted visage, and realized that she was believing the worse, so he hurried to explain: "They rid down southways to confabulate with Cherokees about gettin' you ransomed, mum. Uh, might be they're back now, even . . . It's three weeks since we was at the settlement. Yup, could be they're home by now. Soon's y'r strong enough to ride, we'll all go up an' see." He cleared his throat again. "How's 'em feet? Hank, sop up them rags an' lets tend to these poor feet again . . . "

While these ministrations were being done, old Harmon tried to reassure her of the likelihood that Will was safe. He was not really that confident—it seemed to him that Mister Ingles' sojourn was very long on risk—but he did not want her recovery to be complicated by worry and low spirits.

Hank, for all his burly appearance, was a gentle nurse, and his careful treatment of her feet was soothing, and sometimes he would wince and shake his head as if he were suffering the pain of her mauled and seeping extremities himself. There was a severe case of chilblains, and perhaps some frostbite damage, but no smell of mortification yet.

"Ma'am," he said in awe, "looks t'me like these trailbeaters o' your'n got a good hunnert mile on 'em."

She smiled strangely down over the bear robe at him. "*Nay, friend,*" she whispered, "*more like a thousand.*"

"Yup," he agreed, looking back down at her feet with a shy smile, thinking she was joking. "More like a thousand. They do look it."

"Reckon where you been?" old Harmon asked.

She looked at the ceiling for so long, eyes glistening wet, that he thought she'd drifted off and ignored or forgotten his question. But then she whispered: "*To th' O-y-o, then way down it too.*"

Mister Harmon's eyebrows raised slightly and he gazed at

her thoughtfully, wondering whether she really had any idea what she was saying. Hank looked at his father and shook his head in pity. After a while, Mister Harmon leaned close to her and said: "It's told that this river here," he pointed, "goes plumb through the mountains to the O-hee-o. What say'ee to that, mum?"

She kept gazing through the roof with those wet glittering eyes. *"It does."*

"You, uhm, you *know* it does?"

"Aye," she whispered. *"It's where I been."*

Adam and Hank Harmon looked at her for a long time, still not quite believing. If it were true, they were thinking, this little woman was the first white person ever to have gone through that uncharted vastness. Old Harmon didn't want to wear her out just now with further questions about that, thought his mind was suddenly boiling with questions. So instead, he said after a while:

"Them as was with 'ee—your boys an' all—what o' them?"

It was not a good question to have asked. Mary Ingles dissolved into a fit of quaking, voiceless weeping that went on until she descended into sleep again at evening.

They heard her trying to say something in her sleep. Old Harmon leaned close over her and listened, but the sound made no sense. It was like a whispered chant: *"Ten times ten times ten a—way . . ."*

On waking and asking the Harmon men for a moment's privacy late that night, Mary realized that the soothing broths and soups had restored her voice. The men went out into the night, with their rifles, leaving her with a pail to use as chamberpot. Rising from the bed brought an onslaught of extreme pains, but these pains were not so soul-shaking; she felt stronger and these were the pains of knitting, not dying, flesh and sinew.

The unaccustomed richness of meat had flooded her bowels, but it was a miracle to be passing something more than seed-husks and beetle-wings and wood fiber; at least it was not the debilitating flux she had suffered so many recent times after eating poisonous roots. She crawled back under the bearskin and looked at the rediscovered beauty of glowing wood-embers and wick-flame. She was utterly overwhelmed by amazement and gratitude for the miracle of fire. She thought back on the soul's comfort she had derived from the distant burning spring one long-ago cold night, and knew that she would never again look at fire as merely another useful tool. Now flame was like a picture of the light of living; it was as if she had seen the bright flames of life burn down to embers, and then to a spark, and nearly down to ashes, in the hearth of her own bosom in these past six weeks in the cold wilderness, and she knew she would always understand this whenever she looked at fire, for the rest of her life.

The rest of my life! she thought, with a leap of the heart. *There will be such a thing!*

The men, two inside at a time while one prowled outside as sentry, stayed up most of the night coaxing Mary's story out of her, and were dizzied by it as it wore on. They kept gasping at this, wincing at that. They uttered profanities when she told of the gauntlet and the burnings at the stake. They were aghast, trembling in fury, as she related Ghetel's desperate attempt to kill and cannibalize her.

"I fear she be dead out yonder now," Mary said softly, wistfully.

"I'd hope it," growled Hank Harmon through clenched teeth. "Like t' see th' wolves in 'er guts and buzzards at 'er eyes!"

"Oh, no," Mary exclaimed. "O, listen to this . . . " And then she told them the wonderful story about Ghetel lying down and playing dead to ambush buzzards. She smiled and waited for them to laugh, but they failed to laugh. And then she thought: No, I reckon y' just couldn't understand it lest y'd seen it, lest y'd knowed 'er.

"Pray, Mister Harmon, send y'r lads down th' river a ways to look for her. Surely she's within a day's ride. If she lives yet, y' might save 'er."

"By God, I'd not go a-lookin' for a cannibal," Hank snarled, "save maybe t' see 'er dead!"

"Nor me," growled Junior Harmon.

"Then t' bring 'er poor bones back, or t' bury 'em," Mary pleaded. Mister Harmon was equally outraged. He set his broad face in resolution. "They don't want to. And I'm o' their mind, about such a witch as that, so I'll sure not make 'em."

Her pleadings could not change their minds. She sighed. They just couldn't understand how it had been with her and Ghetel.

She sighed and thought back over it all.

Of course not, she thought. How on earth could they know?

Mary told them what she had heard of General Braddock's defeat in July. They nodded and told her that the news of it had rolled down through the English colonies in August like a dark cloud.

She told them of the account given by the warrior Red Hawk at the Shawnee town. "It was Colonel Washington he couldn't kill, I'd wager," she exclaimed.

Old Harmon nodded. "'Tis told two horses was kilt under him that day. And several musketballs went through his clothes, but he wa'n't nicked. It was our Lord God watched over 'im that day, as He watched over y'se'f, Missus Ingles." The two sons murmured. They were hovering almost worshipfully around her. They seemed to be connecting her somehow with the imagined drama at Fort Duquesne, as if by surviving her ordeal she brought hope that English colonists might yet triumph over the military disaster whose pall had hung over them for so long.

Mary knew her arrival and recuperation had delayed the Harmons' return to the settlement. She could see, by the preoccupation with sentinel duties, that they were anxious about Indian expeditions. And she, so recently a victim of Indian captivity, had even more reason than they for fearing an Indian surprise here in this remote outpost. They were sturdy and brave men, and acted as if they would die to protect her from further harm and suffering, but she well knew that three men in a pole-and-bark hut, burdened with cattle and corn, beef, venison, hides and a sick woman, would have little hope of surviving a raid.

And so, on waking the next morning, she declared that she felt fit to travel whenever they wanted to leave, and the earlier the better. "I just sense it," she said, "that Will and Johnny have got back. And it's too long since I've seen them two."

The Harmons protested a little about her weakness and fatigue, but when she reassured them that she felt up to it, they were glad to saddle up. It took them but a few minutes to strike camp, load the pack horses with everything portable and start leading their fat cows up the valley of the sinking creek toward Draper's Meadows, the sun rising in their eyes.

Mary had been dressed in old Adam Harmon's spare linsey-woolsey hunting shirt, which was big enough to wrap thrice around her gaunt frame and hung below her knees. They had given her a pair of Henry's woolen stockings, wrapped her in a blanket that was draped over her head like a monk's hood and lifted her onto the saddle of Junior's bay horse. The young man was riding on a pack horse, behind its load. They passed up the valley between the snowy mountains, this valley that had been full of mosquitoes and dense green foliage when she had come down it. The men kept an anxious eye upon the little woman on the bay, watching her wobble and lurch as the horse picked its way over the rough ground, but she was sitting well. Hank rode up beside her, his horse snorting steam. "How d'y?" he asked. She turned and smiled at him from under the blanket, looking pathetically like a frail grandmother in a wimple. "A nice ride," she said, and then he saw a tear drop off her nose.

Mary was thinking about the last horse she had ridden.

There was nobody at Draper's Meadows. The partially re-built cabins stood open and deserted. Mary sat on the horse and clenched her jaws and looked over the snowy meadow in front of her scorched cabin, the massacre passing behind her eyes, faint screams and gunshots echoing in her memory, and when she could not look any more, she turned and gazed westward over the Alleghenies whence she had come.

Ten times ten times ten, she heard her mother saying. *Ten times ten times ten,* she heard Tommy's voice reply.

Hank Harmon walked down through the snow from one of

he cabins and swung up onto his saddle. He pointed to tracks n the snow leading up off the meadow. "Looks like folks left quick. 'Bout yesterday. Indian scare, 'd reckon. These tracks head f'r Dunkard's Fort."

"So do we, then," said old Adam Harmon.

And as they rode, Mary looked down at the traces in the snow, and wondered if they had been left by the horses of Johnny and Will.

A few miles further up the New River, they stopped on a low shore. Mister Harmon startled Mary out of her torpor with a sudden loud whoop. She looked up and noticed a thick rope, running through a pulley lashed to a sycamore tree and running to the other shore of the river. At that moment the rope began moving through the pulley, and then from the far shore a wide log raft with pole handrails came forth, a man on it turning a windlass.

"'Ey, now," she said. "This new?"

Old Adam grinned at her. "It's Ingles' Ferry," he said. "Will built it 'fore he went down t' Cherokee land. Best way over t' Dunkard's Bottom."

"Might he be . . . "

"We'll see." Harmon patted her shoulder.

But the youth operating the ferry said that Will Ingles and Johnny Draper had not come across with the people from Draper's Meadows. They hadn't yet been heard from, he said. He was a tall, bony youth Mary had never seen, and had his musket alongside him on the raft. He seemed quite nervous as he cranked them across. After he had gone back and brought the cattle over, he asked if he might go with them to Dunkard's Fort.

"Might's well," Adam Harmon said. "If I was you, I wouldn't stay out here alone these days."

Mary looked back at the ingenious contraption as they rode off, and was proud of Will. "Imagine," she said, almost to herself, "gettin' acrost that dadblame river so easy as that."

They reached the fort about dark. It was only the McCorkle family compound, with a new stockade of upright logs around it—not much of a fortification, but well situated for a watchful defense. There were about twenty people crowded within: the McCorkles; two small families of Dunkard German Baptists; James Cull, who had survived the July massacre at Draper's Meadows by hiding wounded in the brush nearby; and Mr. and Mrs. Philip Lybrook from Sinking Creek, who had come here by way of Draper's Meadows after an Indian alarm. These latter people, Mary's old neighbors, first fell back in shock at the sight of her, then practically smothered her with their amazed and joyous greeting. She was finally laid out on a real bedstead and the last thing she remembered seeing, through a new curtain of tears, before slipping off in a swoon, was the halo of a candle held by Alice Lybrook beside the bed.

No one here had heard from Will Ingles or Johnny Draper.

Will Ingles stood naked at the head of two parallel ranks of armed Indians. The chief struck him across the back with a staff and Will started running down the line, being slashed and bruised by many of the Indians' switches and clubs. He was tripped by a stick thrust between his legs and when he fell, a silent yell on his lips, the Indians closed around him, yelling and flailing . . .

Mary Ingles woke up sweating and whimpering, and the people who were sleeping in blankets on the floor around her bed were getting up to soothe her. The gray of early daylight showed through chinks in the log walls.

"It's no wonder," murmured Mrs. Lybrook to Mrs. Mc-Corkle as they stoked up the cooking fire, "that th' poor thing has nightmares. O heaven, what she's suffered!"

"Reckon what become o' th' baby she was a-carryin'?" Diane McCorkle wondered in a low voice.

"Well," said Mrs. Lybrook, in a near-whisper, "Mister Harmon say he ask'er just that, an' she didn't give no answer." She shook her head. "Poor thang, poor thang. Reckon there's matters she won't never tell about."

"Such as what?" whispered Mrs. McCorkle, pausing with the iron poker in her hand, still looking into the rising flames.

"Well, you know. Like what outrages them naked heathens

might afflict on a he'pless woman . . . " She left it hanging
there, and Mrs. McCorkle stole a look over her shoulder at
the little white head on the pillow, as if something might
show. Mrs. Lybrook's musings had given her some deliciously
ghastly scenes to nurture in her imagination. Her heart beat
rapidly all the rest of the morning and she stole many more
glances at the remarkable little white-headed young-old skeleton of a woman over there in Diane McCorkle's own bed.

"Mister Harmon?"

"Aye, Missus Ingles?"

"Stoop down close here."

"Mhm?"

"Y've not told anybody here what I said, have y', aboot
poor old Ghetel a-trying t'hurt me?"

"Nup, I ain't."

"Have y'r boys?"

"Not that I've heerd."

"Well, good. 'Cause I don't want 'em to think ill of 'er."

"*I* think ill of 'er."

"Well, y' can just stop that, Mister Harmon, if'ee please,
'cause I'm askin' y' once again, as a good Christian man—
y're a good Christian man, an' no savage, ain't that so?—t'
ride back down where I told 'ee, an' try to find 'er . . . "

"Now, mum . . . "

"Mister Harmon, if *I* don't begrudge 'er, I surely don' see
how you nor anyone else can do!"

He cast his eyes down. "Aye, there's summat in that, I'll
allow."

"Do it then, I beg 'ee, Mister Harmon."

He sat staring across the bed and through the far wall, his
lips bitten. Then he seemed to ease down inside from a great
tension. "Very well, I shall."

Mary was genuinely surprised. She had seldom known
strong men of Adam Harmon's ilk to acquiesce, against their
better judgment, to the wishes of womenfolk. Mary was, she
now realized, a much more influential person than she ever
had been.

"And one more favor," she said.

"What?"

"Tell your boys t' keep th' secret, too. If y' should find poor Ghetel an' bring 'er among these folk, I don't want 'er t' be hated out."

But it was too late for that. Junior Harmon had already related it to Jim Cull out by the stockade, and Cull had related it to Mr. McCorkle, and by the time old Adam Harmon had ridden down the west bank to search for the old Dutch woman or her remains, everyone in the fort knew and was aghast at that part of the ordeal of Mary Ingles.

As Mr. Harmon trotted his horse down the west bank of the New River on his dubious favor for Mrs. Ingles, he was concentrating too hard on the frozen and snowy path ahead to notice three armed horsemen approaching the Dunkard's Bottom Fort from the south. They came out of a ravine, leading a pack horse, and went at a walk down through the stark and leafless woods toward the little stockade which stood dark and square in the blue-shadowed snow beside the river.

"Ol' Adam's off down th' river again," said Will Ingles, who had recognized him even at this distance. "That feller worries me; just won't stay put, no matter how things be in the countryside."

"Just like a couple others I know of," observed Gander Jack, with a half-smile and a sidelong glance at Will and Johnny.

They had spent the night alongside the New River, about eight or ten miles upstream from Dunkard's Bottom, and had got up at the first hint of daybreak this morning to make this last leg of their long journey back to the settlements. To Gander Jack the little fortification looked wonderful indeed; he had seen signs of Indian passage almost every day for the last week and felt they were getting in by the skin of their teeth.

"Hayo!"

The greeting came up the ravine to them from the fort. They saw a figure at the stockade, waving at them.

Johnny Draper, who had the deepest lungs among them, called back, "Haaaa!"

The little figure ran across the snow among the cattle and horses and swine that were impounded inside the stockade, and went hollering into the house. In an instant, a dozen people swarmed out of the house, whooping and cheering and waving joyously at them. Will raised his eyebrows. "Kind of an overmuch whoopee, say what? Reckon they've mistook us f'r Cunnel Wash'ton?" Johnny grinned at the joke, then went glum. All these people knew what they had ridden out to do so many weeks ago and were going to be let down by their dismal report.

"Mebbe they's just celebratin' the sight of us alive," Gander Jack said, "an' I'll drink one t' that."

"There," said Mrs. McCorkle, putting another pillow behind Mary. "Now y' just set back an' smile." She bustled around, smoothing back Mary's white hair, which she had brushed for her a few minutes earlier. "Oh, y' look pretty—f'r someone so peaked . . . "

"What's a-goin' on?" Mary asked. Everybody was bustling around like a crowd of simpletons, it seemed to her, and there were excited voices outside every door and wall.

"Someb'dy come t' pay'ee a call, hon. Perk up, now."

And then there was Will Ingles stooping to come under the door lintel, his eyes passing curiously across the room until they stopped on her and went wide. His hand came up to his throat.

O, he's alive! was her first thought. And her second was: *What'll I tell him about th' baby?*

The awful thought did enter his mind the moment he saw the face in the bed across the dim room and realized that it was Mary: *Had she been spiled?*

He shuffled, clumsy as a bear, into the room, that one hand still at his throat, the other starting to raise as if to salute her. The doorway behind him was crowded with breathless people and he could feel them back there. Three steps and he was at the bedside and he had finally grown accustomed to the gloom and he saw her white hair and sunken eyes and hollow cheeks, and then she was distorted by a curtain of tears.

"Well, William," she said.

"F-forgive me, Mary," Will said, dropping to his knees beside the bed. He meant for the thought he had just had, but he disguised it quickly by adding: " . . . f'r not bein' here when y' come . . . "

His hands were on the counterpane near her hand but neither yet could seem to reach and touch the other. Will and Mary just kept staring at each other's faces and seeing only blurred shapes and shades.

"Well," she said, almost strangling, "I did come to y', Will . . ." and let out a long, trembling sigh.

Will was remembering, suddenly, something he had not let himself think of for days: his last sight of her. He remembered running away down through the meadows from that sight with the Indians in pursuit of him and he was wondering how he could ever tell her about that moment.

She slid her left hand down to cover the back of his left hand and they both watched their hands touch and saw their wedding bands glimmering through their tears. He thumbed the tears out of his eyes with his right hand and then he really saw her hands, the swollen knuckles, the scrapes and scars and scabs and mangled blue fingernails, and his chin began trembling and his nose started running.

And then Mary saw somebody else move near the foot of the bed and looked up and saw vaguely the form of her brother Johnny standing there and she knew he was going to ask about Bettie, and she didn't know whether she could handle the answer.

All the things that needed to be said loomed as steep and high before her as the palisade cliff.

"Well, Johnny," she murmured, "how d'ye?"

Old Adam Harmon had made a quick passage down the west side of the river, and by early afternoon was within a league of the hunting camp that his son had abandoned five days before. Adam had run across much Indian sign, most of it several days old: moccasin tracks, in that pigeon-toed pat-

tern left by the Indian stride; grooved impressions left in the
snow at water's edge by canoe-bottoms; and, here and there,
human waste staining the melted snow. At one place not far
above his own outcamp he found the cold, soaked ashes of a
campfire in a trampled hollow, and beds of boughs indicating
that as many as eight or ten braves might have camped here.
Most of the traces led upstream, generally toward the settlements. This meant to him that the feeling in his little finger
had not been wrong; there had indeed been considerable
numbers of warriors in the vicinity at the time of Mrs. Ingles'
rescue and in the days she had lain in his outpost recuperating
from the margins of death.

Of course, there was no sign of this crazy old witch of a
cannibal Mrs. Ingles had sent him a-seeking; he expected to
find none. As close to perishing as young Mrs. Ingles had
been, surely an old woman would have died sooner. Or would
be lying scalpless in the woods somewhere, her gray hair
hanging from some young savage's belt. Or the wolves or
buzzards would have picked her bones by now.

Eh, then, he thought. The easier for me to carry 'em back.

Mr. Harmon had made this trip down mostly to humor Mrs.
Ingles, but he was a practical man above all, and would not
waste his time or effort on bootless errands. Whether he
should find the old Dutch woman's carcass or not, he might at
least salvage what his son had left behind at the hunting
camp; the kettle, the leather butchering-breeches, and, if he
could round her up, the old hobbled pack mare.

He rode through the stark woods, rifle primed and laid
across the pommel, and squinted against the whiteness of the
snow, on constant watch for hints of ambush. He reined in the
horse now and then to listen. A mile ahead, through and
above the trees, loomed the curved blue-gray riverbend cliff
he and his sons called the Big Horse Shoe.

Ahead and to his left was a saddle of land he could ride
through to shortcut the long peninsula that jutted into the
horseshoe. He halted and listened, and stood up slightly in
the stirrups, his eyes darting more keenly now. There was
something unusual in the air. He tuned his ears in and out
through the soft noises of the wilds—gurgle of the river, hush

of space, chink and twitter of winter birds—and then his ear homed in on it, a faint noise not of the wilderness: a dull, metallic sound, just on the threshold of audibility. It repeated, faded, repeated.

And then something else; the back of his neck crawled when he heard it: a short, quavering wail, like a fragment of a wolf's howl. Then the metallic *clunk, clunk,* still so faint; and then again the wail, louder.

It was broad daylight, but Adam Harmon felt the same kind of eerie, half-believing fright he had used to feel at night by a campfire when, with his sons, he had listened to an old half-Indian hunter tell haunt tales about the spirits of this valley— tales about the ghosts of an ancient tribe of Indians that had built mounds and rock walls all through the river valleys. Mr. Harmon was not a particularly superstitious man, but certain moods of landscape and light could make gooseflesh raise under his jaw-whiskers, and in such times he would think very intensely of God's name, and check the powder in the flashpan of his gun, both of which he did now.

He reined his horse to the left and kneed it to a walk and rode into a cleft in a limestone bluff, where he would be hidden on two sides and have a clear view down over the peninsula. He turned and halted there and sat his horse, the butt of his long rifle now resting on his thigh, ready for instant action, his left hand soothing the withers of his horse, which had heard the strange noises and was flicking its ears and puffing steam nervously.

He waited and listened. The noises were coming closer now, and were no longer ghostly. The metallic sound evidently was from a livestock bell of some kind. And the voice was crying:

"*Hallooooo! Hal-LOOOOOOOO!*"

His horse nickered, and another answered nearby.

He could hear the hoofsteps soon, and the bell, and guessed they were going to pass within fifty yards of him. He cocked his flintlock.

And then around the corner of the bluff the rider appeared, and Adam Harmon's hair stood up at the sight, which was a stranger apparition than any of the old haunt stories in his imagination had ever produced:

The afternoon sun glowed in a frizzy halo of white hair, crowning the oldest, ugliest, most cadaverous face Adam Harmon had ever seen on a living body. The wearer of this hollow-cheeked, cave-eyed, wattle-skinned horror-mask was draped in a filthy, tattered gray blanket, and was riding astride a rackabones nag which Harmon instantly recognized as his own strayed pack horse. A bell hanging from its neck clanked at every step.

The horses were already responding to each other before the astonished Adam Harmon realized that this wailing spectre was a woman, and therefore, surely, the old Dutch woman he had come to find. Somehow, apparently she had stumbled onto Junior's abandoned hunting camp down below and caught the mare.

He kneed his horse and rode down toward her. "Ay, there!" he said loudly. The old horse had stopped, and the old woman turned a blank, dulled stare at him, her gnawed, sunken, sore-covered mouth hanging open.

"Could y' be Missus Stump?" he asked, looking at her without friendliness.

She sat gaping wordlessly at him for so long, swaying on the horse's back and seeming to try to focus her eyes, that he thought she was perhaps about to faint. But she closed and opened her mouth several times, like a fish, and then said:

"Ah . . . ah . . . Missus Stumf, yes . . . " She looked fearfully now at the upraised rifle, slowly raised a scraggy hand toward him. "I vould not hurt 'er," she mumbled. "Please don' shoot me, Mister Inkles."

The womenfolk had shooed all the men out and then had brought Mary Ingles close to the hearth, stripped her, bathed her thoroughly, salved her many wounds and chapped skin, dressed her in one of Diane McCorkle's softest, warmest nightshirts, brushed her hair and fed her fresh milk and soup and hoecake. When the men came back in, she was sitting on a chair looking at the fire and there was a tinge of color on her cheekbones.

Will sat beside her as dusk fell outside, and he held her hand and sipped whiskey and gazed into the firelight with her, now and then turning to look at that strange, skull-like head, the deeply recessed eyes.

They had had difficulty talking to each other about things close to their souls. She had told him the whole story of her captivity and escape, but had left out certain things, and he was not going to pry them out until she seemed ready to say them. He had in turn told her everything about his trip down among the Cherokees. Will looked at her shyly for long moments when her profile was to him, and he thought: with care she'll be a young woman again, I think. But a young woman with snow-white hair, always to remind us.

When he thought this, such a bittersweet pang squeezed his chest that he thought he was going to cry again.

Johnny Draper had sat with them for a while. He had gazed into the fire, as if seeing a thousand miles beyond it, and had tried to act hopeful and cheerful. But Mary had watched the expression in his face and had watched him raise his hand up and gnaw the skin around his thumbnail. She had put her hand, that frail, scarred, raw framework of bird-bones that was her hand, on Johnny's wrist and had gently pushed down, saying:

"'Member, Ma always said a gent don't put his hands about 'is face lest he's a-prayin'."

After a while, Johnny had replied, "Well, then, likely I was a-prayin', eh?"

"Do, Johnny. Have faith. She'll get back someday, somehow. I did."

"Aye. But she wasn't brought up a Draper. She was more . . . delicate, like."

Mary thought for a while. "No. A body's delicate only if she's let t'be."

There was a faint shout outside, then a louder one. People left the room to see what was happening. "It's Adam," someone yelled. Will stood up, across the hearth from Mary, and waited, his face pale and hardened.

A few minutes later, everybody came spilling back into the

room from outside, all muttering and grumbling or arguing in high voices. They filled the candle-lit room, tracking mud and snow all over, the men's hats almost touching the low ceiling-joists, and milled back toward both walls of the room, leaving a sort of an aisle between the front door and the hearth where Mary sat. Mary turned and looked toward the door. Mister Harmon stooped under the lintel and came in, mud-spattered to his thighs, then turned and reached out the door into the darkness and led Ghetel into the candlelight.

Ghetel stood tottering in the doorway, blinking. Her eyes were drawn at once toward the fire, and fell upon Mary Ingles. Her mouth dropped open and started working, as if saying voiceless words. The two women looked at each other down the length of the room. All the people in the room knew this was the foreigner-woman who had tried to kill and eat Mary Ingles, and they stared silently at her with a hostile fascination, watching every expression and tic of her hideous face. She had lost all but the two eyeteeth from the front of her mouth by now and they looked like fangs. However the people at Dunkard's Fort had been imagining this cannibal, she surely was no disappointment.

Mary got up slowly from the chair. Even in woolen stockings and moccasins, her feet exploded with pains as she put her weight on them, and she steadied herself on the chair back. At the door at the far end of the room, between the lines of hating, hard-lipped faces, Ghetel looked as if she were about to start down another tribal gauntlet.

Mary and Ghetel started hobbling toward each other. Ghetel was wearing the blood-stained leather butchering-breeches she had found at the Harmon's hunting camp, and rags of blanket-cloth trailed from her festering feet.

It was only the length of a small room, but it seemed an eternity passed as the two white-haired, limping survivors approached each other, looking straight at each other's eyes, with expressions such as no one here had ever seen before.

They stopped two feet apart, eyes blazing from within their deep, shadowy sockets, and there was not a breath to be heard in the room, only the crackle of the fire on the hearth. Then the old woman said:

"You ought to stayed vit' me, May-ry. I found a pot of meat."

An indignant murmur swept up and down both sides of the room, then died down. Mary replied:

"It's all th' same, dear. I found my folks."

They stood there for another moment, then leaned together as if to hold each other up, and put their arms around each other and patted each other on the back.

They were like this for a long time, while the people in the room stood blinking and swallowing and beginning to understand something they knew they would never forget.

Finally Mary raised her head with a long, unsteady sigh. She took Ghetel's arm and turned to lead her to the hearth.

"Come sit," she said. "Them feet need some tendin' to."

Will Ingles lay in the dark in the big bed with Mary beside him and listened to the snoring and the muttering of the people sleeping on pallets all over the floor of the room. There was no privacy for himself and Mary, and he was grateful for that.

He was afraid of being alone in a bed in a room with her.

She had snuggled up to him when they first got into bed together, and her body had felt like a bundle of broomsticks and hoe handles. She had put her head on his arm and her cold bony arms around his chest and had asked him to keep her warm, and at the feel of her he had got all screamy inside and covered with shivers and had wanted to leap out of bed and go sleep on the floor in a corner someplace.

Then she had touched around on his body and made little m's in her throat while his eyes bugged in the darkness and he wanted to cringe away from her touch. Finally, to his relief, she had fallen asleep.

Will wasn't sure whether she had wanted him to do the love thing with her. Surely not; surely she don't feel fit for that, he thought, and wouldn't in this crowded darkness. But just the question of it made his stomach churn and the sweat run down his temples.

He didn't know why.

It wasn't just because she was a stranger to him now, or that she looked like a brittle old woman. It was that, but that wasn't all of it.

It wasn't just because of that fierce, awful wild-animal blaze in those hollow eyes, either. It was that, too, but that still wasn't all of it.

It wasn't just because of the way she had greeted that old Dutch hag, either, the way she had greeted her better than she had greeted him, as if she knew her better than she knew him, as if she loved her better than she loved him. It was that, too, because that had hurt him and scared him, but it was more than that, too.

It was something inside himself, maybe. It had been shaming him, that recollection he had had of running away when the Indians had her. And it was that humility he had felt, that sinking-down inside, while he heard about where she had been and what she had done, and about those six weeks of coming back to him.

He lay in the bed now feeling her arm-bones across his chest and thought about the cold and the hunger and the rocks and rivers and mountains she had seen that nobody else had ever seen, and he realized that he could not have done what she had done.

That seemed to be it. Along with the other things, that was what was the matter.

CHAPTER 32

MARY WAS HAVING PREMONITIONS AGAIN. SHE WAS GETTING SO spooked she would cry out in her sleep every night. And Will, who wanted desperately to assure her some peace of mind until she could become whole again, proposed to take her to a bigger stronghold, called Vass' Fort, about seven leagues

father east. There the settlers from the Roanoke River headwaters had gathered. Among them were Will Ingles' two
younger brothers, John, a bachelor, and Matthew, who had a
wife and child. There was a small militia detachment at Vass'
Fort, and Will believed there would be more security there
for Mary, whose emotions were in a fragile condition. The
iron will that had brought her through her ordeal seemed
about to crumble now that the trial was past, and every night
she had nightmares about being recaptured by Indians.

Mrs. Stumf had been accepted by the German Dunkards,
who were in the process of healing her and fattening her up,
with the intention of taking her back up to Pennsylvania when
her health and the weather would permit. Her name, they had
explained to Mary, was Gretel. It was her back-of-the-throat
"r" that had made it sound like "Ghetel," and they had a
hearty laugh over that business.

Mary made her good-byes to the little group of people at
Dunkard's Bottom who had cared for her so tenderly. She
lingered several minutes with Adam Harmon and his sons,
holding their hands and trying to express her inexpressible
gratitude to them. "Just thank the Heavenly Father," Adam
said, his eyes brimming with love and religious faith. "'Twas
His miracle that brought ye where we was."

Then she sat by the bed where Gretel lay, and held her hand
for a long time. Tears kept puddling in the old woman's
sunken hazel eyes, and her chin trembled, and Mary knew
she wanted to be forgiven for her assaults. But Mary simply
squeezed her hand to try to reassure her nothing needed to be
said about it. Out there in the dark, cold valley, they had been
ruled by the law of survival, not the law of men, and now that
both had survived, the episode could be forgotten more easily
than any breach of the laws of men could be.

Still, Gretel had to allude to it before they parted. She said,
just above a whisper:

"Ven you vas across the river from me, O my heart vas
more emptier than my stomach."

"Aye. Mine too. Well, Gretel. No two souls was ever closer
than you'n me." She pressed her cheek against the scabby,
scaled, gnarled hand that had once in a different world tried

to kill her for food, and she thought of that: there are no two souls closer than predator and prey are, in their moment, she understood. But she did not think it in words.

The chieftain, Captain Wildcat, raised his eyes from the creek valley below to the afternoon sun above, grimaced, then looked back at the valley, running his eagle-eyes far up the game trace that ran along the creek bank. The six Shawnee braves squatting at their posts along the bluff-top looked to him now and then and resumed their scrutiny of the valley.

Captain Wildcat knew the Virginia country better than any other Kispokotha Shawnee chieftain, and his braves had much faith in him. On a raid the previous summer he had taken much booty and several scalps and prisoners from a settlement near the Chi-no-da-ce-pe, not far from this very place where they now lay in ambush. Wildcat had become guardian of the two young sons of one of the white women he had captured. The younger of the two boys had become sick and died, but the other was becoming a good Shawnee child. It was said that a baby girl child of that same woman had been adopted by the squaw of one of the French traders, but Wildcat and his warriors had been on the war path for many weeks and had not been to Shawnee Town to learn whether that was true.

Lying in ambush here now, Wildcat thought often about the boy, and he thought often about the boy's mother, who was a brave and dignified woman and very handsome but had been too stupid to want to became a Shawnee chieftain's wife. He could still remember the summer day at the trading post when she had put his hand off of her. She should have come to live with Wildcat. If she had, she would be alive now and living a pleasant life. Instead, she had gone to the salt lick of the big bones with those greedy French fools and had got lost in the wilderness and had never been found.

But such were the ways of white people: very much trouble and never wise. Wildcat would never again be so foolish as to want a white woman. He was a warrior chieftain, and a warrior chieftain could not afford to be confused; to want a white woman was to be confused. Now he must put that white woman out of his thoughts and pay attention to this ambush, because it was the most important thing he had ever done.

They had been here a long time manning this ambush, almost a full day. The famous American militia colonel named Washington and two of his officers were supposed to have come down this trace this morning on their way to inspect the place called Vass' Fort, which stood a league down the creek. They should have been here by now: they were on good, fresh horses, with no extra baggage, and it did not make sense that they should take this long to come through the valley.

Captain Wildcat keenly desired the reddish scalp of the young colonel. He had heard Red Hawk, second chief of the Shawnee town on the Scioto-cepe, tell in council about his futile attempts to shoot the Virginia colonel in the great battle near Fort Duquesne. To kill an officer whom Red Hawk had been unable to kill would be a great coup. But it would require skill and watchfulness and thoughtful action.

Now the chieftain realized that though he had been lying here a long time dreaming of that glory, it might yet slip out of his hands.

He rose from the place where he had been crouched, and went to his first warrior. I must be sure the Virginia colonel has not already passed to the fort, he told him. I am going to go up over the ridge and down the other side to see if he has gone down that branch instead. The warrior nodded. You have heard, said Wildcat, that this officer is very hard to kill, and so he must be caught by complete surprise, before he has time to draw over him the cloak of the Great Spirit. Again the warrior nodded. Therefore, said the chieftain, no one of you must make a sound or fire a gun until I have looked at the other trail and returned. Tell them that. The warrior nodded and went and told them that, and Wildcat went over the mountain.

While he was gone, Colonel George Washington, Major Andrew Lewis and Captain William Preston of the Virginia militia rode down the creekbed toward Vass' Fort. Captain Preston was a nephew of the late Colonel Patton, who had been killed the previous summer in the massacre at Draper's

Meadows, and Preston was relating to Colonel Washington that he himself had been spared the same fate only by blind chance, having been sent down Sinking Creek to fetch a neighbor to help at the harvest. The young colonel nodded, allowing that even the best of soldiers often survive or die according to sheer luck, or God's will in the disguise of sheer luck.

This is what Colonel Washington and his aides were discussing as they rode under the guns of the six Shawnees hidden along the bluff above them. The warriors were squirming with agitation, and kept their gunsights on the white officers for a good five minutes as they passed below. But they had been ordered not to fire their weapons under any circumstances until their chieftain returned. And as Shawnee soldiers, they were, above all, disciplined.

And by the time the chieftain returned from the other side of the mountain and learned of the escape of his prey, Colonel Washington and the other officers were safe within sight of Vass' Fort.

Captain Preston opened the door to the room in which Colonel Washington was conferring with the leaders of Vass' Fort. There was a jug of rum on the table and an oil lantern hanging on a chain from a ceiling joist. Preston was smiling. "Colonel, sir, if I may interrupt: I find an old neighbor of mine is here, by a miracle, and she has a wondrous tale to tell."

Washington stood as the little, white-haired wraith of a woman limped into the room, supported by a sturdy, bearded young man he vaguely remembered. "This is William Ingles and his wife, Mary," Preston said. A chair was vacated for her, and the colonel sat down with hands folded on the table, looking across at her. The half-wild eyes in the gaunt young face arrested him. In recent years he had learned to recognize the peculiar look of people who had survived every kind of extremity and horror, and he felt a profound pity and respect for them.

"These gentlemen here have already spoken of you," he said. "Is it true that the New River leads straight through the

mountains to the Ohio?" He was a man uncommonly inter-
ested in land.

"Not straight, sir, no, not straight by no means. But it does
go there, sir. I reckon it's some two hundred mile by water to
th' O-y-o. But it's no route y'd take if y' could find any easier
one, sir."

He listened with keen interest as she described such things
as the salt spring and the burning spring and the river of coal.
She told him about the Shawnee town on the Scioto-cepe, and
about the prisoners from Fort Duquesne who had been there,
about the other salt lick where the big bones were. He was
leaning far over the table on his elbows by now, enraptured.
"And how far is that?" he said.

"I reckoned five hundred mile by water. I came a good bit
farther, havin' many a walk-around."

"Pray, ma'am," he pursued with his surveyor's yearning for
creditable measurement, "how did you make these esti-
mates?" He suspected they might be far wrong, wild guesses
exaggerated in her mind by the enormity of her suffering.

She placed a rope of yarn on the table, a strange, limp,
greasy, frayed strand tied in knots from one end to the other.
And she began to explain. "These thirty knots show a day
each on th' way down, in captivity. To th' Shawnee town.
Some fifteen mile a day, with a few days at the salt spring.
These forty-four knots each show a day o' walkin' back a free
woman from th' big bone lick."

Colonel Washington looked up from the yarn into her eyes,
and his scalp crawled. One of his most vivid memories among
the harrowing experiences of the last three years was his own
five-hundred mile winter ride to Fort LeBoeuf in the winter
of 1753, whose accomplishment had made him famous
throughout the Colonies. He had done it mostly on horseback,
with a guide, interpreter and armed escort, yet it had nearly
killed him. And now here before him sat this little woman of
his own age with her haunted eyes who, without provisions or
weapons, had made a far more awesome passage, through
utterly uncharted territory. The young colonel was not a man
often overtaken by humility, but for this moment he felt hum-
ble. He cleared his throat.

"Madame, as I was saying to Captain Preston only today: Some of us seem to have God's eye on us, and his hand ready to intervene for us." He stood up to his towering height, then bowed. "Thank you, Mrs. Ingles. I am honored."

William Ingles stood with his brother Matthew at the gate of Vass' Fort in the early morning light. Matthew wore his long, woolen hunting shirt and his chest was crisscrossed with straps supporting his powder horn and bullet bag and a game bag. He was setting out for a day's hunting, to supplement the monotonous diet of corncake and milk that prevailed in the fort. He grinned at Will's rueful expression. Will was a little embarrassed. He felt that his Mary was making him look something of a fool with her fears and premonitions. Now she had been having strong presentiments that Vass' Fort itself was about to be attacked, and had been urging its inhabitants to vacate it and cross over the Blue Ridge to safer places. She had started up that refrain right after Colonel Washington's departure, and finally Will had agreed to take her across the ridge to a still larger fort near the Peaks of Otter.

"Well, Matt," Will said, "by spring, maybe, she'll have it all out of 'er system, an' then we'll come back over and finish buildin' at the Ferry. I, uhm . . . "

Matthew put his hand on Will's shoulder. "Y' don't have t' say more. If I's her, I'd be scared too, an' prob'ly would be, till I was back in County Donegal. So, Godspeed, ol' feller, an' I'll be a-seeing you come spring, I reckon."

Will and Mary said their good-byes a little later to Matthew's wife and to John and to the other twoscore inhabitants of the fort, and rode southeastward toward the pass over the Blue Ridge, saying little to each other. They were still somewhat like strangers to each other; they had talked and talked about their travels and about Tommy and Georgie and Bettie and Henry, but there were still some things they had not talked about. There were a few patches of wet snow still lying in northerly hollows, but most of the ground was brown and bare and hard.

*   *   *

That afternoon Matthew Ingles was returning to Vass' Fort with a hare in his pouch and a wild turkey hen slung head down over his shoulder when he heard gunfire. He broke into a trot, the dead bird banging heavily against his flank. He thought for a moment of his sister-in-law's premonitions.

Blue gunsmoke was billowing over the stockade of the fort and from the woods around it. The quavering cries of Indians wove through the rattle of gunshots. Matthew's heart rose into his throat and he thought of his wife and child inside. Crouching and staying in the thickest brush, he ran zigzagging toward the stockade. There was nothing for it but to get inside. He ran. His moccasins thudded on the frozen ground and the turkey bumped heavily against him. He threw it off and sprinted toward the fort, which was now but a hundred yards away.

Then there were Indians between him and the fort, a small group of them running across his path from one defilade to another. Painted faces turned and saw him coming.

Matthew ran straight toward one and, at point-blank range, discharged his rifle into his face. The warrior spun to the ground and Matthew leaped over him, but there was now another in his way. All of them seemed to have forgotten the fort now and were stopping and veering and coming toward him with fierce glee in their faces, as if now they were involved in a game of sport, their purpose being to keep this lone white man from reaching the wall of the fort. Matthew roared with an equally fierce exuberance; his muscles felt like steel springs, his feet felt winged. He held his rifle like a quarterstaff, by its barrel. A brown face painted with ochre and blue stripes rose before him and he swung the rifle stock around and felt it thud against flesh and bone, and that Indian was gone. He swung it at another face and with a loud snap the stock broke off. There were hands all over him now. He jabbed the splintered rifle stock into a buckskin-covered abdomen and then the broken gun was wrenched from his hand. He roared with joy and surged on toward the fort, now so near, feeling himself dragged down by the gripping hands. Something was striking his back and shoulders.

He was on the ground, disarmed, the weight of bodies

squirming on him. A few inches ahead of him on the ground there was a great long-handled fry pan. Why it was there he had no idea. But he got out from under the howling attackers somehow, grabbed the pan and scrambled to his feet. It had the weight and heft of an axe, and he killed two warriors with it before sharp things slamming into his back took his breath away and he saw the brown earth coming up to his face.

John Ingles, peering through a loophole in the stockade, wrapped a ball in a greased patch and rammed it down the barrel of his long rifle, tipped a pinch of powder into the flashpan and stuck the barrel out through the loophole. A man behind him yelped and dropped to the ground. There were two dead men and three wounded women on the ground inside the stockade, and John Ingles could not understand where the shots had come from that had hit them. The fort was on a small rise. Any shots that were coming inside the compound had to be coming from someplace higher. John squinted against the powder smoke smarting in his eyes and looked for a target.

"There 'e be!" someone yelled. "Up that poplar!"

John stooped to the loophole again and scanned the surrounding woods until he saw the sniper: the warrior was on a high limb of an immense poplar tree two hundred yards from the fort. Now it seemed that a number of the defenders in that fort had seen him and were sending shots off into that tree. John drew a bead on the tiny figure in the distant branches and fired. Missed. He drew the weapon in to reload, and this time he risked putting in an extra-heavy charge of powder. He rammed the ball down and charged the pan, heart racing, afraid someone else would hit the sniper before he could. He aimed into the high branches again. A puff of smoke floated out from the tree and a ball thwacked into a roof behind him. John Ingles aimed a half a degree high, braced the gun butt tight against his shoulder and squeezed the trigger. The stock wrenched his shoulder back as the super-charge went off, but then through the veil of drifting smoke he saw the warrior pitch sideways and fall fifty feet to the ground. He grinned at the cheers he got.

John Ingles lay on the ground half an hour later, feeling the blood gurgle in his lungs. He had done all he could. He had caught a ball in one of his lungs and was too weak to get up, and the stockade was on fire. The gate had been burned and then rammed open and there were Indians running through the stockade with their damnable yowling, cutting babies apart and slashing women to ribbons with knives, and the screaming and sobbing was just too much to bear. He groaned with rage at his helplessness and watched as a scowling Indian with a bear-claw necklace bent over him and grabbed his hair and sliced into his scalp.

By midafternoon everyone in Vass' Fort was dead or standing naked in the cold mud roped together by the necks, watching the buildings burn. Those with any wits left about them were remembering how they had ignored the warnings of that poor strange Ingles woman.

The westerly wind at their backs all but blew them over the pass through the Blue Ridge; their cloaks flapped forward and the horses' manes shivered and ruffled and parted. Before and below, the rolling lowlands sloped away and away into a pearl-pale haze toward the seaboard. Real civilization was down there, a day's downhill ride away.

They halted their horses in the pass and looked back once, the wind wailing and making them squint and weep; they looked back at the somber ranks of crests stretching westward under the sinking sun. That was the wild world where these two had wed, and had raised and lost their children, and had lost any softness that once might have been in their souls: back in those dark and merciless mountains their souls had been forged.

Will reined his horse around as if to shelter her from that whipping wind, and they sat close together now, facing each other for a moment, seeing the distance and the longings and the sorrow in each other's eyes, the big ruddy man and the little pale woman, now knowing each other's feelings enough to understand that they would one day go back, as westward was where the future lay.

Then Will saw a special darkness go over her face, like the shadow of a cloud blowing over a meadow.

"Reckon what?" he asked.

"I just wish they'd a-come with us," she said. "I still feel it strong, about Vass'."

"Well, I pray y're wrong for once." He sighed. "Now tell me," he said. "What d'yre foreshow on Tommy and Georgie and Bet?"

"Only that we sh'll never stop a-looking' till we know for sure."

"That I swear," he said. And then he said: "Now, Mary, y'know there's one big matter y've not told me yet. Let's get it over with, while there's just us two t' hear't."

She leveled her gaze at him and set her jaw and squinted against the wind and the winter sun behind him, or against whatever would be in his eyes when she told him. "She was born on th' ground three days after th' massacree," Mary said. She saw his eyes moisten and saw his lips forming the silent word *she*. "I toted an' suckled 'er three months. Then . . . " Her gaze fell and her brow knotted.

"What?" he said. He thought the wind had blown her words away.

" . . . Then," she said, looking defiantly at her husband, braced for whatever he might say, " . . . then I had to leave 'er with a nurse squaw. Or she'd 'a' perished, as y' can see by th' sight o' me." There. She had dared to say it.

A blast of wind buffeted her ears and the hood of her cape and Will had to reach up and hold his hat to keep it on his head. He stared at her, and finally he said:

"And did y' give this girleen a name?"

"Aye. But you oughtn't t' know it. I intend to forget, quick as I can."

He sat there and looked at her. She did not know how he was going to take this. Finally, he said:

"As it should be." His mouth was firm and the tears in the corners of his eyes could as well have been from the cold gale.

"And hav'ee somethin' t' say to me?" she asked after a while.

He ran his tongue across his lower teeth and inhaled.

"Only this: When I saw the savages takin' y'off, I had t' run t'other way." He sighed and looked as if he wanted to gaze off somewhere, but kept his eyes on hers.

And she said:

"As it should be. If y'd been fool enough t' run into a massacree, where would *I* be now?"

They both bared their teeth in unsmiling grins now and allowed themselves to gaze off over each other's shoulders. Finally Will reached and took her hand.

"We'll start us a new family, when y're well. Look'ee." He gazed westward over the Alleghenies. "We're just where we were five year back. On Blue Ridge. Just us two. Lookin' yonder."

"Aye. And I love'ee more, Will Ingles."

He swallowed hard, hearing this at last. "Is that true, Mary Ingles?"

"Proof of it: ain't I here?"

Now they both were really smiling.

"Come," he said. "Let's ride down out o' this wind-blast 'fore it blows us plumb away."

CHAPTER
33

October, 1768

WILLIAM INGLES SPURRED HIS HORSE AND GALLOPED AHEAD OF his two traveling companions, up a road through a yellow-green meadow to the rounded shoulder of a hill. He reined his horse to a standstill, rose in his stirrups and looked down into the New River Valley. There it all lay, his domain, peaceful among the golden leaves of the woods: Ingle's Ferry and Inn, the neat house and barn and public house close by the ferry

road, woodsmoke curling up from the chimneys, the cornfields yellowing on the gentle slope above the buildings, the
stone well in the yard beside the inn, all as peaceful as he had
left it three months before to go on this mission.

Will Ingles, now prosperous and sturdy, mantled in a fine
wool cape, wearing a blue and white checked flannel shirt
under his buckskin coat, turned, grinning through his white-
streaked whiskers, as his companions rode up beside him.
One of them was Bill Baker, a rugged, black-haired adventurer who had spent many years as a captive among the
Shawnees. Baker had learned the Shawnee tongue and was a
superb guide and interpreter.

The other rider was a lad of seventeen years, in the buck-
skins and blanket and headband of a Shawnee. He rode his
horse bareback. Across the horse's withers were slung a bow
and a quiver of arrows.

When the youth reached the shoulder of the hill, Bill Baker
said something to him in Shawnee and pointed down the hill
to the cluster of buildings. The lad leaned forward, hands
braced on the horse's neck, and looked at the place very
intently. He looked then at the distant mountains with their
woods in autumn color and looked up and down the curving
river. Expressionless, he took it all in, and Will Ingles
watched him anxiously. At last the youth nodded once, still
without expression.

The three riders trotted their horses down the road into the
valley. Will Ingles looked happy and proud enough to burst.
Chickens clucked and hurried out of the road and a pig
waatched from the yard as the men rode toward the house.
Suddenly Will Ingles cupped his hands around his mouth and
yelled in a piercing voice:

"Heyo! Mary! Heyo, Mary, we're home!"

And when the three riders stopped their horses in front of
the stoop of the log house, a door opened and a very handsome woman in a long blue linsey-woolsey dress, with a white
shawl over her shoulders, stepped out onto the stoop and
looked at them. She was straight-backed and statuesque, with
a youthful ruddy complexion and a crown of thick, snow-
white hair. She looked first at Will, just for a second, and

winked at him. Then she glanced at the other man and said, "Mister Baker, how d'ye?"

"Right well, Missus Ingles, and you too, I hope."

"Tolerable," she replied to him, but her blazing eyes had already moved on to the youth, and she stared at him. While she was studying him, her face growing pale, three little girls appeared in the open door. One was about eight years old, another six, the last, four. At once, seeing Will Ingles, they began bouncing and chorusing, "Papa! Papa!"

"Hush," said Mary Ingles, and without taking her eyes off the youth, she spread her hands back to bar the girls from running down into the yard. Then another figure appeared in the doorway. She was a dark-haired, hard-face, slender woman of about thirty-five.

"How d'ye, Will?" this woman said.

"How d'ye, Bettie," Will said. "Didn't 'spect you."

"Wouldn't a' missed this," she said. "Johnny couldn't leave the harvest, though." Her eyes were glinting with wet and now she turned to look at the mounted youth. Johnny Draper had traced her to the Shawnee town of Chillicothe seven years before and ransomed her from the chief who had adopted her. Her face looked permanently hard and sad, but she was very sentimental and wept easily, often for no apparent reason.

"Well, Mary," said Will Ingles.

"Well, William," said Mary.

"Tell him," Will said to Bill Baker. Baker reached over and tapped the shoulder of the Shawnee boy, who was staring at the white-haired woman. The boy turned to look at him and Mister Baker pointed to her and said:

"Nik-yah."

The boy turned back to Mary Ingles and kept staring at her. Mary Ingles stared back at him.

He carries himself like Wildcat, she was thinking.

Then she nodded to the boy. He was studying her without expression but a great deal was going on in his eyes. Suddenly he threw a leg over his horse and dropped lightly to the ground on the balls of his feet.

He handed his horse's lead to Mister Baker and walked

toward the stoop. He was tall and slender and very dignified
for someone so young.

Mary Ingles began trembling as he walked closer. The little
girls were gawking at him open-mouthed and silent.

He halted a few paces from the stoop and looked at her. She
took two shaky steps down onto the ground and came to
stand an arm's length in front of him. She looked at his dark
eyes and his reddish-brown hair that was neatly held by a
beaded headband. Her eyelids began fluttering and tears
came from the corners of her eyes.

"Nee-gah," the boy said.

She looked a question at Mister Baker.

"He says, 'My mother.'"

Her chin was crumpling up with crying but her mouth
smiled. She reached out and took his hand. Then with a
sudden outburst of snuffling, she flung her arms around him
and buried her face against his neck, and cried uncontrollably. He stood there, his hands rising slowly from his sides,
and then timidly wrapped his arms around her heaving shoulders, and now his nose was running and his eyes were spilling
over. Bettie on the stoop and Will on his horse were now
shaking with constrained sobs and clenched teeth and their
cheeks were wet.

Mary Ingles raised her head after a while and, red-nosed,
the little pain-wrinkles around her mouth etched deep by her
half-grimace, half-smile, searched his glimmering eyes with
her own and put her palms up to the sides of his face, and she
said:

"Ten times ten times ten, Tommy-lad. O, welcome home,
my son!"

AUTHOR'S NOTE

MARY DRAPER INGLES' CAPTIVITY WAS BUT ONE OF AN ESTI-mated 2,000 incidents of kidnapping of white settlers, male and female, adult and child, during the French and Indian War. The ordeals of captivity, torture and escape provided grist for the artistic imagination for many years. The tales, both factual and fictional, that grew out of these adventures made a thrilling undercurrent in American folklore, fired the prejudices that resulted in the implacable and merciless treatment of Indian nations during the westward march of American settlement and, of course, contributed to the shaping of the national character.

Many personal accounts of such escapades were printed in booklet form during and after the French and Indian War, often in florid, dramatic style, and were read with horrified fascination by people whose fantasies dwelt on the "naked and undisciplined savage" with whom they shared the continent. To the religious, such perilous adventures could be interpreted as supreme tests of faith, or often as the symbolic equivalent of a journey into hell—complete with naked demons and the burning of flesh. Often the booklets served also to convey anti-Catholic propaganda among Colonials of Anglican Protestant faith. Many such tales referred to French Catholic priests who moved among the Indians and allegedly granted them absolution for their murders and tortures.

Among the annals of Indian captivity there are many which recount sufferings and tortures one can scarcely imagine, and there were several escapes that seem all but incredible.

But the one I have treated in this book is, to me, the most amazing and inspiring. It is one of those focused demonstrations of what the human spirit—not just the hardened, trained

spirit of the professional soldier or adventurer, but the spirit
of a vulnerable, frightened, "ordinary" person—can endure.

Mary Draper Ingles did recover from the odyssey described
in this book. She bore four more children—three daughters
and a son—by her husband William, raising them in the
wilderness around Ingles' Ferry and surviving, alongside her
husband, at least one other Indian raid on their frontier home.
William Ingles left her a widow when he died in 1782 at the
age of 53 years.

She died in 1815 at 83 years of age, sixty eventful years after
her great ordeal, and was, according to the accounts of rela-
tives and acquaintances, vigorous, self-reliant and robust into
the very last year of her life.

Her son Georgie, aged two at the time of their capture,
reportedly died in the Shawnee nation shortly after being
separated from his mother. The elder son, Thomas, had all
but forgotten his native tongue and his white parents during
his thirteen years as an adopted Shawnee.

William and Mary Ingles, however, had not forgotten him.
They continued inquiries until 1768, when the freed captive
William Baker brought news of him. William Ingles and
Baker made two trips into the Shawnee country before suc-
ceeding in buying Tommy back from his Shawnee parents for
the equivalent of about $150. But Thomas was reluctant to
return to the white man's civilization and would disappear
into the wilderness for long periods of time, armed with his
bow and arrows. Gradually he was re-educated in the white
man's culture, studying for a while in Albermarle County of
Virginia, becoming acquainted with Thomas Jefferson, Pa-
trick Henry and James Madison.

Eventually young Thomas Ingles married and determined
to settle and farm, but the pull of the wilderness caused him
to uproot himself from time to time and stay on the farthest
points of white advance into the Virginia country. When he
could, he visited in the Ohio country with old fellow tribes-
men of the Shawnees.

His determination to live far ahead of the general settlement eventually led, in April, 1782, to an incident so similar
to his own parents' ordeal in 1755 that it is almost uncanny:
While Thomas was in his fields, a large party of Indians

surrounded his house, kidnapped his wife and three children, and looted and burned the property. Thomas, drawn to the scene by the smoke and the noise, was unarmed and helpless to intervene and so was forced to watch his family being carried away—just as he and his mother and brother had been carried away twenty-seven years earlier while his own father watched. As he knew the history of the Draper's Meadows massacre quite well, his emotions in that moment can be imagined.

Thomas joined and led a rescue expedition that caught up with the Indians on the fifth night after the capture. In an early-morning melee, the Indians tomahawked Thomas Ingles' five-year-old daughter, named Mary after her grandmother, and three-year-old son, named William after his grandfather. Thomas Ingles rushed into the camp and seized his wife, Eleanor, just as she was being struck on the head with a tomahawk. An infant daughter was spared when her mother fell over her. The escaping Indians then killed a militia captain in their retreat. The son and daughter died of their wounds, but Thomas' wife recovered after several pieces of skull bone were extracted from her head by a frontier doctor.

John and Bettie Draper lived at Draper's Meadows after John ransomed her in 1761. Four sons and three daughters were born to the Drapers after her return; she died in 1774 at the age of 42.

That same year, John Draper and Thomas Ingles served as lieutenants in the great wilderness battle of Point Pleasant, the spot where the captive Bettie and Mary had reached the Ohio nineteen years before.

John Draper remarried two years later, fathering two more daughters, and lived to the age of 94.

Matthew Ingles, William's younger brother who killed at least two Indians in hand-to-hand combat outside Vass' Fort, did not die immediately after he was overpowered. As brave and formidable fighters often did, Matthew Ingles excited the admiration of his Indian captors. He was either released or he made an escape from the war party soon after the massacre, but never recovered from his wounds, and died at Ingles' Ferry a few months later. His wife and child were murdered in the fort.

The Shawnees had indeed presumed that their prisoners, Mary Ingles and the old Dutch woman, were lost or killed by wild animals in the wilderness around Big Bone Lick. It was not until a certain meeting of Virginians and Shawnees some years later that the Indians learned of their long walk home. They were thrilled and awed by the account, which became something of a legend among the Indians.

The real name and eventual fate of the old Dutch woman who accompanied Mary Draper Ingles in her trek to freedom have, unfortunately, been lost to history. Historical sources dealing with the Ingles-Draper story say she eventually found transportation back to Pennsylvania and was never heard of again in the New River settlements. Historians of the region contend that her name was Stump or Stumf, and that she had been captured at the time of Braddock's defeat near Fort Duquesne, Pennsylvania, and brought down the Ohio to the Shawnee town on the Scioto where she met Mary Ingles. This is her history as I have chosen to see it, as there are no serious contentions to it and such movements seem quite feasible in the light of accounts of other prisoners taken after Braddock's defeat.

Because of the scarcity of Ingles family records concerning the period covered in this novel (many old family papers having been destroyed in fires and raids), I have relied most heavily on an account published in 1886, in a book entitled *Trans-Allegheny Pioneers*, by Dr. John P. Hale (1824-1902), a great-grandson of William and Mary Ingles. Dr. Hale, who was a physician, industrialist, banker and historian, seems to have based his grandmother's account mainly on a narrative, handwritten by Mary Ingles' youngest son, John Ingles (1766-1836), who had heard the tale many times from his parents. Dr. Hale fleshed out that spare narrative with a great deal of research, and by his extensive and detailed knowledge of the New River-Kanawha River Valley was able to fix the locations of most of the incidents in her narrative. Most of those places, of course, had been nameless at the time of her passage. In my novel, the entire length of this valley, to its mouth at the Ohio, is referred to as the New River Valley. It was not until years later that the stretch below the Gauley River's influx was named the Kanawha.

It is fascinating to note that Dr. Hale's major commercial enterprise was a salt-manufacturing complex on the Kanawha at the very place where Mary Draper Ingles was forced by her Indian captors to boil salt on their journey down this wild valley a century before. For many years the largest salt manufactory in the United States, it was a short distance upstream from Charleston, West Virginia.

The accounts of Mary Ingles' ordeal written by these two descendants agree almost exactly in the sequence and details of events, with but one curious difference: John Ingles' version makes no reference to his mother's pregnancy at the time of her capture, nor the delivery of a baby during her captivity.

That John Ingles failed to mention the birth and abandonment of that baby girl indicates either that his parents had never mentioned her in his presence, or that he chose not to include it in his narrative.

Dr. Hale credits the details of the baby's birth to papers authored by Mrs. Letitia Preston Floyd, a daughter of William Preston, longtime neighbor of Mrs. Ingles, and wife of Governor John Floyd II of Virginia, and indicates but does not name other sources.

He relates his information about the baby with such certainty and such richness of detail that I am convinced he was sure of his facts, and I have based my treatment of this part of the story on his information. I can readily believe that the desertion of one's infant—even for the expedient of improving its survival prospects—would be such a traumatic and complex emotional experience that one would not discuss it thereafter in the family.

Trying to recreate the character of someone who lived two centuries ago can only be an act of faith and imagination, with the hope that the fictional character will in some respect do justice to the real one. In writing of other historical figures, I have had pictures of them to indicate how they looked, and memoirs, diaries and letters to indicate what they thought and how they expressed those thoughts. For the creation of the fictional Mary Ingles, I had none of these. There were, of course, no cameras in her lifetime, and if any portrait painter roamed the rugged New River Valley in her time and painted her portrait, nothing is known of any such portrait. Not having seen any likeness, then, I have for physical description only her great-grandson's statement that she was athletic and strong.

Nothing is known, either, of any word or thought ever written by Mary Ingles; one of her descendants suggested to me the explanation that Mary Ingles likely was illiterate, as a large proportion of American frontier colonials were at that time.

Working, therefore, without either her visage or her words to inspire and give me hints of her personality, I had to create her character out of her deeds alone.

And here was inspiration aplenty.

Mary Ingles' main adversary in the forty-three days of her remarkable trek was the wilderness—in particular, the sombre, precipitous roaring New River-Kanawha River Valley, through which she had to pass in the inhospitable season of early winter. For my development of the character of this intimidating and merciless antagonist, I had more to go on: The valley is still there, and the researcher afoot, climbing, walking and sleeping down between its forested slopes and craggy cliffs, quickly comes to know it intimately and to respect it. It is a landscape worthy of myths and legends. It changes moods with the light and the weather. Sometimes it is stark and sometimes it is enchanting, but it is always beautiful. I spent many weeks retracing Mary Ingles' steps through the mountains and, though I have hiked and made my bed on the ground since childhood, I have seldom felt as tiny and overawed as I felt in the confines of that valley. In the morning mists I could see ghosts of Mary Ingles and the old Dutch woman toiling along the shores; in the endless symphony of rock and water I could hear the after-echoes of their voices calling across to each other. I could understand why they were afraid to lose sight of each other. Toward the end of my familiarization with that terrain, I climbed over the palisade cliffs she traversed on the last day of her odyssey. One can walk around the base of the cliff now; a railroad bed had long since been carved into the river's edge. But the pillars of the cliff still stand out above the river, and Mary Ingles' route can still be followed—on all fours, of course. I climbed it, on a dry, moderate morning, fortified by a good night's rest in a sleeping bag and a breakfast of tinned beef, and the crossing took me three hours. That she crossed it on an icy day after six weeks of starvation and fatigue is marvelous.

After my familiarization with the terrain that tried her body and soul, I felt that I had as much understanding of the essential Mary Draper Ingles as one could have. What better study of a human spirit is there than a study of the trials it has overcome?

Of the several appearances of young George Washington in this novel, all are substantiated by historical documentation. There is no record that he did meet or speak to Mary Ingles at Vass' Fort, but I find it conceivable that he did, as he was inspecting the fort in his capacity as Virginia militia commander at about the time Mary Ingles was sheltered there. His keen interest in land speculation would have caused him, I am sure, to ask such questions as he asked her in this novel's dialogue.

My search for the probable Mary Ingles led me eventually to those parts of West Virginia that were first opened up and developed by the Ingleses and the Drapers, and by good fortune I was directed to a great-great-great-granddaughter of that dauntless woman.

Roberta Ingles Steele of Radford, Virginia, might well have met me with reserve and suspicion. She feels the Mary Draper Ingles story has been distorted in many of its retellings through the years, and here I came, another outsider bent on doing another version of it. I could sense her reserve, but she did not hesitate to offer me her hospitality and a good hearing.

Mrs. Steele is, of course, a guardian of Ingles family history. Her great-great-grandfather was John Ingles, Sr., who was born in 1776, about a decade after his mother's return from captivity. His handwritten manuscript, the first known written account of her journey, is for Mrs. Steele the most authentic documentation of the story. That manuscript is preserved in the library of the University of Virginia. In 1969, Mrs. Steele and her brother, Andrew Lewis Ingles, edited and published an annotated version of that manuscript, under the title, *Escape From Indian Captivity* (Commonwealth Press Inc., Radford, Va.). They tried to decipher the original manuscript accurately, preserving John Ingles' spelling, word choice, style and punctuation.

Mrs. Steele sat with me on the broad, pleasant porch of her splendid Radford home, and we did our best to share our conceptions of the brave woman. Little by little she began to give me hints and leads for additional research, and also gave me a copy of *Escape From Indian Captivity*. She made a special trip away from the house to fetch a facsimile of the original manuscript for me. When I returned to Radford a few months later to continue my research, she arranged to drive me out to the site of Ingles' Ferry for a look at the hewn-log structure William Ingles had built there as an adjunct to his wayside inn. Mrs. Steele was at this time much bothered by the encroachments of vandals on the properties, and, indeed, by the general decline in morality and character that she professed to see going on throughout modern society. It was obvious that she had high expectations of people and probably not much patience with moral sloppiness. The world built here through such risk and work and suffering by her ancestors was being eroded by modernity. I felt that her keen sense of worth and family pride, stemming from the pioneer heroism of Mary and William Ingles, is still trying to withstand the long siege of easier times, the slow softening of fiber. Through all her helpfulness and hospitality and dry humor, I could detect a sadder, more severe side. There was a vestige, I thought, of the pioneer woman, looking down the centuries through the eyes of her descendants onto an undreamed-of world. It may be only my writer's fancy, but I think I glimpsed the character of Mary Draper Ingles, that doughty survivor, in the face and the demeanor of this keeper of her legend.

And so my special thanks go to Roberta Steele for lending me her ancestor so that I might try to tell an inspiring story. I am also grateful to Rev. Harold J. Dudley of Raleigh, North Carolina, editor of the Third Edition of John P. Hale's *Trans-Allegheny Pioneers* (Derreth Printing Co., Raleigh, North Carolina), for making his thoughts and his insights available to me; and to dozens of Virginians and West Virginians living along the New River Valley who gave me directions, hospitality and friendship, guided me to great views and campsites at the tops and bottoms of mountains and paddled me here and there in their fishing boats because, knowing I was writing a book about their legendary Mary Ingles, they apparently wanted to make my passage up the valley easier than hers.

About the Author

James Alexander Thom has been a U.S. Marine, a
journalist, and a free-lance magazine writer. Home
is southern Indiana near Bloomington, where he is
rebuilding an old log cabin on 25 acres of wooded hill
country. Thom was until 1980 a member of the
Indiana University Journalism School faculty, and
now devotes full time to traveling, researching, and
writing fiction. He walked, climbed, and camped
along much of the New River gorge in preparation
for writing FOLLOW THE RIVER.